Secrets at
Bletchley Park

Margaret Dickinson, a *Sunday Times* top ten best-seller, was born and brought up in Lincolnshire and, until very recently, lived in Skegness where she raised her family. Her ambition to be a writer began early and she had her first novel published at the age of twenty-five. She has now written over twenty-five novels – set mostly in her home county but also in Nottinghamshire, Derbyshire and South Yorkshire.

Margaret Dickinson

Secrets at Bletchley Park

PAN BOOKS

First published 2021 by Macmillan

This paperback edition first published 2021 by Pan Books
an imprint of Pan Macmillan
The Smithson, 6 Briset Street, London EC1M 5NR
EU representative: Macmillan Publishers Ireland Limited
Mallard Lodge, Lansdowne Village, Dublin 4
Associated companies throughout the world
www.panmacmillan.com

ISBN 978-1-5290-1851-6

3 5 7 9 8 6 4

A CIP catalogue record for this book is available from the British Library.

Typeset in Sabon by Palimpsest Book Production Ltd, Falkirk, Stirlingshire
Printed and bound by CPI Group (UK) Ltd, Croydon, CR0 4YY

MIX
Paper from
responsible sources
FSC® C116313

Visit **www.panmacmillan.com** to read more about all our books
and to buy them. You will also find features, author interviews and
news of any author events, and you can sign up for e-newsletters
so that you're always first to hear about our new releases.

For Dennis
With My Love Always

Acknowledgements

Although this is a work of fiction, I do try to get the background facts right – but because this book was mainly written during the lockdown for Covid-19, I was unable to visit locations to do research as I would normally do. I am sincerely grateful to Peronel Craddock, head of collections and exhibitions for the Bletchley Park Trust, for her help with particular queries, the answers to which I could not find in books or on the internet.

Several other sources have also been valuable for research, most notably: *The Secret Life of Bletchley Park* by Sinclair McKay (Aurum, 2010); *The Lost World of Bletchley Park* by Sinclair McKay (Aurum, 2013); *The Debs of Bletchley Park* by Michael Smith, (Aurum, 2015); and *The Hut Six Story* by Gordon Welchman (M&M Baldwin, 2018).

My love and grateful thanks to Helen Lawton and Pauline Griggs for reading and commenting on the first draft. Their help and support is hugely appreciated. And, as always, my special thanks to my wonderful agent, Darley Anderson, and his team, to my fantastic editor, Trisha Jackson, and to all the marvellous team at Pan Macmillan.

Prologue

'I'm organizing a shooting party at Bletchley Park next weekend. Care to come along?' The tall, middle-aged man with smooth, greying hair spoke casually as he packed the bowl of his pipe methodically.

The younger man blinked behind owlish spectacles. 'Bletchley Park? Where's that?'

'About fifty miles north of London. In Buckinghamshire.'

'A shooting party? Aren't we a bit busy with all this talk of war being imminent?' Almost as an afterthought he added, respectfully, 'Sir.'

The other man took a moment to answer whilst he lit his pipe and gave a few experimental puffs, sending out clouds of smoke. Then he chuckled. 'Our boss has acquired a country estate with the intention of running our intelligence activity from there, should there indeed be a war.'

'What? He intends to move us – the whole of the Government Code and Cypher School – out of London?'

'It'll be a lot safer than being here. Our capital will – sadly – be a prime target for Hitler's bombers.

1

I doubt he'd see a country estate as being important.'

'Unless he got wind of what was there.'

'Then he mustn't, must he? It will all be very hush-hush.'

'You'll expect everyone who works there to sign the Official Secrets Act?'

'Naturally.'

'And what about personnel? You're going to need a lot more than we've got now.'

'The plan is to trawl the universities for the brightest and the best. Mathematical geniuses. Expert chess players. Crossword puzzle addicts. You get the idea?'

'What about translators?'

'There are a lot of bright young women amongst the debutante class in our society, who have been to finishing school abroad. Some of them speak French and German fluently, I understand.'

'But – but won't they – chatter?'

The older man chuckled again. 'They have been well brought up. They know how to conduct themselves in all sorts of situations. So the answer is, no, they won't.'

'And this – shooting party?'

'Oh, that's just a cover for us to check the place out – to see if we think it'll work. We'll only be there for a couple of weeks or so, but if war does come, we'll be ready. So, are you coming?'

The young man's eyes sparkled. 'Try keeping me away.'

PART ONE

Mattie

One

'Don't go near her. She's got nits.'

'And she smells.'

'Her house is the dirtiest in our street. My mum won't let me play with the Price kids.'

'Lets the whole neighbourhood down, my dad says.'

Mattie walked on, her head down, as the taunts continued. School had only reopened the previous week for the autumn term. The long summer holidays had been an oasis of calm in the young girl's tormented life, but now the nightmare was beginning again. She couldn't remember a time when she had not been ridiculed and bullied by her peers. There was the usual gang of them, six or seven from her class, following her home from school. Someone pulled her plait and Mattie clenched her fists. She didn't turn round to look, but she knew it would be Daniel Spencer, the acknowledged leader of the little gang. The worst of it was that he lived at the top end of their street and always seemed to be on the lookout for her, waiting at the end of their ginnel to waylay her.

'We had games today,' one of the girls said. 'She's got cardboard in her shoes.'

'And her vest has got three holes in it,' said another. 'I wouldn't be seen dead in a vest like that.'

'And her dad's a tea leaf.' This was from Arthur, a boy whose family had recently moved north from London. Arthur – pronounced by the boy himself as 'Arfer' – was something of a novelty to the Sheffield school children and his new classmates revelled in learning the cockney rhyming slang he used. No doubt to show off in front of the newcomer, Daniel yanked her plait again, harder this time so that it pulled her head backwards. Mattie felt tears smart her eyes, but she wouldn't let them see her cry. Never in a million years. She would have run, but he was still holding her hair. Something snapped inside the ten-year-old girl. She swung her right arm round in a wide arc. Her fist connected with his nose and she heard a satisfying crunch. There was a brief moment of stillness as they stared at each other before Daniel yelped, let go of her hair and put his hand to his face.

Mattie turned and ran.

She reached the street where she lived and ran pell-mell down the road, almost to the very bottom, skidding to turn sharply left and into the alleyway – the ginnel – between her home and the next terraced house. She pushed open the wooden door into the yard, crashing it back so that it shuddered on its hinges. Taking refuge in the privy at the end of the yard, she pushed the bolt into place and sent up a silent prayer of gratitude that it had been unoccupied. She leaned against the closed door, breathing in the fetid air, but at least she was safe – for the moment.

It seemed an age until she heard raised voices coming nearer and nearer, and then the yard door crashed open again and the shrill voice of Daniel's mother, Bella Spencer, was now far too close for Mattie's comfort. The girl peeped through the gap in the wooden panels and saw the large woman pounding on the back door of the house.

'Elsie Price,' she shouted. 'Come and see what your little bitch of a daughter has done to my Daniel.' She paused for a moment and, when no one appeared, she bellowed, 'Get out here now, else I'm coming in.'

The door opened slowly and Mattie could just see her mother standing there, a cigarette dangling from her lips, her eyes screwed up against the smoke.

'W'as all the noise about?' Elsie's voice was slurred and she leaned against the door jamb for support.

Mattie closed her eyes briefly and groaned inwardly. Her mother was drunk again in the middle of the afternoon. Mattie opened her eyes and peered through the gap once more.

'Gi o'er, Mum. It's not Mattie's fault. I pulled her hair.'

'Tha's no reason to break yer bliddy nose.'

In the darkness of the privy, Mattie blinked. Daniel Spencer sticking up for her? Saying she wasn't to blame? Wonders would never cease.

''Sides,' Daniel went on and this, Mattie thought wryly, was probably nearer the reason why he was trying to prevent his mother having a full-blown row

7

with her mum. 'Their Joe'll batter me into the middle of next week when he finds out.'

Mattie pressed her hand to her mouth to stop the giggle. There wasn't much fun or laughter in the girl's life, but the thought of her older brother, Joe, always brought a smile to her lips. He was her champion – her protector – even from their own father now and again. At thirteen, he was already stronger than their puny father and he dared to stand up to Sid Price's fists. In a year's time Joe would be leaving school, but already he took any part-time job he could find outside school hours – usually amongst the market traders – to bring a few extra shillings to the starved household of two adults and five children. But he was sharp enough not to hand the money to either of his parents for it to be spent on booze or fags. Instead, Joe brought food home. Saturday night was eagerly awaited by all the family when Joe scoured the market stalls for cheap food being sold off at the end of the week. Several of the stall holders for whom he worked often gave him the leftovers that they had no chance of selling. Sometimes, if he'd had a good week, Joe brought home fish and chips and the family ate like kings. Even their father, Sid, waited for Joe to arrive home on a Saturday night before going to the pub.

'Leave it, Mum. Please.' Daniel was still pleading with his mother.

'I won't leave it, our Dan. That little firebrand ought to be taught a lesson and if—'

'W'as going on here?'

Mattie froze as she heard her father's voice and

the sound of bicycle wheels coming across the yard towards the shed next to the privy. She heard the rattle as he flung it against the wall and emerged again into the yard.

'Oh aye, Sid. Another of your little acquisitions, is it?' Bella said sarcastically. 'What poor sod's lost 'is bike this afternoon, then?'

'Mind yer business, yer nosy old bat. And stand aside, will yer? I want me tea.'

Bella sniffed. 'I doubt there'll be much on t'table, Sid.'

'What d'you want, anyway?' Sid asked.

'Your brat of a daughter, that's what. Just look what she's done to my Daniel. He'll not be able to breathe if it swells much more.'

There was a short silence when Mattie guessed her father was assessing the damage she'd caused to Daniel's nose.

'Get some ice on it,' was his only comment.

'Ice? Where d'you think I'm going to find ice?'

'Trout'll let you have some. He's always got plenty.' 'Trout' was Herbert Troughton. He was a fishmonger two streets away.

'An' you think that'll put everything reet, do you? Well, it won't. Wait till 'is dad sees his face. He'll be round 'ere, Sid Price, so you'd better watch out.'

'Oh I'm quivering in me boots,' Sid said and pushed past his wife, who was still being propped up by the doorway. 'Where's me tea, woman?'

With an exasperated shake of her head, Bella wagged her finger at Elsie. 'I feel for you, Elsie love, I really do, but just sometimes, I could shake you.

You'd better get that lass of yours sorted out else she'll be getting herself into trouble.'

Her temper was dying a little now. Kids will be kids, Bella thought, and lads'll always fight, but it had shocked her to hear that it had been Mattie Price who'd inflicted such damage on Daniel. A straight-forward fight between two boys was one thing; this was quite another. She turned and gave him a little push. 'Come on with you, then. Let's go round to Trout's.' As they left the yard she raised her voice. 'If you can hear me, Mattie Price, you just watch your step in future else I'll tan your backside for you.'

With a slam of the yard door they were gone, and Mattie breathed a sigh of relief and escaped from her putrid, self-inflicted prison. She entered by the back door, tiptoed through the scullery and tried to sidle past her father sitting at the table in the kitchen.

'You watch your step, girl,' he muttered, though he did not turn his head to look at her. 'I've enough trouble with the neighbours as it is. And don't touch them things under your bed either. Keep your nose out.'

Mattie fled upstairs to the attic bedroom. She shared a bed with her younger sister, Nancy, whilst Joe and Lewis shared another. Between the two beds hung a moth-eaten brown curtain in a half-hearted attempt to separate them. The baby, Toby, still slept in a drawer in their parents' bedroom, but no doubt he'd soon be put in the battered cot in the corner of the attic room. Their home was a one-up-one-down house, next but one to the end of a street of terraced houses. Only the addition of a scullery added a little more room to the overcrowded house. Across the yard was the privy and a shed which housed a copper for boiling laundry and a sink for washing clothes by hand. A tin bath hung from a hook on the wall, though it wasn't in use every Friday night as were the baths of most of the families in their street.

'Mucky lot, them Prices,' was the general opinion of their neighbours who, though poor, were proud and good-living folk. 'Bit o' soap and water doesn't cost much.'

'I dread to think what them kids are going to grow up like.'

And heads would nod sagely.

Mattie crept into bed. Her tummy was rumbling with hunger but she daren't go down and ask for something to eat. The meagre tea set before her father – bread that was already going mouldy and a piece of hard cheese – was enough to tell her that there wasn't much food in the house. Today was only Friday, but there was a slight chance that Joe might bring something home later . . . She snuggled down beneath the one blanket, worn thin with age and use, and old coats that made up the children's bedcovers. There were three pillows with black and white ticking, but no pillowcases or sheets.

Mattie, exhausted by the struggles of her daily life, fell asleep. Friday night. Two whole days without the taunts and the bullying . . .

Two

On the Monday, Mattie arrived early at school. During playtimes, she hid in the cloakroom and at the end of afternoon school, she loitered in the classroom, sitting at her desk with a maths book taken from a shelf in the bookcase at the back of the room. Books about sums and puzzles of any kind fascinated her. She read and devoured them as other children read story books. She enjoyed all the subjects Miss Donaldson taught her class of mixed ages and abilities. Mattie loved hearing about faraway places and dreamed of one day visiting them. She liked history and learning about how people had lived in the olden days. Some of them, she thought wryly, had had better lives than she had now. And she liked words, especially the ones which were long and difficult to spell and pronounce, but arithmetic was Mattie's favourite subject.

The classroom door opened and her teacher came back into the room.

'Hello, Mattie. You still here?' The kindly young woman didn't add the obvious jocular phrase, 'No home to go to?' She was well aware of Mattie's home life and she'd even heard about the tortuous journeys to and from school that the girl suffered.

'Yes, miss. D'you mind?'

'Not at all, Mattie. Are you waiting for Joe?'

Mattie shook her head. 'No. He always goes to—' She hesitated, unwilling to say 'work'. She wasn't sure at what age a boy was legally allowed to work. She didn't want any kind of authority arriving at their door to make enquiries. If she were the cause of such a visit, her father would undoubtedly give her a good hiding. Though what was 'good' about it, Mattie could never understand. 'To the market after school,' she added now.

Patricia Donaldson perched herself on her high seat behind the tall desk from where she viewed all her class. 'I've some marking to do, so you can stay here until I go home, if you like.' She opened the first exercise book, but her glance went back to the bent head of her pupil and she chewed her bottom lip thoughtfully. Every so often Mattie scratched her head. Patricia hoped the poor child hadn't got nits yet again. Only the previous evening she had been talking to her brother about the girl. Hugh Donaldson was a professor – one of the youngest – at the city's university, which had been founded in 1905. Patricia and Hugh still lived together in the family home. Their parents had died and the house had been bequeathed to them jointly. They'd both been born in Sheffield and had lived on the outskirts of the city all their lives except for the time they had been away at university or, in Patricia's case, teacher training college.

'She's such a bright kid,' Patricia had told him over their tea, 'but her home life is appalling. Her father is reportedly a thief and her mother is drunk most of the time, though how she gets the money for it, God alone knows. Poor Mattie doesn't stand a chance of getting the further education that would help her fulfil her potential.'

'And you think she's got potential?'

'Oh I do. She's the cleverest child I've ever come across.'

'Presumably she'll leave school at fourteen.'

'Before, I'm guessing, if her father has his way.'

'He'll have to be careful he doesn't run up against the law if he takes her out of school illegally.'

Patricia sniffed and said tartly, 'I don't think that would bother him. He seems to escape the law with remarkable facility.'

'So you don't think there's any chance of her being able to go to the girls' secondary school?'

Patricia gave a most unladylike snort of derision. 'Even if she got a scholarship, was provided with the uniform and all the books and equipment needed, there'd be no way her parents – her father in particular – would allow it. He wants her earning money as soon as possible. Her brother, Joe, is thirteen. He already works at the market outside school hours helping the stall holders. His form teacher, Anthony Carter, says he falls asleep in class quite often.'

'Is he bright too?'

'A good average, Anthony says, but the lad has ambitions. He wants to join the army.'

'To get away from home, I expect. It's the best thing he could do. Life in the army would probably be the making of him. He's not following in his father's footsteps, though, is he? Becoming involved in criminal activities, I mean?'

Patricia shook her head. 'Not as far as I know. Evidently, the market traders think very highly of him. At the end of the week he's given any perishable food that's unsold and won't be saleable at the next market. I expect it's what keeps his family going, if truth be told.'

There was silence between them as they finished eating. When Patricia served coffee, Hugh said tentatively, 'He won't – the father, I mean – involve the little lass in his thieving ways, will he?'

'I would hate to accuse any father – however reprehensible he is in many ways – of anything like that. But I will keep a close eye on her whilst she's in my class and maybe have a quiet word with her next teacher too.'

Now, as Patricia regarded Mattie's bent head, the marking forgotten for the moment, she recalled the conversation with her brother and also what she had heard this morning in the staffroom about the fracas between Mattie and Daniel Spencer on Friday after school. She understood exactly why Mattie was lingering in the classroom with her books and puzzles; it was the child's haven.

They both worked quietly for half an hour until Patricia closed the last exercise book and laid down her red pen. She stood and walked to where Mattie was still engrossed in her books. Patricia sat down on the child's chair next to her and leaned across to see what Mattie was writing on scraps of paper. She was copying sums from the open textbook and then working out the answers. The teacher wasn't really surprised to see that the book was one used by children at least two years older than Mattie.

'I have to go home now, Mattie, and the school cleaners will be wanting to do this room. I'm sorry, but we have to leave.'

Mattie glanced up and smiled at her. Patricia was startled. How pretty the child was when she smiled, which sadly wasn't very often. Her cheeks dimpled and her green eyes, which usually looked so sad, lit up.

'Would you like me to mark your sums?'

'Only if you've time, miss. I did struggle a bit with the last two, but I think the rest are right.'

She gathered the scraps of paper together and handed them to the teacher. Patricia glanced through them, nodding as she finished reading through each one, until she came to the last page. 'Ah yes, now here's where you've gone wrong, Mattie, but these are problems; something we've not learnt in class yet.'

'No, miss. I read the explanation in this book, but it was a bit hard to understand.'

'Let me show you.' Swiftly, Patricia explained the workings of a mathematical problem. When she finished, Mattie beamed. 'I understand it now.'

'Would you like to take this book home with you and try some more?'

For a moment Mattie looked longingly at the book, but then she shook her head. 'I'd better not, miss. It – it might get – lost.'

It was more likely, Patricia thought, that the girl's father would sell or pawn it.

'Very well, then.'

'Could I stay here again tomorrow night after school and do some more?' The hope in the girl's eyes was touching.

'I don't stay after school every night,' Patricia said, 'but I'll speak to Mr Musgrave and see what he says. All right?'

Mr Musgrave was the headmaster, a tall, imposing figure who rarely smiled. Mattie was a little afraid of him and kept out of his way as much as possible.

'Will he – will he be cross?'

'I wouldn't think so for a moment. Mr Musgrave likes to encourage anyone who wants to learn.'

'Even me?' Mattie whispered, and Patricia's heart ached as she said a little unsteadily, 'Especially you, Mattie.' More briskly, she said, 'Now, I'll walk a little way home with you, if you like. It's not out of my way.'

Mattie thanked her. Her teacher wasn't to know that the danger no longer lay on the walk home – all her classmates would have gone by now – but when she got to her own street, her nemesis might be waiting for her.

It was about a mile from the school to Mattie's home and Patricia left her about halfway. 'I have to go this way now, Mattie. Will you be all right?'

'Yes, miss. Thank you. See you tomorrow.'

As she turned the corner at the top of the street where she lived, she could see a group of boys kicking a battered football. Few vehicles ever visited this street and so it was a relatively safe playground. Her brother Lewis was amongst them – and so was Daniel.

She wondered whether she should go on to the parallel street, walk to the bottom end and reach her home that way, but then she lifted her chin, squared her shoulders and marched bravely down the street, quickening her pace as she passed the Spencers' house. As she drew level with the boys, Daniel detached himself from the game and came towards her. Mattie had the urge to run but, instead, she faced him, her fists clenched at her side. Her brother Lewis, a thin little boy of eight, ran across the road towards Daniel. 'Don't you hurt our Mattie, Dan. Joe'll come looking for you.'

'I won't,' Daniel shouted to him and then grinned at her.

Slowly Mattie let out the breath she had been holding and loosened her fists, but she continued to stare at him and to be ready for flight should he make a move towards her.

'It's all right, Mattie. I'm not going to pull your hair. I – I just wanted to tell you I'm sorry for teasing you.'

Mattie gaped at him. This wasn't the Daniel Spencer she knew. Had her blow to his face damaged his brain? His nose was still swollen and turning purple now. There were even dark shadows under his eyes where the bruising was spreading.

In a small voice she said, 'I'm sorry I hit you so hard.'

He laughed and then winced as if the movement

on his face hurt a little. 'But you're not sorry you hit me?'

Mattie lifted her chin. 'You shouldn't have pulled my hair. That hurt too.'

Daniel nodded. 'I won't do it again.'

Mattie grinned. 'Not till next time.'

'No, I mean it. I won't.'

'Pigs might fly.'

They stood staring at each other. Two ten-year-old kids locked together in the poverty of one of the poorer areas of the city.

'Is your mum still mad at me?' Mattie asked.

'Don't worry about her. She'll forget about it once the bruise has gone. 'Sides, she's got more to worry about than me getting into a fight.' He bit his lip and then burst out. 'Me dad got laid off on Friday.'

'I'm sorry.'

Daniel's father, Rod, was known to be a hard worker at the steel works, but in these difficult times, people were getting laid off. He wasn't the first and even the children knew he probably wouldn't be the last.

Mattie pulled in a deep breath. 'I'll go and see her.'

'Who?'

'Your mum.'

Daniel tried to pull a face, but winced again. 'I wouldn't. She'll smack your legs.'

Mattie shrugged. 'Wouldn't be the first time I've had my legs smacked.'

She turned and marched purposefully back up the street towards the passageway between the houses leading to Dan's home before her courage deserted her.

Bella Spencer was in her backyard, standing with her arms on the top of the fence chatting to her neighbour. Both women turned towards Mattie. There was a moment's surprised pause before Bella said, 'And what have you to say for yourself, Mattie Price?'

Her legs were trembling, but Mattie spoke up, her words coming out in a rush. 'I'm sorry I hurt Dan's nose, but he pulled my hair and that hurt.'

'Oh so you're a little tell-tale now, an' all, are you?'

'No, I'm not,' Mattie said quietly. 'Dan told you himself what he'd done when you were shouting at my mum.'

Bella's eyes narrowed. 'Has he done it before?'

Mattie held the woman's gaze, realizing she could be walking into a trap. To answer would, indeed, be telling tales. She pressed her lips together and remained silent.

Bella sighed and moved away from the fence. Her neighbour, Aggie, turned towards her own house, but not before saying, 'She's got some guts to face you, Bella. I'll give her that.'

Now Bella stood before Mattie, looking down at her. Bella Spencer was a big woman in all ways. She was tall and somewhat overweight and both her children – and probably her husband too – were in awe of her. Her greying hair was short and she was never seen without her overall except when she went shopping. Then she wore a black coat and a black felt hat. She was formidable in many ways with a quick temper, but she also had a kindly heart and would help her neighbours if they were in trouble. She had often helped the Price family in the past and Mattie wondered if she had caused Bella to turn her back on the most needy family in the street in the future.

'Aye well, love, you haven't got it easy, have you?' Her tone was gentle as she bent towards Mattie. Volatile though she was, Bella never bore a grudge for long and certainly not towards a child. 'Tell you what, you come round to our house after your tea and I'll wash your hair with my special shampoo, because if what our Jane said is true, the nit nurse is visiting your school tomorrow and we wouldn't like her to find anything nasty in your hair, now would we?'

Three

'Now, bend your head over the sink. This'll get rid of t'little blighters.'

Bella scrubbed hard at Mattie's head with strong fingers, soaping and rinsing in turn. Three times Mattie submitted silently to her ministrations. When Bella was done, she sat Mattie in front of the kitchen range and combed her long hair. 'Now we'll dry it. First with a towel and then you can sit here in front of t'fire with Jane and both dry your hair. You know, love, t'isn't my business, I know, but you'd be much better with short hair like Jane's. It'd be so much easier to keep it clean. And it's such a pretty colour when it's washed. Auburn with reddish tints in it, an' there's a bit o' curl in it, an' all.'

'I don't think Mum would let me have it cut.'

Bella sniffed and muttered, half to herself, 'She mebbe wouldn't even notice.' She sat down in the battered easy chair at the side of the hearth and picked up her knitting. Mattie glanced at the garment Bella was creating; it looked like a pullover for Daniel. The two girls sat side by side, their heads bent forward to dry their hair. They didn't speak to each other; not because they were unfriendly, but Jane, at two years younger than Mattie, was a little in awe of her.

And Mattie? Well, she kept herself to herself at school and in the street. She rarely played outside with the other children even though her brother, Lewis, and even six-year-old Nancy, ran riot with the other local children. But for Mattie, the walks to and from school were torture enough without asking for trouble nearer home. When not at school, she did jobs about the house. Not only did it help her mother but it also gave her an excuse not to go out.

When Nancy begged, 'Come and play, Mattie,' she would say, 'I'm too busy. There's the baby to mind. Mum's not well again.'

She washed the pots in the deep sink that had once been white, but was now cracked and stained. She tidied the kitchen and scrubbed the floors and, on Saturdays, she lit the fire in the copper in the shed across the yard and washed and mangled her father's shirt and those of her brothers. Then she would wash her own blouse and Nancy's too, but she dare not wash their underwear. It was already too holey and would most likely disintegrate if exposed to too much soap and water. She washed the baby's nappies, wrinkling her nose at the dreadful smell. Even Mattie was amazed at how little Toby could thrive in such a hovel. He was a happy, placid little chap. But then, she thought, Joe always made sure to bring home milk for him before anyone else.

When Mattie arrived home after having her hair washed at Bella's, her mother was sitting by the cold range, with the baby on her lap.

'Mum,' Mattie stood on the hearth in front of her, 'can I have my hair cut?'

Elsie blinked and tried to focus on her daughter's face. 'Cut your hair?' she repeated. 'Whatever for? It's pretty hair.' She touched her own prematurely greying hair saying wistfully, 'I had hair like yours once.'

'It'd be easier to keep it . . .' Mattie hesitated over what word to use. She didn't want to upset her mother. Elsie was prone to fits of weeping and wailing if something upset her, which usually ended with Sid smacking her across the face. So Mattie finished her sentence lamely with the word, 'Nice.'

'Get me a drink, love, will you?' Elsie said. 'There's a bottle in the copper in the wash house. Don't let your dad see it though. Just a little nip, Mattie love. Just to steady me nerves.'

Mattie sighed, took a cracked mug from the kitchen and crossed the yard to the shed. She opened the door a little way, but it came up against something hard. There was just enough room for her to squeeze in but she couldn't get to the copper now that two bicycles stood in front of it.

She put the cup down and grasped the nearest bike and tugged at it. Then she tried to manoeuvre it so that she could get to the copper.

'What d'you think you're doing?'

Mattie jumped and let go of the bike so that it crashed back against the other one. At the same moment, her father smacked her on the side of the head. 'I've told you to leave my things alone.'

'How can I get to the copper to do the washing?' she retorted, rubbing the side of her head.

He laughed, but the sound was without humour.

'Washing? More likely to be after the bottle she hides in there.' Mattie felt colour suffuse her face. 'Aye, I thought so. How she gets it, I don't know.' He glared at her. 'D'you get it for her?'

'No, Dad, I don't.'

'Is it Joe, then?'

'I don't think so. He always brings food home.'

'Must be that little tyke Lewis, then. I'll have words with him.'

Mattie trembled for her younger brother. She knew only too well what her father's 'words' were. But for now all he did was nod towards the copper. 'Leave it where it is. If she wants it, she can fetch it 'erssen.'

'Now then, let's have a look at you.' Nurse Burton, the 'nit nurse', was a young woman in her thirties. Mattie had seen her once before and that time the nurse had found 'the little blighters', as Bella called them, in her hair. Gently, the nurse unwound Mattie's plait and parted her hair into sections, searching the scalp for tell-tale signs. After a few moments, she declared, 'No, all clear, Mattie. And your hair is nice and clean. Strangely, though, head lice like clean hair the best. That seems funny, doesn't it? But you're fine this time.' She paused and then added, 'My notes tell me that you did have a problem last time I visited.'

Mattie was an honest child. She took a deep breath. 'I did have them, nurse, but a lady in our street washed my hair last night with what she calls her special shampoo. And they've gone.'

'Ah, I see,' Nurse Burton said. 'You know, it would be so much easier if you had short hair. It's so difficult to get them out of long hair. Your neighbour has certainly done a good job, but it's likely you might get them again.'

'That's what Mrs Spencer said. That I should have short hair, I mean, but Mum doesn't want me to have it cut.'

The nurse was very tempted to say, 'Then she should help you look after your hair better', but she bit back the words and instead said kindly, 'Couldn't you explain to your mum what's happening? Perhaps she would agree then.'

'I'll try,' Mattie whispered.

Mattie stayed late after school each afternoon. It wasn't so much now that she was trying to avoid the taunts and the name-calling, but that she actually enjoyed the quiet of being in the classroom on her own and being able to choose books to work on or to read.

'It's all right for you to stay after school whenever you want to, Mattie,' Patricia Donaldson told her. 'I've cleared it with Mr Musgrave. Help yourself to whatever books you want and you can get paper out of the store cupboard – and, if you'd like your work marked, leave it on my desk and I'll have a look at it.' Mattie had beamed and Patricia marvelled again at the change in the child when she smiled. 'You must leave when the cleaners come to do this classroom. That's all.'

Mattie had been working peacefully for half an hour, struggling to understand the concept of algebra in a maths book that was meant for pupils two or three years ahead of her, when the door opened and the headmaster came in. Mattie felt a twinge of panic. Was she in trouble? But the usually dour man was actually smiling and Mattie's heartbeat settled back to its usual rhythm.

Ben Musgrave cultivated the severe look deliberately to give him the gravitas he believed his position needed. He found that it propagated the idea that he was a strict and formidable headmaster amongst his pupils and even his staff. He rarely had to inflict corporal punishment; a mere look from Mr Musgrave's stern face would quell the naughtiest child. But even those in awe of him recognized that he was always fair. Faced with an altercation between pupils, or even between pupil and teacher, he would always listen to each side of the argument and then adjudicate impartially. No one could ever accuse him of being biased.

'Hello, Mattie,' he said, still standing in the doorway of the classroom. That was another thing that made everyone like him, even if they were a little in awe of him; he knew every child and member of staff – including the non-teaching staff – by name and he made it his business to know something of their background and home life too. And so, as he moved into the room and sat down in front of Mattie, he knew all about her, even more since his talk with Patricia the previous day.

'Miss Donaldson says you're doing very well in all your lessons but that your favourite is maths. Is that right?'

'Yes, sir.'

'Would you like to show me what you're doing?'

Mattie turned the textbook towards him and then showed him her jottings on the scraps of paper. He studied them carefully.

'Very good, Mattie. Very good indeed, but just a couple of points. What is that figure there?'

'It's a seven, sir.'

'Ah, now, you need to write your figures more carefully. That could be mistaken for a one and in an examination it could be marked as incorrect even though, in fact, it is quite right. Now, let me show you how the Europeans write a seven.' He took up her pencil and wrote a number seven with a line through the downward stroke. 'See,' he said, turning the page towards her. 'Now, it can't be confused with a one, can it?'

'No, sir.'

'And now I see that those figures are both sevens, then all your sums are correct.' He smiled at the solemn-faced child. 'Well done, Mattie. Now, is there anything I can help you with? Before I became headmaster of this school, I was a maths teacher at a secondary school.' He leaned a little closer as if imparting a confidence. 'It was always my favourite subject too.'

'Well,' she said hesitantly, hardly able to believe that Mr Musgrave was taking such an interest in her. 'I've been reading in this book about algebra, but it's very difficult to understand.'

'Ah, yes, now, you're right, it is, but once you get the hang of it, Mattie, it can be fascinating. Here, let me explain.'

They spent almost another hour, their heads bent together over the book, until one of the cleaners tapped tentatively on the door.

'Oh sorry, sir, I thought it was just the little lass still in here. We can come back . . .'

'No, no, Mrs Kemp. Come in. We ought to finish anyway.' He glanced at his wristwatch. 'My goodness, I didn't realize it was that time already. I hope your mother won't have been worried, Mattie. Off you go. Quickly now.'

Mattie smiled thinly but didn't tell him that it was unlikely her mother would even notice that she had not come home from school. It would have sounded very disloyal. She returned the books to the shelf and tidied her papers.

'Good night, Mr Musgrave, and thank you for helping me. Good night, Mrs Kemp.'

As the two adults watched the child go, Mrs Kemp murmured, 'Poor little scrap and such a nice, polite kid too. I'm not one to gossip, Mr Musgrave, as you well know. The parents of most of the kids who come to this school are struggling in these difficult times, but that child has a harder time than most.'

The headmaster nodded. 'Yes, Mrs Kemp, I do know. And the irony of it is that the child is bright – very bright – but it's unlikely she will have the opportunity to reach her potential.'

'Unless, of course, sir,' Mrs Kemp said quietly, 'you were able to do something to help her.'

'Mm,' Ben Musgrave said, his gaze still on the door through which Mattie had left. 'I will certainly give the matter some thought.'

There was silence between them for a moment before Mrs Kemp cleared her throat and said hesitantly, 'If you'll excuse me, sir, I must get on.'

Mr Musgrave jumped, startled from his reverie. 'Of course, Mrs Kemp. I'm so sorry to have held you up.'

The headmaster returned to his office, where he sat for some time, deep in thought.

Four

Mattie ran home, not because she was afraid of being in trouble for being late, but because she felt the exhilaration of having learnt something new. She ran and skipped her way home. Algebra. The very name sounded something far beyond her comprehension. And yet it wasn't. The way Mr Musgrave had described it all to her was perfectly clear. Now she had something else to fill her mind with and to take her away from the hardships of her daily existence.

'Where've you been till now?' her father demanded harshly as she stepped in through the back door. 'Lewis and Nancy have been home ages.' He smirked. 'Goody two-shoes been kept in, have you?'

Mattie had to think quickly. She daren't tell her father – or anyone at home – the real reason she now stayed behind at school. 'I've been playing, Dad.'

Sid glowered. 'You've no time to be playing. Your mum needs help.' He jerked his thumb towards the ceiling. 'Can't you hear that little bleeder squealing?'

'Mebbe he's hungry.'

Her mother spoke up from her chair near the cold range. 'I've just fed him.'

'Then – then mebbe he needs winding – or changing.'

Elsie shrugged as if she neither knew nor cared.

'Are there any clean nappies?' Mattie asked. Nappies were rather a grand name for the rags that served that purpose in the Price household.

'No. There's a bucketful in the shed need washing, but I can't get to the copper for bikes.' Elsie cast a resentful look at her husband. 'How am I expected to cope if I can't even get to the copper?'

As if you've tried, Mattie thought, but Sid was not so reticent. 'Can't get to your stash of booze, more like.' He heaved himself to his feet. 'You see to him,' he said to Mattie, gesturing again towards the ceiling, 'and I'll move the bikes, but just you mind you don't breathe a word about them. Not to anyone. You hear me?'

'Yes, Dad.'

When she'd settled the baby, she tackled the dirty nappies, screwing up her face against the smell. She left them in a bucket just inside the shed. She'd hang them on the line strung across the yard before she went to school tomorrow.

'Mum.' Once again Mattie stood in front of her mother, the following afternoon after school. She had stayed for a short while, but had been careful not to be as late again. But today, her father was out anyway. 'Mum, can I have my hair cut? The nit nurse said it would be a good idea.'

Elsie glared at her. 'Did she now? And what business is it of hers?'

'She – er – she has to be sure we haven't got nits.'

'And have you?'

'Not this time, but I did have last time she came to the school.'

'So there's no need to cut your hair now, is there?'

'Well – no – but . . .'

Elsie was frowning and Mattie felt a quiver of fear. That look was sometimes a prelude to an outburst of booze-fuelled temper. 'But what?'

Mattie pulled in a deep breath. 'It'd be easier to *keep* it right.'

With a sudden swift movement that belied her normal lethargy, Elsie grabbed Mattie's plait and pulled it towards her, making the girl twist round. 'Mum, you're hurting.'

'I'll hurt you, you ungrateful little sod.' Still holding the plait, Elsie stood up and reached for a pair of scissors from the mantelpiece above the range. Then she hacked off the plait just below the level of Mattie's ears.

'There. That suit you? Now get up to bed and stay there. I don't want to set eyes on you again tonight.'

Mattie stumbled up the stairs, fighting back the tears. She wouldn't let her mother see her cry; she wouldn't let anyone see her cry, but her head still hurt and the humiliation cut deep. She'd wanted her hair cut short, but not like that, not savagely hacked off with no proper trimming of the ends. She'd be a laughing stock at school tomorrow. *As if I'm not already*, she thought ruefully. She buried her head beneath the pile of old coats until one by one her sister and brothers came up to bed. It was dark by the time Joe tiptoed into the room. It was him she'd been waiting for. She idolized her older brother; he looked out for her. He looked out for them all. Mattie eased herself out of the bed and stood at the end of the curtain separating the two halves of the room.

'Joe,' she whispered.

He held the candle he carried high to look at her. 'You all right, Mattie?'

'No. Look.' She pulled at the end of her hair. 'Look what Mum did.'

Joe came closer. 'Why'd she do that?'

'I – I asked if I could have my hair cut. I get nits, Joe, and the nurse that visits the school said it'd be better if I had shorter hair, but when I told Mum she got mad, grabbed the scissors and just – just cut the plait off.'

'Poor Mattie,' he said and the genuine sympathy in his tone made tears well in her eyes again. 'She only gets a bit lairy when she's been drinking too much. Look, get up early in the morning – when I get up – and I'll see what I can do with it before I go to the early market.' Mattie knew that Joe could sometimes get an hour or so's work in before school, helping the farmers from the countryside unpack and set out their stalls with locally grown produce. It was they who often said, 'Come back this afternoon, lad, when we're packing up. There's bound to be a bit o' summat not worth the bother of us tecking home.' Several of them knew Joe's family circumstances and none of them liked to hear of bairns going hungry because of a feckless father. 'Try to get some sleep,' Joe said now. 'And don't worry. We'll sort something out.'

Mattie flung her arms round his waist and hugged

him hard. 'Oh Joe, I don't know what I'd do without you – what we'd all do without you.'

He patted her shoulder awkwardly. 'Get back into bed, Mattie.'

She climbed back in carefully so that she didn't disturb Nancy. Joe pulled the coats over her.

She snuggled down. She felt better now Joe was here. Things were always better when Joe was here.

The following morning her classmates stared at her, but, surprisingly, no one pointed a finger and laughed. Earlier, Joe had done his best to trim the back of her hair and Nancy had given her two of her slides to hold it back behind her ears. Nancy had always had shorter hair; blonde curls which, if washed regularly, would have been very pretty. As it was, her hair was always greasy and unkempt.

In the dinner break, Dan whispered, 'Come to our house tonight, Mattie. My mum's a dab hand at cutting hair. She does all ours. Even me dad's.' He'd been much nicer to her since their altercation and she saw now that the bruising on his face was fading. 'I'll walk home with you, if you like,' he added.

Mattie gaped at him. She wondered if he was planning something horrible to pay her back. She bit her lip but nodded agreement. She'd just have to take that risk.

As they left the school later that afternoon, Dan walked beside her, whistling jauntily, his hands in his pockets. Mattie glanced behind her once or twice, wondering if the other kids were following them, but there was no sign of anyone.

'It's all right, Mattie, they won't tease you while you're with me.'

Mattie swallowed, still unsure whether to believe him or not. He'd always been the ringleader amongst her tormentors. She glanced at him. Dan was tall for his age with dark brown, wavy hair and deep brown eyes. He was quite good-looking, she supposed, but not as handsome as Joe, who had fair hair and bright blue eyes. In Mattie's estimation no one was as wonderful as her brother.

When they reached the top of their street, Mattie began to breathe more easily. He could hardly do much to her now that they were so close to both their homes.

'Come on in. Mum won't mind.'

He led the way down the ginnel and into the Spencers' backyard. Bella was just gathering her day's washing off the line.

'Now what have you two scallywags been up to? Not fighting again, I hope.'

Dan grinned. 'No, Mum. Me and Mattie aren't going to fall out anymore. We're mates now, aren't we, Mattie?'

Mattie smiled weakly whilst Bella looked up to the sky as if searching for something. 'I'm looking for flying pigs.'

'No, I mean it, Mum. 'Sides, I want to keep me nose the shape it is.'

Mattie hung her head.

'I'm only joking,' Dan said. 'You'll have to get used to me teasing you now and then, but it won't be nasty anymore. I promise.'

'Oh, now it's all coming out, is it?' Bella said. 'Been unkind to her, have you?'

'All of us were.'

'I've told you before, Dan,' Bella said sternly, 'you don't have to follow what others do. That'll get you into trouble.'

The two youngsters glanced at each other. Dan certainly wasn't going to admit that he'd been the ringleader. There was pleading in his eyes; please don't tell her. Mattie gave a little shake of her head that only he saw. Dan smiled again and said, 'Come on in and let's show Mum your hair.'

'Hair?' For the first time Bella noticed the absence of Mattie's plait. 'Whatever's been happening? The kids didn't do that to you, did they, because . . . ?'

'No, Mrs Spencer. It was my mum.'

For a moment Bella stared at her, then her face softened. 'Come on in, love, and tell me all about it.'

'Right,' Dan said, 'I'm off out to play footie.'

When Mattie had finished explaining what had happened, Bella said kindly, 'Sit down on the stool and I'll see what I can do with it.' As she combed Mattie's hair and then began to wield her scissors, Bella said, 'I would've loved to have trained to be a hairdresser, but the wages for a trainee were pitiful and I needed to earn money like we all did, I suppose. There . . .' She stood back to admire her handiwork. 'We'll give it a wash now and see how it looks, shall we?'

Half an hour later, Bella was rubbing Mattie's hair vigorously with a towel to dry it. Then she combed it again. 'Oh Mattie, now you haven't got that long plait dragging it down, it's all wavy. Just look in the mirror.'

Mattie stared into the big mirror hanging over the mantelpiece. She didn't recognize herself. It was her thin little face with big eyes staring back at her, but now it was framed by a mass of auburn waves falling almost to her shoulders.

'You've got really pretty hair, Mattie.' Bella hesitated and then added, 'You're welcome to come here each week to wash it if – if it's – er – difficult at home.'

'That's very kind of you, Mrs Spencer, but I – I don't want to be a nuisance, specially if – if . . .'

'If what, love?'

'Well, erm, you've got your own problems.'

Bella frowned for a minute and then, her face clearing, said, 'Oh you heard my Rod got laid off, did you?'

Mattie nodded.

Bella smiled, 'Well, I'm pleased to say he's found a job with one of the little mesters, on'y a couple of streets away. He used to work in t'cutlery industry years ago before he went to one of t'steel works. He'll soon pick it up again. His pay won't be as good, mind you, but at least he's got a job.'

Mattie nodded. She would have loved to have confided in Bella, but she was not going to be disloyal to her own family. Up and down their street Sid Price was known as 'a wrong 'un', but she wasn't going to be the one to confirm or deny it.

Some things were best kept secret.

Five

'So, Miss Donaldson,' Ben Musgrave sat behind his desk, leaning his elbows on it and steepling his fingers, 'what can you tell me about Mattie Price? Can you tell me a little more about her home life?'

Patricia sat down in front of him and sighed. 'It's pretty appalling, from what I know. The father doesn't work and the mother hits the bottle on a regular basis, though where she gets the money from, I don't know. The kids are often hungry. There's only the eldest boy, Joe, who keeps the family together.'

'Ah yes, Joe Price. I know him. He's a good worker at practical subjects, I understand.'

'So Anthony – Mr Carter – says.' Patricia referred to the boy's form teacher and went on to repeat all that she'd told her brother during their recent conversation about the Price family.

'We must do what we can to help him get into the army when the time comes – if that's what he wants,' Ben said, 'but my main concern is how to help little Mattie. Her ability for her age and – I have to say it – her background is amazing. It would be a travesty if she didn't get a proper chance in life. But for the present, we'll carry on helping her outside of school hours, if you're happy to do that.'

'Of course, anything I can do. Have you seen her recently?'

Ben shook his head. 'Not for a few days. Why?'

Patricia smiled. 'She's had her hair cut short. She looks like a different child. Oh, she's still dressed in rags and as thin as ever, but she looks so much happier and I think the bullying has stopped.'

'Bullying?' Ben frowned. 'I didn't know about that. I won't have that in my school.'

'It was mainly on her way home, so there wasn't much we could do.'

'Did she tell you that?'

'No. That's one thing about Mattie, she doesn't tell tales.' Patricia went on to tell him about the altercation between Mattie and Dan that she'd heard about. 'It's incredible, but he's her champion now and seems to hold sway over the other kids. At first, I think she stayed behind after school to avoid the teasing, but now she stays because she's eager to learn.'

'Then we must do all we can to help her to.'

Mattie was indeed much happier, but life was still tough. It was she and her brother, Joe, who held the family together. Whilst Joe worked outside school hours and brought food home, Mattie did her best to keep the house clean and the family's clothes washed. Usually, her father disappeared for most of the day, but just sometimes he would stay at home taking a bicycle to pieces in the yard, cleaning and painting it. That bike would then disappear to be replaced by another in need of repair. In wet weather, he would bring down the curious items from under the children's beds in the attic room and sit at the kitchen table assembling them into a wireless. But there was never one for the family to enjoy; the completed sets disappeared too, just like the bicycles. Elsie, always more nervous when Sid was at home, spent most of her day sitting by the hearth, rousing herself only to attend to the baby, Toby. Surprisingly, he was a chubby, healthy child, always beaming and rarely crying unless he was hungry or needed changing.

The other two children, Lewis at eight and Nancy at six, spent most of their time away from the house; playing in the street or venturing further away to the nearest park or playground. They appeared at meal-times – even when there was little to eat – and at bedtime. But neither of their parents worried where they were or ever asked what they were doing. At least, not until the day that Mr Wilkinson, from the corner shop in the next street, appeared in their yard, grasping Lewis's left ear firmly between his strong finger and thumb.

'Ouch, you're hurting.'

'I'll hurt you, you little sod. Think you can steal from me, do you?' He stopped when he saw Mattie pegging out washing on the line, but he did not release Lewis. 'Where's your dad?' he asked Mattie harshly.

'Out.'

'Aye, I bet he is.' His tone was laced with sarcasm. 'And your mum?'

'In the house, but . . .'

'Right, then. I'll have a word with her.'

'Oh I don't think —' Mattie began, but Mr Wilkinson was already marching towards the back door, dragging his captive with him.

'You there, Mrs Price. I need a word . . .' He opened the door and went inside without waiting for an invitation. Mattie hurried after him.

Elsie looked up startled. She was cuddling Toby, but Mattie noticed that there was a half-empty bottle of whisky on the floor beside her chair. She sighed inwardly; Dad must have been spending more time at home and upsetting her mum.

At that moment, Mr Wilkinson's beady eyes spotted the bottle too. 'Ah,' he said triumphantly. 'So today's not the first time this little varmint has stolen from my shop.'

Elsie frowned and glanced at Lewis, but her eyes were glazed over and, when she spoke, her words were slurred. 'I don't know what you're talking about, Mr Wilkinson.'

'Well, I'll tell you.' At last, he released his grip on Lewis but before the boy could escape entirely, the shopkeeper smacked him sharply on the side of the head. 'He's been stealing from my shop, probably for a while. I knew me stock was disappearing, but I couldn't catch the criminal. But, this morning, I did. Red-handed. Picking up a bottle of my best whisky from the shelf as brazen as you like. Oh, he thought he was being clever, waiting till I'd gone into me storeroom at the back of the shop, but I came back a bit quicker than he was expecting and saw him. Now, I'm not one to cause trouble for folks in this neighbourhood. I've me living to make, so I need to keep folks' good will. So, if you give me the money for one bottle—' he nodded towards the bottle on the hearth – 'because I can see that's one of mine, then we'll say no more about it, except that I don't want to see him in my shop anymore. His brother, Joe, or young Mattie here, yes, but not this little tyke.'

'I haven't got the money, Mr Wilkinson, but I'll send Joe round tonight before you close.'

'Aye well, see that you do.' He turned once again towards Lewis. 'And as for you, I'll be warning all the shopkeepers around here, so don't think you can go nicking from them instead.'

He turned and marched out of the house, indignation in every stride.

'Oh Lewis, you shouldn't go stealing. We don't want a thief in the family.'

Mattie and her brother exchanged a wry glance and, if it hadn't been so serious, Mattie would have giggled. Where on earth did their mother think all those bicycles and wireless parts that Sid brought home came from? Later, in their bedroom, Mattie remonstrated with him.

'Lewis, you mustn't go stealing anymore.'

'I'll go further away from round here. Into town, mebbe.'

'That's not the point. It's wrong. You'll get caught.'

Lewis shrugged. 'No, I won't. I'm quick.'

'Not quick enough for Mr Wilkinson.'

Lewis grinned. 'It's taken him months to catch me, Mattie. I've had a lot more than just one bottle off him.'

Mattie groaned. 'Don't you see? You'll end up in prison.'

'They don't send kids to prison.'

'No, but they send 'em – somewhere.' Mattie's knowledge on the subject was vague, but she knew the young boy would not escape punishment of some sort if he was caught.

But Lewis only shrugged. 'Then I'll mind they don't catch me. There's plenty of shops in town. I don't need to go to the same one for weeks.'

'Oh Lewis, please don't.' But the boy was deaf to her pleas.

'I'm not a tell-tale normally, Joe,' Mattie whispered late that night. 'But this is serious. Lewis has been stealing whisky for Mum from Mr Wilkinson's shop.'

'Don't worry, Mattie. I know all about it. I've tried to talk to him time and again, but he won't listen. I reckon we've got another thief in the family.'

He watched Mattie's stricken face in the flickering candlelight. He touched her arm. 'You just look out for yourself. You're clever, Mattie. You could really go places, if only you had the chance.'

'Miss Donaldson . . .' Ben Musgrave approached her in the staffroom during the dinner break. During school time the teachers always called each other by their surnames. One or two might use Christian names outside school, but no one ever called the headmaster anything but 'Mr Musgrave'. 'I've spoken to my colleague who is headmistress at the girls' secondary school about Mattie Price.' A small smile quirked his mouth. 'She's intrigued.'

Patricia raised her eyebrows quizzically. 'But is she "intrigued" enough to want to help her?'

'I'm hoping so. She wants to meet Mattie.'

'Oh dear.' Patricia's face fell.

'Is that a problem? I thought you said she looked much better since she'd had her hair cut.'

'I did – she does. But – but her clothes . . .'

Ben's smile widened. 'Oh, I think I can sort that out. My wife is involved in various charitable organizations which hold regular jumble sales . . .'

Patricia opened her mouth to protest, but he held up his hand to forestall her. 'Don't worry. Some of the stuff is quite good quality and Mavis would wash it and alter it to fit the girl, if necessary.'

Then Patricia remembered: Mavis Musgrave was the domestic science teacher at the very school Ben was talking about. And she taught sewing and simple dressmaking too. Ben and Mavis Musgrave were in their mid-fifties and had never been able to have children of their own. Patricia wasn't sure whether being a teacher amongst children all day helped or not. In her case – she was one of the many young women doomed to spinsterhood by the Great War – it did help. She loved all the children she taught and they were a great solace to her – even if they were only 'on loan' for a few hours each school day.

Patricia beamed. 'Oh, that would be so kind of her. And of you, too, to take such an interest in Mattie. She just deserves a chance, that's all.'

'Then she shall have it.' Ben paused and then added, 'But you still look worried.'

'I am because even if we managed – somehow – to get her a place there, I don't know what her family will say – or do.'

Mattie didn't know what to do. When Miss Donaldson had told her that the headmistress of the girls' secondary school wanted to interview her, she stared at her teacher open-mouthed. 'But – but – why, miss?'

'It's nothing to worry about, Mattie, I promise. She's coming here next Monday after we finish school and she'll see you in Mr Musgrave's office.'

'But – why?' Mattie asked again. 'I mean – I can't go to her school.' She paused and then added so wistfully that it almost broke Patricia's heart, 'Can I?'

'The truth is, Mattie, I don't know. All I know for now is that Miss Parsons wants to meet you.' Patricia hesitated briefly before adding carefully, 'Do you think you'd be able to wash your hair the night before?'

Mattie thought quickly. Mrs Spencer had said she could go to their house to wash her hair and she'd even said Mattie could have a bath there if she wanted. And oh, how she wanted to now. But then she glanced down at the grubby, ragged dress she was wearing. 'I don't have any other dress than this one, miss,' she said in a small voice.

'Don't worry about that. I'll be bringing something on Monday for you to wear.'

Mattie didn't stay after school; she ran all the way

home, though it was not to her own house she went first, but to the Spencers' at the top of the street.

'Hello, Mattie love. What brings you here? And where's Dan?'

'I – I didn't wait for him. I wanted to see you on your own.'

Bella laughed loudly. 'Ooo, secrets, is it? Go on, then, love.'

Swiftly, Mattie explained what Miss Donaldson had told her. 'She said she's going to bring me something better to wear on Monday if I could wash my hair and – and maybe have a bath too. I just wondered if . . .' Her voice faded away, but Bella understood.

'Of course you can. You come up on Friday evening about seven. I'll even ask Rod if you can have first dip. He'll not mind for once.'

It was the custom in many households that on bath nights in the tin bath in front of the range, the man of the household had first turn in the clean, hot water, followed by his wife and then any children from the oldest to the youngest. The Spencers only had the two: Dan and Jane.

'I always wash my hair and Jane's at the sink in the scullery,' Bella explained. 'By the time we get to the bath the water's that murky, we'd be putting more dirt in our hair than we'd be washing out. So, we'll do yours along with ours. Yours doesn't take much drying now, does it?'

Mattie shook her head, her eyes shining. 'No, it doesn't. Thanks to you.'

Bella touched the girl's cheek in a tender gesture. She was becoming quite fond of Mattie even though she had no time for the rest of the Price family, except perhaps Joe. Years ago, she'd been friendly with Elsie, but now she was irritated by the woman's lack of spirit to stand up to her husband. And the neglect of her children disgusted the maternal Bella.

'See you Friday night, then, Mattie love.'

Six

Once the two girls had washed their hair with Bella's help and had had their bath, the three women went up the stairs to the bedroom where Bella and her husband slept whilst Rod and Dan bathed in turn in front of the range. For once, Jane too had been allowed to bathe before her dad.

'Come on in and let's get your hair dried,' Bella invited and Mattie tiptoed into the room, almost afraid to intrude. She stopped in the doorway and stared in amazement. Sturdy, mahogany furniture – a wardrobe, dressing table and washstand stood against the walls, whilst in the centre of the room, its head against one wall, was a double bed and on the top was the most glorious sight; a pink, silk eiderdown.

'Oh,' Mattie breathed.

'Come on, love. Water's dripping down your neck.'

Slowly, Mattie moved into the room to sit on the stool in front of the dressing table, but her gaze was still on the pretty bedcover.

'My mum and dad bought me that when I got married,' Bella explained.

'It's beautiful,' Mattie breathed. Now she glanced around the rest of the room. The furniture gleamed, polished every week by a house-proud Bella. In the centre of the floor was a square of carpet. True, it was a little threadbare in places, but to have a carpet in a bedroom at all seemed the height of luxury to Mattie. In their house, there were no floor coverings of any sort, not even a hearthrug in front of the range, just bare stone slabs.

Bella stood behind Mattie, rubbing her hair dry with a towel, whilst Jane dried her own.

'Have you always lived in this house?' Mattie asked Bella.

'Since I got married, yes. Before that, I lived with my parents in the next street – the one where Mr Wilkinson has his corner shop.'

At the mention of the shopkeeper, Mattie shuddered. She wondered if Bella had heard about Lewis.

'My dad was a little mester with a workshop only a few streets away,' Bella went on.

Mattie knew about the 'little mesters' of Sheffield, skilled workers in the cutlery industry. They were self-employed, working at various processes, usually as an outworker for a larger firm. It was with one of these that Mr Spencer had now found work.

'And I was a buffer girl at one of the factories.'

Mattie knew what they were too. Girls and young women who polished the cutlery until it shone.

'I'm going to be a buffer girl when I grow up.' Jane, usually so quiet and shy, piped up. 'I'll learn the trade in a factory but one day I'll own my own buffing workshop and have lots of girls working for me. You can come and work for me, Mattie, if you like. I'd always find you a job.'

Through the mirror, Bella winked at Mattie. 'Our

Jane has grand ideas, but it's good to have ambition, isn't it, love?'

Mattie nodded, but couldn't think of anything to say. Who would ever want to employ her? A member of the notorious Price family? Perhaps it would take someone like Jane, who could see beneath the surface, to even think of employing her.

'There you are, all done,' Bella said, with a final gentle touch of Mattie's springy curls. 'You've got such pretty hair, Mattie, just like your mum's when she was your age.'

Mattie turned to her in surprise. 'You knew my mum then? When she was ten?'

'We were at primary school together and were friends. We used to go to each other's homes for tea sometimes.'

Mattie gaped. She'd never been asked to anyone's house for tea and certainly she'd never been able to invite a friend to her home. That's if she'd had any friends.

'What – what was she like?'

'Very pretty and her hair was the same colour as yours – and curly too. She was always so lively and such good fun.'

It didn't sound like the same person, who now sat all day by the cheerless grate in the uncared-for house.

'And she was clever too. She went to the girls' secondary school.' Bella sighed. 'Then, when she left school, she got a job in an office. A really *nice* job, you know. But she wasn't there long. Such a shame. She could really have made something of herself if she hadn't got mixed up with Sid Price and got pregnant.'

'Pregnant? Before she was married?'

Bella stared at Mattie for a moment, mortified that she had let her tongue run away with her. The girl was so grown up for her age that Bella had completely forgotten she was only ten. Still, it was done now, so Bella took a deep breath and went on, "Fraid so, love, but they did get married just before Joe was born, though I reckon she'd have been better to have brought the bairn up herself. All her friends – and she had a lot in those days, Mattie – would have stood by her. Trouble was, her parents wouldn't. They threw her out, so she hadn't any choice, really.'

'How – how awful.'

'You wouldn't do that to me, Mum, would you?' Jane asked. 'If I got pregnant.'

Bella scowled. 'No, lass, I wouldn't, but that doesn't mean I'd be happy about it, so you'd better just watch yourself.'

'Do my grandparents still live around here?'

Now Bella seemed wary, as if thinking she'd already said too much. 'To be honest with you, love, I don't know, because when that happened they moved away to the outskirts of Sheffield. Totley way, I heard say.'

'Did – did Mum ever see them again?'

Bella shook her head. 'You see, Elsie was an only one and they'd doted on her. So her getting pregnant was a bitter blow for them. Besides, her dad had never liked Sid Price. He couldn't abide the fact that Sid wasn't in uniform. All the lads had volunteered at the outbreak of t'war. Sid reckoned he was refused on medical grounds, but we all thought he'd skived the conscription somehow. You can get all sorts of forged documents if you know the right people. Anyway, your granddad wouldn't have him in the house and we all reckoned that's what drove your mum all the more to Sid.'

Mattie thought about her father: a puny man with sharp eyes, a mean mouth and thinning greasy hair. Before she could stop the words tumbling out of her mouth, she'd asked, 'But what did Mum see in him?'

Bella laughed wryly. 'He didn't always look like he does now, love, any more than your mum does. Oh no, back then he was quite a catch. He was good-looking, he dressed smartly and always seemed to have plenty of money to splash around. All the girls were after him and he played the field, but, I'll give him his due . . .' Bella always tried to be fair, but she sounded reluctent to be so now. 'He did stand by your mum and marry her.' She paused and then added bitterly, 'More's the pity for her.' She sniffed contemptuously. 'He even tried it on with me once, but I'd met my Rod by then and there was never anyone else for either of us. I was very lucky he came back from the war in one piece.'

Mattie thought about Rod Spencer, a big, cheerful man with broad shoulders and strong arms. He always seemed to be smiling and though his deep voice had frightened Mattie when she'd been younger, he'd always been kind to her. He still was, she thought now. Not many men would have given up their trad-itional place in the line for the bath to a scruffy little urchin from down the street.

'Right, I'll go down and see if the coast's clear for you to go home, Mattie. Wait here with Jane.'

Minutes later, Mattie was scurrying through the kitchen trying not to glance at Dan sitting in the tin bath in front of the fire or at Mr Spencer standing at the kitchen sink, in only his trousers, his braces hanging down on either side and his chest bare. 'Thank you, Mr Spencer. 'Night.'

''Night, love . . .' Rod began, but Mattie had gone. He shrugged and asked, 'What's all this about, Bella?'

'She's got some sort of interview with the headmistress from the girls' secondary school on Monday morning.'

'*Has* she, indeed? You do surprise me.'

'Oh no, Dad,' Dan said, standing up and sloshing water over the side of the bath onto the cocoa matting. 'Mattie's clever. Cleverer than the rest of us put together. I reckon she deserves a chance.'

'You sticking up for Mattie Price, our Dan?' Rod teased his son. 'Wonders never cease.'

But Dan only ginned.

'I'm sure you're right, lad,' Rod went on, 'but is she likely to get it with her background?' His tone hardened. 'I can't see Sid taking kindly to that. Besides, how's she going to get the uniform she'd need? He'll never provide it.'

'I reckon the church might help,' Bella murmured. The Spencers were not regular churchgoers, but they attended a Sunday morning service at their nearest church now and again and Bella always helped out at fundraising events, especially jumble sales and the like.

Rod grimaced. 'If you find her summat, he'll likely flog it or pawn it.'

'I'll just have to take that chance. But if he does,' Bella added grimly, 'he'll have me to reckon with.'

'Now, Mattie,' Patricia Donaldson said, as she led the girl to the headmaster's study after school on the Monday afternoon. 'Don't be shy. Miss Parsons is very nice and Mr Musgrave will be with you all the time. And you like Mr Musgrave, don't you?'

Mattie nodded. Her stomach felt as if it was tying itself into knots. She nodded and smoothed her hands down the pretty floral dress that Miss Donaldson had just given her to wear for this special occasion. It was the nicest thing she'd ever worn, though she realized she might not be able to keep it. The dress hung a little loosely on her thin frame, but with her face washed in the cloakroom and her hair brushed by Miss Donaldson, at this moment, she looked as good as anyone else in her class.

Patricia opened the door and ushered her pupil in with a gentle push. 'Here she is, Mr Musgrave.'

'Come in, Mattie. Please sit down.'

Mr Musgrave and Miss Parsons were both sitting behind the headmaster's desk and Mr Musgrave indicated a chair in front of them. Her legs were trembling and Mattie sat down gratefully as Patricia left the room, closing the door quietly behind her. She glanced at them both and was heartened to see that the stranger was smiling at her gently. Cecily Parsons was slim with short dark hair, even features and dark eyebrows. She wore a navy blue skirt and blouse, black stockings and lace-up shoes. Mattie guessed she was probably a similar age to her mother, Elsie.

'Don't be frightened, my dear,' she said in a soft voice that somehow strangely commanded attention. 'Mr Musgrave has been telling me about you. I understand from him that your favourite subject is maths. Is that right?'

Mattie nodded and then realized she should answer politely. 'Yes, Miss Parsons,' she whispered. She regarded them both solemnly and suddenly her fears fell away. She felt she could confide in them. She felt they would not judge her for her background, but would assess her on her own merit. 'I really enjoy working out problems like if a car travels at fifty miles an hour, how far will it travel in forty minutes – that sort of thing. And now algebra too. I didn't understand it at first, but then Mr Musgrave explained it all to me and now I do. It's almost like working out a code, isn't it?' She smiled suddenly and the two teachers in front of her were startled by the change in the girl's face. It became animated; her eyes shone and her whole face seemed to light up.

'And what other subjects do you like?'

Mattie wrinkled her brow thoughtfully. 'All of them really, but my favourite is maths, then perhaps English. I like writing stories – fictional ones, that is.'

Miss Parsons's eyebrows rose fractionally. That was a good word for a ten-year-old to use, she was thinking, and the girl obviously understood its meaning too.

'And can you tell me what you're learning in other subjects, such as history and geography?'

'Kings and queens in history. We're on Henry the Eighth at the moment. You know, if Jane Seymour hadn't died, I don't think he would have married his last three wives. She gave him a son and that was all he wanted really.'

They stared at her, astonished at her adult way of analysing.

'And in geography, we're doing capital cities in Europe and learning a little bit about each one.'

Miss Parsons nodded, leaned on the desk and linked her fingers together. 'Now, Mattie, would you be prepared to take a test for us?'

'What would I have to do?'

'You'd spend a day at my school and sit in a classroom with me or another teacher with you. There may be one or two other children taking the test too, but I'm not sure how many yet. And you'd be given questions on various subjects to answer within a certain time.'

'Exams,' Mattie said and glanced at Mr Musgrave, 'like we do at the end of the school year?'

Ben tried to hide a smile and failed. 'Yes, Mattie, though the questions might be a little harder than you're used to.'

But Mattie only beamed. 'I'd like to do that.'

'Then Mr Musgrave and I will arrange it and he will let you know. It probably won't take place until early next year.'

As Mattie walked home, she felt as if her insides were fizzing with excitement. She was bursting to tell someone and yet instinct made her cautious. Just as she'd had the sense to ask Miss Donaldson to keep the dress she'd provided for Mattie's interview at school for her. She'd been thrilled when the teacher said she could keep it, but soon realized it would be unwise to take it home. It would soon disappear into the pawn shop. She'd like to tell Mrs Spencer, who'd been so kind in helping her get ready for her special meeting with the two head teachers, but she was so afraid that it might be seen as boasting in front of Dan and Jane. And then the bullying might start again.

She couldn't tell either of her parents; she doubted her mother would even take the news in and her father would most likely do his best to stop it happening. 'I'll not have her getting ideas above her station,' he would say. 'She'll leave school as soon as she's old enough and get a job.'

But there was one person whom she could always depend on to be on her side. Joe. She couldn't wait to tell Joe.

Seven

Back at the school, the two head teachers, who knew each other very well, sat together over a cup of tea and discussed how they could help Mattie. They would both have preferred something a little stronger, but Ben never allowed alcohol on school premises.

'She's certainly a very bright child, Ben, and ought to attend my school.'

'I agree, but how can we make it happen?'

Cecily Parsons stirred her tea. 'I've long been an advocate of the notion that bright children from poorer families should have the same chance of higher education as their better-off peers.'

Ben nodded. 'But it's an uphill struggle, isn't it?'

'I am fortunate in having a very philanthropic board of governors at my school. One of our governors is a director of one of the big steel works here. His company sponsors three scholarships a year for children of poorer families, who would not otherwise be able to attend my school.'

Ben sat forward in excitement. 'And you think Mattie might be eligible to be considered?'

'I do indeed, though, like I told her, she would have to sit an examination as they all do. How old is she?'

'Ten.'

'And when is she eleven?'

'Er – I don't know that off the top of my head, but I can find out.' He rose at once and went through a communicating door from his own office to that of the school secretary. He returned a few moments later, carrying a buff-coloured file. He sat down and leafed through the contents. 'She's eleven next May.'

'Perfect.' Cecily beamed. 'She can sit the examination at the end of January next year and, if successful, she can start in September. Everything will be paid for her, all her uniform, any books and equipment she'll need – everything.'

Ben closed the file and laid it on his desk. 'That's very generous.'

Cecily regarded him with her head on one side. 'You still look concerned.'

'The real problem is her home life. I don't think her father will allow it.'

'What about the mother?'

'According to what Miss Donaldson tells me, she's not with it half the time.' He mimed drinking.

'Oh dear.'

'What you saw today is not quite the reality. Until recently the child had a long, greasy plait and was infected with head lice. Then, one day, she arrived with her hair cut short and washed. She looks a different girl now.'

'Her dress looked clean and neat.'

Ben pulled a face. 'Miss Donaldson found that for her and my wife took the hem up.'

They were silent for a few moments, until Cecily asked, a little hesitantly as if, already, she feared the answer, 'What does her father do?'

'As little as possible,' Ben answered tartly. 'Rumour has it he lives by his wits, which I think is a euphemism for stealing.'

'But he's never been caught?'

'Not yet.'

'What other family is there?'

'The eldest is Joe. He's a real good lad. He's in the top class here. He's not as clever as Mattie, but he's a hard worker. I understand from my staff that it's he who holds the family together. He works in the market before and after school. There are three other children, all younger than Mattie. Lewis and Nancy are at this school and I believe there's a baby too.'

'Then I think,' Cecily said slowly, 'you should have a quiet word with Joe. He might be able to help.'

'Joe,' Mattie whispered, 'I need a word with you, but I don't want anyone to hear.'

'We'll go out into t'yard. We won't be overheard there – as long as no one's in t'bog. Put your coat on.'

'I haven't got one. I grew out of it and Nancy's got it now.'

Joe looked down at her, assessing her size. 'I'll see what I can do. There's a second-hand stall on the market. I do quite a lot of work for them. They might let me have summat cheap. You'll need one by the time winter sets in.'

When they were outside and standing in the middle of the yard, Joe said, 'What is it, Mattie? Are you in bother?'

Mattie shook her head and swiftly explained all that had been happening. As she finished speaking, Joe's beam seemed to stretch from ear to ear. 'Eeh, Mattie, that's grand. If you pass t'test, you must go to that school.'

Mattie looked up at her brother. 'But Dad wouldn't let me, would he?'

Joe frowned. 'Probably not, but I'll do whatever I can to help you. I'll be fourteen next July and leaving school. I'll be working full-time then.'

'How do you know you'll get a job? It's so hard round here.' Mattie thought about Mr Spencer. A harder-working man you couldn't find and yet he'd been laid off.

But Joe's face lightened again; he was never down for very long. He moved closer and lowered his voice even more. 'I've already got summat lined up. I'll be working in the market for two or three of the traders on different days.'

'Oh Joe,' she breathed. 'That's wonderful.'

'It'll only be until I'm eighteen, Mattie. I'm going in the army then – if they'll have me.'

Mattie's face was stricken. 'I'll miss you, but I know it's what you want to do and it'll be right for you.'

He touched her arm. 'Anyway, that's a long way off. Let's get you to this posh school first.'

Mattie giggled. 'If I pass the exam.'

'Oh you will, Mattie. No doubt about that. Right,

let's go in. I've got a bag of what one of my bosses at t'market calls his "specky apples".'

'Ooo, lovely.'

That evening, the children sat around the table munching on what was left of the apples after Joe had cut out the bruised bits. There was some stale bread he'd brought home too and even a scraping of margarine.

For the first time in a week, the children went to bed with full tummies.

On a bright, frosty morning in January, Mattie walked to Miss Parsons's school, once again wearing the dress that Patricia had found for her and a coat that Joe had bought for next to nothing. Second-hand, of course, but Mattie didn't care. It was a thick, warm coat. But her hands were gloveless and purple with the biting cold wind that whistled through the city's streets. There was to be a full day of test papers, Mr Musgrave had told her; three in the morning and two in the afternoon.

'There will be six of you taking the examination,' he warned, 'but there are only three places to be had. Good luck, Mattie.'

Her knees were shaking as she entered the school gates and found the way to the main entrance hall, where she waited uncertainly. Soon, five other girls, who looked as bewildered as she felt, arrived and they all stood waiting whilst the regular pupils hurried to and fro through the entrance hall on their way to various classrooms. The girls belonging to the school were all dressed in a similar manner; navy-blue gym slips with white or cream blouses, black stockings and sturdy, sensible shoes.

'Ah, there you are, children.' Miss Parsons approached, beaming at them over her spectacles and wearing a black schoolteacher's gown. 'Very punctual, I see. Well done. Now, follow me.' She led them into the vast assembly hall which had a stage at one end with rich royal-blue curtains and hangings. Mattie gasped at the beauty of it. On the pelmet was the school crest, which Mattie had noticed all the pupils wore on their blazer pockets. But today the chairs had all been removed and six desks, placed a few feet apart from each other, were set in the centre of the room.

Mattie was still trembling as Miss Parsons said, 'Now, take a seat. I will give out paper, pencils and pens and then the examination paper, which you must leave face down until I tell you that you can turn it over and begin. The first paper is mathematics. Remember to read each question carefully before you begin. You have one hour to complete your answers.'

As permission was given for the pupils to turn the paper over, Mattie began to read the questions. Her fears fell away and she smiled.

'How did it go?' Joe whispered when he came into the children's shared bedroom later that night.

'All right, I think. The maths paper was easy, but I'm not sure if my essay was good enough. Then there was what they called an intelligence test. It was all sorts of puzzles like saying which shape fitted into a missing piece in a square. I liked that. I like working puzzles out, Joe.'

Joe squeezed her hand in the darkness. 'You'll pass it, Mattie, I know you will.'

'Even if I do, I won't be allowed to go, will I?'

'Let me worry about that, Mattie. You just keep on doing well at school.'

'But—'

'No "buts". Go to sleep.'

Mattie snuggled down, confident that her wonderful brother would sort out all her problems.

One hot Saturday afternoon in May, when the sun shone mercilessly onto the cobbles of the street and the odour from the 'bog', as Joe called it, permeated the backyard and even encroached into the house, Ben Musgrave fought his way through a line of washing that Mattie was hanging out.

'Hello, Mattie. You've got fine weather for a wash day,' he greeted her cheerfully, but his heart sank to see that this was how his clever pupil spent her Saturdays.

Mattie, pegging the last corner of her father's shirt to the line, turned wide eyes on him. 'Oh sir. What are you doing here?'

'I have some good news for you, Mattie.'

'Oh but . . .' She glanced fearfully towards the back door. Her father was at home and she didn't want him to meet Mr Musgrave. Or rather she didn't want Mr Musgrave to meet Sid Price. She actually began to tremble as the headmaster asked, 'Is your father at home? I'd like a word with him.'

Before she could answer, the back door opened and Sid stood on the step. 'I heard voices. Who . . . ?'

As he saw Ben standing there, dressed in a smart suit and wearing a trilby hat, Sid frowned. The visitor looked like authority. Sid didn't like authority.

'Dad,' Mattie said hastily before her father could speak. 'This is Mr Musgrave. The headmaster at my school.'

Sid glanced away from the man and his scowl deepened. 'You in trouble, girl? Because if you are, I'll tek me belt to you.'

'No trouble, Mr Price, I assure you,' Ben said hastily. 'Quite the opposite. We're all very proud of Mattie and I expect you will be too. She's won a scholarship to attend the girls' secondary school. She'll start in September.'

For a brief moment, Sid gaped at the man, his mouth hanging open. When he recovered his senses, he said harshly, 'Oh no, she won't. How d'you think I could afford to buy t'fancy uniform?'

'You don't have to, Mr Price,' Ben said smoothly, still fighting to keep the smile on his face. 'That's part of the scholarship. Everything she'll need will be paid for.'

For a brief moment, Sid's eyes gleamed and both Mattie and Ben guessed he was imagining how much he could get by selling her uniform and other equipment but then his expression turned into a sneer. 'Kids there have to stay on to take exams, don't they?'

'It's usual for them to stay another two years after the statutory leaving age to take their matriculation at least, but—'

'Then she can't go,' Sid said harshly. 'She'll leave school as soon as she can and get a job.'

Ben bit back the retort that sprang automatically to his lips. Instead, he said calmly, 'She'd be able to get a much better job if she stayed on.'

Now Sid's lip curled. 'And what good is a posh education to a girl? They're only good enough to get a job until they're old enough to marry.' He waved his hand towards the washing line. 'This is what they're good at. Keeping house for a man and his bed warm at night.' Sid grinned lewdly and the usually placid Ben had difficulty keeping his temper in check. 'Now,' Sid went on in a more conciliatory tone, 'if it had been Joe you'd come about, that'd have been another matter. Even though he's still at school, he's bringing money in. That lad has nous.'

'Yes, I've recently had a chat with Joe and you're absolutely right, he's a grand lad. But he's the first to admit that he's not as clever as his sister and he wants her to go to the school I'm talking about.'

''Er? Clever? Don't make me laugh. How can a girl be clever?'

'Very easily, Mr Price.' Ben regarded the man with distaste, hoping he was keeping the expression from his face as he delivered what he hoped was a coup de grâce. 'I understand that, years ago, your wife went to the very same school.'

Sid gaped at him. 'How d'you know that?'

'Schools keep records for years.'

There was a slight hesitation before Sid said, 'She had pushy parents. Mebbe they paid for her to go there.'

Ben shrugged. 'If they did, they obviously wanted her to do well.'

Now Sid grinned, showing broken, uneven teeth. 'Didn't do her much good, did it? Didn't stop her getting herself pregnant. Her father got his shotgun out and we had to get wed at seventeen.'

Now Ben could scarcely hide his disgust at the way the man talked about his wife as if she carried all the blame.

'Dad—' Mattie began tentatively, but Sid whirled round on her and shook his fist.

'You keep out of this, girl. While you live in this house, you'll do as I say.'

Ben could see that there was no point in continuing the conversation. 'Then there's no more to be said,' Ben said stiffly. He turned briefly towards the girl, standing clutching the wet shirt tails on the line as if she was clinging to her last hope. 'I'm sorry, Mattie. I tried. I'll bid you "good day", Mr Price.'

As he left the yard, Mattie turned and ran towards the lavatory, slamming the door shut and locking it. Sid went back into the house, smirking. She'd soon come out of there when the smell got too much.

Ben marched up the street, anger and frustration in every step. As he walked off some of the temper he felt, he began to think more rationally and one sentence thrust its way into his mind. Something Sid had said to Mattie.

'While you live in this house . . .' As Ben slowed to a normal walking pace, at last he began to smile. Perhaps, after all, there might be a way.

Eight

'Come in, Joe, and sit down.' Mr Musgrave indicated the chair in front of his desk. 'I thought we'd have a chat during lunch break. I know you're busy after school.'

Joe sat a little nervously on the edge of the chair, wracking his brains to think of something he'd done wrong.

'I wanted to have a word with you about Mattie.'

Joe relaxed and smiled. 'She told me last night. She's passed the exam, hasn't she?'

'She has indeed, Joe, but it seems your father is not at all happy about it. I – um – went to see him on Saturday morning.'

Joe frowned. 'He never said owt.'

'No, I wouldn't have expected him to. He said he won't allow her to go.'

Joe nodded. 'I guessed as much and I've been thinking about how we can get around that.'

'Have you really? Then I'd be delighted to hear any ideas you have.'

'It would need the cooperation of the headmistress of that school.'

'I don't think there'd be any problem there.'

'He takes no interest in our schooling – never has.'

'Not even yours?'

Joe shook his head. 'No, but he knows that it's the law that we all have to keep attending school until we're fourteen. He has to abide by that, even though I know he doesn't like it. He left school at twelve and sees no reason for anyone to stay on any longer. Not our sort, anyway.'

Ben winced and said gently, 'Education should be for everyone, Joe. Whatever walk of life they come from.'

'It's a nice idea, sir, but it doesn't work in practice.'

'Then what are you suggesting?'

'That Mattie just keeps going to school as normal. I don't think he'll even bother *where* she's going.'

Ben stared at him. 'You mean she should attend Miss Parsons's school without telling your parents?'

Joe nodded. 'That's why I said we'd need the headmistress's help. Mattie'll need to leave all her uniform and stuff at the school and change each morning and evening.'

'What about her homework? They get homework there.'

Joe was thoughtful for a moment. 'Couldn't she stay at school to do it? He never bothers what time any of us get home.'

'As she gets older, the amount of work will increase and I – um – noticed on Saturday that she does some of the household chores.'

'She does all of them. Me mum does nothing.'

'Is she ill?'

Joe laughed wryly. 'You could call it that.'

Ben waited, but Joe did not explain further. He

hated to be disloyal to his mother; he understood how hard life was for her though he could not excuse her for her neglect of her family.

'Are there any neighbours who could help?'

'Mrs Spencer might. She's been good to Mattie.'

'Is that Daniel Spencer's mother?' When Joe nodded, Ben added, 'I thought he and Mattie were sworn enemies. They had a fisticuffs a while back, didn't they?'

'They did, but ever since then they've become friends. He's quite protective of her now.'

'Ah, it sometimes happens like that.' Ben was thoughtful for some moments before murmuring, 'I'm not happy about deceiving your parents. It's most irregular and I'm sure it's against some rule or other.'

'We're not exactly *deceiving* them. We're just not telling them.'

'Doesn't that amount to the same thing?'

Joe shrugged. 'We won't lie about it. If they ask, then we'll tell 'em the truth.'

'Perhaps you could tell your mother, then at least we've told one of them.'

Joe thought quickly. If he told Elsie, he wasn't sure she would take it in but that wouldn't be his fault. She'd have been told. He'd have done enough to satisfy Mr Musgrave's conscience. 'That's a good idea, sir. Once you've cleared it with the headmistress, I'll tell Mum what's happening.'

Ben sighed. 'I worry about what will happen when she reaches school-leaving age, Joe.'

Joe grinned. 'Let's cross that bridge when we come to it.'

*

Three days later, Ben called Joe to his office again. 'It's all settled. Miss Parsons is happy to help. Mattie is to go to the school the day before they start in September and see her. They'll then arrange the practicalities of how it's going to work. My wife has suggested that Mattie should leave her uniform and all her belongings at our house. She's willing to wash her clothes each week and Mattie can call each morning and evening to change.'

'You're all being very good helping Mattie,' Joe said. 'I do appreciate it and so does she.'

'Mattie's a very clever girl,' Ben told him seriously. 'It would be a travesty if she didn't have a chance at a good education.' He paused and then looked sternly at Joe. 'Have you told your mother yet?'

'I was waiting until you'd settled it with Miss Parsons. I'll tell her tonight.'

'Do I have your word?'

Solemnly Joe said, 'You do, Mr Musgrave.'

'Mum.' Joe sat on a small stool beside his mother and took her hand. He looked up into her face and saw that this evening her eyes were not quite so dull and glazed over as they sometimes were. Sid was out, as he was most evenings, and Lewis and Nancy were playing in the street. Mattie was upstairs, trying to settle Toby into the drawer that served as his cradle in her parents' bedroom. The baby was teething and for the first time in his young life, he was fretful.

'I've got something to tell you but you must promise me you won't tell Dad.'

Elsie focussed on his face and stroked his hair. 'Oh Joe,' she whispered. 'You're not in trouble, are you?'

'No, Mum. I'm not. I'm doing well. I leave school in a few weeks at the end of term and I've got plenty of work lined up at t'markets. Things'll be a bit easier then. No, it's about Mattie.'

Elsie pulled in a sharp breath and her eyes widened. 'It's all right, Mum, she's not in trouble either. It's good news. Very good news, but Dad won't like it.'

Elsie breathed again. 'Go on.'

'Mattie has won a scholarship to go to the girls' secondary school from September.'

For the first time in ages, Elsie's eyes lit up. 'Oh, that's wonderful. That's my old school,' she began and then the light in her eyes died as suddenly as it had come. 'Her dad will never allow it. He'll want her to leave at fourteen and get a job to bring some money in.'

'I know, but I've hatched a plan with the head-master of the primary school and the headmistress of the girls' school has agreed to it.' Joe went on, but he wasn't sure whether or not his mother was taking it all in.

Elsie frowned. 'A plan? What plan?'

As Joe explained, Elsie nodded slowly, seeming to understand what he was saying. Only at the end did she whisper, 'But if he finds out . . .'

Joe patted her hand again and said philosoph-ically, 'He probably will, eventually, but I don't think he'll actually do anything about it until he wants her to leave school to find work. That'll be the crunch time. But, Mum, she's really clever. She deserves a chance.'

'She does. I ruined my chances. I let myself fall in love with your dad.' A solitary tear trickled down her cheek. 'He hasn't always been like he is now, Joe. Oh, he's always been a bit of a rogue, but he was quite good-looking as a young man. Lewis is going to be very like him.'

Joe sighed. 'And not only in looks, Mum, I'm sorry to say.'

Elsie sighed deeply and said flatly. 'I know, and it breaks my heart.'

'And you were even prettier then too, weren't you? I've seen a photograph.'

A small smiled wavered on her mouth. 'I had all the boys after me. I could have had my pick. I made a big mistake. I know that now, but it's too late.'

'But it's not too late for Mattie. She can achieve what you didn't have the chance to do.'

'They said at the school that I could have gone to university if I'd worked hard,' Elsie murmured, still lost in her memories.

'And so can Mattie. I'm sure of it.'

'But how, Joe?'

'For the time being we'll just get her to this new school. By the time she gets to fourteen, we'll have worked something out.'

'But you'll be going into the army as soon as you're old enough, won't you?'

Joe shrugged. 'Maybe – maybe not. I'd like to see Mattie all right first. The army can always wait. It'll still be there when I'm ready to go.'

Elsie touched his cheek. 'You mustn't sacrifice your own ambitions for Mattie. I don't want that and neither would she.'

'There's another four years before I can go anyway. A lot can happen in that time.'

Elsie sighed again. 'Don't I know it,' she said bitterly. There was a long silence between them, but Joe still stayed where he was, holding her hand. He sensed that there was more Elsie wanted to say.

At last, very softly, she said, 'I hurt my parents dreadfully when I got pregnant with you. They'd trusted me and I let them down. Badly. I'd never seen my father so angry and my poor mother was in tears. He – he told me to pack my bags. "After all we've done for you," he said, "if that's what – and who – you want, then you'd better go."'

'Where *did* you go?'

'To Sid's. There was nowhere else. I'd lost all my girlfriends after I took up with him. They could all see him for what he was. Only I was blind. They'd tried to warn me, but I wouldn't listen.'

'So – you got married?'

Elsie nodded. 'His mother was delighted. You see, she thought I came from a well-off family. I suppose I did compared to theirs and I think she thought that once Sid had done the decent thing and married me, my parents would come round. But . . .' Fresh tears flooded down her hollow cheeks. 'They never did.'

'What happened to them?'

'I don't know. I never saw them again. I heard they'd moved away. I don't even know if they're still alive.'

Nine

Joe was determined to find his grandparents, if possible, but he was reluctant to question his mother any further. Being reminded of them caused her distress; he could see that. But he needed to know where Elsie had lived as a child to begin his search. A way forward came about quite by chance when he was telling Mattie about his conversation with their mother.

'Mum went to that school,' he said, as they talked about the future that was opening up for her. 'You'll be following in her footsteps.'

'Yes, I know,' she said casually. 'Mrs Spencer told me.'

'Eh?'

'Mrs Spencer. She was young with Mum. They used to be friends. They went to the same primary school together.'

'Did they now?' Joe said thoughtfully. 'I wonder . . .'

'Wonder what, Joe?'

'Oh never mind.'

Later that evening, on his way home from his work in the market, Joe knocked on the back door of the Spencers' home.

'Good evening, Mrs Spencer,' he said, pulling his flat cap from his head. 'I wonder if I might have a word with you.'

''Course you can, love. Come in. I hope there's nowt wrong.'

'No, no, but I think you might be able to help me solve a bit of a mystery.'

'I will if I can, Joe. Sit down. We've got the place to ourselves for a bit. The kids are out playing and Rod hasn't come home from work yet. Like a cuppa, would you?'

'Please, Mrs Spencer.'

As Bella bustled about her kitchen she noticed Joe eyeing the remnants of the children's tea with hungry eyes. Feigning casualness she said, 'You'll not have been home yet for your tea, will you? I bet you're famished. I've a bit of pie and mash left over. Would you like it?'

'Isn't it for Mr Spencer's tea?'

'Oh no. He's not too fond of pie and mash.' Mentally, Bella crossed her fingers against the little white lie. It was, in fact, one of her husband's favourites. But she knew that when she explained, her kindly husband would not mind that Joe was feeling happily full for the first time in weeks with Rod's tea inside him. *I'll do ham, egg and chips for Rod*, Bella thought, *he likes that an' all.*

'There you are, love.' Bella smiled as she set the plate before Joe. 'Get yourself around that.'

Joe didn't speak for several minutes whilst he wolfed down the food. Bella shook her head sadly. Those poor mites in that household; she wished she could do more to help, but she didn't know where to begin without getting a flea in her ear from Sid. Not that she was frightened of the odious little man – Bella was in awe of no one – but it was a very awkward situation. She didn't want to cause more trouble for Elsie and the kids instead of helping.

As Joe wiped the last scrap of gravy from his plate with a round of bread, Bella said, 'Now, love, how can I help you?'

'Mattie said you knew our mum when you were young.'

Bella nodded. 'We were at primary school together.' She sighed. 'We were quite friendly then. Used to play together. Go on.'

'Did you live near each other? I mean, did you ever go to her home?'

Bella eyed him sharply, wondering what was coming. 'We both lived in the next street then, but after your mum got involved with Sid Price, got pregnant and married him, her parents moved away. I expect her mum, Mrs Ashmore, couldn't stand the shame. She could be a bit grand when she wanted to be and to have all her hopes and dreams for her daughter – her only child – dashed in that way, well, you can understand it, can't you?

'Ashmore? Was that Mum's maiden name?'

'Yes. She was doted on by her parents. Nothing was too good for their Elsie when she was little. The prettiest dresses, her hair always done in ringlets and the shoes she wore – oh my, Joe, it was the only time I was ever envious of anyone. She had the most beautiful shoes.' She paused, waiting for Joe to speak.

Softly he said, 'I do know what happened. Mum told me. She's never seen her parents again since she left home to marry my dad. She doesn't even know if they're still alive, but I want to find out. Can you help me? Do you know where they moved to?'

Slowly, Bella said, 'They moved to Totley.' She wrinkled her forehead. 'Now, I should know the name of the street. Let me think.' There was a long silence before she smiled and said, 'I've got it! Baslow Road. That was it, though I can't remember a name or a number. I never visited them, you see. But be careful, lad, if you go looking for them. I don't reckon they'll kill the fatted calf for you.'

He eyed her soberly. 'You think they'll still be bitter? Even after all this time?'

'They were dreadfully hurt and upset, Joe. They had high hopes for Elsie. And well-founded, I have to say. She was cleverer than the rest of our class put together.'

'Mattie's clever,' Joe said softly. 'She's won that scholarship to the girls' secondary school.' Swiftly, he explained all that had happened, finishing, 'So you see, we're having to keep it secret from Dad, but as long as one of her parents knows, Mr Musgrave's quite happy.'

Bella clapped her hands. 'Oh, that's grand news. If there's owt I can do to help, you let me know.'

Joe nodded. 'That's so kind of you, Mrs Spencer. I think it'll work for a bit.' He smiled wryly. 'It's not as if Dad ever takes any interest in any of us. Unless, of course,' he added a little bitterly, 'we're bringing in some money. The only trouble that might happen is when she gets to school-leaving age because, of course, that school will want her to stay on and he – won't. But I'll be leaving school at the end of July. I've already been promised jobs with one or two of the market traders, so I'll be able to contribute a bit more to the family finances then.' He took a deep breath. 'And I'm determined Mattie will have her chance, even if it means I'll not be able to go into the army as early as I'd planned.'

Bella patted his shoulder. 'That's some way off yet.' She paused and then said seriously, 'I expect that's perhaps why you're trying to find your grandparents, is it? You think they might help Mattie?'

Joe shrugged. 'I had wondered, but from what you say, it doesn't sound too likely, does it?'

'No, love, it doesn't,' Bella said bluntly, 'so don't get your hopes up.'

On the Sunday morning, Joe set off to the outskirts of the city where Bella said his grandparents had moved to. It was quite a walk, but he was used to going wherever he wanted to go on foot. When he reached the road Bella had mentioned, he paused and gazed about him. It was a long road of detached and semi-detached houses, with terraces of a few adjoining houses here and there. Some even had a tiny plot of garden in the front and, he guessed, perhaps a larger garden at the back, though he couldn't see for himself. And there were trees too. Had his grandparents really lived here? It was streets away – literally and metaphorically – from the kind of house his mother lived in now. No wonder they had been so upset that she had – in their eyes – fallen so low. He walked slowly down the road. He would just have to take a chance and knock on someone's door to ask if they knew anything about a Mr and Mrs Ashmore. He reasoned that someone living further along the road might know of several people living on either side, whereas someone living at the end might only know a few. About halfway down he stood for a moment gazing up at the windows of a house. He felt a little uncertain now. Was he about to open a can of worms that could not be closed?

He walked up the path and knocked on the door. It seemed an age before it was opened by a little old lady, with white hair, a wrinkled face and stooping shoulders. Her eyes were sharp, yet kindly. Was this his grandmother standing in front of him? He guessed his grandparents would be in their late fifties or even early sixties. This lady looked too old, Joe thought, but he would ask her anyway.

'I'm sorry to trouble you,' he said, pulling off his cap. 'But are you Mrs Ashmore?'

She stared at him for a long moment before shaking her head slowly. 'Sorry, love, no. I've only lived here for five years and before that it was a Mr and Mrs Wilson. Before them, I don't know.' She paused and then added, 'You might try next door. The lady there has lived in that house for years, so I understand. She knows a lot of folk in the road. She might remember her.'

'Thank you.' Joe smiled and apologized again for troubling her.

The door of the next house was opened by a tall,

straight-backed woman. Her hair was grey and pulled back into a severe bun at the nape of her neck. Her eyes were beady and suspicious, without the kindliness of her neighbour. Joe's heart sank. Now he hoped that this woman was *not* his grandmother.

'I don't buy at the door, boy, nor have I any jobs that need doing, thank you. Good afternoon.'

She began to close the door, but Joe spoke up. 'I'm not selling owt, missis, just looking for a bit of information, that's all.'

The woman frowned. 'Go on,' she said sharply.

'I'm looking for a Mr and Mrs Ashmore.'

The woman was very still for a moment before asking, 'Why?'

Joe shifted uncomfortably from one foot to the other and twirled his cap between his hands. 'I – um – think I might be related to them.'

Now she stared at him before murmuring, 'Do you now? And what makes you think that?'

Joe thought quickly. 'One of our neighbours used to know me mum when she was young and she told me that her parents moved to Baslow Road. It'd be about thirteen or fourteen years ago.'

The woman's mouth tightened as she asked, 'Are you Elsie's lad?'

'Yes, missis.'

Without warning, the woman stepped forward and thrust her face close to Joe's, so close that he felt her spittle on his face as she spat out the words. 'Then you can get back to where you came from and stay there. Elsie Ashmore broke her parents' hearts when she took up with that ne'er do well. And I'll tell you this much. I reckon – and I'm not the only one to think so – it probably helped to kill 'em.' Shocked, Joe took a step back, but the woman was not finished yet. 'They caught the dreadful flu that raged through the country at the end of the war and they didn't have the will to fight it. They died within a week of one another.' She stepped back now and straightened her shoulders. 'And you can tell Elsie Ashmore from me that I hope she rots in hell, 'cos that's where she ought to be.'

Joe turned and ran.

He didn't slow down until he felt as if his lungs were bursting. He leaned against a low wall in front of one of the houses, but he had no idea what street he was in now. He had just run and run until he could run no more. When he'd recovered his breath a little, he pushed himself off the wall and walked on slowly. He didn't really care where he was or which direction he was going; he'd just had to get as far away as possible from that horrible woman. He was saddened to know that his grandparents were no longer alive; now there was no chance of a reconciliation. And he was ashamed to think his mother's actions had so undermined her parents' health that they had had no vitality left to fight the dreadful so-called Spanish flu which had taken the lives of so many. As he walked on, now finding himself back in familiar streets, Joe decided he would not tell his mother anything about his visit to try to find her parents or what he had learnt. In fact, he would tell no one.

It was a secret he would have to carry.

Ten

It was going to be hard to avoid Bella's questions, so he decided he would tell her the truth, but only part of it. So when she greeted him with the expected question 'How did it go?' he was ready with an answer.

'I found the street. A neighbour told me that Mum's parents died several years ago within a short time of each other.'

Bella eyed him keenly. Joe was avoiding her gaze and, intuitively, she guessed that perhaps he was not telling her everything.

'Are you going to tell your mum?'

'No – well, not now, anyway. She's not . . .' he paused, searching for a kindly word. 'She's not fit enough just now.'

Bella nodded, understandingly. Joe was a good lad and growing into a fine young man. Just how he was turning out so well with his appalling background, she didn't know. He was growing tall and strong from working at the market in his out-of-school time and he was honest and kind. He was a son to be proud of.

'You won't tell her, Mrs Spencer, will you?' he asked earnestly.

'No, love, I won't, though perhaps one day – when she gets a little stronger – you ought to.'

Joe nodded, but could make no promise. There was silence between them until Bella said softly. 'So, we're back to square one as regards Mattie, are we?'

Joe sighed. ''Fraid so.'

Bella patted him on the shoulder. 'Don't worry, lad, we'll think of summat. Now, how about a nice cup of tea and one of my scones I've baked this morning?'

'Ooh, please, Mrs Spencer.' As he stirred his tea, his thoughts once again turned to his sister. 'I think we'll be able to manage for a while when she starts there. Just as long as me dad doesn't find out.'

Bella gave an unladylike snort. 'He's not interested, Joe. We just need to work out what to do when it's time for you to join the army.'

Joe nodded. 'If I could make sure she'd be able to stay on without him putting a stop to it, then I'd go, but—' Although he left the sentence hanging, Bella understood.

'Don't put your own life on hold for your sister, Joe. Mattie wouldn't want you to do that and neither would your mum.'

'Yes, she said as much.' He sighed heavily, but managed a weak smile. 'I know a lot can happen in the next three or four years, Mrs Spencer. As long as we can get her there, then we'll worry about keeping her there when the time comes.'

Bella nodded. *Aye,* she was thinking, *and the best thing that could happen would be for Sid Price to scarper.* Although she didn't wish the man any harm, she knew the family would be better off without him. But she kept these thoughts to herself. All she could do right now was to help Mattie in whatever way she could.

Mattie was the happiest she could ever remember being. With her smart new uniform – kept at the Musgraves' home – and being able to have a bath and her hair washed every week at Bella's, she fitted in with all the other girls at the school. She was no longer the scruffy, smelly kid with nits. Each week Mavis Musgrave washed Mattie's school blouses and ensured the rest of her uniform was clean and pressed ready for Monday morning. Of course, it was natural that at first Mattie was shy and reluctant to try to make friends; she had suffered years of teasing and taunting. But, to her surprise, she was soon included in a small circle of four friends who paired off nicely so that no one felt left out. She also found that several of the girls were clever too so that, although she came top in all subjects except one at the end of the first term, and received a glowing report from her form teacher – which was also endorsed by the head-mistress – there was no resentment amongst her classmates; they just vied with each other to catch up with her.

'She really is the most remarkable child,' Jane Bamforth, Mattie's form teacher, who was also her maths teacher, remarked to the rest of her colleagues during a staff meeting. Miss Parsons had confided in her staff the details of Mattie's home life and the steps that were being taken to ensure she kept her place at their school. All those who now taught Mattie nodded. 'She certainly deserves to be here,' Jane Bamforth went on, 'and if you need any further help of any kind, Miss Parsons, don't hesitate to say.' This too was greeted with murmurs of agreement from the rest of the staff. 'She's so good at *everything*.'

'Not quite,' Felicity Arnold, the sports teacher, smiled wryly. 'In the gym and on the playing field she's – well, to be perfectly honest – hopeless.'

The all-female staff around the table tittered as Felicity elaborated. 'She has no co-ordination. She can't catch a ball for toffee and if I put her in a hockey team she usually misses the ball altogether and often swipes at another girl's ankle. As for the gym, I daren't let her climb anything.' She rolled her eyes. 'I have visions of having to call an ambulance.'

'Then it's a blessing she's academically clever,' Cecily Parsons murmured.

'I know she's only young yet,' Louella Armstrong, who taught general science subjects, said, 'but I think she's university material.'

Now there were louder voices of assent around the table. 'Most definitely,' Cecily Parsons agreed. 'But how on earth are we ever to achieve that?'

Now, no one had an answer.

Joe, too, was amazingly happy. He had left school and was employed by various stallholders in the market. He was blossoming in a working environment. He'd never been a scholar like his sister, but the market traders loved his willingness to do anything asked of him. He still brought home leftover food and earned good money too. The Price family were now better fed. Mattie still did her best to wash the family's clothes and keep the house clean, though it was an uphill struggle for the young girl now that she had school homework to do. She found the only way to cope – and also not to risk her books getting lost, damaged or, it had to be said, even stolen – was to stay late after school each afternoon.

'Just let her work in one of the classrooms, Mr Cooper,' Miss Parsons told the school caretaker. 'She'll leave when you're ready to lock up.'

But with Mattie's natural ability, it was rare that she stayed so late. Homework for her was the easy part; the difficult part was the physical work that awaited her at home.

Although in some ways the family was faring much better, there were areas that none of the children could tackle, not even Joe. One was their father's thieving activities, which, sadly, Lewis seemed to be copying. The other was their mother's habitual drinking. As the children grew older, they began to understand that this was related to Sid's behaviour towards her. But there was one person who felt she could at least try with Elsie: Bella. One Monday morning when she knew all the older children would be at work or at school, and after she had seen Sid riding up the street on a refurbished bicycle that, no doubt, someone had 'lost' a couple of weeks earlier, Bella marched down the street and entered the back door of the Prices' home.

'It's only me, Elsie love,' she called, wrinkling her nose at the frowzy smell that met her. She heard the clatter of glass against the tiles of the hearth as Elsie tried, unsuccessfully, to hide her bottle. Pretending not to notice, Bella advanced to sit down – a little gingerly – in the chair on the opposite side of the cold range.

'Mattie seems to have settled in at her new school. She's doing very well, from what Joe tells me.'

Elsie blinked and tried to focus on Bella's face. 'New school?' There was a pause before she asked, 'What new school?'

'The girls' school. Joe told you all about it. Don't you remember?'

Elsie frowned and then murmured, 'Oh yes. My old school.'

'But you mustn't breathe a word to Sid. You do understand that, don't you, Elsie?'

'Yes, yes, I do. He'd put a stop to it.' Her frown deepened. 'But – she's not wearing a uniform. We all had to wear a uniform.'

'That's all been taken care of,' Bella said. She sat watching Elsie for a few minutes before leaning towards her and saying softly, 'Oh Elsie love, how have you come to this? You used to be such a bright, fun-loving girl. And so clever too. You could have done anything you wanted. What has he done to you?'

Elsie sighed heavily. 'It's just – life, Bella. I can't seem to cope.'

Bella pointed to the bottle half-hidden behind Elsie's chair. 'Well, that's not helping,' she said bluntly.

Tears glistened in Elsie's eyes. 'I know. I do try to stop, Bella, truly I do. Every morning I get up and I tell myself, today, Elsie girl, you will stop drinking, but then—' The tears spilt down her cheeks. 'I get the shakes and I think, well, one little tipple won't hurt – just to steady me – you know. But then one drink leads to another . . .' Her voice faltered and faded away.

'Do you *want* to get better, Elsie? Because if so, I'll do whatever I can to help you.'

'Oh Bella, would you really?' Now Elsie leaned forward and grasped Bella's hands like a drowning person.

'I will,' Bella promised solemnly. 'And we'll start right now, but you'll have to cut down on the drink steadily. I wouldn't recommend "cold turkey".'

'I will, Bella. I promise I will. I'll start today. Just tell me what I ought to do.'

As the weeks and months passed, life in the Price household became a little easier. Elsie's attempt to stop drinking progressed in fits and starts but, overall, there was an improvement. Once she started to feel better, to do a little housework, then she had an incentive. She only slipped backwards when there was trouble, but Bella, true to her word, was always there to lend a sympathetic ear and to give guidance.

'Don't put up with Sid's snide remarks, Elsie love. Answer him back. I wouldn't put up with owt like that from my Rod.'

'Your Rod,' Elsie said bitterly, 'would never say such things to you.'

Bella regarded her steadily. 'Does he ever hit you?'

Elsie sighed. 'Now and again. If I cheek him, I'll feel the back of his hand.'

Bella frowned. She had been brought up to believe that a man never hit a woman. There were ways a man could feel he was master in his own house without resorting to violence.

'What about the kids? Does he hit them?'

'They keep out of his way as much as they can. And Joe . . .' Here Elsie's tone softened as she thought about her eldest child. 'He's bigger – and stronger – than his dad now. Sid daren't touch him.'

'And Mattie – what about Mattie?'

Elsie's smiled widened. 'Oh Bella, she's doing so well at school. I'm so proud of her. I want her to do all the things I should have done and never did. Just so long as Sid doesn't find out.'

'Amen to that,' Bella said.

Eleven

Elsie was sitting by the fire with Toby on her knee, when a loud knock came at the back door. She'd washed up the breakfast pots, done a little washing and even put a meat and potato pie in the oven made from the leftovers which Joe had brought home from the market the previous evening. She was feeling quite proud of herself when the sudden noise startled her. Carrying the toddler on her hip, she opened the door to see a tall, dour-faced policeman standing there. Beside him was a sulky Lewis.

'This your lad, Mrs?' the policeman asked without preamble.

Elsie, her heart hammering in her chest, nodded.

'He's been caught nicking sweets from Mr Wilkinson's corner shop.'

At least it wasn't booze, she thought thankfully, but at the constable's next words her hopes sank. 'I understand from the shopkeeper that this isn't the first time. Now, Mrs, as he's only young, I'm giving him an official caution this time, but if he's caught stealing again it'll be the juvenile court. Understood?'

Elsie nodded again, still not having uttered a word.

'Right, then, I'll be off.' He looked down at Lewis. 'Mind what I said, m'lad.'

Lewis adopted an expression of contrition. 'Yes, officer,' he said meekly and hung his head.

As the policeman left by the yard gate, Nancy came in on her way home from school. 'What's a copper doing here?'

Elsie didn't answer her question. Instead, she thrust a startled Toby into the girl's arms. 'Here, hold him a minute. I've got to go across the yard.'

But instead of visiting the privy, Elsie went into the wash house and reached behind the mangle, scrabbling for the bottle she knew was hidden there.

Sid arrived home just as the younger children were going to bed. Elsie had hoped they'd be safely upstairs before he appeared and her heart sank at the rattle of the back door. She'd saved him a generous portion of the meat pie and hoped that would mollify him, but she hadn't reckoned on Nancy's gleeful tale-telling before Sid had even got through the door into the kitchen.

'A copper's been here.'

For a moment, real fear crossed Sid's face. 'What – what for?' he managed to say in a strangulated whisper.

'Lewis was caught nicking sweets.'

Sid relaxed visibly and gazed around his family as they all waited for his temper to erupt. Elsie sat in her usual chair, looking anxious. He turned to Lewis. 'Is this true?'

Lewis, his eyes wary, nodded.

'Yer silly little fool. 'Aven't I taught you better than that? You mind you don't get caught.' With a swift, unexpected grin Sid ruffled Lewis's hair.

Joe, still sitting at the table as he finished his share of the pie, stood up suddenly. With a glare of disgust at his father, he left the house without a word, banging the back door behind him.

He marched up the road towards the Spencers' home.

'Come in, Joe,' Bella said, as she opened the back door to his soft knock. 'I've been expecting you.'

Joe sighed. 'You've heard already?'

'Aye, Aggie next door couldn't wait to impart a bit of juicy gossip. She saw the copper marching your Lewis home, put two and two together and made five as she always does. So, what's been going on? Sit down and I'll get you summat to eat.'

'I've already had me tea, Mrs Spencer, thanks.'

She smiled knowingly at him. 'But I reckon you'll have room for a bit more, won't you?'

Despite his worry, Joe grinned and nodded.

'Go and sit with Mr Spencer near the fire and tell us what's happened.'

The older man nodded at Joe as he sat down. 'Now then, lad, what's to do?'

Joe explained as he bit into the slice of treacle tart Bella had given him. 'Worst thing is,' he ended, 'this is the kind of thing which will make Mum go back on the bottle. And she was doing so well.'

'Don't worry too much about that, Joe. Your mum's not an alcoholic. It's just her way of coping with upset, especially,' Bella added drily, 'when your dad's around. She'll have setbacks, but as long as the trend is on the up – which I think it is – we'll keep working on it. How's Mattie? Does she know?'

'I'm not sure. She was upstairs. Working on some algebra problem, I expect,' he added with a laugh, but it was said proudly.

'She's doing ever so well,' Bella said. 'Dan still meets her every night when she comes home after school.'

Joe blinked. 'Does he? But – but she stays late to do her homework there. She must come home at different times.'

Bella laughed. 'She does, but he stands at the end of our ginnel watching out for her.'

'I knew he did that when she first started there, but I didn't realize he was still doing it. It's over a year now. She's just started her second year.'

'Ah well, he's the faithful type,' Bella laughed. 'Like his dad. He's trying to persuade her to go to the pictures with him on Saturday night. A group of them are going.'

Husband and wife exchanged a fond glance and Joe felt a moment's envy. What a lovely family this was. 'You know,' he mused, confident that whatever he said to them, it would go no further. 'It's a miracle Dad hasn't found out about Mattie.'

'Not really, Joe.' Bella shook her head. 'He's not that interested in any of your schooling. He only wants you to be out at work and earning money. You mark my words, we're safe until she gets to fourteen, but then the balloon will go up.'

'That's only a couple of years away, so I'd better get me thinking cap on and plan ahead.'

'You'll be seventeen by then, won't you?' Rod put

in. 'You'll be wanting to go into the army as soon as you can.'

'It depends. I want to be sure Mattie's going to be all right.' His jaw hardened. 'I'm determined that, somehow, she's going to have her chance.'

For the next year or so, life settled into a routine for the Price and Spencer families and indeed for everyone in their street. Unemployment was rife throughout the nation. In Sheffield, whenever a job advertisement appeared, more than a hundred applicants would turn up. Rod Spencer was fortunate; the 'little mester' he worked for seemed to have enough work to keep them both occupied. And, for Sid, it made no difference if there was work to be had or not; he wasn't having any of it. No one took much notice of the events happening outside their own little world. Daily life was hard enough; just surviving without worrying what was going on in the rest of the country was a challenge – and, certainly, the rest of the world was far too remote. Most of their street had only a hazy idea of where other countries actually were and none of them owned one of the new-fangled wireless sets – except for the parts that Sid kept under the children's beds and assembled into a set from time to time. But he never tried to sell them to neighbours. Sid Price wasn't that daft.

No one in the back streets of Sheffield, struggling with their day-to-day life, took much notice when, in January 1933, a former army corporal became Chancellor of Germany.

*

'How's it going, then?' Dan greeted Mattie in the usual way as she neared home one warm evening in early May. 'You look a bit down in the mouth. Summat up?'

'Not – really.'

'Yes, there is. I know you well enough now, Mattie Price, to know when you're not your usually sparkling self.'

They regarded each other, realizing how they'd both altered in the last two years. Dan had grown tall and had filled out. He was not quite as tall as her brother, Joe, but maybe he still had some growing to do. He had turned fourteen and would be leaving school in July. Rod had already found him a place as an apprentice to a 'little mester', so that he could learn the cutlery trade.

Mattie too had altered. She was still slim but was now developing a womanly shape. She'd grown her auburn hair longer so that it fell naturally in soft curls and waves to her shoulders. Her skin was clear and smooth but this evening her green eyes, usually sparkling with mischief, were dull and worried.

'Want to come in and talk to my mum?' Dan said softly. 'Jane's gone round to a friend and Dad's not home yet. There's only her and me and if you don't want to tell me,' he grinned, 'I can soon disappear.'

'Oh Dan, you know I don't have secrets from you.' She hesitated for a brief moment and then nodded. 'All right, I will come in, if you think it'll be all right.'

"Course it will. Ever known my mum not to make you welcome?'

Mattie smiled weakly. 'No, I haven't.'

They walked down the ginnel between the houses and into the Spencers' backyard. Dan took her hand and squeezed it. 'Whatever it is, don't be afraid to tell us.' He paused and then added, a little self-consciously, 'Or just Mum, if it's – well, you know – girl stuff.'

Mattie giggled nervously. 'It's nothing like that.'

'Come in, then.'

He pushed open the back door to the smell of freshly baked bread, which made Mattie's mouth water.

'Hello, love,' Bella greeted her as she reached for a bread knife to cut two slices and spread them thickly with butter. 'Sit down and tuck into that, the pair of you. Had a good day, Mattie love?'

'Sort of.'

'There's summat worrying her, Mum. I can tell.'

Bella eyed Mattie tenderly. She'd become very fond of the young girl and treated her almost like another daughter. 'What is it, love? You can tell us. It's your birthday next week, isn't it? Is that it?'

'Sort of,' Mattie repeated and then sighed heavily. 'At school today we all had to go into the headmistress's office one by one.'

'Oh dear. What had you all been up to?'

Mattie shook her head. 'Oh, nothing wrong. We weren't in trouble. It's just that – in September we all move up into the fourth form and – and that's when we start to work for our School Certificate that we take in two years' time when we're sixteen but – but I don't think I'll still be there then.' She raised such sorrowful eyes towards Bella that it almost broke the older woman's heart. 'When Dad remembers that I'm fourteen next week, he'll make me leave school and find a job.'

'And has he remembered?'

'He's not said anything, but – but he will. I know he will.'

'Well, when he does, love, you come and tell me. I'll deal with him because me and your Joe have got a plan all worked out.'

'What?' Mattie asked.

'Best you don't know. Leave it all to us.'

'But Joe'll be wanting to go into the army soon, won't he?'

'Aye, he'll be thinking about it, but he's not eighteen until next July, is he? And I don't think he can go in before then. Besides, if necessary, he'll put off going until he knows you're all right.'

'Oh, I don't want him to do that. The army's what he's always wanted to do.'

'He'll get his chance, don't you worry.'

But Mattie did continue to worry. It was a black cloud hanging over her; a constant threat. By the morning of her birthday, she was trembling with anxiety. No one said a word before she went to school, not even to wish her a happy birthday, and when neither of the Musgraves nor anyone at school remarked upon this special day, Mattie began to hope that no one had remembered. She especially hoped that her father had forgotten.

When she arrived at the top of the road on her way home late in the afternoon, she was surprised to see that Dan wasn't waiting for her as usual. She shrugged and walked on down the street to her own home. As she opened the door into the kitchen, a chorus of voices met her with a tuneless rendition of 'Happy Birthday'. On the table was a cake with fourteen candles already lit and ranged around the table were her mother, her brothers and sister – even Joe was there, home early for once. And Bella, Dan and Jane had joined the party.

'Mrs Spencer made the cake,' Nancy said. 'You've got to blow the candles out in one go. Come on, Mattie, before Dad gets home.'

It was a merry little party and yet they were all on edge for fear that Sid would arrive home and be reminded just what day it was. They were all eating a piece of cake when the door into the yard crashed back against the wall. They glanced at one another in fear and Mattie almost choked on a crumb. Elsie retreated to her chair by the range and took Toby onto her knee, hugging him to her as if for protection. In silence, they all listened to the sound of a bicycle being wheeled across the yard, the wash-house door being opened and then, after a moment, closed again. Sid's footsteps came across the yard. The back door opened and then the door into the kitchen and he was there, staring at them all. They were all staring back at him, holding their breath, until his gaze came to rest on the demolished birthday cake. Quietly, Joe stood up to face his father, but Sid only smiled slyly. 'You might have waited for me. I didn't want to miss my daughter's fourteenth birthday party, now did I? Have you left me a piece?'

''Course we have, Sid,' Bella said, moving to cut that last section of cake into two pieces. 'There you are. I'll take this last piece home for my Rod.' She turned to Elsie. 'We'll be going, then, love. See you tomorrow.'

She kissed Mattie on the cheek and whispered, 'Don't worry, love.'

When they'd left, an uneasy silence fell upon the family as Sid gazed around at them all, his glance resting on each of them for a few moments. Lastly, he turned to Mattie. 'I've got a present for you. It's in the shed. It's for you to get to work on because I've also arranged a nice little job for you at Coles.' Cole Brothers was a large department store in the city. With a triumphant grin, Sid added, 'You start the day after school ends in July.'

'Oh no, she won't,' Joe said. 'She's staying on at school to take her School Certificate in two years' time.'

Sid frowned. 'What on earth are you talking about, boy? She can't stay on at that school any longer.'

'Yes, she can, because she's at the girls' secondary school – has been since she was eleven.'

Sid gaped at him. 'How the hell have you managed that without me knowing?'

'Quite easily,' Joe said smoothly, 'since you never take any notice of any of us and our schooling. All you're waiting for is the day we can leave and get out there to earn money. Well, that's not going to happen to Mattie. She's cleverer than the rest of us put together and she's going to have her chance.'

'Oh no, she isn't.' Sid shook his fist in his son's

face, but Joe didn't flinch. Instead, he took a step closer to his father, standing over him by at least four inches.

'Yes, she is.' If it hadn't been so serious, their conversation could have been straight out of a panto-mime. But this wasn't in the least funny.

Sid glanced at Elsie. 'Did you know about this, because if you did . . . ?'

'Don't go blaming Mum. You ruined her chances when *she* was young, you're not going to do the same to Mattie.'

Sid's lip curled. 'Oh aye, and who's going to stop me, eh?'

'I am.'

'And just how are you going to do that?'

'By suggesting to the coppers that they take a look in our wash house for any bicycles that might have been reported missing recently. To say nothing of all those wireless parts under our beds.'

'You wouldn't.'

'Try me.'

Father and son stood toe to toe, staring each other out, but it was the older man who gave way first and turned away, muttering, 'Blackmail, that's what it is.'

'Whatever it takes, Dad,' Joe said softly now. 'Whatever it takes.'

As Sid pulled open the door, Joe raised his voice. 'Oh and by the way, Dad, I've taken up boxing. I'm getting quite handy with me fists.'

Sid slammed the door behind him. They heard him leave the house and the yard, his footsteps clomping angrily up the ginnel.

'Oh, Joe, I know you mean well – I know you're doing it for Mattie – but you shouldn't have said all that. He'll have gone to the pub now and come home roaring drunk and start knocking me about.' She hugged Toby all the tighter until the little boy squirmed to free himself.

'No, he won't, Mum,' Joe said calmly. 'That's why I told him about me boxing. It was a warning.'

Elsie reached down to feel the comforting shape of the bottle at the side of her chair.

Twelve

On the Saturday morning following her birthday, Mattie, dressed in her school uniform, walked into the city centre. The bicycle her father had promised her had already disappeared. She stepped inside the huge department store and gazed around her in awe. Had her father really found her a job here?

Tentatively, she approached one of the assistants on the cosmetics counter.

'Excuse me, could you tell me who I should see about a job?'

The girl, tall, slender and beautifully made up, looked Mattie up and down and then smiled kindly. 'That'd be Miss Jenkins in personnel. The offices are on the top floor. You'll see a sign when you get up there.'

'Thank you,' Mattie said politely.

She found the offices easily and knocked on the door. Bidden to enter, she found herself in a large room with several girls and three men sitting at desks either typing or working on huge ledgers.

'And what can I do for you, young lady?' One of the men sitting nearest the door rose and came towards her.

Mattie swallowed nervously. 'Could I speak to Miss Jenkins, please?'

'Have you an appointment?'

'No. Sorry.'

He smiled at her. Mattie was surprised at how friendly everyone was. She'd thought they'd send her packing with a flea in her ear. It was one of Bella's favourite sayings and the thought of the woman gave Mattie strength.

'I'll see if she can spare you a moment.' He turned away, crossed the room and knocked on the frosted-glass panel of a door, which Mattie guessed led into a smaller office.

Moments later, Mattie was sitting down in a chair on the opposite side of a desk to a tall, slim middle-aged woman wearing spectacles and with her hair scraped back into a severe bun. Mattie guessed she was in her thirties. But when she smiled at Mattie, the severity left her face.

'How may I help you, my dear?'

'My father said he had secured a job for me here when I leave school in July, but you see, I don't want to leave school. I know I'm old enough now, but I want to take my School Certificate.'

Miss Jenkins's glance took in Mattie's uniform, which she obviously recognized. 'I see you attend my old school,' she murmured. She picked up a heavy ledger and opened it. 'Let me have a look. What's your name?'

'Mattie Price.'

Miss Jenkins slid her finger down the columns. 'No. I've not seen anyone of that name. You say your father came to see me, did he? Perhaps it was one of the other stores, was it?'

'He said he'd got me a job at Coles.'

'I'm sorry, we don't seem to have any record of his visit, and besides, I wouldn't have promised a job for you without interviewing you first.'

Mattie felt a flash of anger. Another of her father's deceits.

'I'm so sorry to have taken up your time,' Mattie said, starting to get up.

'Wait a moment. Sit down and we'll have a little chat. Are you really looking for a job? Because you said a moment ago that you wanted to stay on at school, which is very commendable, I might add.'

Mattie sank back into the chair. 'Yes, I do, so it wouldn't be a full-time one, Miss Jenkins. But I wondered if you had any vacancies for someone like me to work on Saturdays and in the school holidays.'

'Ah, I see.' For a moment, the woman was thoughtful. 'Well, as it happens, one of our Saturday girls, as we call them, though they do work in the holidays as well, is leaving school in July and we are taking her on full-time, so, yes, there might well be a place for you.' She smiled again. 'So, if you're agreeable, I have some time to spare now; we'll do a formal interview here and now. Is that all right?'

Mattie beamed. 'Oh yes, please, Miss Jenkins.'

'Joe, I've got a job.'

'Oh Mattie, not after all I've done for you to try to keep you at school—'

'No, no, listen. It's a Saturday and holiday job at Coles. I – thought it'd appease Dad a bit.'

Joe frowned. 'But what about all the work you do at home to help Mum?'

'It's high time Nancy did a bit more around the house. She's ten now and quite old enough to help. Just think what I was doing at ten years old.' It was said without any hint of resentment, but Joe felt the poignancy of her words.

'That's true and, yes, I suppose you're right. It might make Dad back down a bit.'

'I'll give him every penny I earn.'

'I wouldn't do that. Keep a bit of pocket money for yourself. He'll not know what you're earning and even he wouldn't have the nerve to go and ask your employers.'

'So you're not angry with me, are you, Joe? I couldn't bear it if you were.'

'Silly,' he ruffled her hair. 'I could never be cross with you. I just want you to have your chance, that's all.'

Mattie grinned at him. 'And what about you? Will you apply to join the army next year?'

'We'll see,' Joe said guardedly. He was afraid that if he was away from home, Sid might take advantage of his absence to get what he wanted.

Sid was not really appeased, as Mattie had put it. 'This is a miserable pittance to what you could be earning,' he grumbled, when Mattie handed him most of the money from her first pay packet. But there was nothing he could do with Joe's threat hanging over him. At least, not yet, he promised himself.

He moaned to one or two of his drinking cronies; men who lived like him – just on the wrong side of the law. But to his surprise, he didn't get the sympathy he sought.

'I've heard your lass is right clever,' one said.

A well-known pickpocket, known as Dave the Dipper, who had served time on at least three occasions, said, 'My Patsy was in her class at school before your girl went to the secondary.' He glanced warily at Sid, wondering if he knew that his daughter had been bullied by her classmates, one of whom would have been Patsy. But when Sid said nothing, he went on, 'Look at it this way, Sid – if you let her stay on and get that there certificate, she'll get a much better job at the end of it and bring home more money.'

Sid sniffed contemptuously. 'Oh aye, but I've got to wait two years for that to happen.'

'Well, I would, if my girl got the chance of a better education.'

'And what good will that do, eh? They'll only get 'emselves pregnant and what good would education be to them then, eh? You tell me that.'

'Your Joe's doing all right for himself, I've heard. Think a lot of him round the market, they do.'

Sid sniffed again, but said nothing. He was still smarting from Joe's blackmail. For the moment, he'd do nothing, but once Joe went into the army, well, then they'd all see who was really master in his own house.

Thirteen

Joe had deferred his application to the army until the summer of 1935 when Mattie took her School Certificate. Once she had finished her examinations, he felt able to leave and he had joined the army in July that year. Elsie and Mattie had hugged him hard on the morning he left, making him promise to come home whenever he could.

'And you write to me the minute you know your results,' Joe had said, smiling at Mattie. 'I know you'll do well, but I still want to hear.'

Mattie had nodded, unable to speak for the huge lump in her throat. However were they going to manage without Joe?

She had studied very hard at school as well as working at Coles on Saturdays and during the holidays, but one morning in August, Mattie found that all her dedication had paid off. She had passed every subject with top marks.

'You really should be staying on to take the Higher,' Cecily Parsons told her as she handed her the paper listing her remarkable results. 'You're university material.'

The previous two years had gone surprisingly well for Mattie, despite an uneasy tension at home. Elsie

109

continued to battle with her demons. She still drank more than was good for her, but she had reduced the quantity and now managed to do most of the housework. Money was still tight but, thanks to Joe, the family ate reasonably well. Sid still carried on his nefarious activities and it was a miracle to all of them that he had not yet been caught. Lewis, however, did not fare so well. He had twice appeared before the juvenile court to be bound over.

'Next time it'll be borstal,' Sid warned him. 'You're a fool to let yourself get caught.'

'I don't do it on purpose,' Lewis retorted moodily.

'Well, if you can't do it without getting nicked, you'd better get yourself a proper job. Ask Joe to get you one at the market.'

'I have and he won't. Ses they all know about me. They won't touch me with a barge pole, he ses.'

'Tell 'em you've turned over a new leaf. That going to court scared the livin' daylights out of you and you're never going to thieve again.'

Lewis stared at his father. 'Am I?'

'A' you what?'

'Going to stop stealin'?'

Sid grinned. ''Course not, but that's what you've got to tell 'em and you've got to make it sound convincing.' He ruffled his son's hair. 'Chip off the old block you are, lad, but you've just got to mind you don't get caught.'

'How d'you manage it?'

Sid tapped the side of his nose. 'Ah, that's my secret. Luck of the devil, I've got.' Then he paused and appeared to reconsider. 'Look, I'll give you a few pointers. One, never mess on your own doorstep. No more nicking stuff from Mr Wilkinson's or any of the shops round here. Go into the city and choose the big stores.'

'They've got store detectives in some of them. Isn't it more dangerous?'

'Not if you're fly. Kit yourself out with a loose overcoat and stitch a big pocket on the inside. If you nick summat, don't be in a hurry to leave the store. Walk around casually and keep your wits about you. You'll soon see if anyone's keeping an eye on you and you can go to the changing rooms, or the toilet, if they have one, and drop the stuff. Then, if you are stopped, you'll have nowt on you. See?'

Lewis nodded, his eyes shining.

On the same evening that Mattie got her results, Cecily Parsons visited her domestic science teacher at her home. Although the employment of married women was in general frowned upon because so many men were unemployed, Cecily had gained special approval to appoint Mavis Musgrave because of the shortage of capable domestic science teachers in the area.

'Do come in, Miss Parsons,' Mavis greeted her when she opened the door.

'Oh do call me "Cecily" when we're not at school, Mavis,' she said as she shook hands with Ben and sat down. Whilst Mavis brought in a tray of tea and biscuits, Cecily chatted with Ben.

'I understand you want to talk to us about Mattie Price,' he said, clearing away a pile of papers for his wife to set down the tray.

'I do indeed. I was wondering if there is any way we can help her between us. She's done so well in her exams, it will be a tragedy if she's forced to leave school now.'

'Yes, Mavis was telling me how well she's done. The highest marks achieved this year in your school, I understand.'

Cecily nodded. 'Yes, and in all subjects too. She really is gifted.'

'Have you anything in mind, Cecily?' Mavis asked as she handed the headmistress a cup of tea.

Cecily laughed wryly. 'Not really, just – is there any way we can get her father to agree to her staying on to take her Higher Certificate?'

Ben pulled a face. 'I very much doubt it. He's a horrible man.'

'I understand that Joe has gone now,' Mavis said.

'Yes.' Ben nodded. 'He came to see me just before he left at the end of July. What a good lad he is; he'd stayed on until Mattie had safely finished her exams.'

Cecily nodded. 'Yes. He promised he would make sure that Mattie took her School Certificate and that's what he's done. But the young man has a right to carve his own future – away, I might add, from that dreadful home life. But how on earth we can keep Mattie at school for another two years, I just don't know.'

Ben was thoughtful as he said slowly, 'Mavis, do you remember when I went to see Mr Price at their home to try to persuade him to let Mattie attend Cecily's school?'

Mavis wrinkled her forehead for a moment before saying, 'Yes, I do, now you mention it.'

'He said something very telling at the time. He refused to let her go to your school, Cecily, though somehow Joe managed it. I don't quite know how and, to be honest, I didn't enquire too closely. I don't think I've ever met such a bigoted individual as the father. He thought a good education was wasted on a girl. When Mattie tried to plead with him, he shook his fist at her and said, "While you live in this house, you'll do as I say".'

Mavis brightened. 'Then she could come and live with us, Ben. I'd like that. I've become very fond of Mattie.'

'Woah, hold your horses, Mavis. We don't want to be dragged through the court by her father.'

Cecily laughed. 'From what you say, I hardly think Sid Price is going to put himself deliberately in the sight of the law.'

Ben laughed. 'You're probably right, but I'll have a word with someone at the Education Office. They'll be able to advise us.'

'I'll leave that with you, then, Ben,' Cecily said. 'Let me know what you find out, though Mattie might be reluctant to leave her mother.'

Even through the school summer holidays, Mattie still visited the Spencers' house every week for a bath and to wash her hair. As she knelt in front of their range to dry it, she asked Dan, 'How are you getting on at work? D'you think you'll like the cutlery industry?'

'It's great, Mattie. Much better than school.' He grinned at her. 'Well, for me anyway. I'm a working man.' He puffed out his chest proudly. 'And I'm learning a trade. Mr Marshall treats me very well.' Harry Marshall was the 'little mester' in the city to whom Dan was apprenticed. 'One day, I hope I'll be a little mester like him.'

'I'm surprised you didn't try for the steel works.'

'I would've done, but Dad says times are hard right now with a lot of unemployment in the city. He thought that if I learnt the cutlery business, I'd always have a trade at my fingertips.'

Mattie laughed. 'Literally.' Then her smile faded. 'Maybe I ought to become a buffer girl.'

'Oh no, you won't. Joe didn't give up going into the army for a whole year just so you could go and do summat like that. You stick to your book learning, Mattie. We're all that proud of you.'

'Are you?'

'You know we are.'

'I just—' she began and then stopped.

'What is it, Mattie?'

'Oh, I'm being silly.'

There were only the two of them in the room.

'Go on,' he prompted gently. 'You can tell me anything.'

'I just don't want it to – to come between us.'

'Why would you think that?'

'Some of the other kids we were at primary school with – if I bump into them – say I'm a stuck-up prig now.'

'Tek no notice. They're only jealous.'

'Mm.' Mattie sounded doubtful. 'But they're out earning their own money,' she added in a quiet voice.

'And I'm not. The bit I earn on a Saturday and in the holidays all goes to Dad. I'd like to give it to Mum, but he takes it off me the minute I get home on pay day.'

'You will one day. You'll be able to get a fantastic job. Maybe you'll be a teacher.'

'I think I'd like that, but d'you think they'd let someone with my background do that? My family's hardly a shining example.'

'You'll be your own person, Mattie. You can't be responsible for what other members of your family do.'

Sometimes, she thought, Dan – like Joe – could be very wise. She sat back on her haunches, brushed the hair out of her eyes and looked up at him. 'As long as you and me will always be friends, Dan.'

''Course we will be.'

'Have you quite forgiven me for punching your nose?'

'Have you forgiven me for pulling your plait?'

They grinned at each other. Their friendship since that day had only grown stronger. He leaned forward. 'How are you going to keep going to school to sit your Higher?'

Mattie sighed and shrugged. 'I just don't know. I wish I did.'

'Mum said you can come and live with us, if that'd help.'

'That's so kind of her, but I wouldn't want to cause you trouble, because my dad would go berserk.'

'I don't reckon my mum's frightened of your dad, do you?'

'No, I don't, but I just don't want to cause trouble,' she said again. 'Your mum's been so good to mine, helping her to cut down on the drinking. She's so much better. She manages to cook meals and to do most of the washing now.'

'Are you managing all right now Joe has gone?'

'For money, you mean?' Mattie grimaced. 'More or less. We don't get quite as much leftover stuff from the market as when Joe worked there, but I go round on a Saturday night after I finish work. Most of the traders know me now. Joe introduced me to some of them before he left. They're very kind. They all thought a lot of Joe and still ask after him every time I see them. And Joe still sends part of his army pay home.' She grinned suddenly. 'Did you already know that, because he sends it to your mum to give to me? He doesn't want my dad getting his hands on it.'

'He's a good lad, your Joe. Everyone says so. I wish I was like him.'

'Oh you are,' Mattie said, without thinking. Suddenly, she felt embarrassed and blushed.

Dan grinned. 'Thanks, Mattie. I take that as a real compliment.'

There was silence between them for a while before Dan said softly, 'So, what are you going to do about school?'

Mattie sighed. 'I only wish I knew.'

Fourteen

Only two days after their conversation, Mattie was walking home after work when she heard Dan's voice behind her. 'Mattie! Mattie! Wait!'

She stopped and turned to see him running down the street towards her. 'I saw Mr Musgrave on my way home from work. He wants you to go to his house to see him. Tonight, he said, if you can.'

Mattie wrinkled her forehead. 'Mr Musgrave? Oh, right. I'll go after tea, then. That's if there is any.'

'Why don't you come to ours? Mum's just cooking our tea.'

Mattie shook her head. 'That's kind of you, Dan, but I want to see how Mum is.'

Dan nodded understandingly. 'Righto. See you later, then.'

But a nice surprise awaited Mattie as she opened the back door; she was met by an appetizing aroma. She sniffed the air. 'Meat and potato pie, Mum?'

Elsie, smiling proudly, was just putting the hot pie on the table. 'It's come out really well, Mattie. Even the pastry's come out a treat. I haven't quite lost me touch.'

''Course you haven't, Mum,' she said, giving Elsie a quick hug. 'Where are the others?'

'Upstairs. Give them a shout, will you, and bring Toby down.'

Nancy and Toby – a sturdy little boy of six now – appeared at once, but there was no sign of Lewis or of their father.

'All the more for us,' Nancy said gleefully, sitting down at the table. Nancy was growing into quite a pretty girl with blonde hair, which she now washed regularly. She also loved getting new clothes, though they were hardly 'new', being passed down from Mattie. But as Mattie always looked after her things, when they became Nancy's they still looked presentable.

'I'll put some on two plates for your dad and Lewis,' Elsie said, 'and then we can divide the rest between us.'

As they ate, Mattie said, 'Nancy, will you help Mum with the washing-up tonight, please? I have to go out.'

Nancy pouted. 'I was going round to Jenny's. Can't you do it?' Nancy's friend, Jenny Waterfield, lived two streets away. The two friends spent a lot of time together at Jenny's home and Nancy was often reluctant to do her share of the chores.

'It's all right,' Elsie said. 'I'll manage tonight. You both deserve a night off.'

When both girls glanced at her doubtfully, Elsie added, 'I mean it. Bella came round first thing this morning and got me going, so today's been a good day.' And she actually laughed. 'I'd make the most of it, if I were you.'

'Well, if you're sure, Mum –' Mattie said and then

turned to Nancy. 'You just mind you're not late back.'

Nancy nodded but avoided meeting her elder sister's eyes.

'Come in, Mattie. It's nice to see you.'

Ben Musgrave opened the front door and then ushered her into the living room.

Mattie stopped in surprise. 'Oh, hello, Miss Parsons.'

Cecily patted the seat beside her on the couch. 'Come and sit down, dear. We have something we want to discuss with you.' When they were all seated, she continued, 'Mattie, we've been trying to think of ways we can enable you to stay on at school to take your Higher School Certificate in two years' time. Mr and Mrs Musgrave have enjoyed helping you in our little subterfuge so far and, in fact, they are now willing to have you come to live with them.'

Mattie's mouth dropped open and, for a moment, she couldn't speak.

'I've been taking advice on the legality of you leaving home at sixteen and it seems, even if your father were to take us to court, that their ruling – certainly in the circumstances – would be to allow it.'

'We understand it's a huge decision for you to make, Mattie,' Mavis put in, 'especially with Joe no longer around to help you decide.'

Mattie found her voice. 'We've had a letter from Joe. He's coming home on leave next week. I'll talk it over with him. See what he thinks about me leaving Mum. It's her I'm worried about.'

'That's fine,' Ben said. 'There are still three weeks of the summer holidays left. You've plenty of time to decide before the autumn term starts.'

Mattie cleared her throat. 'I wouldn't be able to pay you any board and lodging, though.'

Mavis shook her head. 'We wouldn't want any. Besides, Miss Parsons is going to look into the possibility of some sort of grant from the Education Authority to help.'

'But, that aside,' Ben added, 'we want to do it anyway.'

'Miss Jenkins – she's the head of personnel at the store where I work at weekends and in the holidays – has offered me a full-time position starting at the beginning of September.' Mattie bit her lip. 'She sent an official letter to my home and my dad opened it and read it, so of course—' Her voice shook and she spread her hands in a helpless gesture.

'Oh dear, that's a shame,' Ben murmured. This was going to complicate matters, he was sure, but Mattie's head was already whirling with ideas.

'Perhaps if I ask Miss Jenkins if she'd let me carry on working Saturdays and school holidays, my dad would let me stay on at school.' But there was no mistaking the doubt in her tone as she said the words aloud.

'We wouldn't want to stop you doing that, even if you came to live here,' Mavis said gently. 'We understand you would still need to help the situation at home.'

Mattie glanced at her and then looked away.

'But the work for the Higher would be much harder than up to now,' Cecily warned.

Mattie nodded. At last she said, 'I'll talk to Joe when he comes home next week.'

'Wha's up, Mattie?' Dan asked her. 'You look as if you've lost a shilling and found a ha'penny.' He was loitering outside the ginnel to their homes as she walked down the street.

She sighed and said bitterly, 'More like I've found nowt.'

'Want to come in?'

Mattie hesitated, torn between longing to go into the Spencers' welcoming home and going to her own home to make sure her mother was all right.

'I'd better not. I'm not sure Nancy can be trusted to come home when she should.'

Dan nodded but as she turned away, he asked, 'Did you get on all right at the Musgraves'?'

Mattie hesitated. 'Sort of, Dan. I'll tell you all about it tomorrow. I'll come and see you and your mum when I come home after work.'

Dan nodded. 'Look forward to that, Mattie.' He turned and disappeared down the ginnel, whistling as he went.

Despite her worries, Mattie smiled.

Mattie spent the days until Joe was due home battling with a mixture of emotions. She was flattered and excited that not only did her teachers think she was clever enough to sit the Higher Certificate, but also the Musgraves were prepared to do so much for her. Yet she was apprehensive too that somehow her father would stop it happening. And she was worried for her mum. If only she was stronger and would stand up to Sid. Elsie was much better, on the whole, these days, but the slightest hint of trouble sent her reaching for the bottle again.

Joe was due to arrive on the Sunday – the only day of the week on which Mattie was at home. She spent the morning doing household chores, but every so often she would run to the end of their ginnel to watch for the first sight of him at the top of the street. At last she saw him, marching down the road, swinging his arms, his kitbag on his back. Mattie ran towards him. He held out his arms, caught her and swung her round. Already, after the first few weeks of basic training, he looked even taller and broader. His lean face was wreathed in smiles as he set her down on the pavement.

'Here, let's have a look at you. My – you're prettier than ever. I bet you've got all the boys chasing after you.'

'Oh, I haven't got time for all that. Joe – I've got a chance to stay on at school and take the Higher. What d'you think?'

'Has Dad agreed?' His tone sounded doubtful.

Mattie bit her lip and shook her head. 'He – he doesn't know. Nor Mum. Mr and Mrs Musgrave have suggested I leave home and go and live with them.'

Joe frowned. 'How would that work, then? Look,' he added before she could answer, 'let's get home first and you can tell me all about it later.'

'How long are you here for?'

'Seventy-two hours.'

'That's not long.'

'Long enough, Mattie. We'll sort it out, I promise.'

'So, what are we going to do, then?' Joe asked. They were sitting together in the attic bedroom. He listened patiently as she explained everything that the Musgraves and Miss Parsons had suggested.

Joe was thoughtful for several minutes before saying slowly, 'Mattie, you know I would never stand in your way – that more than anything I want you to take all the chances you can – but . . .'

'I know what you're going to say, Joe,' she said softly, knowing instinctively what was worrying him, though he was finding it difficult to put into words. 'Mum. You're worried about what will happen to Mum if I leave home.'

Joe nodded. 'Nancy's not as hardworking or as considerate as you. She does what she's asked to do, yes, but only when she's cornered and she'll never think of doing jobs of her own accord, like you've always done. And as for Lewis, well, he ought to be the one leaving home. He's going to bring trouble to our door one day. But, having said all that,' Joe went on with a smile, 'you won't stay at home forever, so now's as good a time as any and you have a real chance to go on to higher education. Has university been mentioned?'

'Oh heavens, not yet.' Mattie giggled. 'I'm only sixteen, though Miss Parsons did once say I was "university material".'

Seriously, Joe said, 'A few very clever people go early.'

'I'm not that bright, Joe.'

'Oh I think you are. Anyway, let's deal with this problem first shall we? Have you told Mum?'

Mattie shook her head. 'I daren't. She's been quite a bit better recently, especially this last week, looking forward to you coming home.'

'Then we'll tell her together tomorrow night when you get home from work. Hopefully, Dad will be out.'

Mattie spent a restless night, mulling over the problem. Just beyond the curtain that separated the two sides of the attic bedroom, Joe too lay awake.

The following evening when Lewis was still out and Nancy had scuttled off to her friend's home to avoid the washing-up after tea, Mattie and Joe sat down beside their mother. Sid was at home but he was outside in the yard tinkering with a bicycle he had 'acquired' that day. Toby was playing on the hearthrug with a box of coloured bricks that Joe had brought home for him.

'Mum,' Joe said in a low voice and taking her hand into his. 'We want to talk to you.'

Elsie's eyes were startled and fearful. 'Go on,' she whispered.

'Mattie's got the most marvellous chance to stay on at school for another two years. She might even be able to try to go to university.'

'Oh Mattie, that's wonderful.' Elsie relaxed visibly. 'How clever you are,' she added wistfully.

'But Dad won't let me, will he?'

Elsie ran her tongue around her lips. 'We'll stand up to him. This is your future.' Joe and Mattie glanced at each other in surprise. This was something they hadn't seen in their mother for a long time.

'The Musgraves have asked me to go and live with them if I have to leave home. But – but I don't want to leave you.'

Elsie smiled tremulously. 'And I don't want to lose you. It's bad enough with you gone, Joe, but I wouldn't want to be the one to hold you back. If it comes to it, Mattie, you must go.'

'But—'

'No "buts",' Elsie said, her voice stronger than they had heard for some time. 'We'll tell your dad when he comes in.'

When Sid came in through the back door about half an hour later, Joe and Mattie stood up to face him. As if sensing something unusual, Sid said, 'What's this?'

'Dad,' Joe took the lead. 'Mattie wants to stay on at school another two years.'

Sid's eyes narrowed and his mouth became a thin, hard line. 'Does she now? Well, she isn't going to.' He turned towards Mattie and shook his fist. 'You'll do as you're told and take that full-time job where you're working. You won't hide owt from me again, so don't think you can. You're getting far too big for your boots, girl. You'll toe the line now that your precious brother isn't here all the time to threaten me.' He turned to Joe. 'And as for you, you can sling yer hook. I don't want you back in the house ever. You hear me?'

'Loud and clear,' Joe muttered, but he did not move.

Mattie was still standing close to her mother and Elsie reached out and grasped her hand. 'Go, Mattie,' she whispered. 'You should go while you've the chance.'

'Mum, I can't leave you—'

'Yes, you can. You must. You'll never get another chance like this. Take it, love.'

'What are you whispering about?' Sid glanced from one to the other. 'I hope you're not taking her side, Elsie, or you'll feel the back of my hand.'

Elsie withered in the face of his onslaught. Her moment of bravado had come and gone, but she'd managed to tell her daughter what she wanted her to do. She just hoped Mattie had more courage than she had.

Mattie squeezed her mother's hand, communicating to her by touch that she understood. She squared her shoulders and faced her father. 'Then I shall leave home.'

'You can't,' Sid sneered. 'You aren't old enough. And if you think you can go to them bloody Spencers up the road, then you can think again. I'll make their life such a misery that they'll wish they'd never been born. I'll have 'em in court faster than their feet could touch the ground.'

Mattie gasped as fear flooded through her. Was she going to bring trouble to the kindly Musgraves if she moved in with them? And to Miss Parsons too? But then she remembered that Ben Musgrave had said that the courts would be unlikely to force her to return home. She didn't know what the law was exactly, but she knew there were certain things that were legal now that she was sixteen. She didn't think her father knew the law that well either, although there was the possibility that he did; he always seemed adept at avoiding it.

'You'll forget all these fancy ideas and settle down to earning your keep. You'll start working full-time at the beginning of September.'

Mattie felt Elsie squeeze her hand. She pulled in a deep breath. 'No, I won't, Dad. I'm staying on at school.'

For a brief moment Sid stared at her. He raised his fist and seemed about to hit her, but a movement from Joe made him drop his arm.

'Then you can pack your bags and leave,' he spat. 'Right now. Tonight, and we'll see if you've got somewhere to go.' Then he turned and pointed his finger at Joe. 'And you, an' all. And don't come back. Either of you.'

As Mattie and Joe turned and moved towards the stairs to collect their meagre belongings, Elsie reached for the comforting feel of the bottle still hidden behind her chair for moments like these.

Fifteen

It was late by the time they knocked on the Spencers' back door, but there was the soft glow of a light coming through the window. 'Someone's still up,' Joe murmured.

'We shouldn't have come here, Joe,' Mattie whispered 'If Dad finds out . . .'

'We'll be gone in the morning. We'll not bring trouble on them.'

The door was opened tentatively by Dan. 'Hello, you two. Come in.'

'I'm sorry it's late—' Joe began, but Dan waved his apologies aside.

'Never too late for you two to call.'

Bella and Rod looked up in surprise when Dan ushered them into the kitchen and Joe began to apologize again. Bella got up from her chair as she noticed both Joe and Mattie were carrying bundles. 'Summat's wrong, isn't it? Come and sit down and tell us all about it. I expect it's to do with what Mattie told us the other day, is it? I was afraid the balloon would go up when Sid found out. Don't look so worried, Mattie love. We'll work summat out.'

Over a mug of cocoa, Joe explained all that had happened. 'I'll be all right,' he ended. 'I can just go

Joe took her to the Musgraves before he caught his train back to camp. But we've told him to come and stay with us whenever he gets leave. He can come down and see you when Sid's out of the way. Now, Elsie, let's get rid of that bottle I can see not quite hiding behind your chair.'

'I've got further to come to see you now, Mattie.' Dan grinned as he waited outside the store at closing time on the following Saturday. 'I'll walk you home.'

'Oh, but—'

'Don't worry, I'm going to come in and have a word with Mr Musgrave. I don't want them thinking I'm going to take your attention away from your studies. There's no one wants you to succeed more than I do, Mattie. I hope you know that.'

'I do, Dan,' she said solemnly. 'Come on, then.'

They walked to the Musgraves' home where Mattie, now entrusted with her own back door key, let them into the house. She took him into the kitchen where Mavis was preparing the evening meal. 'Hello, Mattie. And who's this?'

Before Mattie could answer, Ben, coming into the kitchen, said, 'It's Dan Spencer. Hello, Dan, how are you?' He held out his hand to shake the young man's.

'Very well, Mr Musgrave, thank you. I won't disturb your evening, but I just wanted to see you to explain about me and Mattie.'

Ben and Mavis exchanged a glance that was tinged with anxiety. Were all their best laid plans going to be thrown into chaos? Was Mattie going to throw away her chances because of a romantic attachment?

Whilst they would fully understand – they had met at sixteen whilst still at school – they didn't want Mattie to be diverted from realizing her potential.

'I think you know, sir,' Dan began, the old habit of addressing his former headmaster was difficult to shake off, 'that me and Mattie are just friends and I want to reassure you that that's all it is. I don't want you to think that I shall be getting in Mattie's way or taking her away from her studies, but I do want to see her now and again, if that would be all right.'

Relief spread across Ben's face. 'Of course it is, Dan. We don't want her to lose touch with any of her friends.' Tactfully, he did not mention her family. 'You come round whenever you like. You'll be very welcome.'

'Thank you, sir. Mrs Musgrave,' he added politely as he turned to leave.

Ben followed him to the back door. 'How are you settling in to being a working man? I heard you're working for a little mester in the city? Are you enjoying the work?'

'I love it, Mr Musgrave. I'm not clever like Mattie, but my employer ses I've got a real talent in me hands. I'd like to have me own workshop one day.'

'Then I'm sure you will, Dan. It's good to have ambition.'

As Ben closed the door behind Dan and came back into the kitchen, Mattie still had not moved or spoken. She was startled by the overwhelming disappointment that had flooded through her hearing Dan say the words 'me and Mattie are just friends'.

Sixteen

Living with the Musgraves was a whole new life for Mattie; a world away from her own family and home. She had never before had a bedroom all to herself or clean sheets every week and proper warm blankets. There was even an eiderdown similar to the one she had seen on Bella Spencer's bed. And with three proper meals a day, she began to fill out in all the right places and become the young woman she was meant to be. The Musgraves were very easy-going; they didn't try to stop her continuing to work at the department store on Saturdays and during the school holidays. They understood her need to feel she was still contributing to her family's finances, though, like Joe, she gave the money to Bella to buy food for them. She didn't want her father getting his hands on it or her mother spending it on alcohol. But best of all for the young girl, who was thirsty for knowledge and learning, was the access she now had to the huge bookcase that the Musgraves had in their sitting room. Her greatest joy was to be able to read the daily newspaper; she'd only ever seen old ones wrapping up fish and chips or fruit from the market. Now, each evening, she could spread the day's paper out on the kitchen table and devour every word. The

Musgraves were always on hand to explain anything she didn't understand as she came to terms with the wider world outside the narrow existence that had been her home life.

But, sadly, with this widening knowledge, came disturbing truths. Previously sheltered from national and international news, Mattie was now learning of the unrest throughout Europe. At school she was studying mathematics and science subjects, so her knowledge of history was basic. She knew more about the Stone Age, the Iron Age and the industrial revolution than she did about the politics of the present day or the recent history of her own country.

'Who's this Adolf Hitler?' she asked Ben over their evening meal shortly after the new term had begun in September 1935. She had settled into the work immediately and now she had a comfortable space at her new home to do her homework.

'A very dangerous man,' Ben said.

'It says in your newspaper that he's stopped Jews and Aryans marrying? How can he do that?'

'By threatening that they will be sent to concentration camps.'

'What is an Aryan?'

'Hitler, who now rules Germany, is obsessed with creating what he calls a "master race" and he has adopted the name Aryan to describe what he thinks is perfect; pale skin, blonde hair and blue eyes. But that is actually a misnomer. The origin of the word "Aryan" is completely different. However, no one, it seems, dares to argue with the Führer, as he now calls himself.'

'So, he doesn't want any what *he* would call mixed-race marriages?'

Ben smiled. How very quickly Mattie understood. 'That's about the size of it.'

'How dreadful.'

'I have to admit that he has done a lot for the German people since the catastrophe of the Great War. He has given them back their national pride and the country is prospering, but I am very much afraid that he is a fanatic who will push his ambitions too far. He's power mad and that can be very dangerous. There are rumblings that the Italian dictator is planning to invade Abyssinia and it is my belief that Hitler is watching Mussolini very closely.'

'What, you mean that Hitler might start to invade other countries to gain even more power?'

Ben nodded solemnly.

In the weeks and months that followed, Mattie read the news even more avidly, but her priority was still her schoolwork and seeing some members of her family whenever she could. She visited the Spencers frequently and one Saturday evening, Bella said, 'Mr Spencer has gone to the pub with your dad. He'll try to keep him there for an hour so you can go down and see your mum. Dan'll go with you just in case . . .'

To Mattie's surprise, when she and Dan entered the back door of the Prices' home, her mother was standing at the sink in the scullery washing up the tea things.

'Where's Nancy? She should be doing that.'

'It's all right, Mattie. She's gone round to her

friend's house. She does help me quite a bit, but she's only twelve.'

Mattie bit back the retort that she'd done nearly all the housework at twelve years old. She didn't want to upset her mother, who looked a lot better.

'Come in, both of you. Sid's out.'

'We know. Dan's dad has taken him off to the pub so I could come here.'

Elsie smiled and, for a brief moment, Mattie had a glimpse of the pretty woman she'd once been.

'I don't know what I'd do without your mum, Dan,' Elsie said as she dried her hands and they sat down near the range. 'She's been absolutely wonderful to me.'

'She's very fond of you, Mrs Price. And of Mattie. She's glad to help.'

'She does a lot of shopping for me with the money Joe sends and what Mattie gives her. She always tells me exactly what's happening. I'm so proud of you both.' Tears filled her eyes. 'I just wish I was a better mother.'

Mattie took her hand. 'Mum, it's not your fault things are the way they are. But you're looking so much better.'

'I am because I'm not drinking so much. Bella's helping me with that too. The only time I lapse is if there's trouble.'

Tentatively, hoping it wasn't going to distress her mother, Mattie asked, 'How's Lewis? Has he got a job yet?'

Lewis had left school in July and should be working by now.

Elsie laughed wryly. 'Nobody will take him on. I

think word's got round that he's following in his father's footsteps. But he's not as sharp as Sid. Every time there's a knock on the back door, I open it, dreading to see a policeman standing there.'

'It's a wonder Dad's never been caught.'

Elsie sighed deeply. 'He always says he's got the luck of the Devil, but if the Devil is ever looking the other way . . .'

They stayed with her an hour and then, reluctantly, decided they'd better leave. They'd just arrived back at the Spencers' home when they heard footsteps down the ginnel and Rod came in the back door.

'Phew, that was just in time,' Dan muttered.

'Oh, you're safe enough. Sid's still there and will be, I reckon, until they chuck him out. It's good to see you, Mattie. Now sit down and tell us everything you've been doing. Dan will walk you back to the Musgraves.'

Over the next two years until Mattie took her Higher School Certificate, life continued in much the same pattern. When the exams loomed, Ben said, 'Mavis, do you think we should try to persuade her to stop working on Saturdays and concentrate wholly on her studies?'

'To be honest, darling,' Mavis said, 'I don't think it's having a detrimental effect. She works at her books all day on Sunday and Cecily tells me she's top of the class in all her subjects. Besides, maybe a break on one day a week might even be beneficial.'

'There is that. Mm, well, I'll be guided by you and the redoubtable Cecily Parsons.' He paused and then added, 'Has anything been said about university?'

'Oh that's all been taken care of. Applications were sent in at the beginning of this school year and Cecily has been busy writing letters to all and sundry to try to get funding for Mattie.'

'And if they don't get all she needs, are you willing for us to continue to support her?'

Mavis smiled. 'Of course.'

Ben kissed her forehead. 'Good.'

There was change and upheaval throughout 1936. It began with King George V's death in the January and ended with the abdication of Edward VIII, an event that no one had expected.

'I feel sorry for Bertie,' Ben said, referring to the brother who had now become King George VI. 'He was never trained to be a king as his elder brother was, but I think he will be a good one. He has a stable family life and his wife will be stalwart in her support of him.'

'Presumably his eldest daughter is now heir to the throne, is she?' Mattie asked.

'Yes. Let's hope she has plenty of years ahead to learn all she'll need to know.'

But the changes were not confined to Britain. There was great unrest in Europe; Germany entered the Rhineland and Mussolini conquered Abyssinia, whilst in Spain there was civil war. Quietly, many in Britain began to prepare for another war. Unaware that it could affect her in any way, Mattie continued her studies, though Ben and Mavis were fearful that a new worldwide conflict could engulf another generation of fine young people.

Seventeen

In the summer of 1937, Mattie passed the Higher
School Certificate with the topmost grades in all
subjects and had firm offers from three universities.
With Cecily's guidance, she chose Oxford. There were
great celebrations at the school and in the Musgrave
and Spencer homes.

'We must have a little party,' Mavis declared. 'We
can't let such a momentous occasion pass by. We'll
ask Cecily Parsons to come and perhaps one or two
of your teachers, but you must invite whoever you
wish, Mattie.'

There were only four people she could invite; the
Spencer family. She would dearly loved to have asked
her mother, but it was impossible and, of course, Joe
was away.

On the evening of the party, Mattie stood up and
shyly thanked all those who had helped her. 'I couldn't
have done it without any of you.'

Sadly, there was no such celebrating in the Price
household. Only Elsie knew of Mattie's great success
and was quietly proud, but she said nothing to either
Sid or the other members of her family, though of
course Mattie had written at once to tell her beloved
brother.

Joe was loving his life in the regular army and doing very well. In the July of that year, he celebrated his twenty-first birthday with his fellow soldiers. Although he could have stopped sending part of his pay home, he continued to send regular payments to Bella. On one of his visits home, she'd suggested that he should now keep all the money for himself.

'Things are a bit easier for your mum now, Joe. Sid coughs up once in a while. If he doesn't, he doesn't get fed. You should save up your own money.' She eyed him archly. 'You'll be wanting to get married one day.'

Joe laughed. 'Haven't met the right girl yet, Mrs Spencer.'

'I'm surprised – you're a nice-looking young feller.'

'So, how's things down here, then?' Joe said, tactfully steering the conversation away from himself. 'Nancy is leaving school this summer, isn't she? Has she got a job yet?'

'Oh yes. At the store in town where Mattie still works part-time.'

'Do you know if she contributes at home?'

Bella snorted. 'Not that little madam. She spends all her money on cosmetics and fancy clothes. She doesn't do much about the house either. Not like Mattie used to do. Still, don't you worry about that, Joe. Your mum is a lot better than she used to be and a bit of housework will do her good. Keeps her busy and takes her mind off – other things.'

'If you're sure, because I could have a word with Nancy.'

'Best not. I'll keep an eye on things.'

'I'll keep sending part of my pay to you for the moment anyway. What about Toby? He's eight now.'

Bella's eyes softened. 'He's a grand little lad. Always smiling and cheerful. Not much gets Toby down and, from what I hear, he's getting on well at school. Oh, not in Mattie's league, but I think he's what they call "a good average".'

'And dare I ask about Lewis?'

Bella grimaced. 'He's a real chip off the old block. A petty crook, just like Sid, but he must be learning his "trade" a bit better now. There haven't been any visits from the coppers recently.' She was thoughtful for a moment before adding, 'Actually, he's not exactly like your dad. Sid always looks a right scruff, but Lewis – even though he's only sixteen – always dresses smartly and carries a little suitcase, just as if he's a door-to-door salesman.'

'Are you sure he isn't?'

Bella laughed. 'Don't kid yourself, Joe. He'll never do a proper day's work. By the way, if you want to see your mum, I should go down now. I saw Sid cycling up the road about an hour ago. He won't be back till closing time.'

'I'll do that and then tomorrow I'll see Mattie. She'll be off to university soon. I want to catch her before she leaves.'

Mattie took her place at Oxford in the autumn of 1937. She fitted very well into university life. Now, she was amongst people just as clever as she was. In fact, one or two were perhaps even more intellectually gifted than Mattie. But she enjoyed the challenge of pitting her wits against them and worked hard to achieve even greater heights. Having lived in the Musgraves' home for the past two years, she also knew how to conduct herself in what might be termed middle-class society. She never volunteered information about her family; she talked only about her former school and the kindness and generosity of her benefactors. Her peers were given the impression that perhaps she'd been an only child and had lost her parents. Tactfully, no one asked probing questions and Mattie was able to keep her disreputable home life secret.

A whole new world opened up to her. Though still rather shy, she joined various clubs and activities; she learnt to play chess and joined a choir, finding that she could sing reasonably well. And she was quietly proud to be admitted to a prestigious mathematical group; here she was accepted for her outstanding talent and not because of where she came from. The only thing she did not join was sport of any kind. As the games mistress at school had remarked drily, she was still hopeless. She wrote regularly to Joe and to the Spencer family; she knew Bella would share the letters with Elsie whenever she could. And of course she did not forget the Musgraves or Cecily Parsons, but, cocooned in the academic and social life of the university, it was only when she was back at the Musgraves' home during the Christmas holidays that she read the newspapers and caught up with what was happening in the outside world.

'What's going on in Europe now? I must admit

the outside world seems very far away when we're wrapped up in our own academic life,' she asked, and was startled by Ben's solemn look.

'It's not good, Mattie. It rather looks as if Franco is going to rule Spain. But to my mind, he's not the biggest threat – not to the rest of us, that is. It's Hitler I fear. He has a stranglehold on the German people and he's talking about needing more "living space" for Germany and that can only mean one thing.'

Mattie glanced at him wide-eyed. 'Invading another country, you mean?'

Ben nodded. 'How else could he achieve it?'

Mattie's mind worked quickly. 'Do you – do you really think there might be another war?'

'It's – not impossible, Mattie.'

'But they'd try talks first, wouldn't they? Our Government, I mean.'

'We might not be involved, Mattie. I doubt Hitler would try to invade us. No, it'll be just those countries bordering Germany he'll have his eye on. They lost some territory as part of the Versailles Treaty after the Great War and I think it's those lands he wants back. He's already violated the treaty by re-arming Germany and occupying the Rhineland, so I don't think anything's going to stop him taking what he believes rightly belongs to his country. Maybe he would get away with that, but if he decides to try to conquer other countries, I think he will meet with opposition and that could very well escalate into conflict.'

'And if it did involve us,' Mattie said quietly. 'Joe would have to go, wouldn't he?'

'I'm afraid so, Mattie, yes. But not you, Mattie. You'll be quite safe at university, even if they brought in conscription.'

'Is that what they did in the Great War?'

'They brought in conscription for men of certain ages in 1916 and then they mobilized women to fill the work places left by the men.'

'And you think that's what might happen again – *if* we were to get involved in a war?'

'I'm afraid so.'

At that moment Mavis brought in a tray of coffee. She sat down on the couch and handed the cups round. 'What are you two looking so serious about?'

Ben and Mattie glanced at each other before Ben said, 'War.'

The cup Mavis was holding rattled in its saucer and she turned wide eyes on her husband. 'Has there been some news?'

'No, no. Mattie and I were just talking about the situation, that's all.'

'We feel a bit cut off at university, but I really must keep up with the newspapers now and keep abreast of what's happening. I'm just so worried about Joe.'

But as 1938 dawned, Joe and his fellow soldiers were quietly preparing for whatever might happen. They weren't anxious; they were excited and ready for action. Where Joe was stationed, training intensified and lectures on the state of the nations increased in number and even military tactics were discussed in greater detail. Whether this went on throughout the British Army, Joe didn't know, but his officers seemed to think it was a good idea.

Even civilians were beginning to prepare themselves. In January, just before Mattie was due to return to Oxford, it was announced in the papers that all schoolchildren were to be issued with gas masks.

'The Government wouldn't go to all that trouble and expense if they weren't worried,' Mattie said reasonably. Towards the end of the month, some cities carried out a simulated wartime blackout to prepare their citizens.

'What ought I to do?' Mattie asked, when she came home at the end of March for the Easter break.

'At the moment, nothing,' Ben assured her.

'But a lot of the boys at Oxford are talking about joining up.'

'If war comes, then they probably will.'

'But – what about their studies? Their courses? What will happen?'

'I would fully expect that universities would run some sort of scheme that allowed their students to resume their studies once any conflict was over. But, of course, I don't *know* that.'

'You might find,' Mavis put in quietly, 'that some students might actually be commandeered into war service. They'll want that calibre of person for the intelligence services, won't they?'

Ben chuckled. 'To say nothing of spies.'

Mattie returned to university life more worried and uncertain than ever. Though she continued to work at her studies just as hard as she had always done, she now followed the newspapers avidly. When she read about the massive annual Nuremberg rally at the beginning of September, she shuddered at the display of raw fanaticism and the power the gathering exuded; tanks, aircraft and seemingly endless lines of marching soldiers, all with their arms extended in the Nazi salute or carrying the flag displaying the threatening swastika.

But with the end of September came a glimmer of hope that a full-scale war might, after all, be avoided. The Prime Minister attended a meeting in Munich with Hitler and Mussolini. It was not an unqualified success, for the German-speaking area of Czechoslovakia – the Sudetenland region – was handed over to the Germans, but for the moment it seemed to push back the threat of hostilities between Germany and Britain. 'Peace for our time,' Mr Chamberlain called it, as he waved the piece of paper which he said bore Herr Hitler's name alongside his own.

'He's done his best,' Ben said. 'He shouldn't be blamed for trying to keep this country out of a war.'

'Do you think he's managed it?' Mattie asked.

'Not for a moment,' Ben said solemnly. 'He's virtually handed over the Sudetenland to Hitler, and the Czechs have a right to feel aggrieved.'

'And you don't think Hitler will stop there, do you?'

'No, I don't, and it's caused a lot of dissension in our parliament.'

'I don't like the news that's coming out of Germany about how they're treating their Jews. It's abominable,' Mattie said.

'I fear it will only get worse.'

Mattie trusted Chamberlain's piece of paper as little as Ben did, and in November, when she read accounts of Kristallnacht – the Night of Broken Glass – when thousands of Jewish shops throughout Germany were smashed and looted, hundreds of synagogues burnt down and many Jews killed, any hope that this violence would not escalate into full-scale war died.

Mattie believed that it was only a matter of time, but she kept these thoughts to herself. All she could do for the moment was to work hard and finish her studies, but her anxiety over Joe only increased. By the beginning of 1939, she hadn't seen him for months and Bella hadn't heard anything from him either.

'He'll be busy, love. Try not to worry,' she said, trying to comfort Mattie. 'Not much of a letter writer, your Joe, is he?'

Mattie smiled fondly. 'That's very true.'

'I'll let you know if I hear anything,' Bella promised.

In February, free air-raid shelters were distributed in London and the threat of war loomed ever closer. In the same month, more turmoil and bitterness in the British parliament erupted when the Government of the day – Mr Chamberlain's Tory Party – recognized General Franco's rule in Spain.

By March, however, when Hitler marched into Prague, even Mr Chamberlain could see that he had been cruelly duped by the Führer, who was now occupying lands not populated by German-speaking people. At the end of the month, Britain and France promised to aid Poland if it should be attacked.

When Mattie came home for the Easter holidays, the threat of war was very real. Sitting with the family in the Spencers' kitchen on a visit one evening, the conversation was very solemn.

'If war does come, I shall volunteer,' Dan said. 'I see they're already doubling the Territorial Army.'

Mattie, feeling a sudden tremor of fear, waited for Bella or Rod to argue with their son, but neither of them did so. They just exchanged a look and Bella sighed.

'You must do what you think best, son,' Rod said quietly.

'Can I volunteer for anything?' Jane asked. True to her word, Jane now worked as a buffer girl in one of the large cutlery-making factories.

'I think you'd be too young, love?' Rod said.

'I'm eighteen in August,' Jane declared stoutly. 'I'd want to do something, to help the war effort, 'specially if Dan goes.'

'I'd join a local women's organization of some sort,' Bella said. She glanced at Mattie. 'Did you see the piece in the paper last Wednesday that plans are being made to evacuate children from the city within days of war breaking out? There'd be a lot of work to do if that happens. I'd volunteer to do that and I'd encourage your mum to come along with me. It'd be just the thing to give her a bit of independence, making her feel she was "doing her bit".'

Mattie opened her mouth to agree, but at that moment a knock sounded at the back door.

'I'll go.' Jane jumped up and a moment later they heard her squeal. '*Joe!* Come in, come in. Mattie's here too.'

As he came into the kitchen Mattie rushed to him and flung her arms around him, burying her face against the rough khaki of his jacket. He held her tightly for a moment, before gently easing himself out of her grasp and holding her at arm's length to look down at her. 'You look as if you've grown, though I don't expect you have really.'

'And the same to you,' she said, laughing through her tears of joy at seeing him. 'You're positively *huge*.'

'It's all the drill and the cross-country runs.'

Dan grinned as he held out his hand in welcome. 'I feel positively puny at the side of you.' They all laughed, because Dan too was tall and broad shouldered. He now stood a head taller than Mattie.

'Have you come to stay?' Bella said. 'Your bed in Dan's room is always kept aired – just in case.'

'If it's no trouble, Mrs Spencer. A lot of us have been given leave now because there's a strong feeling that things are hotting up.'

Bella stood up. 'Come and sit down. I'll get you summat to eat.'

'I'm sorry I haven't been in touch lately. It's been hectic.'

'We'll watch for your dad going past in the morning and then you can go and visit your mum,' Bella said, pouring a cup of strong tea for him.

'How's she doing, Mrs Spencer?'

'A lot better, Joe. I take her the news from Mattie regularly.' She smiled and pinched his ear lobe. 'And from you, you young scallywag, when we get some.'

'I'll try to do better, Mrs Spencer. Honest I will.'

'It need only be a few lines, Joe. Just to let us know you're OK.'

The family talked for two hours, exchanging news and gossip.

'Everything going all right at university, Mattie?' Joe was anxious to know.

Mattie grinned, a little embarrassed. 'I shouldn't say so myself, but, yes, thanks. Wonderfully.'

'Still coming top of the class in everything?' Dan teased gently.

Now Mattie blushed.

''Course she is,' Bella said. She couldn't have been prouder of Mattie – and of Joe – than if they'd been her own children.

Suddenly, Mattie glanced at the clock on the mantelpiece. 'It's getting late. I must get back. Mrs Musgrave will be worrying.'

'I'll walk you home,' Joe began, but Dan stood up quickly and put his hand on Joe's shoulder. 'I'll see her back. I usually do and you look like you could do with some kip.'

'Well—' Joe hesitated, but Mattie kissed his cheek. 'I'll come back in the morning and we can go and see Mum together if the coast's clear.'

They walked through the familiar streets in the deepening dusk and when they reached the Musgraves' home, Mattie said at once, 'I'm sorry I'm a bit later than usual, but Joe arrived unexpectedly.'

'Don't worry,' Mavis said cheerfully. 'We know Dan always sees you back here. Are you coming in for a moment, Dan?'

'Not tonight, Mrs Musgrave, if you don't mind.

I'll get off back. I'd like a talk with Joe about the army, if he's not already tucked up in bed. 'Night, Mattie. See you soon.'

With a wave of farewell to Mavis, he set off down the street, his hands in his pockets and whistling jauntily. But Mattie's worried eyes followed him.

'He's a grand lad,' Mavis said as she closed the door and locked up for the night. 'Is he contemplating joining up?'

'He said tonight that if war comes, he will.'

Mavis put her arms around Mattie's shoulders. 'You're very fond of Dan, aren't you Mattie?'

'I hadn't realized it until recently, but, yes, I am.' Then she added hastily, 'But don't think I'm going to let anything come between me and my studies. I'll never let that happen.'

'No, I know you won't. And besides,' Mavis said, with a twinkle in her eyes, 'Dan's every bit as anxious for you to succeed as we all are.'

'Do you think so?'

'I don't "think" so, Mattie, I know so.'

Eighteen

The following morning, Mattie and Joe managed to see their mother. Elsie cried tears of joy when she saw them together.

'Oh, I miss you both so much.'

'You're looking so much better, Mum,' Joe said hugging her. 'How are things?'

'Not too bad really,' Elsie said carefully. 'As long as I don't try to interfere in whatever your dad and Lewis get up to, life trundles along. Nancy's working now.'

'Does she give you any money?' Joe asked bluntly.

Elsie hesitated, but was forced to admit that she did not. 'She doesn't earn a lot yet and – and there's always something she needs. She has to dress smartly for work. It's difficult for her . . .' Elsie's voice faded away lamely.

'Don't make excuses for her, Mum. I'm sure she could give you something even if it's only a few shillings.'

'What about Toby?' Mattie asked.

Now Elsie's face brightened. 'He's a grand little lad. Never a moment's trouble. He helps about the house more than—' She stopped and then said, 'Well, with whatever a little lad of ten can manage.' Her face clouded as she added, 'I expect if war comes, he'll have to be evacuated to somewhere safer.'

'You could go with him, couldn't you, Mum?' Joe said.

Elsie shook her head. 'He'll be too old for me to go too. Mothers with babies will be able to go, but not someone with a ten-year-old. Besides, I'd have to stay here and look after your dad, Lewis and Nancy.'

'That's a shame,' Joe said. 'A bit of country air would do you the world of good.'

Suddenly, they all heard footsteps in the ginnel and a look of fear crossed over Elsie's face. 'If that's your dad . . .'

The three of them stood as if transfixed until the back door opened and Lewis came in. For a moment he was startled but then his natural bravado re-asserted itself. 'I thought for a moment you were the army come to march me off, seein' as I'm almost eighteen. How are you, matey?' He shook Joe's hand and kissed Mattie's cheek. 'It's good to see you both, but I wouldn't let Dad catch you here. Your names are still mud in this house.'

'We'll be off, then,' Joe remarked as he took in his younger brother's dapper appearance; a well-cut suit, with a white shirt and tie and sporting a trilby hat. 'We don't want to cause trouble for Mum.'

'Oh, I watch out for her, don't I, Mum? You've no need to worry about our mum whilst I'm still here.'

Elsie smiled weakly as Joe said stiffly, 'I'm glad to hear it, Lewis. And just mind you keep watching out for her and our Nancy and Toby too.' He said no more, but there was a veiled warning in his tone that none of them failed to notice. Lewis, however, only grinned.

Joe returned to camp and the following week Mattie went back to university. She was now in the last term of the second year of her three-year course. The work was getting harder, but she revelled in the challenge. And now she was keeping abreast of the daily news. It was not pleasant reading. In May, Germany and Italy agreed a 'Pact of Steel', a political and military alliance. At the same time, an approach by Britain to form an alliance with Russia was met with a less-than-lukewarm response. It seemed to some that Stalin was also considering closer ties with Germany. By the time Mattie came down from university for the summer holidays at the end of her second year, the crisis was deepening, but, for the moment, everyone tried to carry on as normal.

Each long holiday from university, Mattie always went back to the city store to work. Now, of course, she saw a little more of her sister Nancy, who worked there full-time. Nancy had grown into a pretty sixteen-year-old with blonde hair and blue eyes and a curvaceous figure that was the envy of many of her contemporaries. She had a merry, almost flirtatious manner which actually went down very well with the customers but was not so popular with her work-mates, who gossiped about her amongst themselves.

'She gets all the sales because she's so chatty with everyone.'

'True, but mind you don't cross her. That friendliness hides a vicious temper if you upset her.'

'*Does* it?'

''Fraid so. But her sister's back on Monday for the summer. Now, she is really nice. Pretty, too, but not in such a – such a brassy way. Mattie's a real sweetie. Apparently, she's very clever, but she never lets it show. She'll help anyone.'

'If she's so clever, what's she doing working here?'

'Oh, she's at university most of the time. Oxford, I think. She just comes back in the holidays.'

Her workmate gaped at her, quite lost for words.

Her days at the department store were busy, but Mattie always found time to seek out Nancy and ask after her family.

'How's Mum?' was always her first question.

Nancy shrugged. 'All right.'

'I hope you help her with the housework.'

Nancy frowned. 'She manages fine now, Mattie. I can't do a full day's work here and then go home and start cleaning.'

'You still find time to go out with Jennifer though, don't you?'

Nancy's face turned ugly. 'Don't you get on your high horse with me, lady. You're the one who left home to live in a posh house with the Musgraves and go to university, and we're the ones left to pick up the pieces.'

Mattie turned away. She had no answer to that. For the next few weeks, the sisters avoided each other.

By the end of July, it looked as if war was inevitable.

'It seems to be because of a quarrel over the port of Danzig which, under the Treaty of Versailles, gives

Poland its only access to the sea,' Ben explained to Mattie.

'Hitler's already ignored most of the points in that agreement,' Mattie said. 'Why would this be any different?'

'Exactly. That's what everyone is afraid of.'

'And we, I suppose, are supporting Poland like we promised?'

Ben nodded.

'Good,' Mattie said firmly. 'I don't like people – or countries – who break their promises.'

'Even if it means we go to war?' Mavis put in softly.

Now Mattie hesitated. 'I don't want a war,' she said slowly. 'Of course I don't, but . . .' She bit her lip. 'It's my gut feeling that Hitler won't stop there anyway. He annexed Austria last year, didn't he? Then he got the Sudetenland and now he wants bits of Poland. He's not going to stop. I'm sure of it.'

Ben sighed heavily. 'You could well be right, Mattie. The one thing we've got to hope for is that he doesn't sign an alliance with Stalin.'

But Ben's hopes came to nothing when, towards the end of August, a Non-Aggression Pact was agreed between Germany and Russia. All Britain's efforts to get Stalin on their side had failed and now war seemed inevitable.

'Mattie,' Ben said, 'I've had word that plans are in place for a lot of our children to be evacuated from the city for safety reasons. The authorities are sure that if war does come – and it's looking more likely every day – Sheffield will be a prime target for bombing because of its industry. We've sent letters out today to all the parents – including yours about Toby.'

'I don't think my mum will be happy about that.'

'It's up to the parents to decide, of course.'

Mattie sighed. 'He ought to go, but I expect you'll get a "no" from my mum.'

But on the last day of the month, Nancy sought out Mattie. 'Mum's got herself in a right state mithering about Toby. She's drinking again.'

'What's happened?'

'He's going to be evacuated and she can't go with him because he's too old. He has to go on his own.'

'Where are they being sent to?'

Nancy shrugged. 'Somewhere in Derbyshire, I think.'

'That's not too far away. Maybe she'll be able to go and see him.'

'Can you come and see her? Talk some sense into her. She always listens to you.'

'But what about Dad?'

'He goes out to the pub most evenings. Come tonight after seven. He'll be out by then and won't come home before chucking-out time.'

'Right. I'll come round about half past seven. I'll get Dan to come with me.'

Nancy smirked. ''A' you walking out with him?'

'Heavens, no. We're just good friends.'

'I've heard that one before. Boys and girls can't be friends. Not properly.'

'Why ever not?'

159

'You know, for someone who's supposed to be so clever, you're very naive at times. Because, my dear sister, one of them will always start to get romantic feelings. That's why.'

'Well, Dan and I will be the exception to the rule,' Mattie said, adopting a lofty air. But somewhere deep inside her a little voice told her she wasn't being entirely truthful.

That evening, Mattie called at the Spencers' home.

'Dan, will you come to our house with me? Nancy says Mum's fretting about Toby being sent away from the city.'

'Of course. I've just seen your dad pedalling up the street, so t'coast should be clear.'

'I'll come with you, love,' Bella said. 'I've been worried about her too. I reckon she's drinking more again.'

Mattie nodded. 'Nancy said as much.'

'Right. Come on, then.'

Minutes later they were all entering the back door of the Price home.

'Nah then, Elsie,' Bella greeted her as they entered the kitchen. There was a rattle of glass against stone as Elsie tried to hide the bottle behind her chair. 'Aw love, you're not up to that game again, a' ye? You were doing so well.'

'I'm sorry, Bella.' Elsie sank into her chair and her eyes filled with tears. 'It's just – so hard. They're sending Toby away. I didn't want him to go, but Sid said he must. He's to be at school in the morning. Then a bus will take them all to the station. Oh Mattie, I – I can't bear it.'

Nancy, who was sitting at the table eating her tea, rolled her eyes. 'What did I tell you, Mattie?'

Mattie sat down beside her mother and took her hands. 'Look, Mum, you want him to be safe, don't you?'

'But we can have a shelter,' Elsie argued. 'They've said so. An Anderson for the backyard or a Morrison for inside. I can look after him.' Her glance swivelled to Bella. 'I swear I'll stop drinking altogether, if he stays.'

'It's not really about that, is it, love? You can't keep him at home all the time. He'd still have to go to school and he'd be in danger then, wouldn't he?'

'They'll have shelters at the school.'

'But he's still got to run between home and school. You've got to be strong, Elsie love, and let him go. Besides, if he gets sent to nice people in the country-side, think how he'll thrive.'

Elsie frowned. 'But what if he doesn't get to be with nice people? What if they're unkind to him?'

'Then he can write and tell you so and you can do something about it.'

'They'd read his letters. He wouldn't be allowed to send them if he didn't put nice things about the people in them.'

'Your Toby's an enterprising lad. He'd find a way to let you know. And you'd be able to go and see him for yourself. You'd soon know then how he was.'

Elsie leaned back in her chair. 'You're all against me,' she moaned.

'No, we're not, love. We're trying to help you see that it would be the best for Toby. He's not going to be that far away, now is he? In fact,' she smiled broadly, 'I'd come with you to see him. You an' me could take a little trip into the countryside. A day out, Elsie. How would that be, eh?'

They were still trying to persuade her, to reason with her gently, when footsteps sounded in the ginnel.

They glanced at each other, but Nancy said, 'It'll be Lewis.'

But it wasn't Lewis; it was Sid.

Nineteen

'What the hell are you lot doing in my house?' He pointed an accusing finger at Mattie. 'Especially *you*! I told you to get out and stay out and I meant it.' Before Mattie could say a word, he sneered, 'Your fancy friends thrown you out, have they? Got tired of do-gooding?'

It was Nancy who leapt up from her seat at the table and went towards her father. 'Why don't you throw me out, an' all? You'd like to do that, wouldn't you? With Toby gone, there'd be only you and Lewis to carry on your thieving ways, cos Mum won't stand up to you. She'd just end up dead in a gutter somewhere, having drunk herself into a stupor. And I don't reckon you'd give a damn. Well, we *do* give a damn, Dad. All of us and that's why they're here. Mrs Spencer—'

'She can keep her nose out of our business,' he spluttered, but Nancy moved even closer and thrust her face towards his.

'She's the only reason Mum's been a lot better just lately. She's been helping her for months, years even. This news about Toby has upskittled Mum, but she'll be all right. I'll make sure she's all right and you'll help me, won't you, Mrs Spencer?'

'Too right I will, love.'

With an angry curse, Sid gestured helplessly with a clenched fist, before turning and leaving the house again, banging the back door. Now everyone looked at Nancy, whose face was red, her eyes still glittering with temper.

'Well, well, well.' Bella smiled. 'Who'd have thought it – little Nancy, eh?'

Nancy grinned and brushed her hands together as if wiping away something nasty. Calmer now, she said, 'I know you all think I'm an idle little cow for not helping about the house, but you see, it's deliberate. If Mum has summat to do, she's much better.' She glanced towards Elsie, still sitting in her chair. In a much gentler tone she said, 'Now, come on, Mum, we've got to get Toby's stuff together, because he's going tomorrow. I've got the morning off work to take you up to the station to wave him off. Mebbe—' She paused and glanced at Bella. 'Could you come with us, Mrs Spencer?'

'Of course.'

'Shall I . . . ?' Mattie began, but Nancy said quickly, 'You'd best stay at work if I'm taking the morning off.'

As they took their leave, Mattie put her arms around her sister. 'Oh Nancy, I'm sorry I misjudged you. You've not got it easy here, I can see that.'

'If only,' Nancy said with heartfelt irony, but she was smiling as she hugged Mattie in return. It was the closest Mattie had felt to her sister since they'd been young children.

As Bella, Dan and Mattie walked back up the

street, Bella said, 'If I hadn't seen it with me own eyes, I wouldn't have believed it. Young Nancy standing up to her dad like that.'

'She's always had a bit of a temper,' Mattie murmured.

'I'll tell you summat else,' Dan said. 'She not only knows that she's got our backing, but also that the whole street would soon come out in support. It would only take one word from my mum. The neighbours'd likely run him out of the street, if they really knew what went on in that house.'

Bella laughed. 'That's true, lad, and the best thing about it is, Sid knows it an' all.'

But Mattie was still frowning. 'I'm just worried he'll take it out on Mum when none of us are there.'

'If he does, Mattie,' Bella said firmly, 'he'll soon regret it, I promise you that.'

The following day was hard for Elsie but with the support of Nancy and Bella, she got to the station to wave Toby off, even though tears were streaming down her face. But she wasn't the only weeping mother on the platform. Sending their young children off to live with strangers was the hardest thing most of them had ever had to do. Elsie refused to move until the train was out of sight and even then it took both Nancy and Bella, one on either side of her, to guide her out of the station and back home.

'You'll get a letter or a postcard in a day or two,' Bella soothed. 'That'll put your mind at rest when you know where he is and who he's with.'

'Will it?' Elsie sounded doubtful.

Two days after the exodus of children from the cities, the grim news was finally confirmed in a broadcast by the Prime Minister that Britain was at war with Germany.

'Even though we all expected it,' Bella said, 'I still feel shocked. I always had hope that, somehow, even at the last minute, they'd do summat to stop it.' She sighed. 'Ah well, we'll just have to deal with it and get on with whatever's thrown at us. I must go down and see Elsie. If she's heard the news, she'll be in a right state. Drinking herself into oblivion, I shouldn't wonder. I still think she believed that Toby would come back home if nowt happened.'

But when Bella went down the street to see Elsie, another surprise awaited her. This time, a pleasant one. Elsie was standing at the kitchen table kneading bread, as sober as the proverbial judge.

'Come in, Bella, love,' she called out. 'I saw you come past the window. Make us a cuppa, would you, while I finish this? Kettle's on the hob.'

As Elsie put the dough on the hearth to prove, the two women sat down on either side of the kitchen table.

'You'll be pleased to know, Bella,' Elsie began, a tiny smile quirking the corners of her mouth, 'that when I got home the other day after seeing Toby off, I poured all the drink I had in the house down the sink and threw away the bottles. I've made a promise to myself that I won't touch another drop until he's home again.'

Bella gaped at her. 'Well, "it's an ill wind that blows nobody any good," as my old mum used to say. Good for you, Elsie. Mind you stick to it.'

'I will, Bella. It's for Toby.'

Mattie returned to university that autumn for her final year with very mixed feelings. Even though life there sheltered its students to some extent, news from the outside world still filtered through. Everyone was concerned about their loved ones at home and what was happening to them, and Mattie had so many people to worry about now; her own family, the Spencers, the Musgraves and, of course, uppermost in her mind, Joe. She knew, from what he had told her, that he would be one of the first to go to war, so when, in October, she heard that over one hundred and fifty thousand men of the British Expeditionary Force had landed in France, she knew he would be amongst them.

And then, of course, there was Dan. What was he going to do?

She found out at Christmas.

'I'm thinking of volunteering for the army,' he told her as she sat in the Spencers' kitchen.

Before Mattie could answer, Bella said, 'I really don't know why he wants to go yet. Nothing much is happening. A lot of folks are calling it the "phoney" war. It could all fizzle out and then he's wasted his time. You'd do better to stick at your apprenticeship, lad, and wait until you really have to go. If you ever do.'

'What does your dad say?'

'Same as Mum,' Dan said dolefully. 'Wait and see.'

'Would that be so bad?' Mattie asked.

Dan shrugged. 'A lot of me mates are joining up and I don't want to look like a coward.'

'They all know that's not the case, surely?'

'No one's said anything, but I've had some very funny looks and the conversation always gets round to who's gone already, who's going next . . . You know, that sort of thing.'

Mattie sighed. She did know, yes, because a lot of the talk amongst her fellow students – especially the young men – was just the same.

'If I were you,' Mattie said carefully, 'I'd leave it until something really starts to happen and then go. Your mam's right about that. If it all gets sorted out without a lot of fisticuffs, then you'd have wasted your time and probably jeopardized your career. Even if you do have to go eventually, you want something to come back to, don't you?'

Dan glanced at her swiftly and then looked away again. Mattie felt her heart leap in her chest. She knew exactly what that look had meant.

If I do come back.

Still, nothing much happened which involved British troops for the rest of the year and even into 1940. The heaviest action was between Russia and Finland. But when Hitler invaded Denmark and Norway in April, it really began to feel as if the war was going to escalate instead of 'fizzle out', as Bella had hoped.

Back at university, during her final term, Mattie received a letter from Dan:

I've done it: I've joined the same regiment as Joe. I don't expect our paths will cross much in reality, but I'd like to think I'm fighting alongside him in spirit at least . . .

Mattie folded his letter thoughtfully. *I wonder what I ought to do*, she pondered. *I really want to do something to help the war effort other than joining the women's land army to dig potatoes. Perhaps one of the services?*

Twenty

On the last day in April, Mattie was sitting in the university's library, cramming for her last exam paper, when a shadow fell across her book. She glanced up to see her tutor taking a seat across the table from her. He glanced around, almost furtively, she thought.

'Mattie,' he said in a low voice, 'have you decided what you're going to do when you leave here?'

'Not exactly, no. I'd like to do something to help the war effort, of course, but I don't quite know what.'

'Then perhaps I can help you.' He gave another glance around to make sure no one could overhear their conversation. 'May I suggest you go to the Foreign Office in London to be interviewed for some very important work for which, I can tell you, you would be eminently suited? But you must tell no one – not even your family – where or why you are going.'

Mattie stared at him. 'Well, you haven't even really told *me* why . . .'

'Precisely.'

'I've never been to London. Can I take someone with me?'

'Certainly not. I am trying to impress upon you how secretive this must be. Do you understand?'

'I – think so.'

'I will book an appointment for you on Friday of this week. I believe your train fare will be reimbursed.' He stood up. 'Now, not a word to anyone. I will let you know the name of the person you are to see by Thursday. All right?'

He didn't wait for her answer, but turned and left without glancing back at her.

As she was not expected back at the Musgraves until the following weekend, it was quite easy for Mattie to make the trip to London without telling anyone. Rather than being fazed by the big city, she found it exhilarating. It was very like her home town only much bigger. She had a little time to kill before her appointment so, whilst making her way to the Foreign Office, she was able to linger a while to see some of the sights she'd only read about in books. She presented herself at the building at the appointed time and asked where she was to go.

'Up the stairs, miss. Wait in the first room on the left and someone will come to get you.'

It seemed an age that she waited, but it was only about twenty minutes. A thin, severe-looking woman in a grey suit entered, asked her name and then bade her follow her down the corridor to a small office. The woman offered her a seat on the opposite side of the desk and then proceeded to peruse several papers.

At last she looked up and said, 'I see you have a glowing report from your tutors at Oxford. You are expected to get a first.'

Mattie didn't know what to say, but it seemed the woman did not require an answer, as she went on, 'I believe you are exactly the type of person we require for certain work. I see that your last exam is scheduled for the fourteenth and also I see that your home is in Sheffield.'

Here it comes, Mattie thought, questions about her home life. Her hands began to tremble, but, to her surprise, the woman asked her nothing more. It had been a statement of fact rather than a question.

'So, that will give you time to pay a visit home on the weekend of the eleventh and twelfth, take your exam on the fourteenth and then travel from Oxford to Bletchley Park in Buckinghamshire on the fifteenth. I will give you a travel warrant for your journey.' She met Mattie's gaze with a steady stare. 'But I must impress upon you that you must tell no one – absolutely no one – where you are actually going. Obviously, your family will ask questions but all you can tell them is that you have been offered a job at the Foreign Office in London and are required to take it up immediately. They must address any letters to Room One-One-One, care of the Foreign Office, and any letters you send out must purport to come from here at the Foreign Office. Letters will be brought to you by courier and any you wish to send out will be picked up and posted out from here.'

'What about accommodation at Bletchley Park?'

'That will all have been sorted out for you by the time you get there. Now, are you willing to take the job?'

'It all sounds a bit of a puzzle.'

For a moment the woman stared at her and then actually smiled. 'You don't know how right you are,' she murmured and then, unbending a little, added, 'Look, I'm sorry I can't give you details. The only two things I can impress upon you are that it is work that is extremely important for the war effort and that it must be undertaken in the utmost secrecy. So . . . ?'

'Oh yes, I'll do it. It sounds most intriguing.'

On 10 May, two events happened that confirmed everyone's worst fears: Winston Churchill, a man capable of igniting the will to win in the British people, became Prime Minister and formed an all-party coalition government, a sure sign that full-scale war was imminent; and Holland and Belgium were attacked. Everyone realized that Britain really was at war. There was no doubting it now.

Mattie shivered as she squinted through the darkness of the railway station's platform at Bletchley. She had never known such blackness; in the city, despite the blackout, there was always a faint glow from some-where, but here it was like being in the depths of a black hole. The last two weeks had passed so quickly. She had taken the last written exams and, in between them, had travelled home to Sheffield to say goodbye to her family and dearest friends. To their credit, not one of them had pressed her for details about her new job. Her mother and Bella had just said, 'That sounds nice, dear', Nancy wasn't really interested and the Musgraves glanced at each other and asked no questions at all. She was sad not to see Dan, but relieved too; he would have been the one to press her further for answers. It had all passed in rather a whirl and now here she was standing on a draughty platform in a place she'd never heard of until two weeks ago, with no idea about what she was supposed to do next.

As her eyes became a little more used to the night, shadows began to emerge and she heard the sound of a trundling luggage barrow.

'Excuse me . . .' she began hesitantly, but the man pushing the barrow didn't hear her. Then, beside her, another shadow loomed and a woman's cultured voice said, 'Hello, are you lost too?'

'Not exactly lost, but I'm not sure what to do next.'

'Me neither. I expect we're on our way to the same place, though where it is, God alone knows. There doesn't seem to be anyone to meet us. Anyway' – a hand came out of the darkness and touched Mattie's arm – 'I'm Victoria. And you are?'

Am I supposed to answer? Mattie wondered. Was this a test of some kind?

The two women, even though they couldn't see each other properly, shook hands. Then Victoria pointed the thin beam of a torch towards her.

'You look like a little grey mouse in this light. That's what I'll call you. Mouse. Now, let's see if we can find someone to tell us where on earth we have to go. Come along, Mouse, there's a dear.'

PART TWO

Victoria

Twenty-One

Kensington, London, June 1929

'You are going to Miss Taylor's Boarding School for
Young Ladies in Buckinghamshire and that's an end
to it,' Grace Hamilton said. 'And you can take that
sulky look off your face, Victoria. It's one of the best
schools in the country and you're going there at great
expense to me. I shall have to make some serious
economies to be able to afford it.'

Victoria glanced around the lavishly furnished
drawing room of the house where the two of them,
plus two servants, lived.

Like giving up your weekly luncheon at Claridge's?
Victoria wanted to say. Or attending Ascot in a new
outfit every year with the most extravagant hat? But
Victoria knew when to hold her tongue. Her mother's
punishment for being crossed was legendary. The
young girl couldn't count the hours she'd spent locked
in her bedroom with only the maid to bring her food.

So, Victoria said nothing.

'You will start in September and come home in
the holidays at Christmas, Easter and the summer.
You will take your School Certificate at sixteen, after
which you will go to finishing school. Probably

Switzerland or Germany, though I haven't decided yet. And you will work very hard to repay my investment in your future. After that, you will "come out" and find yourself a respectable and wealthy husband.' Grace stared at her hard. 'I never wanted children, Victoria. I've never made a secret of that fact, but your father was thoughtless enough to get himself killed at Passchendaele, leaving me pregnant.' Her face twisted with bitterness. 'I have done my best for you and will continue to do so until you find a husband. In the meantime, we will keep out of each other's way as much as possible. By the way, Miss Gilbert' – Grace was referring to Victoria's governess – 'will be leaving at the end of July. You will have to amuse yourself during August until you go to boarding school.'

Victoria felt a lump in her throat and tears prickle her eyes, but, stoically, she stopped them from falling. Her mother did not approve of any kind of display of emotion. One of Grace's mantras throughout Victoria's childhood had always been, 'You can stop that silly noise or I'll give you something to cry about'. And Victoria had known exactly what that meant: the sting of a thin cane across the back of her legs.

Naomi Gilbert was perhaps the only real friend that Victoria had; she'd never been allowed to mix with girls of her own age and therefore her governess was her only companion. No discipline from her tutor was necessary; Victoria loved Miss Gilbert and would never have dreamed of being disobedient. In front of Grace, Naomi held herself aloof from her charge, but when they were alone, she allowed her fondness for her pupil to show. She felt sorry for the girl who lived in an ivory tower; a comfortable one, certainly, but it was a cold and loveless solitary existence for a child nonetheless, shut away on the second floor of the white stucco-fronted terraced house. This was Victoria's world: her bedroom and bathroom, then the schoolroom and Miss Gilbert's room were on the same floor, but at the back of the house. Victoria was such a pretty little girl, Naomi thought, with blonde curly hair and solemn blue eyes. She could have had a wide circle of friends if only she had been allowed to mix with other children.

Pupil and governess took their customary walk in the nearby park that afternoon and, once out of sight of the house, Victoria slipped her hand into Naomi's.

'You had a conversation with your mother this morning, I understand?' Naomi said in her soft and gentle voice.

'If you could call it that. I never said a word.'

Naomi allowed herself a wry smile. 'Best not.' There was silence between them before she went on. 'So, you know what is to happen?'

Not trusting herself to speak for a moment, Victoria nodded. Then her voice broke as she whispered, 'You're leaving in a few weeks and I'll never see you again.'

'Oh, I think you will, Victoria dear. I shall write to you at the school and come and see you on visiting days.'

Victoria looked up at the sweet face of the young woman walking beside her. Naomi had dark hair and gentle brown eyes. 'Will you? Will you really?'

'But only when I can be sure your mother won't be visiting.'

'I don't think she will.' It was a statement of fact, without a trace of self-pity in the girl's tone.

'I wouldn't want to bump into her. It'll have to be our secret. Now, don't let's waste any more of this lovely sunny afternoon.'

Arriving at the park, they walked to the bench where they usually sat to watch all the nannies wheeling out their charges in huge black perambulators. There were some with older children who twisted themselves free of the restraining grasp and ran across the grass. Boys kicked a football whilst girls played with hoops and sticks.

'I had a nanny before you came,' Victoria murmured. 'She used to bring me here, but she never let me play on the grass or run about. I wasn't even allowed on the swings. She was very strict. "Young ladies should act with decorum," she used to say. I soon learnt what the word meant.'

'Maybe she was strict, but she did a good job teaching you the basics of reading and writing before I arrived.' Naomi paused. 'What's your favourite lesson now?'

'French and drawing,' Victoria said promptly. 'I love the idea of being able to talk to people from other countries in their own language and I like drawing things – and people – I see around me.' She usually brought her sketch pad and pencils with her to the park on fine days and made line drawings of the children at play or the nannies sitting on another bench chatting to each other, their prams parked close by. But today, after her mother's shocking announcement, she had quite forgotten to bring them.

'My knowledge of French is only elementary, I'm afraid,' Naomi said sadly. 'You see, I'm only qualified to teach children up to the age of about eleven. You'll certainly learn a lot more at school. Perhaps even another language too. Like German, for instance.'

Victoria felt torn. She dreaded being parted from Miss Gilbert and yet there was the enticement of having the chance to learn so much more. Leaving home didn't worry her at all. The strictest school rules couldn't be worse than her mother's harsh regime, but she would miss her governess's sweet nature and affection.

'So,' she said slowly, 'there's no chance of you being able to apply for a post at the school I'm going to?'

Naomi laughed. 'I'm afraid not, dear. The teachers at Miss Taylor's renowned establishment will be so much cleverer than I am. You'll learn far more than ever I could teach you.' Her tone was wistful. How she wished she could teach this dear child everything she needed to know. But Victoria had a quick brain; she deserved to have a better chance. And she did seem to have a gift for picking up a foreign language. Naomi had no doubt that her pupil would thrive at a good school. And, as Mrs Hamilton had said, Miss Taylor's was one of the best.

'Look,' Victoria said suddenly, interrupting Naomi's thoughts. 'He's here again.'

Naomi followed the line of Victoria's gaze to see a tall, distinguished-looking man heading for a bench on the opposite side of the stretch of grass a few yards from where they were sitting. He sat down stiffly, his leg stretched out in front of him. He rested the cane he always used against the bench and looked about him. He was clean-shaven with strong features. He wore a light linen suit on this warm summer day. From this distance they couldn't see the colour of his eyes nor of his hair, which was mainly hidden beneath a straw hat.

'Do you think he has hurt his leg?' Victoria asked softly. 'He never bends it.'

'Perhaps he was wounded in the war. He looks like a military gentleman.'

'Have you noticed, he comes here every Friday afternoon, but we've never seen him on any other day of the week?'

'Mm. Maybe he works on other days.'

'D'you think so?' Victoria sounded doubtful. 'He looks far too grand to me to have a job.'

Naomi chuckled. 'Even grand gentlemen sometimes have to work to earn a living now, especially since the war.'

'At least he's not begging or selling matches on street corners. I'm glad he doesn't have to do that.'

On a rare trip into the city centre a few years earlier, Victoria had seen wounded veteran soldiers reduced to such humiliation after years of service for their country. The sight had appalled the young child.

As they walked home, Naomi said, 'If you ever come to the park on your own, dear, you must promise me that you will never talk to strangers, especially men. I know the gentleman we see each week intrigues you, but you mustn't get into conversation with him. You do promise me, don't you, Victoria?'

'Of course, Miss Gilbert.'

The last Friday in July came all too quickly and Naomi had to leave. Victoria had cried the night before in her bed, but on the final morning she was dry-eyed, standing beside her mother, rigidly composed and straight-backed. She would not let her mother see her shed tears. She shook hands solemnly with Naomi; they had said their fond farewells earlier in the privacy of the schoolroom and now both were putting on a brave face in front of Grace Hamilton.

As the cab bearing Naomi away from her disappeared round the corner, Victoria picked up her sketch pad and pencils and, with the young housemaid, Rose, in tow, she walked to the park. She led Rose to where she and Naomi had shared so many happy hours and began to draw the gentleman sitting on the opposite bench, who would look at her and smile kindly.

Twenty-Two

'Where have you been?'

Grace's eyes were bright with anger as Victoria stepped in through the front door.

'To the park, Mother.' Swiftly, she added, 'I had Rose with me.'

'I am fully aware of that. She was missing when I needed her.'

'I'm sorry, Mother. I didn't think you'd want me to go on my own.'

'Of course not, but you should have asked me before you took one of the servants with you. I have a friend coming for afternoon tea at four o'clock so you will go to your room and stay there.'

'Yes, Mother,' Victoria said meekly and headed for the foot of the stairs.

'Just a moment. What is that you're carrying?' Grace held out her hand.

'Just – just my sketch pad and pencils.

'Give them to me.'

Reluctantly, Victoria handed them over. There wasn't much she enjoyed in her mundane life, but drawing and painting were two of her few pleasures. Going to the park, being in the open air with other people not far away – even though she was not allowed to speak to them – was another simple joy.

Grace flicked through the pages; the trees and shrubs which Victoria had drawn, the nannies and their perambulators, two boys playing football, two little girls, their heads bent together as they compared their dolls. Then she turned to the last drawing; the man sitting on the bench. Grace's face turned pale and her body became rigid. Her hands trembled as she gazed down at the face. In that moment she realized that all her schemes and well-laid plans could come crashing down around her. Slowly, she turned her gaze upon her daughter. 'And who, might I ask,' she said in a hoarse voice, 'is this?'

'Just a man in the park, Mother.' Victoria pressed her lips together to stop herself saying more; that she and Naomi had seen him often, that he came to the park every week on a Friday. Some instinct made her remain silent.

As she recovered her composure, Grace asked harshly, 'Did you speak to him?'

'Of course not.'

'Don't use that insolent tone with me.'

'I'm sorry. I didn't mean to, but I never speak to anyone, just like you've always instructed me.'

Grace glared at her as if she didn't really believe her.

Slowly and deliberately, Grace tore the drawings from the pad and ripped each one to shreds, letting the pieces flutter to the floor. Strangely, she paused a moment over the picture of the man and then tore it apart with added venom. Victoria pressed her fingernails into the palms of her hands to stop herself crying.

'Pick them up and dispose of them. There will be no more visits to the park before you go to school. You will take a turn about the garden with Rose every other day to allow you some fresh air. Other than that, you will keep to your room until you go away. You can occupy yourself reading. I will furnish you with plenty of books on different subjects.' Her lip curled. 'I'm sure Miss Gilbert's teaching will not have reached the exacting standards of Miss Taylor's establishment.'

Victoria managed to reach her room before the tears fell. But after a few moments, she dried her eyes and reached for another drawing pad. She still had the case holding her pencils in her pocket. She sat down at the dressing table that doubled as a desk and began to sketch quickly from memory until the man on the bench emerged once more onto the paper. She could still picture his firm jaw, his straight nose and the way his straw hat shaded his eyes. She wished she could have seen his eyes; she would have liked to have known their colour. His hair too. But she'd replicated to perfection the way his leg was stretched out in front of him, his cane leaning against the bench beside him. And the way he glanced across to where she and Miss Gilbert had been sitting. She'd caught the angle of his head exactly.

Victoria bit her lip. Where could she hide the

drawing? She couldn't risk Rose finding it when she cleaned the room. Miss Gilbert's loyalty to her charge had been unquestionable, but Victoria was unsure of Rose's. Perhaps the young maid would feel her loyalty lay with the woman who paid her wages. The girl glanced around her bedroom. The chest of drawers and the wardrobe were no use for hiding things and yet . . . ? Perhaps behind one of them. Victoria crossed the room and knelt down at the end of the chest of drawers. There was a small space between the back of the piece of furniture and the wall. Carefully, she slid the sheet of paper into the gap. It would only be found when the room was spring cleaned and every item of furniture pulled away from the wall. But the major clean was over for this year and the drawers were unlikely to be moved again until next spring.

Victoria would have been surprised if she could have overheard the conversation in the kitchen soon after their return from the park. Rose was recounting their walk and what had happened when they returned home to the cook, Mrs Beddows.

'That poor girl, Cook. She has nothing. Oh she has everything she needs in – in *things*, but she's not loved by her mother. Mrs Hamilton makes it so obvious. How cruel she is.'

'Shh, girl,' Mrs Beddows hissed. 'D'you want to get us both dismissed without a reference?'

'Of course not, but—'

'Then you should guard your tongue.' But as Mrs Beddows squeezed Rose's arm, the young maid knew that the older woman actually agreed with her. She just didn't want to be overheard saying so. Rose smiled weakly and nodded.

'We must try to do everything we can to make Victoria's last few weeks here as comfortable as possible,' the cook whispered. 'You can look after her and I will make her favourite meals.'

'She's to be kept confined to her room until she leaves. She's only to be allowed out into the garden every other day and I must accompany her.'

The cook frowned. 'Whatever can she have done to bring such punishment upon herself?'

Rose shrugged. 'The mistress seemed very angry about the sketches she'd done of people in the park.'

Mrs Beddows frowned. 'Were they people she knew?'

Rose shook her head. 'Who does the poor child know? No one. Madam tore her drawings to shreds and then made her pick up all the pieces of paper from the floor.'

Mrs Beddows shook her head with a sigh. 'She's a strange woman is Mrs Hamilton. I've worked for her for nine years and yet I still know so little about her.' She wrinkled her forehead. 'Nothing, in fact, if I'm honest. She moves in society circles, goes to dinner parties and joins committees for good causes and she holds dinner parties here sometimes. But to my mind they're all *acquaintances* whom she cultivates for her own purposes. She's not got what I would call real friends.'

'And neither has Miss Victoria now that Miss Gilbert has gone. How that poor girl is to get through the next few weeks until she goes to school, I don't know.'

'It's always puzzled me why she's never let Miss Victoria have friends. It's as if she doesn't want anyone to get too close to either of them.'

Rose laughed wryly. 'It's more likely that she doesn't want lively, chattering girls disturbing her peace.'

The following five weeks would have been very tedious for Victoria if it hadn't been for the kindness of both Rose and Mrs Beddows. The housemaid spent as much time as she could in Victoria's room on the pretext of making or changing the bed, tidying and dusting, but as soon as she knew that her mistress was out of the house, she would play board games or cards with the young girl. Victoria taught Rose how to knit and helped her with her reading. And Mrs Beddows played her part too. She sent up tempting meals with titbits that didn't find their way into the dining room.

'Don't tell your mother what you've had for your dinner this evening, there's a dear,' Rose whispered often. 'Mrs Beddows made it specially for you. She knows it's your favourite.'

'Of course I won't. I'll eat it quickly in case Mother comes up.'

But they both knew she was quite safe; her mother never came to see her.

'Where is she? Where's she gone?' Rose burst into the kitchen, panic written all over her face. 'She's not in her room.'

Mrs Beddows turned wide eyes on her fellow servant. There were only the two of them and they did everything in the house that needed doing, though there was a woman who came in five days a week to help with the washing and ironing and some of the heavier cleaning work. 'Did you forget to lock her door?'

'I must have done.' Rose was frantic. 'I'll get the sack. Oh, how could she do this to me?'

'Don't blame poor Victoria. She only turned eleven a couple of months back. You should have been more careful. You can't expect her to understand.'

'She understands all right. She's clever.'

'Have you looked in the garden?'

'Yes. She's not there.'

'Then try the park. That's where she loved to go with Miss Gilbert.'

Rose tore out of the house and ran down the street. She was breathless, her legs trembling, by the time she reached the park gates. She glanced around her in horror; the expanse of grass and trees and paths was so vast. How was she ever to find the girl? She took deep breaths to calm her racing heart, trying to recall what the governess used to tell them about her walks with Victoria.

'We sit on one of the benches and watch the nannies with their perambulators and the little children playing,' Naomi had told them. 'I'd love to be able to let Victoria join in. She watches them with such longing on her face, but I just daren't.'

Rose spotted one of the many gardeners who worked in the park and ran to him.

'Where are the benches where people sit?'

Startled, the young man looked up. 'They're all around the park, miss.'

Rose bit her lip and looked around her wildly.

'Are you looking for someone?'

Close to tears now, Rose nodded. 'A young girl. She's eleven with blonde hair and blue eyes . . .'

The young man wrinkled his forehead thoughtfully and rubbed his chin.

Trying to be helpful, Rose added, 'She used to come to the park most days when it was fine with her governess. They used to sit and watch the little children playing and the nannies with their prams . . .'

The gardener's face cleared. 'Oh they all meet in the middle of the park so the kiddies can play on the grass there.' He waved his arm. 'You could try over there, miss, and there are benches for folks to sit . . .'

But Rose was gone, running in the direction he'd pointed. When she saw the nannies, who had congregated on the benches circling the stretch of grass where the children played, Rose slowed her pace and tried to recover her breath. There was no sign of Victoria there. Then her glance swept wider, encompassing the path that ran around the area. On the outer perimeter of the path there were more benches. Rose scanned them and at last – on the far side – she saw Victoria, her head bowed over her sketch pad, her hand moving swiftly over the paper.

'The little madam,' Rose muttered. 'Sitting there as if butter wouldn't melt.' And then she began to run again.

As she neared her, Victoria looked up and began to smile, but her smile faded when she saw Rose's angry expression.

'Come on, miss, we've got to get you home before the mistress comes back else she'll have my guts for garters.'

Victoria got up at once. 'Oh Rose, I'm sorry. I didn't think.'

As they began to run side by side towards the park gates, Victoria glanced back just once at the man sitting alone on the bench. He was watching them go.

Twenty-Three

The morning came at last when she was to leave. Victoria could hardly contain her excitement. At last, she would be free; free to make friends and to learn so many new subjects. Her trunk was packed with her spare clothing, but she was already dressed in the regulation school uniform. A white blouse under a bottle-green gymslip, beneath which were some strange undergarments; woollen combinations and a sleeveless liberty bodice, buttoned down the front and holding four suspenders to which were attached black stockings. Over these were voluminous dark green knickers. Victoria wriggled in the new clothes; she had never been obliged to wear so many layers and felt hot already. The nicest part about the uniform was the smart green blazer with the school badge emblazoned in gold thread work on the pocket.

'It'll likely be cold in winter, miss,' Rose had tried to mollify her. 'There'll not be the huge fires you're used to at home. You'll be glad of them then.'

At the very bottom, beneath everything, Victoria had managed to hide the drawing of the man in the park. Although she could not have explained why, there was something about him that intrigued her.

Perhaps her interest had been heightened by her mother's strange reaction to the picture.

As she stood in the hallway with her trunk and a smaller suitcase, waiting for the cab to arrive, her mother stood before her. 'Well, Victoria, I hope you are going to behave yourself at school. I don't want to hear any bad reports from Miss Taylor and I certainly don't want to have to visit the school myself.'

'No, Mother,' the girl said meekly.

Grace nodded briskly. 'Ah, now here's the taxi. I'll bid you goodbye. Rose will help you with your belongings and see you onto the train.' She made no move to embrace her daughter or to allow Victoria to kiss her cheek. Instead, she turned and disappeared into the morning room, closing the door firmly behind her as if she had just rid herself of an encumbrance.

Standing on the platform a short while later, Rose handed the ticket to Victoria. 'Take good care of that, miss. Now, let's find you a carriage and I've to tell the guard to mind you get off at the right station. Ah, now here's a carriage with a lady travelling in it. You'll be quite safe, miss.' Both Rose and Mrs Beddows had been surprised and disgusted when they learnt that no one was to travel with the young girl on the train.

'Good luck, miss. We'll see you at Christmas.'

Impetuously, Victoria hugged the maid. Rose had been good to her. Nothing had come of her escapade to the park, but she had realized that she had put the maid in a dangerous position and she was sorry.

Rose could have been dismissed without a reference because of her, and Victoria now understood just how serious that could have been for the young girl. Mrs Beddows had explained it to her.

Now, she climbed into the carriage and leaned out of the window to wave goodbye one last time. As the guard raised his whistle to his lips, a young woman emerged from the shadows on the platform and hurried towards the carriage where Victoria was still leaning out of the window.

'Look sharp, miss,' the guard said, as he waved Victoria to stand back. He opened the door for the woman to climb in. 'Almost left it too late.'

Victoria reached out to grasp the woman's arms and help her to a seat. As the stranger glanced up, Victoria saw that she was no stranger at all.

'Miss Gilbert! Oh how lovely.' Still holding Naomi's hands, Victoria sat down in the opposite seat and beamed at her.

Naomi chuckled. 'I had to wait until the last moment until I was sure no one was travelling on the train with you.'

'How – how did you know which train I'd be on?'

'I didn't. I knew you were going today. I've been here since eight o'clock and I bought a ticket that would allow me to travel on any train, so here I am. Oh Victoria, I have missed you.'

'And I you.'

They sat holding hands across the space between them and drinking in the sight of each other.

'You look well. Have you still been able to go to the park?'

Victoria shook her head and explained all that had happened.

'Oh you poor child, but never mind. You are going to love boarding school. I just know you are.'

When the train pulled into the station, what seemed like hundreds of girls spilt out onto the platform from the other carriages. The air was filled with merry laughter and shouting. The majority seemed to know exactly what to do and where they were going. Obviously, they were older girls and this was not their first time. But there were a few others like Victoria who looked lost and bewildered, clinging to their mothers' hands as if they were drowning. Perhaps, amongst the swirling mass of faces, they felt as if they were.

'I had better not come to the school with you,' Naomi said. 'Look, over there, there seems to be a woman marshalling the newcomers. Let's go across.'

They joined the cluster of girls and their mothers gathering around the tall, thin middle-aged woman dressed in a brown coat and felt hat. 'Come along, girls,' she called out cheerfully. 'I want you to form a line and then we will walk to the school. It's not far. Leave your luggage. It will be collected later.'

'We'd better say goodbye, Victoria. I don't want anyone questioning who I am. If anyone does ask, tell them the truth. That I am your former governess and that I accompanied you on the journey.'

Impulsively, Victoria put her arms around Naomi's slim waist and hugged her hard. 'You will write to me, won't you?'

'Of course I will.' Naomi's voice was a little husky

as she held the little girl close for a moment. 'But you must write to your mother too, you know. Once a week, usually on a Sunday after church, you will be expected to write letters home.'

Victoria nodded, unable to speak now for the lump growing in her throat. As if Naomi thought there might be tears from both of them, she kissed Victoria's cheek swiftly.

'Goodbye, my dear. Be good and work hard.' With that, the young woman turned away and hurried down the platform to wait for the train that would take her back to London.

Victoria watched her go and then, with a little sigh, she turned and joined the group of girls and their mothers clustering around the member of the school staff.

'Now, have we got everyone?' The woman seemed to be speaking more to herself than to the assembled pupils. 'My name is Miss Mills and I teach French, but for the moment,' she smiled and her thin face seemed to light up; she looked ten years younger than she had a moment ago, 'I am charged with getting you all to the school safely and handing you over to Matron. Mothers, you may accompany your daughters, so that you can see where they're going to be, but once there you must say your goodbyes and leave. Now, shall we go?'

It was more of an order than a request and, obediently, mothers and girls formed themselves into a more or less orderly line and followed the straight-backed teacher out of the station. Victoria found herself at the end of the line, on her own, but after only a few yards another girl fell into step beside her.

'I'm on my own too. My mother couldn't come with me. My name's Charlotte Mountjoy. What's yours?'

'Victoria Hamilton.'

'Was that your mother with you?'

Victoria shook her head. 'No, my – my former governess.' As Naomi had suggested, it was better to be honest from the start.

Charlotte was thoughtful for a moment. 'Haven't you been to school before, then?'

Victoria shook her head.

'I went to the village school, but my grandparents are paying for me to come here. My father was wounded in the war and can't work. What about yours?'

Charlotte was like a fresh breeze blowing into Victoria's life. She had curly dark hair and dancing, mischievous brown eyes. Victoria had never known such friendliness from one of her peers; she had never had the chance to get to know any other children. Naomi or Rose had been her only companions.

'My – my father was killed in the war. At Passchendaele.'

Sympathy flickered across Charlotte's face. 'That's awful. Your mother must be heartbroken at sending you away, but I expect she's only trying to do what's best for you.'

'Come along, you two at the back. Keep up,' Miss Mills's voice drifted down the line to them.

The two girls quickened their pace to catch up.

After what seemed miles – but, in fact, was only about a mile and a half – the crocodile of girls passed through a pair of huge iron gates and walked up a long drive towards a huge stone building. Neatly cut lawns bordered by flower beds lay on either side, and beyond them Victoria could see playing fields.

Some of the younger children – Victoria estimated that some were as young as seven or eight – were now crying openly and clinging to their mothers' hands until the last possible moment.

'Oh my,' Charlotte breathed. 'It's huge. How are we ever to find our way around?'

The size of the school was daunting to the newcomers, but the older girls bounded up the stone steps, through the huge brown-stained doors with shining brass handles and then into an enormous high-ceilinged assembly hall. The chattering girls, greeting each other after the long holidays, sounded like a flock of excited starlings. It didn't, however, last for many minutes as a tall, rather plump and imposing figure stood on a stage at the far end and clapped for silence. When she had everyone's attention, she said, 'Welcome back, girls, and a special welcome to all our new girls.' Her glance raked the older pupils. 'I'm sure you will all do your best to help the newcomers settle in.'

A murmur of 'Yes, matron' rippled around the room.

So, Victoria thought, this woman in her long-sleeved navy-blue dress and starched white apron was the matron, who was at that very moment saying that she would be a mother to them all for the next few years. 'Now,' she said at last, 'say goodbye to your mothers. We have much to do.'

The crying of the younger children was now audible. Some clung to their mothers, who had to prise themselves free, even though tears filled their own eyes. At last they were gone, walking away down the driveway, whilst their daughters clustered around the front windows to wave goodbye for the last time. One or two more daring ones stood on the top of the steps. As Victoria, dry-eyed, stood watching them, Charlotte whispered, 'I'm glad my mother didn't come. This is far worse than saying goodbye at home, isn't it? I thought my mother was never going to stop crying when I left.'

'Mm,' Victoria murmured, watching the last of the women disappearing through the gates and hearing the howl of anguish from one of the very smallest girls. How different all this was to the cold, dispassionate farewell of Grace Hamilton. How she longed to be one of those crying copious tears at the departure of a beloved mother.

Twenty-Four

The new pupils were escorted to their dormitory by four of the older girls, who were prefects in the sixth form. Each of them looked after five new girls. When they arrived in the long room with twelve beds down each side, they found their trunks and cases had already been delivered. One of the 'sisters' clapped her hands and took charge.

'I think that's the head girl,' Charlotte whispered. 'Her name's Cressida. I don't know her surname.'

Cressida was speaking, raising her voice to make herself heard. 'Welcome to Miss Taylor's School. You will all sleep here for the first week until you have been assessed and put into the right class for your age and ability. Then you will be transferred to the dormitory shared with your classmates. Now, first, you must unpack your trunks and put away your clothes. You will see that your name has been attached to the bottom of your bed, so that is where you will sleep. Beside each bed there is a small chest of drawers and a wardrobe. These are inspected every week on a Sunday morning before church by Matron, so mind you keep them tidy. Be as quick as you can with your unpacking. It's almost lunchtime.'

*

Victoria didn't know how to make friends; she'd never had the chance before now. She had thought that perhaps Charlotte would be her friend and, in a way, she was. She was never *un*friendly but she seemed to want to be chums with everyone, rather than anyone in particular. She didn't 'pair off', as some of the girls did. When any of the games or activities required twosomes, Victoria was usually the last to be picked and, if she was the odd one out, she ended up being coupled with the games mistress. Not that she minded. Miss Carter was a jolly young woman, probably in her thirties, with a loud voice, which was a necessity to make herself heard above the chattering girls. In fact, Victoria liked all the members of staff. From the headmistress down, they were firm but kind and it seemed as if the girls all respected that. There were some 'high jinks' – of course there were – but Victoria watched the faces of the teachers when they were reprimanding the miscreant and was sure they were trying to stifle their amusement. The headmistress set the tone of the school. She was a commanding presence, though she never had to do anything to demand silence or attention. On the rare occasions she had to punish someone, it was done with an air of disappointment in the pupil, which had far more effect on the girl than angry words. Miss Taylor was in her late forties; a tall, slim woman with greying hair and always immaculately dressed in smart costumes and crisp, white blouses. It was rumoured she had gained a first in languages at university – one of the first women to do so. Educating the next generation of young women to be independently minded was her life's work. She was admired and respected and held in great affection by all her staff, both teaching and non-teaching.

Friday afternoons were devoted to games; hockey and netball in the winter months and tennis and athletics in the summer. By the end of the second week after their arrival the newcomers had been allocated to their classes and had moved into the appropriate dormitories. And now firmer friendships began to form, but Victoria, ignorant of how to make the first approach, hung back. This was fatal; no one took any notice of the tall, shy blonde girl whom they deemed – in their ignorance – to be standoffish and holding herself aloof deliberately. But the thaw in their attitude towards her began the moment Victoria took a hockey stick into her hands. She had never had the chance to play sports of any kind before, yet somehow she liked the feel of the stick in her hands. She absorbed Miss Carter's explanation of the rules and, allocated the position of centre half, attacked the game – and the opposing team – with a gusto that even she hadn't known she possessed. She fought to win the ball and run, dribbling it up the field to hammer it into the back of the goal.

'Well done, Victoria.' Miss Carter beamed. 'You must have played before.'

'No, miss, I haven't.' Victoria was panting hard and red in the face with exhilaration. 'I've never been to school before.'

'Then you're a natural.' Miss Carter blew her whistle for everyone to return to their positions on the field for another bully-off.

Victoria scored two more goals. At the end of the game, the girls in her team – including Charlotte – surrounded her.

'What else do you play? Netball?'

Victoria blushed, unused to being the centre of attention. 'I – no – I mean, I've never played anything before.'

Charlotte linked her arm through Victoria's as they left the playing field. 'Then we must try you out. Lucy,' she called out to the girl who had been voted their form captain, 'you'll have to watch this one. She's going to get serious points for our house.'

Throughout the school, the girls were divided into houses. There were three named after historical figures – Raleigh, Darwin and Columbus – and in each class roughly a third of the pupils were put into each house. Points could be earned – or lost – and at Speech Day a cup was awarded to the house with the highest number of points for the previous school year. Victoria was in Raleigh House alongside Charlotte and Lucy. Misbehaviour or poor work could result in points being deducted. It was the task of the form captain to keep a record of points gained or lost.

After the games lesson, Charlotte attached herself to Victoria for the rest of the day. She saved her a seat at tea-time next to her and set up a game of draughts in the common room afterwards. The following day, they walked together in the weekly outing to the local village and sat together in the church on the Sunday. Charlotte was amusing company and Victoria felt that, at last, she had found a friend, but on the Monday morning there was a surprise for their class. A new girl had arrived.

'Now, girls,' Miss Taylor said, when she brought her into the dining room at breakfast time, 'this is Celia Groves. She has just arrived back from Singapore where her parents live. She is to be in Class 3A. I hope you will all make her feel welcome in our school.'

Victoria glanced up. The girl was tall, with short-cropped fair hair and a disdainful air. Victoria wondered if she was indeed looking down her nose at them or whether it was shyness. The girl was not exactly pretty but she had even features and clear skin. Lucy, as form captain, started to rise to her feet to greet the new classmate, but Charlotte leapt up, almost overturning her chair in her eager-ness.

'Here, Miss Taylor. Celia can sit here. Move along, Victoria. Make room.' She almost pushed Victoria to make her move along to create another place at the table.

The newcomer sat down on the far side of Charlotte who, now with her back towards Victoria, fussed over Celia, pointing out how to help herself to breakfast. As they left the dining room to begin lessons, Charlotte put her arm through Celia's and led her away. Victoria, completely forgotten now, watched them go. Then she felt someone squeeze her arm and she turned to look up into Cressida's eyes. Cressida had been assigned to sit on their table at meal times. She was an elegant seventeen-year-old with her long, dark hair worn in a plait and wound around her head. She had a lovely face and kind, brown eyes. To all the younger girls in the school she was like a big sister.

'Have you noticed that Charlotte,' she whispered to Victoria, 'is like a butterfly fluttering from flower to flower to collect the nectar? I've been watching her for a few days now. Her "friend of the moment" is always someone who has done something notable. The first week of term, I noticed she hung around Lucy when she was made form captain. Then last week it was Diana, wasn't it? I understand she came top of your class in a spelling test. This weekend it was you, because you shone on the hockey field. And now' – she nodded towards the pair walking out of the dining room – 'it's the fascination of a new girl, and especially' – Cressida chuckled – 'one who is from an exotic place like Singapore.'

Victoria smiled uncertainly. 'I'm beginning to understand.'

'You'll find that not all your classmates are like that,' Cressida said. 'Some make friends more slowly. Now, you'd better get to your first lesson or you might be late and lose all those lovely points you got for our house on Friday afternoon.'

'Points? Did I?'

'Oh yes. Didn't you know?' Cressida Phillips happened to be in the same house as Victoria. In fact, she was the overall captain of Raleigh House as well as being head girl of the whole school. 'Miss Carter told your form captain to award you two house points for your efforts at hockey. I can see you being picked for the team to play against other schools. Then you'll really earn some points. No doubt Charlotte will be back at your side then.'

As they walked out of the dining room, Victoria said shyly, 'Thank you for explaining things, Cressida. You see, I've never been to school. Not even a day school. I had a governess at home so – so I've never had any friends.'

Cressida raised her eyebrows. 'None? Not even around where you lived?'

Victoria shook her head. 'No. Mother – wouldn't let me play with other children.'

Cressida stared at her for a moment. 'Do you know why?'

'Not really – no.'

'Did she have friends herself?'

'One or two. She used to go out quite a bit, meeting people for lunch and dinner, but I always had to stay at home with Miss Gilbert. She was my governess.' Victoria smiled. 'She was lovely. I do miss her.'

Cressida smiled. 'Then you must make sure you write to her tomorrow morning. Sunday morning after church is letter-writing time.'

'Will I be allowed to?'

'Of course, though you must be very careful what you write. Miss Taylor reads all your letters – those you send and those you receive.'

Victoria shrugged. 'I'm not likely to put anything derogatory about the school. I like it here.'

'Do you?' There was a note of surprise in Cressida's tone. 'Even though you haven't made any friends yet.' She pulled an ironic face. 'Well, apart from Charlotte. But I think you soon will. Genuine friends,

I mean. Just be yourself and let others come to you. And they will, especially now you've shown yourself to be a promising hockey player.'

As they parted company, Cressida touched Victoria's arm again. 'And don't forget – any problems, you come to me. We prefects aren't all about shouting at you for running in the corridor. We're here to help.'

Victoria hurried to her first lesson of the day. It was French and today they were going to be introduced to a real French woman, an assistant to their teacher. As Victoria took her place, she was amused to see that Charlotte was ushering the new girl into a desk beside her. It was as if Victoria no longer existed. Now, after her conversation with Cressida, Victoria was amused by Charlotte's actions, rather than hurt.

As the two teachers entered the classroom, the pupils stood up.

Speaking in French, Miss Mills bade them sit down and then introduced Mademoiselle Brielle Dubois. Out of the class of twenty-one there were now six newcomers. Four of them, including Celia, stared blankly at Miss Mills. They couldn't understand a word she was saying. Charlotte stood up and replied in French, welcoming the assistant. Though her grammar was reasonable, her pronunciation of the language was appalling. Victoria bowed her head. She didn't want either of the teachers to catch her eye and invite her to speak; she didn't want to be seen to be showing off. Already she had seen one or two of her classmates rolling their eyes when Charlotte had piped up. During the first two weeks of the term Miss Mills had handed out exercise books and text-books and had set them some simple homework to find out what each of them knew already – if anything. Now she was ready to start teaching them properly and, with the help of a native speaker, those with any aptitude for the language would forge ahead.

The lesson, conducted solely in French, went well and Victoria managed to avoid eye contact until the moment that Miss Mills handed back their home-work.

'Very well done, Victoria. I see that you already have a good command of the language for your age. Did you learn it at your previous school?'

'My governess taught me, mademoiselle,' Victoria said softly. She did not feel embarrassed about admit-ting this now; she had learnt that the majority of the girls in the class had been taught at home.

As the lesson ended and the teachers left, the four girls who had never learnt French before clustered around Victoria. She felt a moment's fear and her heart beat a little faster.

'I couldn't understand a word of that,' Celia said. 'But you obviously could. Will you help us, Victoria?'

Relieved, she smiled up at them. 'Of course I will. You only have to say.'

'Right. After homework time each evening, will you give us some basic French lessons in the common room? It'd just help us to get started, don't you think?'

'Oh yes,' came a chorus of agreement from the others.

'Well – yes – all right,' Victoria said. 'If that's what you want.'

'We do,' they said in unison.

'And perhaps,' she said tentatively, 'you could help me with some of the subjects I don't understand. I'm lost in the science lessons. I'd never even seen a Bunsen burner before.'

'What a brilliant idea,' Lucy said. 'As our form captain, I suggest we form a mutual help society. All those that are really good at a subject can help those who find it difficult. What do you say?'

Now there was agreement amongst all the girls.

'Won't Miss Taylor be impressed with our initiative?' Lucy said happily.

Standing at the back of the group, Charlotte pouted.

Twenty-Five

Miss Taylor was indeed delighted to learn how the girls of Form 3A were bonding to help each other.

'I first learnt about it in their letters home,' Miss Taylor said in a staff meeting the following week. 'It seems it arose out of a French lesson. Some of the new girls had never done French before and felt lost. But it seems that one girl – Victoria Hamilton – had done well in the test you set them all, Miss Mills.'

'She did extremely well for an eleven-year-old,' Marianne agreed. 'And in class, her accent is very good.'

Brielle nodded agreement. 'Do you know if she has ever lived in my country?'

'I don't think so,' Miss Taylor said. 'She was taught at home by a governess – a Miss Gilbert – until she came here. She must have been an excellent teacher and I glean that Victoria was very fond of her. She writes to her every Sunday along with her duty letter to her mother.'

'You say "duty letter"?' Lily Carter questioned.

Miss Taylor looked up with a slight frown on her smooth forehead. 'Victoria's letters to her mother are stilted, with no real affection – quite unlike the ones she writes to her former governess.'

'What about her mother's letters to her?'

'She hasn't written to her. Not once.'

'Perhaps it was one of those households where the children were kept in the nursery or schoolroom and lived a life quite remote from their parents,' Marianne Mills suggested.

'Perhaps, but there is no father. I understand he was killed in the war.'

There was a murmur of sympathy. 'It sounds as if the mother lives her own life.'

'The child is well-cared for. I can't fault Mrs Hamilton on that. All her clothes are of the best quality and she certainly seems to have provided her daughter with an excellent governess. Miss Gilbert has asked for permission to visit her on parents' days.' There were three Sundays during each term when parents were able to visit their daughters and take them out to tea.

'And will you allow it?'

'Of course, because I rather suspect that her mother will not come.'

'But at least she had the good sense to send Victoria to our school,' Delores Martin, the science mistress, said with a saucy twinkle in her eyes. The rest of her colleagues – including Miss Taylor – laughed. Then Delores added seriously, 'I have to say, Miss Taylor, that I agree with you wholeheartedly about this help group the girls have formed. Gifted though Victoria might be at French, she certainly has no previous experience of science subjects. Not even an aptitude for it, I'm sorry to say. She will benefit greatly from her classmates as they will from her command of French.'

There was a murmur of agreement around the table.

'Well, she's good at two things: French and sport,' Miss Carter put in, but Peggy Walters, the art teacher, interrupted her, 'She's very good at drawing. In fact, for her age, some of her artwork is excellent.'

And then Joyce Fairbrother joined in. 'She's good at English too and even knows a little Latin. Though we don't offer that as an option here until they're twelve or thirteen, do we?'

Miss Taylor was frowning thoughtfully. 'You know, I'd been thinking about offering German as a subject,' she said slowly. 'What do you think?'

For a long moment there was silence around the table. Brielle looked uncomfortable, bowed her head and remained silent. She was only going to be at this school for a year; this was not her business.

Tentatively, Marianne said, 'It's an idea, but do you think it would be well received amongst the parents? Many of them still have bitter memories from the war.'

'Yes, I realize that, but if we're ever to move forward – to try to win peace – we will need young men and women who speak several languages. We need to unite Europe, not always be at war with each other.'

'And if there is another war,' Joyce said soberly, 'as some are already predicting – there are those who think the Great War wasn't really the war to end all wars as it was supposed to be – a knowledge of German would be very useful.'

'For spies, you mean?' Delores said, trying to lighten the serious tone.

A ripple of nervous laughter ran around the table, but Miss Taylor said quite seriously. 'If – God forbid – there was another war, they would need people who could speak a variety of European languages.'

'I've just realized – you read French *and* German at university, didn't you, Miss Taylor?'

Emily Taylor nodded. 'If we did decide to offer German as a subject, I would take the first classes myself, just until we see how popular it is.'

'Then why don't you write to all the parents and ask for their opinion?' Joyce, as Emily's deputy head, suggested. 'That way you'd see how much interest there was for their daughters.'

'You could offer it alongside Latin when they reach twelve,' Marianne put in. 'Or even as an alternative to Latin, if they didn't want to do both.'

'It would complicate an already difficult timetable,' Joyce, who had charge of planning all the timetables each year throughout the school, commented. 'But I'm sure we could do it somehow.'

One or two of the staff were now warming to the idea.

'It would be a welcome addition for anyone who wanted to study languages,' Marianne added.

'Then I will write to all the parents and see what they feel. We wouldn't be able to include it until the next academic year anyway.'

Brielle breathed a silent sigh of relief. Her childhood had been lived in fear of the Germans who had occupied part of her homeland, but as she was only seconded to this school for one year, she would be gone by the time any such lessons started.

'Miss Gilbert!'

Victoria flew down the driveway and into Naomi's open arms. They hugged each other without embarrassment. At last Naomi held her at arm's length. 'Let me look at you.'

They stood together, smiling at each other, so happy to be together again even just for an afternoon.

'How have you been? Are you happy here, Victoria? Oh, I do so want you to be happy.'

'I am, Miss Gilbert. Truly I am.'

Victoria linked her arm through Naomi's as they turned and walked up to the front door. Today, the girls were allowed to go off the school premises with their visitors and so Victoria planned to take Naomi into the village to a little teashop she had already visited on Saturday-afternoon outings with the other girls. But first she must inform a member of staff where she was going.

'Are you sure your mother won't be coming today?' Naomi asked worriedly as they reached the steps.

Victoria giggled. It was a sound Naomi hadn't heard very often and it cheered her. The girl did indeed sound happy. 'I don't think so. She hasn't written to me once since I've been here. I don't think she's going to turn up unexpectedly, do you?'

'Very unlikely, I would say. Now, who do we have to see before we leave?'

'There's Miss Taylor at the top of the steps. We'll tell her.'

'But she's the headmistress, isn't she? Should we bother her?'

'Oh it's fine, Miss Taylor is lovely.'

As they climbed the steps to reach her, Emily Taylor held out her hand. 'You, I presume, are Miss Gilbert. I am very pleased to meet you.'

Unbeknown to Victoria, Naomi had written to the headmistress to ask permission to visit her former pupil. *I will not, of course, come if her mother is likely to visit*, she had said.

Emily had sent a charming letter in reply:

Mrs Hamilton has informed me that she will be unable to visit Victoria while she is here, so you will be most welcome. Victoria is a lovely girl. She is doing very well here and is a credit to your teaching.

Now the two women were standing face to face. They smiled at each other. They both knew that there was so much they would like to say to each other about Victoria, but now was not the time nor the place.

'What time must we be back?' Naomi asked.

'Six o'clock. It will give them all time to settle down after an exciting afternoon.' She did not add that she expected some of the girls to be in tears at parting with their parents once again.

'She seems very nice,' Naomi said, as they walked back down the drive and out of the gates.

'She is. She's lovely. Not as lovely as you, of course, but she is great. They all are. All the teachers and other staff. They're firm – you have to behave your-self – but they're all so kind. Even the prefects look after us.'

'I'm so glad. Your mother—' Naomi was guarded when she spoke about her former employer. She had never liked Grace Hamilton and was appalled at the way she had treated her daughter. But it would never do to say so to Victoria; Naomi felt it would be most unprofessional. 'She certainly made the right decision to send you here, then, because I really couldn't take you any further and you needed to get out into the world.' It was the closest she would come to criticizing Victoria's mother.

They walked the mile or so into the village and found the teashop, which Victoria had spotted. Entering, they found one or two other girls from the school with their families, including Charlotte, her parents – and Celia.

They both waved to Victoria and she smiled and nodded in acknowledgement.

Charlotte's rather shrill voice carried across the space to the table where Naomi and Victoria found seats. 'That's Victoria Hamilton, but I don't think that's her mother. She never comes. It's weird, isn't it?'

At that point, Charlotte's mother shushed her and the girl lowered her voice. Naomi touched Victoria's arm. 'Don't let it worry you,' she whispered.

'Oh I don't,' Victoria said, minding to keep her voice low. 'That's just Charlotte. She flits from one friend to another, depending on who is the most important at the time. Celia started a couple of weeks after the rest of us. Her parents live in Singapore so they can't visit. But it's so nice of Charlotte to invite her to join her, don't you think?' She glanced at Naomi to see that her veiled sarcasm was not lost on her. Naomi's eyes sparkled with laughter.

'I do indeed. Now, what are we going to order?'

They indulged in a cream tea and talked and talked for two hours until Naomi said regretfully, 'I shall have to see you back to the school now. My train leaves at five-thirty and I mustn't miss it. I don't think there's another one until tomorrow morning.'

As they parted company back at the school half an hour later, Victoria hugged Naomi hard. 'Thank you so much for coming to see me. It's been wonderful.'

'It has. I'm so pleased to see that you have settled in well. I'll come again next visiting day.'

Twenty-Six

The school term moved on; Victoria was chosen to play in the Under 15s school hockey team that visited other schools for matches. She soon became the team's leading goal scorer. When other schools visited theirs to play a match, the whole of Miss Taylor's School surrounded the pitch to watch and to cheer the home team on. On a particular day in November, they beat the visiting opposition by three goals to one. Two of the winning goals had been scored by Victoria. As she left the field, red-faced with exertion and delight, she was surrounded by her fellow players and the members of her own class.

'Oh well done, Victoria,' Charlotte shouted above the clamour. 'I'll save you a place at tea-time.'

When she entered the dining hall a little later, she saw Charlotte waving to her frantically. 'Over here, Victoria. Next to me.'

A little to one side, Celia was waiting, uncertain what to do. The place she usually occupied beside Charlotte was being offered to the victor on the hockey field. The girl looked hurt and mystified. It was clear she had not yet worked out Charlotte's fickle character. Victoria was also aware that several of her classmates and also Cressida were watching the interaction between the three of them. They were waiting to see what Victoria would do.

Victoria smiled and walked straight up to Celia. She took her arm. 'Come, sit with us. This is your place after all.' Adroitly, she engineered a place for Celia to sit between herself and Charlotte.

'Oh but, I wanted—' Charlotte began, but Victoria interrupted. 'How kind of you to save us *both* a place, Charlotte. Do pass the bread and butter, there's a dear.'

Out of the corner of her eye, she saw Cressida trying to hide her laughter. The head girl turned away but not before she had given Victoria a conspiratorial wink of approval.

The Mutual Help Society, as the girls in 3A were calling themselves, was a huge success. After two weeks, every girl in the class had joined and each one of them found they had something to offer or to learn from the others. Even Charlotte, whose favourite subject was domestic science, found she could offer guidance to those who couldn't quite get the hang of making pastry. No one got 'above themselves' and no one was made to feel left out. Even the shy ones found a new confidence.

'It's working so well,' Emily informed her staff at the next meeting. 'I have asked Cressida to spread the word to other classes.'

'Isn't there a danger they'll actually copy each other's work?'

'It's a possibility, I suppose. If you have any suspicion that that's happening, do let me know.'

'Oughtn't they to have a teacher in charge? I mean, they're not qualified to be teaching each other.'

'I don't want it to feel like they're in detention. I think – for the time being – we'll let it carry on as it is, but we'll all keep a close watch on what is happening, especially if other classes follow suit. Now, the next item on the agenda is parents' replies to my letter about offering German as a subject. The majority are in favour of the idea. A few were rather hesitant about it, but didn't openly disagree. Only three were forcefully opposed. Under no circumstances are their girls to be allowed to take the subject. I believe they are families who lost someone in the war and are still very bitter.'

'What about Victoria's mother?'

'Ah—' Emily rifled through the pile of letters in front of her. 'Her reply is the most interesting of all.'

'I'm surprised she bothered to write back,' someone muttered.

Emily cleared her throat and read out a passage from Grace Hamilton's letter.

'. . . *I have placed my daughter in your care at great sacrifice to myself and I expect you to educate her in the manner befitting her station in life. I therefore leave all such decisions to your discretion. However, it may be useful for you to know that I intend to send Victoria to finishing school in Switzerland at the appropriate time . . .*'

'Wonderful,' the French mistress clapped her hands, 'that gives you carte blanche where she's concerned, then. If she turns out to be as good at German as she is at French, then you're in for a treat, Miss Taylor. She's a joy to teach.'

'We'll offer it as a subject and advertise for a qualified teacher for the next academic year, but in the meantime, I will begin lessons with those who wish to take it.'

'Have you time, Miss Taylor?'

'One or two lessons a week for each year shouldn't be too onerous.' Emily smiled. 'Besides, I quite miss being in the classroom. I shall enjoy being back, even if only for a couple of terms. I'll start in January.'

Victoria was dreading going home for Christmas. She guessed she'd be confined to her room again, with only Rose for occasional company. She doubted she'd even be allowed to go to the park. Celia was destined to stay at the school through the holidays, but, back in favour with Charlotte for the moment, she'd been invited to their home for Christmas.

Rose was at the station to meet Victoria. The maid hugged her hard. 'Oh Miss Victoria, it's lovely to see you. Cook has been busy for days preparing all your favourite meals. Now, come along, let's find a porter to help with your luggage. Oh, you haven't got much.'

'I didn't bring my trunk. The holiday is only two weeks and I have clothes at home I can use.'

'If they still fit you.' Rose giggled. 'I'm sure you've grown.'

Sitting side by side in the cab on the way home, Rose asked, 'Are you happy at the school, miss? Me and Mrs Beddows do so want you to be happy.' Her face sobered for a moment. 'We'd've liked to have come to see you, but the mistress wouldn't let us. We did ask.'

'That's all right, Rose, I understand. It's kind of you even to think of it and, yes, I am happy there.'

'Good. I'm so pleased to hear it, miss, and Mrs Beddows will be too. Ah, here we are. I think your mother's out this afternoon, but she'll be home for dinner.' The unspoken words lay between them; would Victoria be invited to dine with her mother? If she was, it would be a first.

The plump cook embraced Victoria, clasping her to her warm bosom. 'You've grown, miss. They must be looking after you well there. What's the food like?'

'Quite good, Mrs B,' Victoria said tactfully, 'but not as good as yours.'

Mrs Beddows beamed.

'That's the front door.' Rose's sharp ears had heard the sound. 'I expect it's the mistress coming back.'

'You'd better go up and say hello to your mother,' Mrs Beddows said, shooing Victoria away good-naturedly.

As Victoria stepped into the hall, her mother was removing her hat and coat and peeling off her gloves.

'Oh, you're back?' Her glance raked Victoria from head to toe. 'I see they're keeping you well-groomed and the end of term report I've received is quite good. You seem to excel at sports, French and – art.' She hesitated over the final word and Victoria was sure her mother was remembering the drawings she'd destroyed, including the one of the man in the park. Recalling the image of him, Victoria wondered if she would be allowed to go to the park whilst she was at home. Grace nodded at her and turned towards the drawing room. It was a dismissal.

As she climbed the stairs to her room, Victoria heard Rose say, 'Mrs Beddows wondered, ma'am, as you have no guests for dinner tonight, if Miss Victoria would be dining with you?'

Grace glanced over her shoulder to glare at the maid. 'Why on earth would I want to do that? An eleven-year-old can hardly make sparkling conversation. She will take her meals in the schoolroom as usual.'

But the following morning, a surprise awaited Victoria. A flustered Rose burst into the schoolroom. 'Quick, miss, get ready. Your mother wants to take you for a walk in the park.'

Victoria's mouth dropped open. 'Really?'

'Yes, really. She's waiting for you in the hall. Oh do hurry up, miss, there's a dear.'

School had broken up on the Friday at lunchtime and the girls had travelled home during the afternoon. So today was a Saturday. She hoped the man in the park would not be there; some instinct told her that this sudden desire of her mother's to accompany her to the park was about him.

In two minutes, Victoria was running down the stairs.

'Come along, Victoria. I haven't got all day.'

They left the house and walked side by side to the park in silence. Reaching the gates, Grace glanced around her. Watching her, Victoria thought her look was wary, as if she might see something – or someone – she'd rather not.

'Now, tell me. Where do you usually go when you come here?'

Victoria pointed. 'Over there, Mother. On one of the benches near where the nannies gather with their prams and the children play on the grass.'

'Did Miss Gilbert ever let you play with the other children? I want the truth, Victoria.'

'No, Mother. Never.'

'Then we'll go and sit on the same bench.'

When they sat down, Victoria glanced around her nervously, but the bench where the man had always sat was empty. Victoria breathed a sigh of relief. It was Saturday. She was sure he wouldn't be here today; at least she fervently hoped not.

They sat in silence, neither knowing what to say to one another. At last, Grace said, 'I trust you are doing your very best at school.'

'Yes, Mother.'

'Have you made any friends?'

Guardedly, not understanding quite why her mother was asking such a question, she said, 'No one special. I try to be friendly towards everyone.'

'I just wondered if there was anyone who was likely to ask you to stay with them during school holidays.'

Victoria thought of Charlotte and her invitation to Celia. 'I don't think so. Besides, I'd have to ask them back, wouldn't I? And – and I don't expect you'd like that.'

'Absolutely not,' Grace said, standing up. 'Come

along, it's time we were going home. Winter's hardly the time to be sitting on park benches. Besides, I have a luncheon appointment.'

Victoria saw her mother's glance sweep around the area, from one bench to another. Seeming satisfied, she began to march towards the gate.

With a sigh, Victoria rose and followed her. She loved being in the park, whatever the weather. And despite not wanting him to be there – she was sure it would have caused some kind of trouble – part of her couldn't help being disappointed at not seeing the man again.

Twenty-Seven

If it hadn't been for Mrs Beddows and Rose, Christmas Day would have. been miserable for Victoria. She received presents from her mother; all useful or educational. A pretty silk scarf arrived by post from Naomi and Mrs Beddows and Rose bought her a Solitaire game; a round wooden board and marbles. It rather accentuated her loneliness and yet, as she attempted to master the difficult game, she found she rather enjoyed the challenge.

'Your mother's out for the whole day. She's lunching with some friends and then going to a grand dinner this evening,' Mrs Beddows told her. Then her eyes twinkled, 'So you're going to come down here to us for Christmas dinner. Would you like that?'

Victoria beamed. 'Oh I would. Thank you.' Then her face clouded for a moment. 'But – don't you have your own families you want to go to?'

'I've only got a sister and she lives in Manchester.'

'And my family are down in Cornwall,' Rose said. 'All too far for us to travel when we only get two days off. Besides, I like to go there in the spring or the summer when the weather's nice.'

Victoria nodded. She remembered Rose taking a fortnight's holiday the previous May. She'd missed her, but Naomi had been here then. She dreaded to think what it would be like if Rose were to go during the long summer holidays when she'd be at home. She very much doubted that her mother would go to the park with her on a regular basis. Perhaps Grace would never go again after that one time and Rose would be her only hope of going on outings, even if it was confined to the local park. Anything was better than being stuck in the house on lovely summer days.

The three of them enjoyed their Christmas Day. They played games; charades, I Spy and several board games. Victoria went to bed happy; she couldn't remember ever having enjoyed Christmas Day so much.

On Boxing Day, her mother was at home and, to her surprise, Victoria was allowed to have luncheon with her in the dining room. There were only the two of them and conversation was stilted.

'Tell me about the other girls in your class,' Grace said. 'Are there any daughters of the aristocracy?'

'I don't think so, though one – Celia, who arrived just after term started – is the daughter of Sir Roland Groves. He works for the British Government in Singapore.'

Grace frowned slightly. 'So – has the girl gone to Singapore for Christmas?'

Victoria shook her head. 'No. One of the other girls – Charlotte – invited her to her home for the holidays.'

'Really?' Grace said softly. 'And is this Charlotte a friend of yours?'

'On and off.'

Grace's frown deepened. 'What is that supposed to mean?'

'Charlotte flits from one friend to another, depending on who's done something special or is particularly – intriguing. Like Celia was when she first arrived. Someone – different.'

'What about you? Has she ever thought you "special"?'

'For a while, when I was picked for the hockey team and scored the goals that won house points for us.' Victoria didn't mention the second time when her goal-scoring had earned Charlotte's gushing attention.

'What would have happened to Celia if Charlotte had not invited her to spend Christmas with her family?'

Victoria wrinkled her forehead. 'I think she'd have stayed at school. One or two girls from other classes were staying because their parents are abroad. If there aren't too many, Miss Taylor has them to stay in her private apartment.'

'Does she now?' Grace murmured.

The holidays dragged. Apart from a few outings to the park with Rose, Victoria hardly left the house. She went shopping once with her mother to buy some items of underwear to take back to school, but, other than that, she stayed in the schoolroom. How she missed Naomi. Often she would glance up from her reading to the desk where her governess had sat, wishing she could magic her there. But the day came at last when she could return to school. Plunged back amongst the merry chatter of her peers, listening to their stories of all that they had done during the holidays and what presents they'd received for Christmas, Victoria could not help but feel a trace of envy.

'Did you have a good time?' Celia asked her, as they stood together to warm their hands against the heating pipes that ran around the walls of the dormitory. 'I bet it was nice to see all your friends again, wasn't it?'

Victoria glanced at her. Was she being genuine? She thought so; Celia couldn't possibly know that Victoria had no friends at home. It was a fact Victoria rather wanted to keep to herself.

'Christmas Day was nice,' she said guardedly, remembering the kindness of Mrs Beddows and Rose. 'How about you? Did you have a nice time at Charlotte's?'

Now it seemed it was Celia's turn to be careful what she said. She glanced around to make sure that no one else was in earshot – especially Charlotte, Victoria guessed.

'It was all right. Her parents are lovely and made me very welcome, but—'

She hesitated until Victoria prompted softly, 'Go on. I'm good at keeping secrets.'

Celia sighed. 'Well, once we got there, she went out a lot to see her friends.'

'Didn't she take you with her? Show you off to all her friends?'

'Not very often and only when her mother

suggested it.' She was thoughtful for a moment before saying slowly, 'I think that when I was with her, they took more notice of me than they did of her. They wanted to know all about my life in Singapore.'

'Ah,' Victoria said. 'That would explain it.'

'She sneaked out without me a lot of the time, leaving me with her parents and little brother. He's only six, but he's adorable. I didn't mind playing games with him.'

'D'you think she'll ask you to stay again?'

Celia shrugged. 'I don't know, but I wouldn't mind staying at school if she didn't. The girls who've stayed here this holiday say that Miss Taylor gave them a marvellous time. There are two members of staff who stay here too. Miss Mills and Miss Carter. They had a great Christmas Day and then they went on outings. One was to a pantomime.'

'Really?' Victoria clamped her mouth shut before it let her down by revealing that that was something she'd only read about.

The bell went for the start of the day and the two girls hurried to their lessons. There was no sign of Charlotte, so Victoria and Celia sat together.

'Isn't Charlotte taking German?' Victoria whispered.

Celia shook her head. 'She says she finds French hard enough without taking on another language.'

'Does she? She never comes to the Help meetings for French.'

'That's because *she*'s the one needing help in French.'

'But she comes to the domestic science sessions.'

Celia chuckled. 'She's the one *giving* the help then. I have to admit, she is rather good at that.'

At that moment, Miss Taylor arrived and all talking stopped. They were about to take their very first lesson in German.

The highlights of the Spring Term of 1930 for the girls at Miss Taylor's School were the hockey and netball matches played against other girls' schools in the area. Whilst Victoria loved hockey, she found that, although she could have been quite competent at netball, it wasn't a game she enjoyed.

'I'm quite happy for you to stick to hockey,' Miss Carter said and then grinned. 'No pun intended. But your friend Celia has taken to netball like the proverbial duck. She's tall and has good ball skills. She's a whizz at scoring.'

Whilst Charlotte still flitted from girl to girl, Victoria and Celia, thrown together when Charlotte was 'elsewhere', grew closer. Celia, though determined to persevere, was finding the German lessons hard, whilst Victoria absorbed everything about the subject.

'You're so good at languages,' Celia moaned.

'We're all good at something, it's just a case of finding out what each one of us is good at. That's why this Mutual Help Society is such a good idea. Besides, you're good at art. I love drawing and painting, but I'm not a patch on you.'

Celia blushed modestly. 'So if I help you improve your drawing skills, will you help me with German?'

'Of course I will.'

Celia grinned. 'Let's not say too much to Charlotte, eh?'

Victoria giggled. 'Our secret.'

Twenty-Eight

As Easter approached, the girls began to look forward to going home. A fortnight before they were due to break up, Miss Taylor called Victoria into her office. She was sitting at her desk with her back to the window and holding a letter in her hand. Her face was so solemn that Victoria's heart started to beat faster. Had she some bad news to impart?

'Sit down, Victoria.'

Her legs trembling, Victoria sat in the chair on the opposite side of the desk facing the head teacher.

'My dear, I have had a letter from your mother. She' – Emily hesitated a moment before continuing – 'asks if you can stay at school during the holidays.'

Victoria wondered if the word 'asks' should be changed to 'demands', but she said nothing. Inside, she was begging silently, *Oh please say 'yes', Miss Taylor*, whilst Emily said, 'Would you mind that very much?'

There was actually no need for Victoria to answer – it was written in her eyes – but she said it anyway. 'No, I wouldn't mind at all, Miss Taylor.'

'Celia will be here. It seems she has not been invited to Charlotte's home this holiday.'

A small smile flickered on Victoria's mouth. She tried to hide it, but Emily's sharp eyes had seen it.

She understood the meaning behind it. She knew a lot more about what went on in her school than the girls ever realized.

'Miss Mills and Miss Carter will both be here too and we plan to take you on various outings. There will be five girls in total. Cressida will be one. Her parents live and work abroad like Celia's. Lucy may also be here. Her mother is to have a serious operation and her father thinks it would be best for Lucy to be amongst friends at such a trying time. And there is another girl, Phyllis Beresford. She's the same age as Cressida.'

Victoria nodded. 'She's a prefect, isn't she?'

'That's right. She and Cressida are friends and, being almost eighteen, they will be allowed to go out together sometimes. They both leave here at the end of the summer term.'

'I'll be sorry to see them go,' Victoria murmured. 'Cressida is a wonderful head girl.'

'Yes, she is. She's an excellent role model for you younger girls.'

The Easter holidays proved to be a happy time for Victoria. Naomi visited and was allowed to take the three younger girls out into the village to the little teashop, whilst the two older girls were allowed a trip into London on their own. Naomi now had a post at the primary school in the village where she lived, she told Victoria.

'It's very different to teaching on a one-to-one basis,' she said, 'but I find I am enjoying it. It's quite a challenge teaching twenty-five children of mixed abilities.'

'She's lovely, your old governess,' Lucy said, linking her arm through Victoria's while they stood on the school steps, waving goodbye to Naomi as she hurried down the drive to catch her train. 'Though "old" is a bit unfair. She can't be more than thirty, can she?'

'She's brilliant,' Celia agreed. 'I wish the governess I had in Singapore had been like her. She was an old trout. She never let me do anything that could be classed as "fun" and she thought my drawing was a waste of time. I had to do it in secret.'

'Did your parents encourage it?' Lucy asked. 'Your drawing, I mean?'

'Daddy did. He liked to paint a bit himself, but Mummy, bless her, was too much of a social butterfly to worry about my education. She loves the life out there.'

'Do you?' Lucy asked.

Celia wrinkled her forehead. 'Parts of it. It's nice to have servants to wait on you hand and foot but, to me, it all seemed a bit – well – not – not real.'

'Superficial?' Lucy volunteered.

'Yes – yes, that's the word.'

'But we have servants in this country,' Lucy said. 'My mother doesn't lift a finger to do any actual work. Oh, she runs the house, supervises everything – tells Cook what meals to make, that sort of thing – but you don't see her lighting fires and polishing the furniture.'

Victoria said nothing; she didn't want to get into a discussion about mothers. But it seemed the other two girls weren't going to let her off quite so lightly.

'What about your home, Victoria? Why have you had to stay here during the holidays?'

Victoria had planned what to say if ever she should be pressed to answer questions about her home life. 'We live quite comfortably in Kensington, though I don't think we have pots of money. Mother said it would be "a great expense" for her to send me here. We have a cook and a housemaid and a daily help and, of course, there was Miss Gilbert before I came here.'

'What about your father?' Lucy asked quietly.

'He was killed at Passchendaele.'

'Oh I'm sorry. So—' Celia thought quickly. 'You can't have known him, then.'

Victoria shook her head.

'But you have photographs of him?'

'No.' Her voice was husky. 'I've never seen one. I don't know what he looks like.'

The other two girls exchanged a glance and Celia said softly, 'Maybe it's too painful for your mother.'

'Perhaps,' Victoria murmured. Until the girls had brought the subject up, she had never queried the fact that there were no photographs anywhere of her father, nor had her mother ever spoken of him except to blame him for her daughter's existence with a bitterness that forbade further questions.

Tactfully changing the subject, Lucy said, 'Did you know that Miss Taylor is taking us to a show in London tomorrow afternoon? A matinee.'

'I've never been to a London show,' Celia said.

Victoria said nothing. Living in London as she did, her friends would no doubt expect that she had. But the truth was she knew very little about the theatre world in her home city. Miss Gilbert had been allowed to take her to museums and art galleries as part of her education, but never to plays or shows.

Victoria scarcely slept that night. The following day was full of exciting prospects.

The trip into London's West End was everything Victoria had hoped it might be – and more. Miss Taylor took all five girls to a variety show and they sat in the front row of the circle.

'I can't believe you've never been to a show before, when you live in London,' Phyllis remarked.

Victoria noticed Cressida give her friend a sharp nudge. She glanced kindly at Victoria. 'She's only eleven, Phyll. Give her time.'

But Phyllis Beresford was known to be outspoken. 'I'd been to several West End shows by the time I was her age and I don't even *live* in London.'

'Well, she's here now,' Cressida said firmly, giving Victoria's hand a quick reassuring squeeze, but Victoria noticed that the other four girls glanced at each other. No doubt they were all wondering about her home life. She had been rather secretive about it, whilst they were 'open books', chattering endlessly about their parents, their siblings, their pets and their friends at home.

But when the show started, Victoria forgot all about them. She was entranced by the leggy dancing girls, the singers and acrobats.

When they returned to school, Victoria thanked Miss Taylor politely. The headmistress smiled down at her. She didn't need to ask the young girl if she had enjoyed herself; the answer was in her sparkling eyes.

Later that evening, after 'lights out' for the girls, Emily sat in her private sitting room with the other two members of her staff who had remained at the school during the holiday. They were drinking cocoa and talking about what she had overheard passing between the girls.

'I thought for a moment I was going to have to step in, but Cressida – bless her – saved the day.'

'But I bet Victoria didn't give anything away about her home life even then,' Marianne said. 'Am I right?'

'You are. All I can glean is that her mother doesn't really care much about her. Can't wait to foist her off on someone else.'

'She's never visited her here, has she? The mother, I mean? The woman who does come is her old governess, isn't she?'

Emily nodded. 'Yes. Miss Gilbert. A lovely woman. Victoria is obviously very fond of her.'

'Do we know anything at all about the rest of her family? What about her father? Or her grandparents?'

'All I know is that her father was killed at Passchendaele.'

Lily was frowning. 'When is Victoria's birthday?'

'I can't remember off the top of my head.'

'Why? What makes you ask?'

'Just curious about the time she could have been conceived. That's all.'

Emily set down her cocoa and walked through to her office, which was attached to her sitting room. A few moments later she returned.

'The sixth of June, 1918.'

Lily counted on her fingers. 'That means she must have been conceived in August or September the previous year.'

Marianne leaned forward. 'But Passchendaele lasted from July to November 1917. I know those dates well because my uncle – my mother's brother – was killed in that battle. And I remember her saying that he hardly ever got home on leave in the latter years of the war.'

'Perhaps Victoria's father was wounded and came home for a while.'

'Possible, I suppose.'

Marianne laughed. 'Perhaps Mrs Hamilton had an affair.'

'That's possible too.' Emily sighed. 'I don't think we ought to speculate. It's not our business. Victoria's fees are always paid on time and her address is in a well-to-do part of London – Kensington. She's been very well brought up. That's not in doubt, but I have to say, her background is a bit of a mystery.'

'I wonder whether,' Lily pondered, 'as she gets older, she will ever have questions of her own?'

'Well, if she does and she comes to me, I'd certainly do my best to help her. I do have some connections at the War Office. But in the meantime, all we can do is try to protect her from the other girls being nosy. I wouldn't like her to get hurt.'

'Oh, I think you'll find that little Miss Hamilton is far tougher than you might think,' Lily said.

Twenty-Nine

When Grace Hamilton wrote again during the summer term to ask if Victoria could stay at school throughout the long summer holidays, Emily wrote back to say that on this occasion it would be impossible. All the girls who stayed for one reason or another during the shorter holidays went home in July and August, even the ones whose parents were abroad. And neither she nor any members of her staff would be in residence at the school.

In fact, she wrote, *we close the school for four weeks so that all staff, including household staff, can take holidays.*

She paused, her pen suspended in mid-air, wondering if she dare suggest that Miss Gilbert might like to have Victoria to stay with her for a couple of weeks, but she decided against it. It was hardly fair, without having asked the woman herself first. Neither did she dare ask if there were grandparents.

But it seemed as if Grace, anxious not to be saddled with her daughter for six whole weeks, had had a similar thought. A fortnight later, Emily received a short note from Grace:

When school breaks up, Victoria is to go to stay with her former governess, Miss Naomi Gilbert, for a month. She will then come home for the last fortnight of the holidays, when I will make sure she has everything in the way of new uniform, etc., for the commencement of the autumn term.

So, Emily thought wryly, Mrs Hamilton had once again delegated her parental duties. When she imparted the news to Victoria, she had steeled herself to expect tears of disappointment from the girl that she would not be going home. However, she was left in no doubt about her young charge's feelings. Victoria positively beamed and almost skipped out of the headmistress's office.

Naomi lived a thirty-minute train ride from the school. Victoria wrote to her to tell her what time she would be arriving and received the welcoming response: *I'll be waiting.* And there she was on the platform, eagerly scanning the carriage windows. Victoria waved animatedly. As the train stopped and the doors were opened, Victoria jumped down, dragging her suitcase with her. Her trunk was to be sent to her home in London ready to be repacked with clothes for the new school year. But Victoria had been careful to place the drawing of the man in the park safely in the bottom of the suitcase, which she carried with her.

'Oh, I'm so pleased to see you.'

'Thank you for having me.'

They both spoke at once as they hugged each other.

'Come along. We'll get a taxi outside the station. It's too far to walk carrying your suitcase.'

Victoria couldn't have been made more welcome. Naomi showed her to her room in the little cottage. A pretty chintz counterpane covered the single bed, with matching curtains. A rug lay at the side of the bed and there was a wardrobe, a chest of drawers and a washstand with bowl and ewer. The small window looked out over a typical cottage garden; a patch of lawn surrounded by flowers of all varieties and colours.

'Oh,' Victoria gasped, 'it's beautiful.'

'I'm afraid it's not what you're used to. The lavatory is down the garden path and I don't have a proper bathroom. When you want a bath, you'll have to give me advance warning. It's a tin bath in front of the kitchen fire with water heated in the back boiler.'

'Oh Miss Gilbert,' Victoria clasped her hands together, 'I don't care about any of that. I'm here – with *you*.'

Naomi smiled. 'I should tell you straight away that your mother sent me some money for your keep whilst you are here, but as I don't really need it, I thought we'd spend it on some trips out. In fact, I've booked us a week in a hotel in Bournemouth. Would you like that?'

'By the sea?'

Naomi nodded.

'Oh! How wonderful. I've never seen the sea.'

Naomi felt a lump in her throat. Though the

statement was made without guile or a trace of self-pity, Victoria had no idea how heartbreaking those words sounded. For a girl of twelve never to have seen the sea was deplorable. If her background had been poor, it would have been understandable, but for Victoria Hamilton, born into a middle-class background, well . . . Naomi could scarcely find the words to describe how she felt.

Their stay in the seaside town was idyllic. The sun shone every day and Victoria revelled in the beach and the sea. They had picnics on the sands, paddled, dug sandcastles, collected seashells and Naomi taught her to swim. Back at Naomi's cottage they still went out for day trips, but often they were just content to laze in the garden, to read or talk as the mood took them.

All too soon the four weeks had flown by. As they parted on the station, Naomi held her close and whispered in her ear, as if it were a secret between them, 'Two weeks will soon be over, and you'll be back at school.'

Naomi had been right; the two weeks would pass quickly enough. Victoria was pleased to see Mrs Beddows and Rose. They made her feel welcome.

'You've grown, Miss Victoria,' the cook said approvingly. 'You're going to be tall.'

'And beautiful,' Rose put in stoutly. 'You'll turn a few heads.'

'Don't let her mother hear you say that,' Cook laughed. 'She'll have her under lock and key before you can say "boyfriend".'

They laughed together at the absurdity of the conversation about a twelve-year-old, but Mrs Beddows's face sobered. She knew the way of the world. Another four years and Victoria would indeed be a very attractive young woman. She would certainly catch the eyes of the boys – and even of men.

'Now,' she said briskly, banishing such worrying thoughts, 'your mother has said you're to dine with her tonight and then tomorrow she is taking you into town to equip you with whatever you need in the way of new uniform. Your trunk from school arrived whilst you were at Miss Gilbert's. Did you have a nice time, by the way?'

'Yes, thank you. She lives in a lovely little cottage in a village. Everyone is very friendly.'

It had been agreed between Naomi and Victoria that she should say nothing about their week in Bournemouth or about the day trips. If asked about her holiday – 'and you will be,' Naomi had said – she should stick to talking about Naomi's home and the village.

More secrets to be kept, Victoria had thought.

So now, she chattered about her stay in the village and found that there was enough to talk about to keep anyone from guessing that she was actually missing out the best times of the holiday.

'There's a sweet little teashop in the village that serves cream teas. It's very like the one near the school. We girls are allowed to go there occasionally on a Saturday afternoon.'

'That's nice, miss. I'm glad you've had a lovely

time. Now, off you and Rose go upstairs to sort out your uniform. Make a list for your mother for tomorrow. She's taking you to Daniel Neal's on Kensington High Street.'

Dinner passed with the usual stilted conversation between mother and daughter, but the following day their trip felt a little easier. Grace obviously enjoyed shopping, even if it was for mundane items like a uniform.

They were just about to enter the store when a high-pitched voice sounded behind them. 'Grace! *Darling!*'

A woman, dressed extravagantly, made as if to kiss Grace on both cheeks, though their faces never actually touched.

Standing back, she glanced at Victoria standing a couple of paces behind her mother. 'And who, might I ask, is this?' Before Grace could speak, the woman provided her own answer. 'Don't tell me. This is your daughter. Now, Grace, I must take issue with you. Why have you kept her hidden away? She's beautiful.' The woman touched Victoria's cheek with manicured fingers. A waft of expensive perfume drifted towards her. She turned back to Grace. 'Now, let's go and have coffee and I can get to know this delightful girl.'

'I'm sorry, Pearl,' Grace said stiffly, 'but we really haven't time. We're here to buy her school uniform and we must get back home by twelve as I have an appointment later. We have to go. I'll see you at the ladies' luncheon club next Thursday as usual.'

But just as they were about to turn away, Grace paused, thinking quickly. Pearl might be very useful in the future. She moved easily in the upper circles of society and would be able to be Victoria's sponsor for the girl to be presented at court. Grace smiled and said, 'When she's older, Pearl, I'd be delighted for you to get to know her. Now, come along, Victoria.'

Pearl pretended to pout that she was not being allowed to meet the young girl properly, and wriggled her fingers in farewell.

As they bought the rest of the items Victoria needed and hurried home, she made no comment about their meeting with one of her mother's friends.

She knew better than to ask questions.

Victoria was due to return to school on the first Sunday in September, so on the Friday beforehand she asked Mrs Beddows if Rose could go with her to the park.

'I don't see why not. If it's fine.'

After Rose had finished her duties, they set off for a couple of hours in the afternoon. The day was fine and warm and they headed to the bench in the park where she had always sat with Naomi, though now it seemed a long time since she had been there. She glanced around, holding her breath. Was he here? Did he still come on a Friday?

But the man was not sitting on the bench on the other side of the stretch of grass and Victoria felt a stab of disappointment. She hoped nothing had happened to him. He wasn't old – about her mother's age, she guessed – but it looked as if he might have been wounded in the war. Perhaps his general health had been undermined too. She had heard dreadful tales of men being gassed and left with wounds that never healed properly.

'Shall we go for a walk before we have to go back?'

'If you like, miss.'

They walked around the park, covering almost every corner of it until Rose said, 'Me legs are aching, miss. Can we go home now?'

'Oh Rose, I'm so sorry. I forget how early you have to get up every morning. Please forgive me.'

'Don't worry, miss. It's been nice to be out in the sunshine. Honest. It's just that I have to help Cook get dinner ready.'

As they left the park by the iron gates, Victoria glanced back. For some reason she could not have explained, she was sorry not to have seen him. It might be a long time before she had a chance to come to the park again.

Thirty

Back at school at the start of her second year, Victoria decided that she would take one or two of the new girls in the lower classes under her wing. If she found a little girl – there were some as young as eight – looking forlorn or lost, she would help her find whatever room she was looking for. She remembered only too well how strange and confusing the big school had seemed to her only the previous year. How grateful she had been for Cressida's kindness and even for Charlotte's intermittent friendship. But Cressida had now left school and there was a new head girl – Ava Burton. She was a good choice. She upheld the disciplinary ethic of the school, though she lacked Cressida's empathy with the younger children. But Victoria, with growing confidence, found that she could keep order with a smile and a kind word. Two or three of the young girls found they would rather approach Victoria than one of the prefects, who already seemed like adults to them.

'I see Charlotte is enamoured with the new girl in our class,' Celia said. She and Victoria had gravitated towards one another again.

'Who is she?'

'Oh, now this one might last a while. She's

Constance Davidson, the daughter of Sir Michael Davidson.'

Victoria linked her arm through Celia's. 'Come on, let's go and get ready for games this afternoon. I'm so glad we're back into the hockey season again.'

As the school year progressed, Victoria was made captain of the Under 15s hockey team. The team won all their matches against other schools bar two and at the end of the year were awarded a cup at Speech Day. Proudly, Victoria mounted the stage to receive the award. As she walked off, carrying the cup, her glance sought a familiar face amongst the rows of parents at the back of the hall. Naomi Gilbert clapped until her hands were sore.

Of course, there was no sign of Grace Hamilton.

And so the pattern was set for the next few years. Victoria remained at the school in the Christmas and Easter holidays alongside Celia and other girls, who could not go home for one reason or another. In the summer break, she spent a month with Naomi and then went home for the final fortnight. She didn't see the man in the park again, even though she went each Friday of the last two weeks she spent in London.

At school, she progressed satisfactorily in all subjects but she shone in both French and German. At thirteen, she had begun Latin lessons and found that, although it was supposed to be a 'dead' language, so much of it helped her with her other languages. Celia, too, took Latin, relying heavily on Victoria's help.

'I can't see the point of it.' Charlotte pulled a face.

'I'm going to do science. Much more useful, my father says. That's what Constance is doing.' She always introduced her new friend as 'Constance, the daughter of Sir Michael Davidson', even though the girl herself had no airs and graces and could have been popular with her other classmates if Charlotte had not monopolized her so completely.

'You were right, Celia, this friendship does seem to be lasting a lot longer than the others,' Victoria remarked.

'You know why, don't you?'

Victoria frowned. 'Not really, no.'

'She's angling for an invitation to Constance's home. They say she lives in a town house in Mayfair, but the family also have a "country seat" that's almost a stately home in the Midlands somewhere.'

'And has an invitation been forthcoming?'

'Not yet. That's why she's hanging on.'

'I feel for Constance. I'm sure she would like to make friends with other people, but Charlotte's like a limpet.'

'Let's try and prise her away, shall we?'

'Yes, let's.'

But Victoria and Celia had met their match with Charlotte. Whatever they tried to do to involve Constance in other activities always failed. Charlotte always stepped in.

'Oh, sorry, we can't. We've permission to go into the village . . .'

'Haven't got time. We're supposed to be supervising class 2B's prep. Miss Mills asked us to do it. She's got a migraine, poor thing.'

And on it went – always some excuse – until everyone gave up trying.

'I'm sure it's not Constance's fault,' Celia said, exasperated when yet another attempt to get her to join them was refused by Charlotte. 'Did you see the look on her face? I'm sure she wanted to come with us on Saturday afternoon's picnic.'

'Anyway, let's forget about them for the moment,' Victoria said. 'What are you going to do after we take our school cert? It's next year, you know.'

'Oh my? Is it really? How the years have flown. We'll be sixteen by then, won't we? I'm not sure. I'm going to write to my father to ask whether I can stay on here to do my Higher.'

'Do you hope to go to university?'

Celia shook her head. 'I'm not clever enough. I want to go to art school, if Daddy will agree. Hasn't the time gone quickly? It doesn't seem five minutes since we arrived as shy little eleven-year-olds.' She glanced at Victoria. 'You've certainly blossomed into a confident young lady. What has your mother got lined up for you?'

Victoria pulled a face. 'She hasn't said lately, but when I came here she told me I was to take the School Certificate, go to finishing school afterwards and then "come out" and find myself a suitable husband.'

'That doesn't sound like the real "you" one bit.'

'It isn't, but how on earth I'm going to get her to change her mind, I don't know. My mother is not someone you argue with.'

Celia was thoughtful. 'Where was she proposing to send you to finishing school?'

'Probably Switzerland.'

'There you are, then.'

Victoria looked puzzled. 'Where am I?'

'Stay on here to do your Higher School Cert – she'll let you do that, won't she?'

'I'm not sure.'

'Then get Miss Taylor on your side.'

Victoria sighed. 'Not even Miss Taylor would be able to change my mother's mind if it's already made up.'

'Worth a try, I'd have said.'

Victoria brightened. 'You're right. It is.'

'And then,' Celia went on with her plan for Victoria's future, 'you'll be eighteen. You go to Switzerland – or wherever – for at least a year and after that – well, I reckon you could duck out of the coming-out and husband-finding nonsense. That's if you want to.'

'Oh I do. Believe me, I do.' Victoria was thoughtful for a moment before saying, 'When the time's right, I'll talk to Miss Taylor.'

Thirty-One

The following year, 1934, was busy for all the girls. Victoria and Celia – though friendly with all the girls in their class – became the best of friends, but neither asked the other home with them. Celia's parents still lived in Singapore and, without anything ever being said, Celia understood that Mrs Hamilton did not invite her daughter's friends to stay. Close though they were, Celia still didn't know very much about Victoria's home life. Despite her mother's coldness, Victoria – who had never known any different – blossomed under the watchful eye of the headmistress and her caring staff and the continuing affection of Naomi Gilbert. And now, Celia's friendship too.

At the end of the summer term, when they had all taken the School Certificate and were excitedly anticipating the holidays, Victoria sought an appointment with Miss Taylor.

'Sit down, my dear,' Emily invited, as the sixteen-year-old entered her study. 'Now, although we won't know the results for a few weeks, how do you feel the examinations went?'

'I think all my languages – including Latin – will be all right and also, hopefully, English and English literature. History and geography I found quite hard.'

'You should be all right with art, too.'

Victoria grimaced. 'Once upon a time, I might have agreed, but compared to Celia . . .'

Miss Taylor laughed. 'The examiners don't make comparisons between the candidates. They set a standard you have to reach and I think you will do that.' She paused. 'So, what did you want to see me about?'

Victoria took a deep breath. 'I would like to stay on here for another two years to do my Higher, but I'm not sure my mother will agree. I just wondered if you could help.'

Emily toyed with a pen on her desk as she said slowly. 'I know she has plans for you to go to finishing school. Although I can understand that, I think sixteen is a little young. Eighteen would be so much better.' When she looked up and met Victoria's gaze, her eyes were sparkling with mischief. 'Perhaps I could use that argument. And, of course, I always advocate that education is never wasted, even if your only ambition is to marry well.'

'It's not *my* ambition,' Victoria said swiftly before she could stop herself. She flushed with embarrassment, feeling she had been disloyal to her mother. 'Oh please, forget I said that.'

Softly, Emily said, 'What is said in confidence in this room goes no further, Victoria. Not even to my staff. And I would crave you keeping my confidence if I say to you that I am pleased to hear it. You have so much potential. You have a gift for languages and should be allowed to use that talent.' Her face clouded as she added, 'I am not against marriage – of course I'm not – but I am against it being regarded as a *career*. The be-all and end-all. If you meet someone and fall in love – and he loves you . . .' For a brief moment her face was anguished. 'Then that is a different matter entirely.'

Victoria didn't ask questions. Perhaps Miss Taylor had had an unhappy love affair. Or, she thought, the headmistress was the right age to be one of the thousands of women left doomed to spinsterhood because of the Great War.

'So,' Emily was saying, 'I will write to your mother, but I will not' – the corner of her mouth twitched with amusement – 'mention that you and I have spoken on this matter. It will seem to come from an ambitious headmistress, who wants kudos for her school.'

No word came back from her mother before the school broke up for the long holidays; Victoria was on her way to Naomi's cottage and Celia began her long journey to Singapore.

'Oh it's so lovely to see you.' Naomi hugged her and then stood back to look at her as she always did.

'You have altered even in the last month since I saw you at school.' Naomi was still a faithful visitor three times a term and had been during the years Victoria had been at the school. 'You're growing into a lovely young woman.'

Victoria blushed at the compliment.

Over supper she told Naomi what had transpired

between herself and the headmistress. 'But she didn't hear from Mother before we broke up.'

'Your mother will tell you when you go home for the last two weeks of this holiday as usual, but in the meantime, try not to let it worry you and spoil your time here.' Naomi leaned forward. 'I've booked for us to go to Bournemouth again.'

'Then I'll put it out of my head and just enjoy myself,' Victoria said with a smile.

'I've had this letter from your headmistress,' Grace greeted her at the end of August when Victoria arrived home. 'Do you know anything about it?'

Victoria pretended to pull in a deep breath. 'Oh Mother, am I in trouble? I can't think of anything I've done wrong.'

'No, no, it's nothing like that. She has sent the results of your School Certificate examinations.' Grace unbent sufficiently to add, 'You have done very well, Victoria. I am pleased to see that my sacrifices have not been in vain.'

Victoria knew better than to ask to see the results for herself. Grace was still glancing down at the letter. 'It seems that Miss Taylor feels you would benefit by staying on another two years and taking the Higher School Certificate. She feels it would equip you for going on to finishing school and then coming out. Of course, you'd be nineteen by then. A little on the older side, but perhaps that would be to the good.' Now it seemed that Grace was thinking aloud. Still, Victoria remained silent. After what seemed a long pause to the impatient girl, Grace said, 'Yes, yes, on balance, I think that is a good idea. So, you will stay on at school for another two years. I hope you will work hard.'

There was no question put to Victoria as to whether that was what she would like to do; that was not in Grace's nature. She was the one to make decisions about her daughter's future, not the girl herself.

Later, in the privacy of Victoria's bedroom as she helped her sort through her clothes in readiness for the usual trip into the city the following day, Rose whispered, 'Are you happy about that – about staying on at school, miss? Mrs Beddows and me are worried you might not want to.'

Victoria hugged the maid. 'I'm ecstatic. It's what I really want.'

Rose looked relieved. 'That's all right, then. I'll tell Mrs Beddows.'

Arriving back at school at the end of the following week, Victoria was stepping out of the taxi when she heard her name being called excitedly. 'Victoria!'

'Celia! Oh, you're here too. How perfectly marvellous. I didn't know if you were coming back.'

'Neither did I for sure, but Daddy has now agreed to me going to art school on the condition that I get my Higher first. I can't believe it and I can't tell you how happy I am.' As the two girls hugged each other, Celia added, 'Charlotte's here too.'

'Really? I thought she said she wasn't coming back.'

Celia chuckled. 'It seems she's changed her mind. You see, Constance has returned.'

'Ah, now that explains it, then.'

The two girls went to report their arrival and then find their way to the part of the sprawling school that was known as the sixth-form block. They were no longer to sleep in dormitories, but would be allocated a room with two beds in it and they could choose with whom they wished to share. Naturally, Victoria and Celia were together – and so were Charlotte and Constance.

'Though whether Constance is too happy about it, I wouldn't like to say,' Celia remarked.

'I say, this is rather jolly, isn't it?' Victoria wasn't listening. She was inspecting their room. There was a large wardrobe that they could share and a chest of drawers with six drawers – three each – a washstand and a rug between the two single beds.

'Very comfy,' Celia declared.

'No desks to work at, though.'

'It'd be a bit cramped. I think we'll still have to work in the library. There is the sixth-form common room, but I'm guessing that will always be a bit noisy.'

'I shan't grumble at that,' Victoria said. 'I've always liked the library. Whoever's on duty always keeps order – and silence.'

'I wonder if we will be prefects?'

Victoria shook her head. 'Not usually in the Lower Sixth. Maybe next year . . .'

After supper that evening, Victoria knocked hesitantly on the headmistress's door. She needn't have worried; Miss Taylor was as welcoming as ever. She never thought of herself as being 'off duty'.

'I apologize for bothering you so late . . .'

'It's not a problem, Victoria. I am so pleased you have come back. I had a letter from your mother telling me so. Now, how can I help you?'

'I just wondered if I could see the details of my results.'

Emily blinked. 'Your results? But I sent them to your mother at the same time as I asked about you staying on into the sixth form.'

'Yes, I know. She told me I'd done well, but she didn't show me the details. I mean, I know I've already chosen my subjects for the Higher, but I just wanted to see how I'd done in – well, everything.'

Emily stared at her and, for a moment, there was a spark of anger in her eyes. What a cold, heartless woman Grace Hamilton must be, the head teacher thought. Completely selfish and self-centred, without a scrap of empathy for her daughter. The fact that the girl's mother had never once visited her during her time at the school had surprised Emily, but this shocked her. Still, keeping her voice level, she said quietly, 'Of course you do.'

Emily went to her desk and found the folder with the results of all the pupils who had taken the School Certificate that year. After a moment leafing through the papers she said, 'Ah, here we are.' She glanced at it briefly to remind herself of the details and then handed it to Victoria.

'You did indeed do very well.' She smiled. 'You had the best results overall of anyone. I think you'll be in line for a prize on Speech Day, especially the Languages Cup. And seeing as you're the captain of

the school hockey team now, I expect you'll be trot-
ting up on stage more than once. I'm very proud of
you, Victoria, and I am extremely glad your mother
agreed to you returning for the sixth form.'

Victoria and Celia worked hard, encouraging and
helping each other. The next two years seemed to fly
by. And then they were leaving the place that had
been home to them for seven years, and going their
separate ways.

'I quite envy you going to Switzerland,' Celia said,
'though it wouldn't suit me. I'm more than happy to
be going to art school. I've got in at the Slade.'

'That's fantastic. So you still won't be going back
to Singapore.'

'Not yet, anyway, but I will eventually.'

Charlotte was also going on to finishing school,
though not to the same one as Victoria. She was
following closely in Constance's footsteps and going
to a well-known one in Geneva, whilst Victoria was
going to a relatively small one in Davos. She was
glad that they were not going to the same school;
although she thought she could have been friends
with Constance, she'd had enough of Charlotte's
weather-vane character. Though she had to admit
that during the last few years, since Constance's
arrival, she had not flitted from one friend to another
quite so much. But Victoria's relief was short-lived.

'Guess what?' Charlotte was smiling. 'Constance
and I are both coming to the Davos Finishing School.
Her father decided it was a better one for her and
I've managed to get in too. Isn't that wonderful?'

Victoria kept her face expressionless, but her glance

went beyond Charlotte to Constance. Her face was thunderous and she shrugged her shoulders helplessly.

Victoria had a struggle not to laugh.

'Are you sure you're going to be all right, miss?' Rose said worriedly. 'It's an awful long way to go on your own and you'll be there nearly a whole year without coming home.'

Both Mrs Beddows and Rose knew about the conversation between mother and daughter.

'I'm arranging for you to remain at the school in Davos during the Christmas and Easter holidays,' Grace had said. 'I understand they find various activities for you to do. Skiing is one of them, I believe. I'm quite happy for you to do that. It is an upper-class sport, after all, and will give you a topic of conversation at your coming out. It is the sort of thing a future husband would approve of. And then when you come home in July, we can start planning for your presentation at court next year.'

'I'll be fine,' Victoria said now in answer to Rose's question.

'All that travelling and on your own too,' Rose shook her head. 'I'm sure I'd get lost.'

Victoria didn't tell her that Naomi was coming south with her to see her onto the ferry which would take her to France. She put her arm around the maid. 'I'm a big girl now. Don't worry about me, Rose.' The phrase that had always belonged to the maid slipped out naturally. 'There's a dear.'

Rose glanced at the girl she'd seen grow from a gawky child into a tall and shapely young woman.

Victoria wore her blonde hair long, falling to her shoulders in soft waves and curls. Her skin was clear and glowing without the need for any artificial aid and her blue eyes sparkled with vitality and excited anticipation. There was no doubting that she was looking forward to her new adventure.

Thirty-Two

The journey was uneventful – even the ferry crossing was smooth – and whilst travelling across France, Victoria chatted to other passengers on the train in their native language.

And then she was crossing the border into Switzerland. She changed trains at Zurich, and now conversation with others was at a minimum. She was entranced by the views from the carriage window: the snow-capped mountains, the rivers and streams, the men and women working in the fields and the pretty, flower-decked chalets halfway up the mountain sides. And then the train was pulling into the station in Davos.

The privately owned finishing school was situated on the outskirts of the town, a little way up a mountain with glorious views across the valley to the soaring mountains opposite.

Victoria was just finishing putting her clothes away in the chest of drawers when a knock came at the door. It had taken some time to unpack because she kept being drawn to the window and the magnificent view beyond it.

She opened it to find Constance standing there. She glanced down the corridor.

'No Charlotte?'

Constance pulled a face. 'Not yet, but no doubt she'll be here soon.'

'Come in. I'll make us a hot chocolate.'

'Thanks.' Constance stepped into the room and, just like Victoria, was drawn to stand near the window. 'Isn't it beautiful?' she breathed.

'Wonderful. I think we're going to be happy here, don't you?'

Constance stirred the drink that Victoria handed to her. 'I – hope so.'

'Are you homesick?'

Constance shook her head. 'No – it's just . . .'

'Go on. You can tell me.'

'It's Charlotte.'

'Oh. Right. Why?'

'I don't want to sound disloyal. In many ways she's a good friend—'

'I don't betray confidences,' Victoria said softly.

'But she's – such a *limpet*. I want to make other friends. I so wanted to at school, but she was so possessive, she hardly let me out of her sight. And when anyone else tried to include me in what they were doing – you did sometimes, I know – she always had some excuse ready.'

'I remember. Go on.'

'Well – that's it, really. Just that I'd like to be friends with you.'

Victoria smiled. 'I'd like that.' She hadn't been able to see much of the real Constance. Like the girl herself said, Charlotte had always been in the way, but maybe here there'd be other girls whom Charlotte would find intriguing and perhaps, just perhaps, she'd give Constance a little more freedom.

'I don't want to be unkind to her,' Constance said. 'She might be feeling lost when she gets here and perhaps even homesick.'

'Let's see what happens, shall we?' Victoria suggested and then she chuckled. 'I could always make out *I'm* feeling homesick and sort of attach myself to the two of you.'

'Do you think you will be?'

'What? Homesick?' Victoria laughed wryly. 'Not for a moment, but Charlotte is not to know that.'

Constance smiled suddenly and her whole face altered. 'Let's give it a try.'

'And now, let's go and explore this place and find out what the rules are so that we can break them. Mind you, we'd better not flout too many in the first week. I don't want to get sent home in disgrace.'

Charlotte arrived a day later than Victoria and Constance. They greeted her warmly. Neither of them were unkind girls and they told her all they had learnt about the school.

'We'll take you on a tour once you've settled in.'

'We've got two days to find our feet before lessons begin. By tomorrow, all the girls will have arrived and there'll be various formalities to go through.'

'Who am I sharing with?' Charlotte glanced from one to the other.

'No one,' Victoria laughed. 'We all have our own rooms. Let's go and find where your room is. I'll carry your case for you. Lead on, Constance.'

They both fussed around her, helping her to unpack and showing her around the whole school and ending up on a balcony leading out from the sitting room.

'Just look at those views, Charlotte. Aren't they breathtaking?'

From where they were standing they could look out over the town nestling in the valley below. Charlotte's gaze took in the view. 'What are all those grand-looking buildings? Hotels?'

'No,' Constance said quietly, 'they're sanatoriums.'

'Evidently, people come from all over the world to be treated for tuberculosis,' Victoria said.

There was a pause before Charlotte said in a small voice, 'My mother's brother died of that when he was in his twenties. Maybe, if he'd been able to come here . . .' Her voice trailed away.

'Come on,' Victoria said, linking her arm through Charlotte's. 'Let's go and see if they're serving dinner or supper – or whatever they call it here.'

The next day, the three girls ventured down into the town.

'Have you noticed how lenient the staff are here?' Constance remarked. 'As long as we tell Matron where we're going, we can more or less do what we like.'

'We have to be in by ten o'clock,' Victoria said. 'That seems to be the only rule, really.'

'We're very lucky, when you think about it,' Constance said. 'Just think – back home, girls born into less privileged circumstances than ours have to leave school and work from the age of about fourteen.'

Victoria's glance roamed over the buildings around her and she looked at the mountains soaring above the town on all sides. She breathed in the fresh, clean air. Yes, she thought, we are lucky. *I* am lucky. For the first time in her young life, she felt she owed her mother a modicum of gratitude. At least she was being given chances in life that many other girls of her age never had.

The rest of the girls arrived the following day and Charlotte was in her element rushing around, introducing herself to each of them.

'Do you know?' she breathed to Constance and Victoria, 'there's a daughter of an earl here. Lady Georgina Haig.'

Victoria and Constance did not dare to exchange a glance; they both knew that they would burst out laughing. Instead, Constance, valiantly keeping a straight face, said, 'Then you must ask her to join us, Charlotte, if she would like to. Perhaps we can help her to settle in.'

'What a good idea,' Charlotte said. 'I'll go now.'

As she turned and almost ran out of the room, Victoria and Constance clutched at each other, stuffing their fists into their mouths. At last, when they thought she could no longer hear, they began to laugh out loud. 'Oh my,' Constance spluttered, holding her ribs. When they had both calmed a little, she added, 'Did you mind me suggesting that?'

'Not at all. We'll pair off nicely,' Victoria's eyes twinkled.

And that is what happened. The four girls went

everywhere together, though occasionally they separated and did different things, but it was always
Charlotte and Georgina, Victoria and Constance.

'It couldn't have worked better. Thank goodness
for Lady G.'

'Is that what you call her?'

'Oh, I'm a terror for shortening people's names or
giving them nicknames,' Constance said.

Victoria laughed. 'Are you now? And what's mine?'

'Oh, Vicky, of course. Not very inspiring, I know.
But it's all I could think of. You're something of an
enigma, you know.'

Victoria pulled a face. 'That name makes me sound
like that vapour rub you use when you've got a cold.
So, what do you like to be called?'

'At home I'm Connie or Con.'

'What do you call Charlotte?'

'Butterfly.'

Victoria stared at her and then began laughing.
'Does she know?'

'Oh yes. I never make a secret of anyone's nickname.'

'Doesn't she mind?'

'I don't think she's cottoned on to the meaning
behind it. She thinks it's a compliment to be likened
to a pretty butterfly.'

As the days passed, Constance gave all the girls
in their group nicknames that were soon adopted by
everyone. Though she wasn't too keen on being called
'Vicky', Victoria shrugged and decided that to protest
would be acting in a superior manner and would
likely lose her friends.

'Isn't it odd,' Constance remarked, 'not to have proper lessons?'

Victoria chuckled, 'I wouldn't let the principal hear you say that. She thinks all the lessons are of vital importance to young ladies of our class. Besides, we're still getting French and German lessons here.'

'Alongside deportment, etiquette, household management . . .' Constance ticked them off on her fingers.

'And, of course, how to act when presented to the royals,' Victoria giggled.

'Have you heard?' Charlotte loved to be the first with a fresh piece of news. 'Those of us who aren't going home for Christmas are going skiing.'

'Where?'

'Well, here, of course. Why go anywhere else when we've got all the ski slopes we need on our doorstep?'

Victoria and Constance exchanged a glance; neither of them were going home for the holidays.

'But I thought *you* were going home,' Constance said.

'Not now,' Charlotte said. 'I'm not missing that. Besides, Lady G is going skiing. You'll both give it a go, won't you?'

'Try and stop us,' Constance and Victoria chorused.

'Have you seen those two young men over there?' Charlotte whispered as they sat down to an après-ski drink. 'They keep looking at us.'

'Well, of course they do,' Constance remarked. 'We're very pretty girls, aren't we?'

They laughed together. 'Modesty's not your strongest point, is it?' Victoria teased.

Constance grinned. 'Not really.'

'Do you think they're locals?'

'No,' Charlotte said. 'They're on a skiing trip. They're from Germany and have been coming here for the last three years.'

The other three stared at her. 'How do you know all that?'

She grinned. 'Because I asked them.'

'And which one did you alight on, Butterfly?' Georgina asked with a languid drawl.

'I tried the tall one with fair curly hair and – what do the romantic novelists call it? – chiselled looks.'

The four girls glanced across. 'He certainly looks like a Greek god,' Constance murmured.

'Hands off,' Charlotte said. 'He's mine.'

'And how do you propose to introduce us to them?'

'Well, I'm not sure yet, I'll have to think about it.'

'No need,' Constance muttered. 'They're coming over.'

Victoria was quaking inside. She'd never had dealings at all with men or boys in her sheltered life. She didn't know what to do or how to behave.

'Oh Connie,' she murmured, 'I'll have to go—'

Her friend turned to her and saw the panic in her eyes. She didn't understand its cause – Victoria said very little, if anything, about her home life – but Constance recognized fear when she saw it.

'It's all right, Vicky,' she whispered. 'Stick close to me.'

It was not the god-like creature who came forward

first – he seemed to hang back a little – but his companion. He was not as handsome as his taller friend, but he had a pleasant, friendly face and a wide smile. Charlotte rose to her feet and held out her hand.

'I saw you skiing earlier. You're very good.'

The young man laughed. He spoke perfect English but with a strong German accent. 'Then you didn't see me fall down? I think it might have been my friend here you saw. Kurt. He's a very good skier. I am Leon.'

Without waiting to be invited, Leon sat down and Kurt, though seeming a little reluctant, took the vacant chair next to Victoria. Her heart was beating so fast she thought he must surely hear it. All at once, in the space of a few minutes, all the confidence she had gained at Miss Taylor's School, and here in Switzerland too, deserted her. She was actually trembling at his nearness. She felt as if she were blushing from head to toe.

Charlotte introduced herself and her three friends and then Leon, taking the lead, asked, 'So what are you all doing here? Where are you from?'

'We're at finishing school here in Davos, but because we haven't gone home for Christmas, here we are. Learning to ski.'

'And where is "home"?'

'England.'

'Ah yes, England. I should very much like to visit there sometime.'

'Where are you from?' Constance asked, feeling that they shouldn't leave all the talking to Charlotte.

'Germany. Berlin.'

Charlotte clasped her hands together, her eyes shining. 'Oh, I've always wanted to visit Berlin.'

Victoria, whose heartbeat was slowing a little, smiled inwardly. She had the feeling that whatever place name Leon had said, Charlotte's answer would have been the same.

'And would you like to visit Germany, *Fräulein*?' a soft, deep voice murmured next to her. She turned and found herself looking into the brightest blue eyes she thought she'd ever seen. She opened her mouth to speak but found that the words wouldn't come.

She cleared her throat and said, huskily, 'I've never really thought about it. This is the first time I've ever been abroad.'

On the other side of the table, Georgina said, 'Girls in our class in Britain lead very sheltered lives. We have governesses at home, then we go to boarding school and possibly on to a finishing school – like we have. We're very closely chaperoned, at least until we've been presented at court and have what they call "come out into society".' She pulled a face. 'That particular delight awaits us when we get home.' She nodded to the other side of the room. 'If you look over there, you'll see Mademoiselle Laurent from the school. She accompanies us every day and has her beady eye on us all the time.'

Leon guffawed. 'And can't you ever escape her?'

Charlotte's eyes twinkled mischievously. 'Maybe tonight at the après-ski in one of the hotels in town. Where are you staying, by the way?'

The six of them chatted for a little longer, until

Georgina said, 'We should be getting back now. They'll be serving dinner very soon and I want a long, hot bath.'

'We'll see you later, then,' Leon said, as they all stood up. 'Do come to our hotel, if you can. We'll look after you.'

In the far corner, Mademoiselle Laurent rose to her feet too.

Thirty-Three

'Do you think we should?' Victoria asked Constance worriedly.

'Should what, Vicky?'

'Meet up with those two young men. Charlotte seems determined to.'

'Well, we won't if you're not happy about it.'

'But – but I don't want to spoil your fun if – if you want to.'

Constance returned from the mirror where she'd been brushing her long, dark brown hair and came and sat down beside Victoria on the bed. They were getting ready together in Victoria's room.

'Vicky, we're friends now, aren't we?'

'Of course. Why do you ask?'

'Because I saw the look in your eyes when those two young men came over and I want to know why you were so terrified. We're all wary of young men we don't know – we have to be – but we're not all quite so frightened as you obviously were. Now, whatever you tell me is just between the two of us. I won't tell the others.'

'I'm being silly, I know that,' Victoria said in a small voice, 'but I've never been used to young men.

I – I had a governess at home. Then I went to Miss Taylor's and now here.'

'Didn't you have any friends at home?'

Victoria shook her head. 'Mother never allowed me to have friends. I spent all my time with Miss Gilbert, my governess, until I went to boarding school.'

'No one? Not even girls?'

Again Victoria shook her head, feeling very foolish. It sounded strange and rather pathetic even to her own ears.

Constance was tempted to say 'You poor thing' but she bit back the words when she realized they would sound critical of Victoria's mother.

'I can see how that could happen,' she murmured instead. 'I was lucky, I suppose. I have two older brothers and I was allowed to mix with their friends.' She squeezed Victoria's hands. 'Don't worry. Stick with me. I'll look after you, but you ought to know – because perhaps you won't recognize the signs – that the good-looking one called Kurt has his eye on you.'

'Oh, but he can't – I mean – Charlotte said . . .'

Constance laughed out loud. 'I rather think that young man will make up his own mind about who he likes, never mind Charlotte's flirting. Now, come on, time we were going down.'

They spent the evening with the two Germans and Kurt made no attempt to hide his interest in Victoria. Even she, in her naivety, could see it.

For the first part of the evening, Charlotte tried

to prise him away from Victoria's side, but when she found it wasn't working, she turned her flattering attentions on Leon. He was far more receptive to her wiles. Both Constance and Georgina were amused rather than put out because the other two girls were getting all the attention. When a local band began to play dance music, Kurt held out his hand to Victoria. Leon was already leading Charlotte onto the floor.

Constance nudged Victoria. 'Go on. You can put all those dance lessons we've been having recently to the test. Nothing can go wrong, Vicky. Mademoiselle Laurent has her eye on all of us.'

'Oh, I—' Victoria began, but at Kurt's earnest 'Please' she relented. Blushing a little, she allowed him to put his arm around her waist.

As they danced close together, he whispered, 'You are a very pretty girl. You are just what we Germans like. Blonde with blue eyes, like me.'

She wasn't used to being paid compliments, especially by a young man, but instinctively, she accepted gracefully with a 'thank you'. She wished she could think of something to say, but she couldn't. She would have to leave opening a conversation to him.

'So, what will you do when you finish your time at the school? What will you do back home?'

'Come out, I suppose.'

'What does that mean, exactly? Come out from where and into what?'

Victoria giggled nervously. 'In England, young women of a certain level in society are presented at court to the King and Queen. And then they attend

a ball and are said to have "come out" into society.'
She pulled a face. 'But really, it is little more than a
marriage market where young women can meet suitable young men. Suitable, that is, in their mothers'
eyes as future husbands.'

'And you are not allowed to choose for yourself?'

'Well, sort of. I mean, we're not *forced* into a
marriage we don't want, like girls used to be.' Her
statement ought to be true, Victoria thought, but she
wondered just what would happen in her own case. If
a suitable young man of her mother's choice made a
proposal, would she be allowed to refuse it if she didn't
like him? She very much doubted it. A cold shudder
ran through her. For a moment her future looked bleak.

'And are you allowed to make friends with young
men that you have not met at this famous ball?'

'I – suppose so.'

'What about a *foreign* friend?' His arm tightened
a little around her waist.

She looked up and was disconcerted by his intense
blue eyes gazing down at her. She found it difficult
to breathe. Fortunately for Victoria, the dance came
to an end. He took his arm from around her but he
did not release her hand as he took a step back and
gave a little bow. Then he led her back to the table
where Constance and Georgina waited. With them
was an irate Mademoiselle Laurent. She turned to
greet Victoria with a small frown creasing her forehead and spoke in rapid French. 'Where is your
friend? Where is Charlotte?'

Victoria glanced around and the other two girls
stood up and scanned the room too.

'I don't know.'

'She was over there a moment ago. I saw her.' Constance said.

'You will find her. Now. This minute.'

'I'll look in the cloakroom,' Constance said. 'You two go and look outside.'

'I will help you—' Kurt began, but Mademoiselle Laurent cut him short. 'There will be no need for that. Thank you. The girls will be going back to the school as soon as we find Charlotte.'

Kurt gave another polite little bow. As he turned away, he said in a whisper that only Victoria heard, 'I will see you tomorrow on the slopes.'

Victoria and Georgina stepped outside into the bitter coldness of the night. It was snowing.

'She can't be out here,' Georgina said, shivering in her thin dress.

'I'm very much afraid she is. Look, over there, though I don't think she's feeling the cold.' In the dim light from a few lanterns strung between the trees, they could see two shadowy figures. Charlotte was wrapped in Leon's arms.

'Oh my goodness,' Georgina said. 'We'll have to put a stop to this or we'll all be sent home in disgrace.'

They crossed the snowy ground and, as they neared the oblivious couple, Victoria hissed, 'Charlotte!'

They sprang guiltily apart.

'Sorry, Leon, but we have to get her back inside,' Georgina said. 'Our chaperone is looking for her. If she's caught with you, she'll be in terrible trouble.'

Without waiting for an answer, they each grabbed

Charlotte by an arm and hustled her towards the door.

'Whatever were you thinking, Charlotte?'

'If Mademoiselle Laurent reports you, we'll all be in trouble.'

'Probably packed off back home. All of us.'

'You're a couple of spoilsports,' Charlotte said morosely. 'Let go of me.'

But their grips only tightened. 'Not until we get you back inside,' Victoria muttered.

'Your reputation will be in shreds,' Georgina said.

At the door they paused before entering, whilst Georgina glanced into the room through the glass. 'I can't see Mademoiselle Laurent. Let's get her back inside before she spots us.'

'You talk to me as if I'm a child. I said, let go of me.'

'You're acting like a child. A very silly one.'

They stamped the snow from their shoes and stepped through the door.

'Now, if we can, let's get back to our table. I'll get us all another drink,' Georgina said. 'Connie should be back in a minute when she can't find you in the cloakroom.'

'Sit down there and don't say a word,' Victoria muttered. She was still angry with Charlotte for her stupidity.

Whilst Georgina struggled through the throng to fetch drinks, Victoria sat guarding a recalcitrant Charlotte, who pouted moodily.

'Why do you have to spoil it? It was only a harmless bit of fun.'

'Mademoiselle Laurent wouldn't see it that way. And neither would Matron.'

Though they saw the principal of the finishing school occasionally, it was the woman in the position of matron who had charge over the girls. She was kindly but firm, though Victoria suspected she would be a tyrant if crossed.

'There you are.' Constance arrived back at the table out of breath. 'I looked everywhere. Where were you?'

Charlotte glared back at Constance but did not answer, leaving it to Victoria to say in a whisper, 'Outside with Leon.'

Constance's mouth formed a round 'oh' just as Georgina arrived back with a tray of drinks. 'Now, everyone, calm down. Charlotte, take that sulky look off your face or Mademoiselle Laurent will suspect something. Where is she, by the way?'

Victoria glanced around. 'She's over there but heading towards us. On guard, everyone.'

When the irate chaperone reached them, they were all sitting chatting and smiling. Constance pre-empted Mademoiselle Laurent's questions by saying cheerfully, 'Here she is, mademoiselle. Safe and sound.' Mentally, she crossed her fingers, hoping that statement was true. 'We found her but then we couldn't find you. Would you sit with us and I'll get you a drink? And then I think we'd better all go back to the school.' Again, she forestalled the chaperone's demand.

Breathless and red in the face from the minutes of anxiety, Mademoiselle Laurent sat down, fanning herself vigorously. 'You must not go out of my sight. Not even for a moment,' she said in French. 'Where were you?'

The others held their breath. Was Charlotte going to tell a deliberate lie?

'When the dance ended I left the floor on the wrong side of the room.' She waved her hand vaguely. 'And it's so crowded in here.'

Neatly, she had avoided telling the whole truth.

Mademoiselle nodded, seeming to accept the explanation. The other girls breathed a sigh of relief but were startled when the woman added, 'You see, if any of you come to harm, I will lose my position at the school.'

'I'll get that drink for you,' Constance murmured, whilst Charlotte said in a small voice, 'I'm sorry, mademoiselle. It won't happen again.'

It most certainly won't, Victoria wanted to say, but she kept silent.

Thirty-Four

'But I want to see Leon again,' Charlotte wailed the next day. 'The holiday's over the day after tomorrow. Lessons start again. There won't be many more chances.' She glanced at Victoria and added craftily, 'And I'm sure Victoria wants to see Kurt.'

Victoria feigned a shrug. Yes, she would like to see the handsome German again, but she was not going to let Charlotte – or the other two – know that.

'You'll no doubt see them on the slopes today and again tomorrow,' Constance said. 'Now, are you both ready? Let's get in a good day's skiing, never mind your romancing.'

They took the ski lift up to the lower slopes. Only Georgina was proficient enough to try the more difficult runs, but she chose to stay with her friends and help them.

'It's wonderful skiing down, but the haul back up is a pain,' Charlotte grumbled as, for the umpteenth time, her gaze swept the slopes. Then her eyes lit up. 'There they are. Look.' She pointed. 'Sitting outside the chalet. Come on.' Without waiting for an answer, she set off towards the two young men.

'We've suddenly found some extra energy from somewhere, have we?' Georgina drawled. Then she sighed. 'Come on, we'd better go with her. That girl is going to get herself into trouble, if we don't watch her.'

Victoria's eyes widened. 'Oh, you don't mean . . . ?'

'No, no, not *that*,' Georgina chuckled. 'I don't think even she's daft enough to let that happen.'

'I'm not so sure,' Constance muttered. 'If last night's escapade is anything to go by. She risked her reputation at the very least.'

As the four of them climbed the last steep slope, Leon spotted them and his smile broadened into a grin. The two young men stood up.

'Are you all right?' Leon asked, his gaze on Charlotte. 'No trouble after we left, was there?'

'Only from these three.' Charlotte pulled a face.

'They were quite right,' he said. 'I hadn't realized you were under quite such strict – surveillance. We should never have gone out of your chaperone's view. I am sorry.' He gave a courteous little bow that was an apology to all of them.

'No harm done,' Constance said generously, but added seriously, 'We'll just have to be a bit more careful. All of us could have been in serious trouble and Charlotte might have been sent home in disgrace. But at least you have a bit more freedom on the slopes. Mademoiselle Laurent can't make it up here.'

They all laughed and then Constance said, 'Come on, Lady G. I want you to try one of the slopes a bit higher up. What about you, Vicky? You're the sportswoman amongst us.'

'I will look after Victoria,' Kurt said at once. 'She will come to no harm with me, I promise you.'

'Right, then. Come on, Connie. We'll leave them to it.'

The two girls skied away to find a slightly more difficult run.

'What did she mean about you being a sports-woman?' Kurt asked. Charlotte and Leon had moved off and the two of them were virtually alone. Suddenly, Victoria was unsure once more.

'Oh, it's just that Connie and I were at school together in England and I – um – was quite good at hockey.'

'I think – from the way your friend spoke – you are being modest.'

Victoria smiled. 'Hockey's not quite the same thing as sliding down a steep snowy mountain.'

'Come, we will go a little higher. I know just the run that would suit you.'

Later, as they sat over mugs of hot chocolate, Kurt said, 'You have the makings of a very good skier, Victoria. You have a natural balance and you are not afraid. I cannot believe this is the first time you have been skiing.'

'Thank you.'

'Leon and I plan to come here again at Easter, if there is plenty of snow. What about you?'

'I – don't know what the school has planned.'

'Would you like to see me again?'

Victoria blushed but managed to keep her voice steady as she said, 'Yes.'

He smiled and touched her hand briefly. 'You finish at the school in the summer, don't you?'

She nodded.

'And then you go home to "come out". Is that right?'

'Yes, but I don't really want to do that. It's all a lot of unnecessary fuss and expense just to—'

She paused, but Kurt finished the sentence softly, 'To find a husband.'

For several moments they gazed at each other across the table. Then Kurt took her hand, grasping it firmly this time. 'Come to Germany when you finish at the school. I am sure you could find work there. Perhaps as a translator. Your German is excellent.'

For a brief moment, Victoria allowed herself to dream, to believe that such a thing was possible. Then common sense prevailed. 'I couldn't possibly. My mother would never agree.'

A cynical smile curled his lips. 'And you never disobey your mother?'

Victoria pulled in a sharp breath. 'No. I never have.'

'Then don't you think it's about time you did?'

This time, Victoria did not answer him.

Victoria and Charlotte spent their last day on the ski slopes with Kurt and Leon. As they parted, Kurt kissed her gently on the mouth and murmured, 'I will see you again. Somehow.'

As they returned to the school, Charlotte walked alongside Victoria. When she was sure that the other two girls could not hear, she whispered, 'Leon wants to see me again. He says he and Kurt are planning come here at Easter. We'll be able to see them. Do you want to see Kurt?'

'I don't see how we can unless the school organizes skiing again for us,' Victoria began. Then she paused and added, 'Can we?'

Charlotte grinned mischievously. 'We could still meet them in town in the evening. The school couldn't stop us, could they?'

'They might be able to. We're in their charge for the year, seeing as we're not going home in the holidays.'

As it turned out, the two girls were in luck. Everyone – not just Victoria and Charlotte – had enjoyed the skiing so much that there was a petition organized for it to happen again during the Easter holidays for those girls who were not travelling home. As no behavioural issues had been reported back to her, the principal gave her approval.

'I'll write and tell Leon,' Charlotte said happily.

'I suppose we'll have to join in,' Georgina said, feigning a bored tone, 'just to keep our eye on these two.'

'I don't mind.' Constance smiled. 'I quite enjoyed it myself. Thanks to you, Lady G, my skiing is coming along very nicely.'

'I'll have to think about charging you for lessons,' Georgina teased.

By the end of the Easter holiday, Charlotte declared herself ecstatically in love with Leon.

'When we finish here in the summer, I am going straight to Germany.'

'Have your parents agreed?'

'Oh yes, I had a letter from Daddy yesterday. He's

very happy for me to continue my education and he agreed there's no better way than visiting other countries.'

'He doesn't know about Leon, then?'

'Er – no.'

'What about your "coming out"?'

Charlotte shrugged. 'Daddy's not too worried about that. He doesn't really agree with it anyway. It was just Mummy who wanted it.'

'Don't you?'

'Not now.'

'What about a chaperone?' Georgina asked.

Charlotte shrugged. 'It's not been mentioned. Look, why don't we all go? The four of us. It'd be such fun.' She smiled archly at Victoria. 'You'd like to see Kurt again, wouldn't you, Vicky?'

'Would your mother agree to you going?' Constance asked Victoria.

'I could write to her, I suppose.'

The expected letter from Grace never arrived and so when the girls had to make arrangements for the journey to Germany, Victoria made the bold decision to go with Charlotte anyway. Money was still being put into her bank account regularly. She hadn't needed to spend very much during the term time, so the amount had built up very nicely. She could easily afford to go and stay as long as she wanted.

'I suppose we'll have to go with them,' Georgina said, her eyes twinkling mischievously. 'What about you, Connie? Shall we all go?'

Constance nodded. 'Yes, my parents have already

agreed to it. They don't mind as we're going to be together.'

'But aren't you planning to "come out"?' Charlotte asked.

'Queen Charlotte's Ball is usually in May, so we've missed it for this year anyway,' Georgina said reasonably. She glanced at Victoria and smiled, 'So, Vicky, you might not escape it after all. There's always next year.'

Victoria pulled a face and then laughed. 'Oh well. We'll see. A lot can happen before then.'

'Well, that all went off quite nicely,' Georgina said, as they sat together on the train travelling from Davos on their way to Germany. 'We've all been "finished" and all got good reports to keep our parents happy. And now, we're off to pastures new. I must admit,' she glanced teasingly at both Charlotte and Victoria, 'I'm rather glad you two are dragging us to Germany. I, for one, am not going under duress. I'm really looking forward to seeing Berlin.'

Victoria laughed. 'I can't imagine you doing anything under duress, Lady G.'

'Well, no, that's true. I don't very often.'

'My father's actually keen for me to go,' Constance added. 'I think he rather wants to find out what's happening there.'

The other three looked at her. 'Why?'

Constance sighed. 'There are all sorts of tales coming out of Germany. Some rather – worrying.'

Charlotte giggled. 'Do you mean he wants us to be spies?'

But Constance was still being serious. 'Not exactly. He just wants to get a general feeling about what life is like now for the ordinary German people since Adolf Hitler came to power. And anything we find out that's – interesting.'

'That sounds like spying to me,' Charlotte said firmly. 'Do you want us to interrogate Leon and Kurt?'

'Heavens, no. We mustn't put ourselves in danger. My father wouldn't want that for a minute. They might both get very suspicious if we start asking searching questions. They just look upon us as four rather silly posh girls.'

'But why the interest?' Georgina asked. 'What does your father do, exactly?'

Constance hesitated for a moment and then lowered her voice. 'He works at the British Foreign Office.'

The other three girls stared at her. This was something they had not known.

Thirty-Five

Charlotte had been in regular communication with Leon and it had been he who had arranged the hotel accommodation for them.

'I'll say this for him,' Georgina approved, 'he's got good taste.'

The hotel was small but beautifully kept, the rooms spotless and the food of the standard they were all used to.

'And it's only a short walk from the centre,' Charlotte said happily, pleased that her friends approved of Leon's choice.

'How long has he booked us in for?'

'A month,' Charlotte said.

'A month!' Georgina repeated. 'I didn't know we were staying that long. I told my parents it'd only be a couple of weeks.'

Charlotte shrugged. 'The boys are hiring a big car – a Mercedes that can take all of us, I think – to take us on all sorts of trips. But you can go home earlier if you want to.'

'I'll see how it goes.' Georgina was non-committal. She wasn't sure how this trip was going to work out. Charlotte and Victoria would want to spend as much time as they could with 'the boys', as Charlotte called

291

them, which would leave herself and Constance to their own devices for much of the time. Much as she liked Constance, a month in the company of just one other person might be hard work. Georgina did not want to be bored.

Her fears, however, were unfounded. It seemed that neither Kurt nor Leon had to work for a living and they devoted their time to taking the four girls out on day trips and even for longer excursions where they stayed overnight in modest hotels, chastely booking three rooms; the four girls pairing off into two and the boys sharing the third. Only during the evenings did Kurt and Leon spend time alone with Charlotte and Victoria, but there was always plenty to occupy Georgina and Constance.

'Isn't the scenery magnificent?' Georgina remarked as they drove through the mountainous region of the Black Forest.

'We are very proud of our country,' Kurt said. He and Leon took it in turns to drive. 'We would like to show you the very best and so wondered if you can stay until the end of September.'

'Why?' Georgina asked.

'Two reasons. We would like to take you to the annual Nuremberg rally and then at the end of September there is to be a wonderful floodlit demonstration. Mussolini is visiting our Führer.'

'I'm sorry,' Georgina said firmly before any of the others could interrupt. 'We really must go home at the beginning of September at the latest.'

'Oh but—' Charlotte began, but Georgina did not let her finish.

'All of us must go. We must stay together. That was the agreement we made with all our parents. It was on that condition that they allowed us to come at all.'

Victoria said nothing; she had made no such agreement with her mother, but neither did she want to stay and certainly not on her own or with just Charlotte.

Kurt shrugged. 'Then will you all promise us that you will come back next year? Come in September for the rally and then stay for two months. Will you at least do that?'

'If we can, then yes,' Georgina said. 'But don't forget, we've all got to go through the coming-out process when we get home.'

'That's in the summer,' Charlotte said. 'We'll be able to come back in September. Oh, do say "yes", Lady G. Please.'

Georgina sighed. 'Very well, then. Like I say, if we can.'

From the back seat of the car, Georgina saw the two young men glance at each other.

'We're disappointed,' Leon said. 'But at least we have next year to look forward to.'

Back at the hotel, once the two young men had left, a full-scale row erupted between Charlotte and Georgina. 'I think you're acting like – like a *chaperone*. I'm seriously thinking of staying here. I want to go to this rally they're talking about.'

'Well, I can't stop you, but would your father be happy about you staying here on your own?'

Charlotte hesitated and then cast an appealing glance at Victoria. 'You'll stay, won't you, Vicky?'

Victoria took a few moments before she said, slowly, 'Actually, no, I don't think I will.'

Charlotte gasped and her eyes widened. 'Why ever not? I thought you and Kurt were close now.'

'We are – but . . .'

'What is it?' Constance said softly.

Victoria frowned. 'I don't know. It's just a feeling I get. There's something a little – odd about the atmosphere here. Kurt and Leon seem so wrapped up in this Nazi Party they belong to. They follow its diktats slavishly. This Führer of theirs can do no wrong in their eyes.'

'Well, I don't think he can,' Charlotte said. 'Leon says he's been the saviour of Germany. They were on their knees at the end of the war and in recent years he's started to re-arm and has brought in conscription again.'

'All totally against the Treaty of Versailles,' Constance put in mildly. 'It's one thing to build your country's confidence up again – its pride – but to re-arm, well, it's tantamount to slapping the rest of Europe across the face with a glove.'

Georgina laughed. 'What, like a challenge to a duel?'

But Constance wasn't laughing. 'Exactly. They could be looking for another war.'

'You're wrong. You're all wrong. I know you are.' Charlotte was almost in tears trying to defend what Leon believed in so ardently.

Feeling sorry for her, Victoria put her arm around the girl's shoulders. 'Look, come home with us now – please don't stay here on your own – and I promise that you and I will come back next year and go to this rally of theirs, even if Lady G and Constance don't want to. But,' she added firmly, 'that's only on the condition that it's safe to come. All right?'

Charlotte bit her lip but nodded agreement. 'All right.'

Later, in the bedroom they shared, Constance said, 'My word, Vicky, you ought to be a diplomat. But don't worry, I'll be coming back here next year too. I really want to see how things progress in this country. Like you, I feel things aren't quite what they seem. My father will be most interested to hear what we've seen already. Would you be willing to come and talk to him?'

'Of course.'

No more was said and the girls travelled home at the beginning of September. All four of them were to be presented at court the following spring. Their mothers were caught up in a whirl of arrangements – even Grace took more notice of her daughter than she ever had done.

'I have arranged for a friend of mine – Pearl Harrington – to be your sponsor.' Grace now regularly called Victoria down to the morning room to discuss her plans. The girl had never known such attention from her mother. She had been rather apprehensive that, on her return from Germany, she might be in disgrace for having gone there, but it seemed Grace viewed the trip as being something that would appeal to the kind of future husband she planned to find for her daughter.

'Can't you sponsor me, Mother?'

'No, sadly I was never presented at court,' Grace

said in clipped tones. Victoria opened her mouth to ask why, but the glare Grace gave her stilled her questions. 'We will be going shopping tomorrow. You will need a presentation gown – white, of course, with short sleeves, white gloves and a train. You will also wear three white ostrich feathers in your hair.' Grace had paused here and then added, with some reluctance, Victoria thought, 'I have a pearl necklace you can borrow. Pearls are traditional. After that, you will attend all sorts of functions through the Season, the most important one being, of course, Queen Charlotte's ball. Although next year, I hear on the society grapevine, a ball is to be held at Buckingham Palace during Derby week. And you will need all sorts of outfits for the rest of the Season. A whole wardrobe, in fact.'

Now, nothing was said about the cost all this would involve. Victoria wondered why.

Preparations for Victoria's coming out took precedence over everything else, even Christmas, which passed by almost unnoticed. Victoria was adamant, however, that she was going to see Naomi for a long weekend.

'You haven't anything arranged for me for New Year, have you, Mother?'

'No. Why?'

'I would like to visit Miss Gilbert. I haven't seen her since before I went to Switzerland.'

For a moment, Grace seemed to struggle inwardly, then she said, rather ungraciously and sighing pointedly, 'Well, go if you must.'

*

Naomi's cottage was a sanctuary of peace and quiet.

'You have no idea what I'll have to endure this summer,' Victoria told her former governess. 'And the money that's been spent on dresses and outfits that will probably never be worn again would feed a poor family from a city's back streets for a week. It's – it's obscene.'

Naomi chuckled. 'She intends to find you a suitable husband. At least she's finally taking notice of you. Surely that's a bonus, isn't it?'

Victoria pulled a face. 'I'm not sure I want her to find me a husband.' She paused for a moment. She'd not told her mother about Kurt, but now she felt the need to confide in Naomi. She explained, but made light of the brief romance. She didn't want Naomi to think she was heartbroken because, to her surprise, she wasn't. 'And as for Mother taking notice of me now – I'm not sure about that either. I just seem to be doing as I'm told. I mean, for Heaven's sake, I'm nearly twenty.'

'I expect that's why your mother's so anxious for you to take part in the Season. She will regard twenty as being "left on the shelf".'

'No doubt,' Victoria said dryly.

'You'll have a wonderful summer, my dear. Just come and tell me all about it when it's all over.'

'I will,' Victoria said and bit back the remark that she would most likely be going back to Germany then. Perhaps she would be able to fit in a quick visit before she and her friends went back.

The social whirl began and Victoria – to her surprise – found that she enjoyed quite a lot of it.

The presentation at the palace was meant to be the highlight, but for Victoria and her friends the most memorable event was the ball given at Buckingham Palace on the day after Derby Day. Apart from the royal procession into the ballroom, and the procession to supper when they watched the King escort his mother and the Brazilian Ambassador escort Queen Elizabeth, the ball seemed quite an informal affair – just like any other party. The King and Queen danced all night, mingling with their guests, and when the last dance ended at three o'clock in the morning, breakfast was served.

'That's a first,' Pearl commented. Victoria had taken to the woman chosen to be her sponsor at the presentation. She had not expected to like her mother's friend, but she did. Pearl had been a tremendous help, and had accompanied Victoria to many of the Season's occasions. Best of all, she was good fun. They sat together through several race meetings and horse shows, wandered around the Chelsea Flower Show, attended Wimbledon, sitting only yards away from Queen Mary, stood on the side of the River Thames to follow the boat race and watched Test matches at Lords.

After such a hectic schedule, Victoria was thankful when the Season came to an end and she was able to pack her suitcase for her trip to Germany. Although, she had to admit, she had enjoyed most of it – thanks to Pearl's companionship.

'But *still* you haven't found a young man,' her mother accused her. 'Surely there must have been someone. I must have a serious talk with Pearl. She *promised* me she would find you a husband. What a waste of time and effort, to say nothing about what it has cost me. Really, Victoria, I am most disappointed in you.'

Thirty-Six

They were booked into the same hotel where they'd stayed on their previous visit, and had even been allocated the same rooms. In the evening, Kurt and Leon arrived.

Charlotte threw herself into Leon's arms. Although Victoria's greeting to Kurt was a little more circumspect, she was surprised how pleased she was to see him again. Her heart seemed to give a little skip; she had forgotten just how handsome he was. She lifted her face to be kissed chastely on the cheek, but he took hold of her chin and turned her to face him, kissing her firmly on the mouth. 'It has been a long year,' he murmured against her mouth.

'It – it's nice to be back,' Victoria said.

'I have missed you, *meine Liebe*. Now . . .' He turned more briskly towards the others. 'Tonight we will take you all out to dine and then tomorrow we go to Nuremberg. The rally lasts for a week, but Leon and I have decided which are the best days to take you. We will stay there for two nights. We have already booked a hotel, though it was hard to find one.' He smiled. 'Everyone wants to be in Nuremberg just now.'

'How deliciously strong and commanding he is,' Charlotte sighed.

Two days later, they all attended a massive demonstration; aircraft flying overhead in formation, tanks and thousands of marching soldiers, many of them holding flags or banners emblazoned with the swastika. And then they heard an impassioned speech from the Führer himself.

'What's he saying, what's he saying?' Charlotte hissed. 'I can't follow all of it.'

'I'll tell you later,' Victoria whispered. She had to admit, Adolf Hitler was charismatic. He carried his people along on a tide of ardent patriotism and now Victoria could understand why they followed him unquestioningly. But there was just something – something she couldn't quite put into words – that frightened her. His words were uplifting for his countrymen, but nevertheless aggressive. As if he carried years of festering resentment. Earlier in the year, he had marched into Austria proclaiming it to be a federal state of Germany. Now, watching this amazing display of strength, Victoria wondered where it would end. The floodlit demonstration went on until late into the night, with the crowds cheering themselves hoarse as their leader drove through the throng to the sound of patriotic songs, standing up in the back of an open-topped car.

'Is he not glorious?' Leon said, when they returned tired and hungry to the hotel. 'You see how his people love him. They will follow him to the ends of the earth.'

'What about you and Kurt,' Constance asked softly, 'will you follow him blindly too?'

A flash of anger crossed Kurt's face. 'It is not "blind", *Fräulein*. He will lead us all to greatness.'

When they returned to Berlin two days later, Georgina said, 'I'm not really sure I want to stay any longer. I found that rally rather disturbing.'

'Me too,' Constance agreed and then, with a sigh, glanced at Victoria and Charlotte. 'But I expect you two would like to stay, wouldn't you?'

'Yes, definitely,' Charlotte said firmly, though Victoria didn't answer. She was torn. She liked Kurt; he was the first man to show a romantic interest in her. Not one of the numerous young men she had met during the Season had shown half the tenderness towards her that Kurt had. Actually, she felt rather a failure when she heard that Constance had received three proposals and Georgina two during the Season, although neither had accepted any of them. Charlotte had been unforthcoming about any romances, declaring that her heart belonged to Leon.

'We'll stay a little longer,' Constance said, 'if you don't mind, Lady G. After what we've witnessed, I rather want to get a bit more information to take back, if I can.'

Charlotte's lip curled. 'Oh, quite the spy, aren't you?'

'Not at all. There's nothing clandestine about what I'm doing. Come on, don't let's argue. Let's go out and see a bit more of the city. There's still a lot we haven't seen. And that's not information-gathering – just seeing a beautiful city.'

Their visit turned into weeks and then, surprisingly, into months and almost before they realized it, it was the beginning of November.

'You know,' Constance remarked, 'we're all incredibly lucky to have such indulgent parents who are allowing us to stay here so long.'

Victoria said nothing. She was sure her mother's motives were more far-reaching than that; all Grace wanted was for her daughter to gain experiences which would attract a suitable husband. Victoria smiled to herself. She was, nevertheless, enjoying herself. Indeed, they were all enjoying themselves; there was so much to see in Berlin, and Leon and Kurt frequently took them on day trips into the countryside in the big car they'd hired once again.

And then it all ended abruptly. One evening at the very beginning of November, Kurt and Leon arrived at the hotel to take the four girls out to dinner. Victoria's mouth dropped open when she saw them and, beside her, she heard gasps of surprise from Constance and Georgina. Charlotte, however, rushed towards the two young men. 'Oh, how handsome you both look.'

Leon and Kurt were dressed in uniform: brown jackets with swastika armbands, brown trousers and caps, and black knee-length boots.

'My God,' Constance breathed. 'They've joined Hitler's storm troopers.'

'I rather think,' Georgina said softly, 'that we should be making tracks for home, girls.'

'Oh I agree, but let's play it carefully in front of them because I somehow think we're going to have

303

a problem with Charlotte.' Constance glanced at Victoria, but said no more.

They went out to dinner as planned, but now they were very aware of the glances from the other diners as they sat with two members of the Nazi Party's military wing. And as they walked back to the hotel, still in their company, they saw people scuttling quickly past them or fading into the shadows at their approach.

As the two young men bade their farewells, Kurt whispered to Victoria, 'You should stay in your hotel in the evenings if we are not with you. I may not see you for a couple of nights. We are going to be – busy.'

'Shall we go out tonight to that same restaurant where the boys took us?' Charlotte said the following evening.

'Kurt said we shouldn't go out without them,' Victoria said.

'Why?' Constance asked, but Victoria only shrugged.

Charlotte laughed out loud. 'I know why. They don't want four pretty *Fräuleins* let loose in the city. Someone might run off with us.'

'We'll be all right, if we stick together. No going off on your own, Charlotte,' Georgina said firmly.

They found the restaurant easily enough, having been there several times with Kurt and Leon. They knew the way even in the dark. Recognized by the waiter, they were served the best food and treated with respect. As they were finishing their pudding, the waiter approached their table, looking harassed.

'I will have to ask you to leave,' he said, glancing around him anxiously.

'Why? What have we done?' Victoria asked him in German.

'Nothing, *Fräulein*, nothing at all. But we have heard that there is trouble in the streets. We wish to close and board up the windows.'

'Board up the windows?' Victoria repeated. 'Why? What's happening?'

'Please, do not ask. Just – just go. You need not pay the bill.'

'Of course we'll pay you,' Constance said, standing up. 'We wouldn't dream of leaving without paying. How much is it?'

With another nervous glance around him at other diners who were also being asked to leave by other waiters, he named a sum and took the money Constance held out to him.

'Please – keep the change. We're going.'

They stepped into the street and stood for a moment. In the distance they heard the sound of breaking glass, of cries and shouts and running feet coming closer to where they were standing. Other diners from the restaurant, leaving too, pushed past them.

'Get home, ladies,' one of them said in broken English. 'As quickly as you can.'

'Come on,' Georgina said, taking charge. 'Take my hand, Charlotte. Connie, you take Victoria's. I don't know what's happening, but it sounds serious. Stick together, if we can, but we'll meet back at the hotel if we get separated.'

And then they began to run up the street, but their way back to the hotel was towards the noise, not away from it.

The sound of breaking glass grew closer and when they turned a corner, they saw figures looming up in the darkness with batons raised and smashing every window in sight; shops, houses – even the synagogue standing at the end of the street was being attacked.

Now the girls clutched each other as they stared in horror at the scene before them. People were crying and screaming; men, women and even children. And then Victoria too let out a cry as she saw a figure she recognized. The dark shape of Kurt, dressed in his uniform, raised his baton and brought it down across the shoulders of an old man who fell to the ground. She started forward as if to help the injured man, but Constance held her fast. 'No, Vicky. Leave it. It's nothing to do with us.'

'But—'

'Quick, down this side road,' Georgina said. 'I recognize it. The hotel's in the next street.'

And then, with one last horrified glance at what was happening, they fled into the darkness.

Thirty-Seven

They knocked and banged on the hotel door.

'Why is it locked?' Charlotte said. 'They don't usually lock it this early?'

'Because of the trouble in the nearby streets, I expect,' Georgina said. She banged on the door again. 'Oh, come on, do open up.'

In the distance, they could still hear the sound of windows being shattered and people screaming and crying.

At last they heard someone come to the other side of the door.

Georgina put her mouth close to the keyhole and shouted. 'Let us in. It's the girls from rooms nineteen and twenty.'

There was a rattle on the other side and the door opened tentatively. 'Are you on your own?'

'Just the four of us who are staying here.'

The door opened wider. 'We don't want your soldier friends here,' the porter said as he finally let them in. 'There's trouble.'

'We know. We've just seen it. Do you know what's happening?'

'They're smashing up houses and shops that belong to Jews.'

'Why?'

The man avoided meeting her gaze, shrugged and turned away. 'I will get you all a drink.'

'Thanks. We need it.'

They sat for a while in the bar trying to calm down, but it was difficult when they could still hear the commotion outside. It seemed to be coming closer.

'Let's go upstairs,' Constance said. 'I think the barman wants to close up and put all the lights out. We'll take our drinks with us.'

They gathered in the room which Georgina and Charlotte shared, but said very little to each other. They could still hear the uproar outside and every sound made them shudder.

'I'm going to bed,' Constance said. 'I don't expect any of us will sleep, but we ought to try.' She and Victoria went to their own room and got ready for bed, neither speaking very much; they were appalled at what was still happening just below their windows.

The following morning as they were dressing, Constance said softly, 'Vicky, we have to leave. We have to get out of here. You do realize that, don't you?'

Victoria was still reeling from the sight of Kurt in the uniform of the storm troopers – the 'Brownshirts', as they were nicknamed.

'I know,' she said huskily. She had hardly slept, but had lain awake, listening to the sounds of destruction that went on for most of the night. Only in the early hours did the noise stop.

Victoria was distraught. She thought she had found someone who really loved her, but she could not reconcile the handsome, courteous man who had held her close when they danced and kissed her gently when they said goodnight with the frightening figure in a threatening uniform, battering a helpless old man. She sighed heavily. 'I don't think Butterfly will agree to leave.'

'She must,' Constance said grimly. 'None of us ought to stay here any longer. Let's go and talk to the others.'

They found Georgina alone in the bedroom next door.

'Where's Butterfly?' Constance asked.

'In the bathroom at the end of the corridor, I think.'

'We need to leave as soon as we can,' Constance said.

Georgina nodded. 'Agreed. I'll go to the station right now and get four tickets.'

'What about your breakfast?'

'I'll get something when I get back. I don't think this ought to wait.'

'Where are we heading?' Constance asked.

'Anywhere as long as it's out of Germany, but I'm going to try for Paris first.'

'If you have any problems, try the British Embassy,' Constance said.

'I don't think I will have. I've got all my identity papers with me.'

'Won't you need ours?'

Georgina hesitated. 'I'll try without first. No doubt they'll check them all before we board the train anyway.'

'Do you want me to come with you?'

309

Georgina glanced meaningfully at Victoria. 'No, Connie, you stay here with Vicky.'

Victoria looked up. 'Don't worry. I'm not going to do anything stupid like trying to find Kurt to say goodbye. I know you're right. We've got to go and the sooner the better. Get tickets for as soon as you can, Lady G.'

'What about Butterfly? Will she try to see Leon again?'

'More than likely,' Constance said dryly. 'We'll just have to keep a sharp eye on her. While you go to the station, Vicky and I will explain things to her.'

'Good luck with that, then.'

A few minutes after Georgina had left, Charlotte returned. 'Where's Lady G gone?'

Constance and Victoria exchanged a glance.

Taking a deep breath, Victoria said, 'She's gone to the station to get train tickets for us all. We're going home, Butterfly.'

'I'm not. I want to see Leon again. He's promised to show me the ruins of the Reichstag that was burnt down about four or five years ago.'

'There'll be a lot more ruins to look at tomorrow if what we saw last night is anything to go by.'

'Whatever do you mean?'

'You saw it. All those soldiers smashing windows and hitting people.'

'Oh, nonsense,' Charlotte scoffed. 'They weren't soldiers. It was just some hooligans. They'll have them here just the same as anywhere else.'

Constance sighed and murmured, '"There is none so blind as those who will not see."'

310

'Charlotte,' Victoria began. The use of her proper name rather than the fun nickname made Charlotte's eyes widen. 'One of those causing the destruction was Kurt.'

Charlotte stared at her for a long moment. 'I don't believe you. You're making it up just to frighten me and to get me to agree to go home. Well, it's not going to work. And don't try telling me that you saw Leon out there last night, because you didn't. I know you didn't.'

'No,' Victoria said flatly, 'no, I didn't see Leon, but I did see Kurt. I saw him hit an old man across the back. The man fell down and didn't get up again. And—' She was seeing the picture in her mind like a film being played over and over again. Her breath caught on a sob as she added, 'And Kurt just stepped over him and left him there.'

She didn't think she would ever forget the sight for as long as she lived.

Georgina bought the tickets without any trouble.

'I couldn't get anything for today or tomorrow. The earliest I could get is the day after tomorrow, leaving early in the morning.'

They spent an uncomfortable day arguing with Charlotte, who wanted to go out to find Leon. She refused to do her packing. 'I'm going nowhere until I've seen Leon again.'

'Then I'll do it,' Georgina said, dragging their suitcases from the bottom of the wardrobe and flinging open drawers.

The hours crawled by and the atmosphere between

the four friends was tense. They were all relieved when it was time to go to bed, though they spent a second restless night, falling into a fitful sleep as dawn broke. But there was no need for them to be up early; they weren't travelling until the next day. Somehow, they would have to keep a tight rein on Charlotte for another whole day. As Georgina rolled out of bed, rubbing her eyes, she glanced at the bedside clock.

'Come on, Butterfly. Rise and shine. It's five past nine. We'd better hurry or we won't get any breakfast.' She turned to look at the mound beneath the clothes on the other bed. 'Charlotte – come on.'

With a sigh she put her hand on what she thought was Charlotte's shoulder, but it was soft and yielded to her touch. She grasped the bedclothes and flung them back. Two pillows lay where Charlotte should be.

'Oh no. *Now* what has she done?'

She checked the bathroom first, but knew already that it was hopeless. Then she rapped sharply on the other bedroom door.

'Come in,' a sleepy voice said and Georgina opened the door.

'She's gone.'

Constance and Victoria both sat up. 'What d'you mean? Gone?'

'Charlotte. She's not in her bed. She must have got dressed and crept out. And, yes, I've checked the bathroom. She meant it because she left two pillows in her bed to look like it was her.'

'Oh Lord, no.'

They both got out of bed and began to dress.

'Let's have breakfast first,' Georgina said, calming down a little now. 'She can't have gone far. All her things are still here.'

'That's a relief. You're right. We'll have breakfast and decide what to do.'

As they ate, they discussed the best plan of action.

'I think one of us should stay here,' Constance suggested. 'Probably you, Lady G, in case she comes back to collect her clothes and to go to stay with Leon.'

'No doubt she's gone to find him to ask him that very question,' Georgina said.

Victoria toyed with her food, only half listening to what the other two were saying. She was still reeling with shock at the sights she had witnessed. And the sight of Kurt's menacing shadow looming over the man on the ground played over and over again in her mind. She felt as if her heart was breaking.

'Where do we start looking?' Georgina said. 'We've no idea where Leon lives, have we?'

Constance shook her head.

Victoria pulled in a deep breath and tried to concentrate, tried to be helpful. 'She said last night that Leon wanted to show her the ruins of the Reichstag that was burnt down a while back.'

'Right, at least that's a start,' Constance said. 'If you've finished, Vicky, we'll go now. Will you stay here, Lady G, in case she comes back?'

Georgina nodded.

'If we do find her, what excuse are we going to

make for dragging her away?' Victoria asked as they fetched their coats from their room. 'We don't want Leon to guess what we're doing. He'll tell Kurt and he's already said he wants to keep me here.'

Constance's eyebrows rose. It must be more serious between Victoria and Kurt than she'd realized. Softly, she asked, 'Are those the exact words he used? That he "wants to keep you here"?'

Victoria nodded.

'That sounds very possessive. Almost like a veiled threat, if you ask me.' When Victoria didn't say anything, Constance added, 'And do you want to stay?'

Victoria pressed her lips together and tears filled her eyes. This more than anything touched Constance. She had never, in all the years she had known her, seen Victoria cry.

'My – my heart says, "yes, I do", but my head says "get out and get out now".'

'And which is going to win?' Constance held her breath as she waited for her friend's reply.

Victoria met Constance's worried gaze. Through her tears, she gave a weak smile. 'Oh, my head, of course.'

Relieved, Constance squeezed her arm before saying, 'Come on, let's go and find her, but I don't think she's going to be as sensible as you.'

They left the hotel and went to where the fire-damaged ruins of the Reichstag stood. They searched around the perimeter, but could see no sign of either Leon or Charlotte.

'They wouldn't go inside, would they?'

'No telling with that pair, if they wanted a bit of privacy.'

Gingerly, they stepped inside the tumbledown walls. It took them an hour searching carefully until they came to the far end of the building.

'There, look. Under that archway.'

Victoria followed the line of Constance's pointing finger to see Charlotte and Leon wrapped in each other's arms. Together, keeping a wary eye on the ruins above their heads, they crunched across the debris-strewn ground. 'Are they going to rebuild this?' Victoria asked. 'It must have been a magnificent building.'

'I really don't know,' Constance said, absently, her whole focus being on reaching Charlotte and extracting her from Leon's clutches.

At the sound of their voices, Charlotte turned towards them, but she did not move out of his embrace. He, too, glanced round and his anger, even from some distance away, was plain to see.

As they drew closer, Leon said sarcastically, 'Here are your faithful bloodhounds making sure I am not deflowering the perfect English rose.'

He's changed, Victoria thought. Where had the friendly, jovial young man they had met on the ski slopes gone? Seeing him wearing a uniform of the Third Reich, a little voice inside her whispered, *He's just like Kurt.*

'Sorry, don't mean to spoil your fun, you two,' Constance said cheerily. 'We didn't know you were together. We were just worried Charlotte might have got lost.'

Charlotte glowered at them. 'How did you know where to find me?'

'We didn't,' Constance said glibly. She was not above lying if the situation warranted it. 'We've been looking for you all morning.'

'Well, you needn't have bothered. I'm quite safe.'

Victoria would have liked to have argued that point, but she kept quiet.

'I have to go on duty later, anyway,' Leon said. 'I'll see her safely back to the hotel. I promise.'

Now he smiled, but to Victoria it was no longer the generous, fun-loving smile she believed she'd seen when they'd first met. Now it looked more like a tiger who had caught his prey.

Constance shrugged. 'That's fine. See you later, then, Charlotte.' She turned, linked her arm casually through Victoria's, and they began to walk away. As if reading her mind, Constance muttered, 'Leave it, Vicky. We don't want him to suspect anything.'

'But what if he doesn't bring her back?'

'I think he will. Besides, if he really is going playing soldiers, she'll have nothing else to do. She'll find her own way back to the hotel.'

'I hope so,' Victoria whispered fervently.

When they got back to the hotel, Georgina asked at once, 'No Charlotte?'

'We found her,' Constance told her. 'She's with Leon.'

'And she wouldn't leave him.'

'We had to play it very casually or he might have smelt a rat.'

'He's not the nice young man he was,' Victoria said sadly. 'He's changed. Just like Kurt has.'

'He's promised to bring her back to the hotel before he goes on duty later.'

'Let's just hope he does,' Georgina said. 'Because I think there could be trouble again tonight.'

The three girls waited and waited and, with each passing hour, they became more and more anxious about their friend.

'She's a silly girl in many ways,' Constance said, 'but I really am quite fond of her.'

Georgina glanced at Victoria. 'We know you really like Kurt, but at least you're seeing common sense.'

'He's not the man I thought he was and this is not the country I'd hoped it would be.'

'As soon as we get home,' Constance said, 'I'm going straight to see my father to tell him all that we've seen.'

'If you need us to come with you, just let us know,' Georgina said. 'I expect my father will be interested too. After all, he sits in the House of Lords.'

And still they waited.

Thirty-Eight

It was dark by the time Charlotte arrived back, thankfully on her own. The other three had gone down to dinner, but none of them had really felt much like eating.

'Where have you been?' Georgina asked sharply.

'With Leon. Didn't the others tell you?'

'Yes . . .' Georgina tapped at her wristwatch. 'But we didn't think you'd be this late. You've missed dinner.'

'I had it with Leon. He took me to this lovely little restaurant. We should try it—'

'We're not trying anything,' Constance snapped. 'We're going home tomorrow. *All* of us.'

Charlotte gaped at her. 'Well, I'm not. I'm staying here with Leon.' She glanced at Victoria. 'Don't you want to stay with Kurt?'

'I'll be honest with you – with all of you. Yes, I'd love to stay with Kurt. In fact, I'd like nothing better. But it'd have to be with the man I first met. I don't like what he's become, Charlotte. I don't like what's happening in this country either. It – it frightens me. I want to go home. We all do.'

'I don't.'

'Well, I'm sorry,' Georgina said firmly, 'but you're coming with us.'

'No, I'm not. You can't make me—'

'Yes, we can.'

'How? Are you going to drag me forcibly to the railway station?'

'If we have to – yes.'

'I've already got all your travel paperwork in my safekeeping,' Georgina said.

'And I've packed your clothes,' Victoria added. 'We're leaving quite early in the morning.'

'You've no right—'

'Look,' Constance said, taking her arm and leading her to the sofa set at one side of the rather large hotel room which she and Victoria shared. 'Please let's just talk this through calmly.'

'Calmly? You expect me to be calm when you're dragging me away from the man I love, from the man I'm going to marry?'

'*Marry!*' the other three chorused.

'Oh Lord,' Georgina groaned, 'this has gone further than I thought.'

'You haven't done anything stupid, have you?'

'What d'you mean?'

'Well, like sleeping with him?'

Charlotte blushed. 'No, I haven't, but—' She bit her lip. 'But I came close to giving in. He – he wants me to stay here and marry him. He—' She hesitated and then hung her head and finished in a whisper, 'He says I'd be safe if I was married to him.'

'Safe?' Constance almost squeaked. 'Is that what he said? He actually said the word "safe"?' Taking a deep breath to calm herself she added, 'And why do you think he said that?'

319

Charlotte shrugged, but now they could see that doubt was creeping into her eyes. 'The Germans don't like foreigners much, do they? Though Leon says they don't mind the British. I could soon brush up on the language.' She glanced at Victoria. 'I wish I'd taken it at school now.' She paused and then added, 'He'd have to get permission to marry me, though.'

'Permission?' Constance was shocked. 'Who from?'

'His superiors.'

'Doesn't that tell you something?'

'Why should it? We have to get permission from our parents to marry when we're still under twenty-one, so why shouldn't he have to ask his superiors?' She frowned. 'Don't the military in Britain have to ask permission?'

'I really have no idea.'

'And do you really think your parents are going to agree to it?' Constance said quietly.

'If they don't, then I'll wait until I'm of age. I've only got a few months to wait.'

'What you do when you get home will be none of our business,' Georgina said. She was beginning to lose patience.

'Actually, I think it still will be,' Constance said. 'We're her friends and Celia told me that when she went to stay at Butterfly's home that time when she couldn't get back to Singapore, they were very kind to her. Butterfly's parents, she said, were – are – lovely people.'

Georgina sighed. 'I suppose you're right.' Then turning to Charlotte she added, 'But you just make me so mad. Can't you feel the tension in the air? There's something – something . . .'

She sought the right word and Victoria supplied it: 'Menacing.'

'Yes, yes, that's it, Vicky. Something menacing in the air.'

'Now you're being silly.'

'No, she's not,' Constance joined in. 'Are you really telling me everything we've seen while we've been here – that huge rally at Nuremberg and then that destruction the other night – that it doesn't tell you anything?'

'All I see is a nation which was crippled by the last war,' Charlotte said doggedly, 'which was on its knees and treated harshly by the Treaty of Versailles, and whose people have found a man they can believe in, a man who has given them back their national pride and lifted them out of despair and ruin.'

'That sounds like Leon talking,' Georgina said.

'It's certainly how Kurt talks,' Victoria murmured.

'And all those thousands of soldiers . . .' Constance said.

'Marching with pride for their country,' Charlotte tried to interrupt, but Constance went on.

'The weaponry, the tanks, the aircraft, the – the *display* of strength. And Adolf Hitler is calling for *lebensraum* – living space. Where's he going to get it from?' Ominously, she added, 'And, more importantly, how?'

Charlotte frowned. 'I don't understand what you mean.'

Patiently, as if explaining to a child, Constance

said, 'If you want more living space for your people, how are you going to get it?' Still, Charlotte appeared mystified. 'Oh, come on, Butterfly. You're a clever girl. Think!'

Slowly, as if the clouds were clearing, she said, 'I suppose you get it by extending your borders.'

'And how do you do that?'

'By – taking it from neighbouring countries.'

'And do you think they're going to give up their territory easily?'

'But some of it is Germany's by rights. Leon said that the Sudetenland is populated by German-speaking people. It *should* be theirs.'

'My word, we have been having a history lesson, haven't we?' Georgina said.

'Besides,' Charlotte was not ready to capitulate yet, 'our Prime Minister came here in September, didn't he? He made an agreement with Hitler. "Peace for our time," he said. There's not going to be a war between us and Germany.'

'I wouldn't hold your breath,' Constance muttered. 'I don't think that agreement is worth the paper it's written on.'

'Well, I'm sorry. You three go home if you want to, but I'm not coming. And that's my final word.'

She flounced out of the room Constance and Victoria shared and into the one next door.

'I'd better go too,' Georgina said. 'I'll try to talk some sense into her, but it's not looking promising. And I don't want her sneaking off again.'

'Good luck,' the others said grimly.

But when Georgina went into their bedroom, Charlotte was already in bed. She refused to talk to Georgina at all. She lay down and turned her back on her friend.

Thirty-Nine

Georgina got ready for bed, but sleep was impossible. She dozed occasionally but was so afraid that Charlotte would disappear again in the night and that they wouldn't be able to find her in the morning in time for the train on which they were now all booked to travel. When she gave up trying to sleep at all at about six o'clock, she went down the corridor to the bathroom and sluiced her face. Already she had a headache, but at least Charlotte was still in her bed, snoring gently. She wondered how the girl could sleep so soundly when she was the cause of so much anxiety to her friends.

At seven o'clock she shook her gently. 'Come on, Butterfly. It's time you were getting up.'

Charlotte grunted and rolled over, pulling the bedclothes up around her ears. 'I'm not coming. I told you.'

For a moment, Georgina stood looking down at her. Then anger surged through her and with an ominous growl that was totally unlike her normally placid nature, she heaved the mattress up and tipped Charlotte out of the bed onto the floor.

The girl gave a squeal of shock, rather than of

injury. She fought her way out of the tangle of bedclothes. 'Whatever did you do that for?'

'Because we're leaving in a couple of hours and you are coming with us.'

'No, I'm not, I –'

'Yes, you are. We should never have come back here. We've put ourselves in awful danger.'

Charlotte laughed. 'Now you're being melodramatic. Do you really think that Kurt and Leon would let anything happen to any of us?'

'They'd be powerless to stop it.' She leaned towards Charlotte to emphasize her point. 'They couldn't stop all that destruction the other night, could they?'

Charlotte stared at her and then said, 'Obviously they didn't want to, if what Vicky said is true.'

'Then that's worse than ever. Do you really want to have anything to do with a man who condones that sort of – of violence?'

'They were only following orders as any good soldier should.'

'Oh yes, that's always the excuse, isn't it?' Georgina said sarcastically. 'You can get away with anything if you're "obeying orders".'

The two girls glared at each other; Georgina was angry, Charlotte mutinous. Where it would have ended, neither of them knew, as a knock at the door came at that moment. Without waiting for a reply, Constance and Victoria walked in.

'Is she ready? It's time we were having a quick breakfast and then leaving. We don't want to miss that train. We might not get on another.'

The two of them now saw that Charlotte was in her nightclothes.

'Is she still refusing to come?' Victoria asked.

'Yes, and now it's time for the rough stuff,' Georgina said. 'Vicky, find her clothes – Connie, pack the rest of her suitcase.'

With a strength that none of them knew she possessed, Georgina hauled Charlotte to her feet and began to pull her nightdress over her head.

'What do – you – think . . . ?' Charlotte began but her protests were futile.

With a struggle, the three of them got her into her clothes.

'I need the bathroom. I haven't washed or—'

'You should have thought of that before.'

'But I need to—'

'I'll go with her,' Victoria said.

'You'll have to go in with her, else she'll lock the door and we won't be able to get her out.'

'You'll do no such thing.'

'Yes, I will. Come on, if you're that desperate.'

Victoria gripped her arm and almost frogmarched her down the landing to the communal bathroom. Luckily, it was vacant.

'You're not to come in.'

'Yes, I am. I'll turn my back.'

A few minutes later, they returned to the bedroom where Constance and Georgina were waiting.

'Right – ready now? You've delayed us so much, Charlotte, we've no time for breakfast.'

'No, I'm *not* ready. I want to say goodbye to Leon.' She turned with one last, desperate plea to Victoria.

'Vicky, surely you don't want to go without saying goodbye to Kurt?'

For a brief moment, tears filled Victoria's eyes. 'Of course I'd like to, but it's just not – sensible. He – they'd – try to stop us.'

'And they'd probably manage it,' Constance muttered darkly. 'Haven't you noticed that everyone obeys the soldiers?'

Georgina and Constance each took hold of one of Charlotte's arms. They carried their own suitcases in their other hands.

'Can you manage her suitcase as well as your own, Vicky?'

Victoria nodded and picked up both suitcases and, before her resolve failed her, she muttered, 'Let's go.'

They checked out of the hotel and then walked down the road towards the railway station. It was the street where they'd seen the destruction two nights ago. Broken glass still littered the ground and the shops had obviously been looted; there was nothing left on display in the windows. Men, women and children moved disconsolately amongst the wreckage trying to salvage anything they could. Some carried small suitcases.

Victoria halted as she glanced about her.

'What is it?' Georgina asked, stopping too.

'Look,' Victoria whispered. 'Look at the names above the doors. I didn't believe what the barman said, but he was right. They're – they're all Jewish shops. Every one that's been damaged is Jewish.'

'And they've daubed the Star of David on the doors.'

They walked on. Further down the street, two soldiers in brown shirts were coming towards them.

Charlotte drew in a breath. 'Is it . . . ?' she began.

'No, it isn't,' Georgina said curtly. 'Come on. Keep moving.'

But as they passed the soldiers, they saw them approach an old woman. They began pushing her backwards and forwards between them until she fell down. As she lay helpless on the ground, one of the soldiers aimed a vicious kick at her. They moved on, laughing, and left her lying there in the road. No one in the street went to her aid. They had all turned away, ignoring what was happening.

Victoria started towards the old woman, but Georgina hissed, 'Leave it, Vicky. We can't help. If you go near her, they'll likely arrest you.'

'But—' Victoria began.

'She's right, Vicky,' Constance said. 'For God's sake, let's get out of here.'

They almost ran the rest of the way to the railway station. When they arrived, they stared about them in shock. The platform was crowded with people and long lines of children, each with a label around their neck, were waiting patiently to board the train. One or two little girls were clinging to their mothers and crying piteously.

'What's happening?' Charlotte's voice was shaky. 'Where are they all going?'

'They're escaping,' Georgina said grimly and added, baldly, 'They're Jewish children.'

'But – but *why*?'

'Oh my.' Georgina rolled her eyes. 'Are you thick, or what? You've just seen what's happened to their homes and their shops – their livelihoods. They're being attacked physically too. The Nazis are persecuting the Jews. God knows why, I don't understand it – but they are. And like it or not, your precious Leon is one of those doing it.'

Victoria bit her lip, but said nothing. She felt a leaden weight in her chest. It was the greatest sadness of her young life to have to admit what the man she thought she'd loved was really like.

Still, Charlotte was not ready to accept what her friend was saying. 'But not *children*. Leon would never hurt children.'

'But he *would* hit old men and women,' Constance muttered.

'Maybe he doesn't want to – deep down,' Georgina acknowledged in a rare moment of generosity towards him. 'But, like you said earlier, he's obeying orders. To be fair, he can't do anything else.'

'Why? What d'you mean?'

'Because if he *dis*obeyed, he'd be in serious trouble himself.'

Charlotte's eyes were suddenly wide with terror. 'Oh, you don't mean . . . ?'

'Yes, I do. Now let's get on this train. I have our tickets.'

'But these children – we can't let them stay here if they're in such danger.'

Georgina stared at her for a moment. Were they really getting through to Charlotte at last?

Charlotte twisted herself free from the restraining

grip of both Georgina and Constance, who let out a startled 'Oh!' But instead of running away, back out of the station as they'd feared she might, Charlotte approached one of the little girls hanging on to her mother's skirts. She was crying bitterly and tears streamed down the woman's face too.

'Can I help you?'

The woman spoke in rapid German. 'She must get on the train. The children must go without their parents. She must get to safety.'

'Where is she going?' Charlotte asked.

'To England. She is going to Hull. There is someone there who will take her in.'

'Is she on her own?'

'No, no. She has no brothers or sisters, but there are other children travelling with her to the same place. She must stay with them.'

Smiling down at her, Charlotte held out her hand to the little girl. 'Let's get you onto the train with your friends. You don't want to get separated from them.'

The mother prised the child's clinging hands from her and gave her a little push. Then she turned and hurried away through the throng.

The girl screamed, '*Mutti!*' and tried to pull away, but Charlotte held her fast.

'Come,' she said gently. 'Your mother wants you to get on the train. Don't upset her. Do as she asks you.'

At last Charlotte managed to persuade the child to climb into the train. She made sure the little girl was sitting with other children she knew and then took a seat in the same carriage where she could watch over her.

Constance, Georgina and Victoria stowed their suitcases and sat down with her.

'Are we supposed to be here?' Constance asked worriedly. 'Maybe they want this carriage just for the children.'

'I'm not letting her out of my sight until the train starts to move.'

'We could say the same about you,' Constance murmured. Charlotte's only reply was to glare at her and then turn her attention back to the little girl.

It seemed an age before the train began to move and they could all breathe a sigh of relief. At every station on their way to Paris, especially if they had to change trains, Charlotte hurried to the girl's side and held her hand, chatting to her.

'I'm just so worried she's going to disappear and try to get a train back to Berlin,' Constance muttered. 'I don't trust her.'

'I've still got her suitcase,' Victoria said.

'And I've still got all her paperwork,' Georgina said. 'I really don't think she can.'

Once they were settled and on their way again, Charlotte returned to her seat and whispered to the others, 'There don't seem to be any grown-ups travelling with them.'

'There are a couple of older children – a boy and a girl. They're about fourteen, I'd say,' Victoria said. From where they were sitting, she had been watching all the children. 'Poor little scraps,' she murmured.

As they neared London on the final leg of their

journey, Constance said, 'I want you all to come with me to meet my father. The sooner he hears about all we've seen, the better. Will you do that?'

'Of course,' Georgina and Victoria said as one, but Charlotte looked wary. With a sigh she said, 'I suppose you're going to tell him all about – about me.'

The other three exchanged a glance before Georgina said, 'Actually, we're not. What happened in Berlin between you and Leon will stay there. I know you're angry with us for dragging you away, but we're very fond of you and we feared for your safety and what would happen to you if we left you there.' She sighed heavily. 'We can't, of course, stop you going back if you're determined to be with him, but I – all of us – really hope you won't.'

Charlotte raised her head and looked at the three of them in turn. Slowly, she said, 'No, I won't be going back. You've made me see sense. I'm heart-broken, I won't deny that, but I know you're right.'

'What made you change your mind?' Victoria asked gently, perhaps the only one amongst them who really understood how Charlotte was feeling.

'The children,' Charlotte said simply. 'Being sent away from their families, their home, their country. How can that be happening? Who's doing it? *Why* are they doing it?'

It was a question none of the other three could answer.

Forty

'Oh, so you're back,' Grace greeted her daughter.

'I am, Mother. And how are you?'

'I'm well, thank you. Are you?' The last two words seemed to be uttered grudgingly, as though she didn't really care one way or the other how Victoria was. She didn't even wait for a reply before saying, 'I'll ring for afternoon tea. I want to talk to you. Come down when you've changed from your travelling clothes. Rose will see to your unpacking.'

Grace turned, went into the drawing room and closed the door behind her.

The welcome from Mrs Beddows and Rose was as warm as her mother's had been cold.

'Oh, it's so good to see you safely back, miss. Here, sit down. I'll make tea for us . . .'

'That'd be lovely, Mrs Beddows, but Mother wants me to take tea with her in the drawing room.'

Mrs Beddows's mouth formed a round 'oh' but all she said was, 'Then you'd best look quick and get out of those clothes. Rose, set the tray.'

Twenty minutes later, Victoria was sitting on the opposite side of the marble fireplace to her mother whilst Grace poured tea and Rose handed round the small fancy cakes.

'That will be all, Rose,' Grace said. The girl bobbed a curtsy and, out of sight of her mistress, winked at Victoria as she left the room.

'So, now you have got all your gallivanting out of your system – at least I hope you have – are you going to settle down and do what I wanted you to do last year? Find yourself a suitable husband? I just hope you haven't left it too late and that all the eligible ones haven't been snapped up in your absence. I see the Honourable Frederick Jones has become engaged to Cynthia Giles. I had high hopes of him for you.'

'Freddie Jones – delightful though he is – is not for me, Mother.'

Grace's brow darkened. 'If you're going to be so choosey, you'll find yourself left on the shelf – an old maid. And just remember, I'm not prepared to support you after you reach your majority. By now you should be safely married and taking your place in society alongside a husband with wealth and position. Why do you think all this money has been spent on your education?'

Victoria ignored her mother's last remarks. Instead she said, 'I'll have my own allowance when I'm twenty-one, won't I? That's what you've always told me.'

'Pah! And how far do you think that will go? A paltry sum like that will scarcely keep you in hat pins. It certainly won't allow you to move in the circles you ought to be moving in.'

'Then I'd better see about earning my own living.'

'What!' Grace's cheeks turned a tinge of bright pink. 'I won't hear of such a thing. No daughter of mine is going to get a *job*. What is the world coming to?'

'The world, Mother, is facing a very uncertain future.'

'What on earth are you talking about?'

'Don't you and your friends ever talk politics over those expensive luncheons, or is the talk confined to the latest fashions, hats and hairstyles?'

'Victoria – how dare you speak to me like that? Of course we take a keen interest in world affairs, but we put our faith in our Prime Minister. He secured peace for our time back in September.'

'I don't think Mr Hitler has any intention of sticking to his promise on that famous piece of paper.'

'Oh and I suppose whilst you've been in Germany you've had an audience with the chancellor and been privy to all his aspirations.'

'No, Mother, of course not,' Victoria said calmly, 'but I have witnessed things that I would rather not have seen. Things that have disturbed me. In fact, my friends and I have an appointment tomorrow morning to see—' For a moment Victoria hesitated. She realized that it was perhaps not such a good idea to tell her mother where she was going, so she finished lamely, 'Someone.'

'And these friends, just who are they?'

'Three girls I was at school with. Constance, Charlotte – I was at Miss Taylor's with them – and then we met Lady Georgina at the finishing school in Switzerland.'

'*Lady* Georgina? Who is she exactly?'

'She's Lady Georgina Haig. That's all I know.'

'What? Do you mean you haven't even asked her about her background, who her family are?'

Victoria met her mother's glare calmly. 'No. I find it better not to ask questions.'

As if sensing the unspoken words – that if Victoria were to ask questions of others, they would quite naturally ask her about her family life – Grace changed the direction of her questioning slightly. 'And they've all been to Germany too?'

'Yes. I did tell you before I left.'

'So you're going to keep in touch with them?'

'Yes.'

'Even Lady Georgina?'

'Yes, Mother.'

'Well, that's something, I suppose.' Grace rose from her chair. 'If you mix in the same circles as her, perhaps you will meet someone.' Grace's tone did not sound too hopeful. She was beginning to realize – much to her disgust – that her daughter was developing a mind – and perhaps even a will – of her own. 'I am going out to dinner tonight. Mrs Beddows will prepare you something on a tray.' She paused before saying stiffly, 'You will see that I have made your old schoolroom into a sitting room for you where you can entertain your friends if you wish, though I don't want hordes of rowdy young people tramping in and out of the house at all hours. But you may invite people of decorum like Lady Georgina.'

Victoria was surprised – shocked even – but she managed to say, 'Thank you, Mother.'

Grace shrugged. 'Well, it seems I have to do something to encourage you to mix with the right people.'

Although she fully intended to keep in touch with her three friends, there was only one person she really wanted to see now that she was back in England. Naomi Gilbert. But she didn't think her mother would think that entirely 'suitable'.

When Victoria left the drawing room, she went at once to look at her old schoolroom. It had indeed been transformed; now it was a comfortable sitting room for a young woman to entertain her friends, with bright, chintz-covered sofas and chairs and low occasional tables for serving drinks. The walls had been redecorated and there was a new carpet square on the floor. There was even a generously filled cocktail cabinet in the corner and a small mahogany dining table set to one side of the room with four chairs round it.

'Do you like it, miss?'

Victoria glanced up and smiled at Rose. 'I do. My mother has been very generous.'

The maid came into the room and gave a sniff and under her breath so that her young mistress would not hear, she muttered, 'Not before time.' Aloud she said, 'Madam has given instructions that when she is at home you are to have luncheon and dinner with her, but when she's out, I am to serve your meals up here. If you have guests of your own, then, of course I will, but' – the maid moved closer – 'when you're on your own, Mrs Beddows said we'd be delighted if you'd take your meals with us. That's if you want to, of course, miss.'

Victoria beamed. 'That'd be lovely. I'll come down

tonight, if I may. Mother will be out to dinner, I understand.'

Rose nodded. 'I'll tell Cook. We're really looking forward to hearing all about your travels.'

Victoria's face sobered, wondering just how much she ought to tell them.

There were no such qualms the following morning when she met up with Constance, Charlotte and Georgina outside the Foreign Office.

'Right,' Constance said, leading the way. 'Let's go and find my father.'

A few minutes later in his office, Constance was introducing her father, Sir Michael Davidson, to her friends.

Sir Michael was tall with a military bearing. His smooth hair was silver and he sported a neat moustache. His eyes were a twinkling blue and yet in their depths was the look of authority. Victoria was sure that those eyes could turn quite icy if he was crossed.

'Sit down, my dears. I've arranged for some coffee to be brought in. It should be here in a moment. Now,' he sat down behind his desk, leaned his elbows on its surface and steepled his fingers, 'how can I help you?'

'We think that it's perhaps how we can help you, Father. We feel there are things we saw in Germany that you should know about first-hand. No doubt you've heard about them, but we've *seen* them for ourselves.'

Sir Michael glanced at his daughter. 'You didn't say anything about this at dinner last night.'

'I didn't want to frighten Mother,' Constance said simply. 'To be honest, I think we only just got out of Germany at the right time.'

'There were thirty, perhaps forty, children on the same train as us, fleeing to safety,' Charlotte began. 'They were Jewish children being sent away on their own – without their parents.'

Sir Michael nodded. 'There are plans afoot to bring Jewish children out of Germany. It will be called the Kindertransport. I understand it's to start at the beginning of December. The transport of those children you've seen must have been privately arranged by their parents or Jewish authorities there.'

'The mother of one little girl told me that she was going to some relatives in Hull. I think they were all going there.'

'Ah, that explains it, then. There is a Jewish community in Hull. No doubt it has been organized between them. Now,' he added, briskly, 'before you proceed any further, I'll call in my secretary. I want notes taken of this meeting.'

When they were all settled with cups of coffee and a pale, thin young man with a notebook and pencil in his hands had joined them, they began to tell their story.

'I think we should start with our visit to Germany last year and then explain why we went back this year,' Constance said. They'd agreed that they would tell Sir Michael about the two young men they had met and with whom they'd become friends.

'Please do. I want the full picture.'

Sir Michael sat back in his chair and prepared to listen.

The four girls told their story succinctly, not interrupting one another but each one adding their own particular experience. Painful though it was, both Victoria and Charlotte bravely talked about Kurt and Leon.

Sir Michael's blue eyes were kindly as he said gently, 'I can see it hurts both of you to talk about those young men, but you have made the right decision to come home. From what you've told me and our own intelligence, things are going to get worse before long. Much worse.'

Though there were unshed tears in her eyes, Charlotte said shakily, 'I have to be honest with you, Sir Michael, at first I resisted. But these three are very difficult to stand up to and it wasn't until I saw that pitiful line of young children at the station that I fully understood. They were right and I was wrong.' She turned towards her friends. 'And I promise you, I won't be trying to go back.'

'Thank goodness for that,' Constance said, with a laugh. 'I didn't fancy having to come after you and drag you home again.'

'There is just one thing, Sir Michael,' Charlotte went on. 'I would like to work with refugee children coming here. Can you put me in touch with anyone?'

'Of course.' He turned to his secretary. 'Perhaps you'd see to that for me, William? Get in touch with the woman who is organizing the Kindertransport and see if she would like Charlotte's help. I can't imagine her refusing. You wouldn't need to return to Germany, if you'd rather not. You could organize things this end for when she brings the children back here.' Then he turned back to the other three. 'And what do you three plan to do?' His mouth quirked. 'Find husbands, I suppose.'

'Heavens, no!' Constance said and then met her father's steady gaze as she said quietly, 'Tell us honestly, are we heading towards another war?'

Sir Michael regarded his daughter gravely.

'We always try to work on facts, my dear, so at the moment the *facts* tell us that no, we're not, but our gut *feeling* is entirely different and, to be honest, what you have told me today is disturbing, to say the least. Now, to get back to my question about your plans – I understand that you all speak German fluently.'

'Yes,' Constance and Georgina said together, although they both pointed towards Victoria at the same time. 'But she,' Constance went on, 'is the best of all of us.'

Charlotte pulled a face. 'I'm not very good, Sir Michael. I could never really get to grips with it. I know enough to make myself understood and understand what people say to me, but if they speak rapidly, I'm lost.'

Sir Michael smiled kindly at her. 'Don't worry, my dear. It sounds as if your talents lie in another direction. Your obvious concern for those poor children does you credit.'

He turned back to the other three as Georgina added with a laugh. 'Most of the time the Germans thought Victoria was a native.'

'And with that blonde hair,' Constance added, 'they wouldn't believe us when we said she was English.'

Sir Michael smiled at Victoria. 'Then would you consider a post here at the Foreign Office?'

Victoria gasped, but answered without hesitation, 'Oh yes. Yes, I would.'

'Of course, you'd have to undergo a strict screening, particularly as you have – um – had a German boyfriend.' He chuckled and his eyes twinkled with mischief. 'I couldn't risk introducing a spy into our midst. Having said that,' he went on, quite serious again now, 'your recent knowledge of what is happening there and – as you say – the mood of the country could be of enormous use to us.'

'I'd like that very much,' Victoria said quietly. 'Thank you, Sir Michael.'

'And what about you two?'

He glanced from his daughter to Georgina, who said, 'I intend – for the present anyway – to go home and learn how to run our estate. You see, there's only me to inherit it.' She smiled. 'Thank goodness there is no primogeniture entailment on the estate, but I really should know how to manage it. If, of course, there is a war, then perhaps I'd have to think again.'

'Not necessarily,' Sir Michael said. 'If war does come, the production of food will be paramount. You'd be doing the country a great service by running your estate efficiently. And what about you, Constance? Would you like to work here? Your German, together with your typewriting skills, would be most useful.'

'Yes, I would.'

'Of course, I can only *recommend* both of you. My colleagues will have to interview you properly. I can't be seen to be indulging in nepotism!'

They all laughed and the meeting ended on a much lighter note than that on which it had begun.

Forty-One

'I have never heard such nonsense. A girl of your class *working*. You will do no such thing, Victoria. I don't want to hear another word about it. I can see I shall have to introduce you to the right people myself.' Grace sighed, as if the mere thought was a heavy burden. 'I thought that at least going to an expensive school in Switzerland would lead you in the right direction, but it seems that all you have done is surround yourself with a group of – of blue stockings, who have forgotten – or, worse still, are totally disregarding – their proper place in the world.'

Victoria pulled in a deep breath. 'Mother, I do not intend to marry for the sake of it. If I ever do get married it will be because I love someone.'

Grace glared at her. 'What nonsense is this? Have you met someone? Some ne'er do well?'

'I did meet someone, yes, but it was a match that was, sadly, quite impossible.'

'Who?' Grace snapped. 'I demand that you tell me who this person is.'

'There is no point. Nothing will come of it.'

'Victoria!' Grace's voice was high-pitched, almost shouting now. 'Tell me. I demand that you tell me.'

Victoria met her mother's gaze quite calmly, though

she was quaking inside. She realized in that moment that from now on – especially if she were to work at the Foreign Office – there were secrets she would have to keep. She would have to stand firm against all sorts of questioning – including from her family and friends. She might as well start now, she thought.

'Whatever it was, Mother – and it wasn't very much – it is over now. I promise you that.'

Grace's lip curled and a look of disgust settled on her face. 'You – you haven't done anything stupid, have you? You're not – soiled goods, are you?'

Victoria almost laughed aloud. 'No, Mother. I haven't and I'm not, but I do intend to follow my own path in life.'

'You ungrateful little hussy. After all I have done for you. I have spent a fortune on your education—'

'And I am very grateful for that. I truly am, but I will not be told who I am going to marry. I am applying for a position at the Foreign Office.'

'You can't. I will put a stop to it. You're underage.'

'Only for another six months, Mother. I hardly think that in that time you can find a suitable husband and force me to marry him. Oh, and may I have my birth certificate, please? I need it to go with my application.'

Grace's face turned white and she sank back in her chair and put her hand to her chest. 'I – I haven't got it. It – it was lost – years ago.'

Victoria shrugged and turned to leave the room. 'Then I'll just have to send for a copy. Somerset House, isn't it?'

*

The interview at the Foreign Office – or rather the interviews, plural, because three different people interrogated her – was thorough and searching. When asked about her friendship with the German soldier, Victoria was open and honest.

'I was very fond of him, but when I saw him dressed in the brown uniform of Hitler's storm troopers and also how the soldiers were treating the Jewish people – and that he was one of them – I was shocked beyond belief.'

'In the eyes of the German people,' her interviewer said mildly, 'Adolf Hitler is some kind of saviour, if I'm not being blasphemous using that word.'

'There is no denying that he has done a tremendous amount for his country. He has given them back their national pride and rebuilt their economy and their lives. That's what those young soldiers believe.' She sighed. 'Kurt amongst them.'

'And, it has to be said, he has rebuilt their military strength too. They were not supposed to re-arm but they have, in direct contravention to the Treaty,' her interviewer said.

'Yes and, from what we saw in September, it's some strength.'

'I rather fear they're way ahead of us in producing armaments.' The man leaned forward, with his arms on his desk. 'I hope you understand how thorough we have to be in vetting you.'

'Of course. But I can't think of any way to reassure you further.'

'Perhaps the production of your birth certificate might help.'

'I've applied for one, but it hasn't arrived yet.'

'Then I'd be grateful if you'd apply again and have it sent here to Sir Michael, marked for his attention. It might also be helpful if you go to Somerset House in person and tell them the reason you need a copy.'

As he stood up and held out his hand, bringing the interview to an end, Victoria too rose. 'Thank you. I'll do that.'

The man at Somerset House said, 'That's no problem, miss. Of course I'll order another one for you. Has the first one not arrived?'

Victoria blinked. 'The – the first one? I don't understand.'

'I have a note here that a copy was sent out last week to your home address.'

'I haven't seen it,' she said quite truthfully as an awful thought entered her mind.

'Never mind. Perhaps it got lost in the post. I'll have another one sent to Sir Michael, as you ask.' His smile broadened. 'We're quite used to requests coming from his office.'

'Thank you. I'm very grateful,' she said as she handed over a second fee.

As she took a cab home, Victoria decided to say nothing to her mother about the missing birth certificate. In fact, for the moment, she would say nothing to her about her interview. But she chewed her lip. Now there was another problem. If her mother – as she suspected – was intercepting her post, how was she going to hear whether her application to work at the Foreign Office had been successful or not? Then she brightened as she remembered she was having lunch with Constance today. She would ask her for advice.

Now that Georgina had returned to her parents' estate in the countryside and Charlotte had thrown herself into the work of helping the refugee children, only Constance and Victoria had arranged to meet every Wednesday for lunch at a Lyons Corner House they liked.

'I don't want to go to Claridge's,' Victoria had told her. 'That's where my mother meets her friends. I don't want to bump into any of them. They're extremely nosy and would ask all sorts of questions I don't want to answer.'

As they sat down, Constance asked with sincere concern, 'How are you?'

'I'm fine,' Victoria said and, to her surprise, she meant it.

'Not too broken-hearted?'

Victoria's laugh was genuine. 'Not anymore. Since we've got back, I've realized how right we were to leave when we did. I'm just glad we managed to bring Charlotte back too. You don't think she'll go back, do you?'

'I hope not.' After a moment's thought, she added, 'No, I don't think so, not now she's got involved with helping those children. She's on to the next thing in her life. Lady G didn't call her "Butterfly" for nothing.'

'I hope you're right.'

'And you really are all right?' Constance asked again. 'You can tell me, you know. I don't break confidences.'

'No, truly. I'm fine.'

With her head on one side, Constance regarded her friend. 'You know, you're quite tough under all that outward serene sophistication and there's a lot going on in that blonde head of yours. I think you're very capable of making a decision with your head rather than your heart, whilst Charlotte is just the opposite. If we hadn't been so forceful, she would have stayed there, you know.'

Victoria nodded. 'Yes, I'm afraid she would have.'

As Victoria volunteered no more, Constance picked up the menu. 'Let's order, shall we?'

As they finished eating and lingered over coffee, Victoria said, 'Actually, I would like your advice, Connie, but this is very confidential.'

'Whatever you tell me is safe with me. I'm not the daughter of someone important at the Foreign Office for nothing. Besides, I'm hoping to get a job there myself *and* on my own merits, I might add.'

'It is about us getting jobs there.' Victoria ran her tongue around her lips a little nervously. 'Things are difficult for me at home. My mother doesn't want me to get a job at all, so when I told her about it she was – well – quite angry.' She paused.

'Go on,' Constance prompted gently.

'She told me that she would forbid me working there – or anywhere – that she would put a stop to it as I'm still under-age.' Victoria frowned. 'The trouble is, I rather think she might be able to. There are quite probably some very influential women amongst her luncheon buddies. However, I did remind her that I am twenty-one in six months' time. And although I didn't say as much, I don't think even she could find a suitable husband and force me to marry him in that time.'

'You poor thing. I would never have guessed. You've never said anything.'

'I'm not particularly proud of the fact that my mother makes it very clear she didn't want me, that I've been a burden to her all my life and that she can't wait to marry me off and have done with me. But, I have to admit, she has given me a very good education and for that I'm grateful.'

Constance's face creased with sympathy. 'Didn't she ever show you any affection, then?'

Victoria shook her head. 'The only real affection I ever had was from my governess, Miss Gilbert, the cook and the housemaid, Rose.'

'Oh, I remember Miss Gilbert coming to see you at school. For a long time, we all thought she was your mother.'

'My mother never came. Not once.'

'And you stayed at school during the Christmas and Easter holidays, didn't you? I remember that.'

Victoria nodded. 'And in the summer, I went to Miss Gilbert's for four weeks and then went home for just the final two weeks so that Mother could take me shopping for a new uniform and anything I needed for school. She was generous in that way.'

'Mm.' Constance made it sound as if she didn't agree and Victoria smiled weakly.

'So when you were home, didn't you see much of her, even then?'

'I lived between my bedroom and the schoolroom upstairs. Occasionally – very occasionally – I had luncheon with her, or dinner, but not often. She went out a lot.'

'And—' Constance began hesitantly, but pressed on, 'your father?'

'I know nothing about him – not even his full name. All I know is that he was killed in the war at Passchendaele.'

Now Constance was open-mouthed. 'What about grandparents on both sides?'

Victoria shrugged. 'Nothing.'

'And you never asked about them?'

Victoria laughed wryly. 'You don't ask my mother those sorts of questions. That's why I'm looking forward to getting my birth certificate. Maybe I'll find out a bit more from that. And that brings me round to what I was going to tell you – to ask you, really. I sent for the certificate over a week ago – straight after we'd first talked to your father. It never arrived, but when I went to Somerset House in person yesterday, the man there said they'd definitely sent one out already. Anyway, he was very nice and promised to send another copy addressed to your father at the Foreign Office. I just wanted to ask you to tell him to expect it. I hope that's all right.'

'Of course it will be.' Constance waved her fears aside, then she frowned. 'You think your mother kept it from you, don't you?'

'Yes, I am afraid I do. And there's something else. If she *did* do that, then she would withhold any letter that comes in reply to my application, whatever the answer is.'

'Ah. Yes, I see. So how can I help?'

'Could you ask your father if he would tell you when there is a letter for me and I will call at the office to collect it?'

'Of course I will. How can I get in touch with you?'

'I'll give you our telephone number. Ring about one o'clock. Mother's often out for lunch then and even if she answers, just ask for me. She may say I'm not there, but just keep trying. And besides, we're going to meet here every Wednesday, aren't we?'

Constance smiled. 'Of course we are.'

Forty-Two

When the two girls met again for lunch two weeks later, Constance handed a rather large, fat envelope across the table to Victoria with a huge smile. 'Father entrusted this to me to bring to you. I hope that's all right.'

'Of course it is.' Her fingers were trembling as she reached across the table.

'I think your birth certificate's in there too.'

Victoria opened the envelope and read the covering letter. It contained an offer of employment at the Foreign Office as a translator. She looked up, a little uncertainly. She really didn't want to get a job there if Constance hadn't been successful too, but her friend was smiling. 'So? Have you got it?'

Victoria nodded. 'What about you?'

She found she was holding her breath until Constance said, 'Yes, me too. As a typist. Just what I wanted.' She paused and then asked, 'Go on. Open your certificate. I know you're dying to.'

'Let's order first and then – then . . .'

As the waiter moved away from taking their order, Victoria opened the folded certificate. Her glance went at once to the section about her father. She read it out to Constance.

'Richard Hamilton. And he was an officer in the British Army.' Then she frowned.

'What is it?' Constance asked.

'I'm not sure. I've never seen a birth certificate before so I don't know what should be on it.'

'Obviously your full name and date of birth. Where you were born. Your father's name and occupation and your mother's maiden name. That's all I know for certain.'

'Would it say if my father was dead?'

'It might say "deceased" in brackets. I know it does on marriage certificates, but I'm not sure about birth certificates.'

'Well, it doesn't.' She glanced up. 'When did Passchendaele end? I know we learnt about it at school, but I've forgotten.'

'I'm rubbish at remembering dates, but we can look it up. It was certainly during 1917, but I can't remember the exact dates. Why?'

'It just seems – odd, somehow. Something doesn't feel quite right but I don't know what it is.' She read through the paper again and then folded it. 'Never mind. I'm determined to find out one day, but what really matters now is how I'm going to persuade my mother to allow me to accept the position. Anyway, here's pudding. Let's enjoy it.'

Telling her mother turned out to be not as difficult as she had imagined. At first Grace told her she was not to accept the offer, but when Victoria stood her ground, at last her mother said, 'Oh very well, then, if you must. At least it's respectable and you might meet some decent young men with acceptable backgrounds.' She gave an exaggerated sigh. 'And, I suppose, if we are to be plunged into war, it would safeguard you against being called up.' She feigned a shudder. 'One hears such dreadful tales about the sort of girl in the services. Their morals leave a lot to be desired, so I've heard.' She cast her eyes to the ceiling.

Victoria heartily disagreed with her mother. She admired the young women who were already volunteering before war had even been declared.

'Just mind you dress smartly for work,' was Grace's parting shot.

The date given in the letter when she should present herself for work was 3 April. There were three weeks to wait, so Victoria wrote to Naomi to ask if she might spend a week with her. The reply came back at once that she would be delighted to see her. The two spent an idyllic week at Naomi's cottage, catching up on each other's news and taking day trips into the surrounding countryside.

Back in London, Victoria readied herself to start work and on the first morning she found she was quite nervous, not knowing exactly what was expected of her. After all the formalities had been completed, which included signing the Official Secrets Act, she was shown into a room where six other people, all men, were sitting at their desks. The man in charge of them, Mr Walters, showed her to the desk she was to occupy.

'You can meet your colleagues at lunchtime,' he told her. 'I would like you to work on this.' He laid a sheaf of papers on her desk. 'You will find paper and writing materials in the drawer. If you need anything, just ask Charlie sitting behind you.'

The room was quiet, each young man bent studiously over his desk scribbling on a foolscap lined writing pad.

Victoria took a deep breath and began to read . . .

She found the work so engrossing that she wasn't aware of the time passing until the young man sitting behind her tapped her on the shoulder and said, 'Pens down. It's lunchtime.'

Victoria stretched her shoulders and rubbed her eyes. She stood up and picked up her handbag. 'Lead on, Macduff.'

Over lunch she met the other translators working in the same room. 'I'll never remember all your names,' she laughed.

'I had the same problem when I started,' Charlie said. 'We ought to wear name badges, really. But we'll remember yours, so we'll just keep reminding you of our names when we speak to you.'

But she found that lunchtime was the only time when there was conversation between any of them. At all other times, unless it was about work, it was a case of 'heads down'.

By lunchtime on the second day, when Victoria had worked through all the papers she had been given, she whispered to Charlie, 'What do I do now?'

'Good Lord, have you finished already? That was quick.' He hesitated and then said, 'Well, you take it to Mr Walters in his office at the end of this corridor but I'd have another read through, if I were you. No offence, but he doesn't like any mistakes. The work is too important.'

Victoria was about to argue that she had worked through it carefully, checking as she went along, but she thought better of it. Instead, she smiled brightly. 'Thank you, Charlie. That's a very helpful tip.'

So, it wasn't until late in the afternoon that she took her work to Mr Walters's office.

He, too, seemed surprised to see her so soon. But he bade her put the folder into his in tray. 'I'll look at it tomorrow. Now here's your second assignment. You might find this a little more difficult, but I have to assess the level of your capabilities. You do understand?'

'Of course, Mr Walters. Thank you.'

She took the folder and returned to her desk, but she had only just sat down when Charlie stood up and trilled, 'Home time, everyone. Who's for the pub? You coming, Vicky?'

'Yes, I'd love to. But it's Victoria, if you don't mind.' She smiled widely to lessen what might be seen as a snub. 'I hate it being shortened. But you don't seem to mind your nickname?'

Charlie shrugged. 'It's what I've always been called since I was a kid. It doesn't worry me.' He grinned. 'But Victoria it is, then.'

As they walked out into the street, she explained further. 'I do have three girlfriends who call me "Vicky". It started when we were at school in Switzerland and I was quite shy then. I didn't have the nerve to say anything.'

'But now you have. Good for you. Start as you mean to go on.'

'You might meet one of them. Constance. She's started as a typist here.'

'Not Constance Davidson?'

'Yes, Sir Michael's daughter. Do you know her?'

He gave a theatrical sigh. 'I worship from afar.'

'Do you really? Then I must introduce you to her.'

'I'd like that, but then it will be me who goes all shy and tongue-tied. And probably bright red in the face.'

Victoria giggled. 'She's not that fearsome.'

'No, but her father might be,' he said wryly.

They reached the pub and Charlie held open the door for her. Inside, the chatter and laughter was noisy. Release from the quietness of their offices, Victoria thought.

'Over here, Vicky.' It was Constance waving from a far corner and beckoning.

'Come on, Charlie. No time like the present.'

'Oh heck,' he muttered, but then grinned sheepishly. 'Go on, then.'

'Connie, this is Charlie. We work in the same office. He's been lovely helping me to settle in.' She turned towards Charlie and saw – just as he had predicted – that he was bright red in the face.

'C-can I get you both a drink?'

Constance smiled at him and gave him her order. Victoria did the same and the two girls sat down together whilst Charlie went to the bar.

'He seems nice,' Constance remarked.

'He is.'

'Quite good-looking too. I've always liked dark-haired men and I prefer clean shaven. I've never liked men with those silly little moustaches.'

Victoria decided not to say anything about Charlie admiring Constance; such a revelation could nip a blossoming romance in the bud. Better to let it take its natural course – if there was to be one.

'So, what's he do?'

'He's a translator. I think we all are in that office. What are the other girls in the typing pool like?'

'All right. Haven't got to know many of them yet, but they seem a friendly bunch. But the noise, Vicky, when we all get typing together, is something else. There's a woman who sits at the front facing us all. Miss Prentiss. She doesn't do much typing. She gives out the work and then checks it when we've done. You can't make even the slightest mistake. If you do, you get it flung back at you to do all over again – so it's a good job my typing's pretty accurate. They're not too bothered about the speed you can do as long as it's perfect.'

Victoria pulled a face. 'I don't think I could do that. My typewriting skills leave a lot to be desired.'

Constance chuckled. 'Each to her own. I don't think my German is good enough for me to be a translator or an interpreter, but Miss Prentiss said I shall be taking dictation from some of the senior members of staff, though not my father. She says that would be unfair on both of us.'

'I think she's right.'

At that moment, Charlie returned with the drinks and they sat chatting for over an hour until Constance said – reluctantly, Victoria thought – 'I ought to be going. Mother organizes dinner for seven o'clock.'

'Yes, I should too.' The two girls got up.

'See you tomorrow, Charlie,' Victoria said.

Constance held out her hand. 'Nice to meet you. Is this a regular meeting place after work?'

Charlie nodded, suddenly tongue-tied again.

'Then I'll no doubt see you again. Bye for now.'

As they left the bar, Victoria glanced back to see Charlie watching them go. His gaze was fastened not on her, but on her friend.

Forty-Three

Through the months that followed, Victoria and Constance heard of Mussolini's capture of Tirana, the capital of Albania, and had first-hand knowledge of the pledges given by Britain to go to the aid of certain other countries if they were attacked, in addition to the promise already given to defend Poland. They knew about the upcoming conscription of single men aged between twenty and twenty-two and the call to all farmers to plough up grazing pastures to produce more crops for food. They worried over Germany and Italy signing a Pact of Steel and were even more alarmed by the non-aggression pact signed by Hitler and Stalin. At the very end of August, British children began to be evacuated from cities and towns.

Constance had taken an apartment in the city, reasonably close to the Foreign Office, and she invited Victoria to move in with her.

'Despite all the doom and gloom, Vicky, we could have such fun. Do say you will?'

When Victoria mooted the idea to her mother, Grace merely shrugged and said, 'You are of age now. I really have no interest in what you decide to do anymore. After all the money that has been lavished on you, I really thought you would make something of your life. You are a sad disappointment to me, Victoria.'

With that final cold dismissal from her mother's life, Victoria bade a tearful farewell to Mrs Beddows and Rose, promising that she would still visit them often, and moved her few belongings from the house in Kensington to the spacious apartment in Westminster. They settled in happily together, sending out invitations to Georgina and to Charlotte to visit whenever they could.

But then, Hitler marched into Poland.

It was almost a relief when war was finally declared, but with it came the conscription of all men between the ages of eighteen and forty-one.

'That's me, then,' Charlie said, as he sat in the pub with Victoria and Constance after work. The conversation and especially the laughter was more subdued now.

'Not necessarily,' Constance said. 'I'm sure your job must come in the category of a reserved occupation.'

Charlie sighed. 'I'll have to find out.'

'I'm sure translating is far more important than being one more soldier to get shot at,' Constance said firmly, as if defying anyone to contradict her.

'I wouldn't want to appear to be a coward,' Charlie murmured.

'No one would think that – at least, not the people who matter. You do an extremely valuable job here and it's likely to become even more important now.'

He smiled at Constance, meeting her eyes. 'It's nice of you to say so.'

Suddenly, Victoria felt she was playing gooseberry.

Nothing much seemed to happen in the first few months of the war, even though thousands of men from the British Expeditionary Force were sent to France in October. People called it 'the phoney war' and began to hope that perhaps this one really would be 'over before Christmas'. But it wasn't, and in early April 1940, when Hitler invaded Denmark and Norway, everyone sighed and accepted that this was probably going to escalate into another worldwide conflict.

Early in May, Victoria was summoned to Sir Michael's office.

'Do come in, Victoria. Sorry, I should call you Miss Hamilton when we're at work, but you've become such good friends with Constance that I always think of you as Victoria.'

'Sir Michael,' Victoria murmured and sat down opposite him, on the visitors' side of his desk.

Sir Michael leaned back in his chair. 'You've done very well here and you're a valued part of the team, but—' He hesitated and Victoria's heart sank. She loved working at the Foreign Office but it sounded as if she was either going to be dismissed or moved.

'We want you for work that is of national importance.' He smiled at her mystified face. 'You have already signed the Official Secrets Act for your work here, so I can tell you a little more than I would normally tell candidates. The work is secret – Top Secret, with a capital T. You would be working at a location outside London, but you would not be able to tell your family or friends where you are. The work is decoding intercepted messages—'

Victoria gasped.

'And you would be involved in the translation of the decrypted messages. A great many brilliant minds have already been sent there. I can't impress upon you enough that not only is it of the highest importance but also secrecy is paramount. So, will you accept the offer?'

'Of course. Anything I can do to help the war effort. Am I allowed to tell Constance?'

Sir Michael hesitated for a moment and then said, 'No. Would you trust me to tell her as much as she ought to know, but no more?'

'Of course, but we share a flat. If I'm to go away, I ought to let her find someone else.'

Sir Michael shook his head. 'No. Your share of the rent will be paid. You will have leave occasionally and you'll want somewhere to come back to, won't you? Besides,' he smiled, 'I don't think Constance would take kindly to a stranger as a flat mate. William will fill you in on travel arrangements and give you everything you need. But remember, not a word to anyone. Any letters you wish to receive must be addressed to you here at the Foreign Office, which shouldn't present a problem, as it's no secret that you work here, is it?'

'When do I go?'

'Next Wednesday. And please, no visiting family or friends to say goodbye. They must all think that you are still physically working here.'

Victoria's eyes widened. 'That's quick.'

'Your particular skills are sorely needed at Station X.'

Even the name didn't give her any clue as to where she was going, but she knew better than to ask any more questions. She guessed it was the code name for the place. She rose and held out her hand. 'Thank you, Sir Michael. I won't let you down.'

'Oh I'm sure of that,' he said, as he too rose and took her hand. 'I wouldn't have recommended you otherwise.'

Victoria stepped down from the train onto the darkened platform. It was very late to be arriving, but this was the train she'd been told to take. She lugged her suitcase with her, stepping blindly into the darkness. She heard the trundling of a barrow, no doubt being pushed by a porter, but he was too far away for her to hail him. She was so conscious of the need to be quiet, to merge into the background and not to be noticed. *Well*, she thought wryly, *that's easy enough to do here on a railway station in the middle of nowhere*. She walked forward where she expected to find offices of some sort or a waiting room at least. Then, to her left, she became aware that there was a figure. As her eyes became accustomed to the darkness, she could make out the small, slim figure of what she thought was a young woman. She moved cautiously towards her.

'Hello, are you lost too?'

'Not exactly lost, but I'm not sure what to do next.' She'd been right; it was a young woman's voice with a strong northern accent.

'Me neither. I expect we're on our way to the same place, though where it is, God alone knows. There doesn't seem to be anyone to meet us. Anyway—' Victoria put out her hand and touched the girl's arm. She didn't think it would matter exchanging just first names. 'I'm Victoria. And you are?'

The girl didn't answer, but she shook the hand that Victoria held out to her. Victoria pointed the thin beam of her torch towards the stranger. The girl was smaller than she was and dressed in some sort of grey suit. Victoria suddenly thought of Lady G and imagined the nickname she would give the stranger.

'You look like a little grey mouse in this light.' Since the girl had offered no name, Victoria laughed and added, 'That's what I'll call you. Mouse. Now, let's see if we can find someone to tell us where on earth we have to go. Come along, Mouse, there's a dear.'

PART THREE

Bletchley Park

Forty-Four

'Excuse me . . .' Victoria hailed the porter trundling the now-empty luggage barrow back along the platform.

'Evenin', miss.' His friendly voice greeted them, even though they could only see his dark shape. 'Oh, there's two of you. Usual place, is it?'

'I – we – haven't the faintest idea, but probably, yes.'

Victoria began to fish in her handbag to retrieve the letter she'd been given, when Mattie nudged her and muttered, 'I wouldn't, if I were you.'

Victoria paused and then whispered, 'Yes, of course. You're right. Silly of me. This is going to take a bit of getting used to.' She raised her voice and said, 'So, can you point us in the right direction to – um – the usual place?'

'Out of the station, miss, and then follow the cinder path.' He glanced at the heavy suitcases they were carrying. 'I'd lend you mi barrow, but the station master'd have my guts fer garters if I let it out of me sight. And I certainly can't leave the station. Sorry.'

'Don't worry about it,' Victoria said, heaving her suitcase into a more comfortable grip.

The two girls stumbled along the path he'd indicated. Their eyes were becoming more accustomed to the gloom now.

'We should have come in the daylight,' Mattie muttered. 'I never realized the countryside could be so pitch-black.'

'You're right, but we weren't to know that there would be no one to greet us with open arms. I wonder how much further it is.' Victoria paused to catch her breath.

Mattie squinted ahead. 'I think I can see a fence. Come on.'

They reached a high chain-link fence with a roll of barbed wire on the top.

'What's this? A prison camp?' Victoria muttered.

'It may well be, considering all the cloak and dagger stuff I've gone through already. I expect you've had much the same as me. I haven't a clue where we are or what we're doing here.'

For a brief moment Victoria felt a stab of fear. Was this legitimate or had she been lured into some sort of internment camp because of her association with a German soldier? Then she shook it off and castigated herself silently for being so foolish. The authorities didn't need to play games. If they'd wanted to intern her, they'd have just done it. It was the darkness and the eeriness of the place getting to her imagination, she told herself. Besides, she trusted Sir Michael.

They pressed on. Now they were walking along a concrete drive and at last they arrived at iron gates with an armed sentry standing on the other side.

'Good evening, ladies. May I see your passes please?'

'I don't think we've been given proper passes,' Victoria said.

'Ah, so are you just arriving for the first time?'

'Yes.'

'So, you should have received a letter.'

Both girls now handed their letters over to be scrutinized. As he handed them back, he said, 'You will be given passes and make sure you have them with you at all times or you won't be allowed back in.'

'Thank you,' they both murmured as he swung open the gate and ushered them through.

'Keep straight ahead and you will come to the house on your left. Enter by the front door and someone will be there to meet you.'

As they walked on further, the sprawling house loomed up in the darkness. They entered by the huge doors and were met, as they had been warned, by another sentry.

'Just go up the stairs, ladies,' the soldier said. 'Someone will meet you.'

'My word, this is a grand place,' Mattie murmured as they mounted the stairs. She stared around her at the high ceilings, panelled walls and marble pillars and arches.

'Ah, good evening, ladies. Welcome to Station X.' A dapper little man met them at the top of the stairs and ushered them into a small room. 'My name is Timothy Branston. Please sit down. Now, I know you won't have been told much.' He smiled broadly at them, his round spectacles lifting as his nose wrinkled. 'And at this stage, I can't tell you very much more. Only that you must read this document – it's quite lengthy – and then you must sign it before we can proceed.'

He pushed two sets of papers across the desk. On the front of each were the words *OFFICIAL SECRETS ACT* and, beneath them, *DECLARATION*.

'I've signed one of these before,' Victoria said, looking up. She was about to say that she'd been working at the Foreign Office, but then decided that it was probably best to keep yet another secret.

'We'd be very grateful if you'd read it again and sign it for us. We like to have our own copy. I'll leave you both to read through it thoroughly. Please be absolutely sure you know what you're signing. Oh, and by the way, are either of you colour blind?'

Mystified, the two girls glanced at each other before shaking their heads. 'No.'

'Blimey,' Mattie said as she finished reading and turned to the section where she had to sign. 'Are we signing our life away?'

'For the next few years,' Victoria murmured, 'I would say "yes".'

'Oh well, I'm not sure what we're getting ourselves into, but here goes.'

As they sat back and waited for Timothy Branston to return, Mattie said, 'I'm sorry I didn't tell you my name. I just wondered if it was some sort of test.'

'I quite understand,' Victoria said. 'You might very well have been right.'

'Anyway, it's Mattie.'

'Pleased to meet you, but I shall still call you "Mouse".'

'Then I shall call you "Vicky",' Mattie replied, but she was smiling as she said it.

'Fair enough,' Victoria laughed.

When Timothy returned and gathered up the documents he said, 'Now I can tell you a little more. Here at Bletchley Park we're all engaged – in different roles, of course, but the aim is the same – in breaking the codes of the enemy's messages. These are intercepted by listening posts dotted around the British Isles, which we call Y Stations. These are manned by men and women from the forces – very often women from the ATS. There are even some civilian volunteers – amateur radio enthusiasts – who work for us too. They track the enemy networks and meticulously copy down all letters and numbers on pre-printed forms. Of course, they can't make any sense of the encrypted messages, which are then sent to us here at Bletchley with great haste, often by motorcycle courier. It is our job to decipher these coded messages.' The little man was smiling. 'Our greatest achievement occurred in January when we first broke an Enigma message.'

The two girls, looking mystified, glanced at each other.

Timothy chuckled and perched himself on the corner of the table. He pulled a pipe from his pocket and proceeded to pack it and light it. 'Do either of you smoke?'

They both shook their heads.

'Well, I hope you won't mind the smell of tobacco

because you'll find that most of the men here do. Now, where was I?'

'You mentioned something called Enigma.'

'Ah yes. The Germans developed a machine just after the last war mainly for commercial use by banks and suchlike. But then the German navy saw its potential for sending encrypted messages and, a little later, the German army adopted it too. Now, of course, it's used by all the German armed forces. It's a fiendishly complicated machine, even though it looks innocent enough. Like a typewriter. You'll see one tomorrow.'

Victoria stifled a yawn and tried to keep her interest focussed, but Timothy had noticed. 'I am so sorry. I should have realized that you've probably both had a long day.' He smiled sheepishly. 'I'm a bit of a bore when I get talking about my favourite topic.'

'No, no,' they both tried to protest, but he could tell they were weary.

'I'll get someone to take you to your billet and I'll see you again in the morning. Eight o'clock sharp. I'll arrange for someone to pick you up tomorrow, but after that you must make your own arrangements for getting back and forth.'

'Understood,' Victoria said and stood up. 'Thank you, Mr Branston.'

'Oh Timothy, or even Tim, please. We tend to go by just Christian names here. We're all about security, you see, as you will find out, and the less you know about other people, the better.'

They went back downstairs and out of the front door again to find a car already waiting for them.

They were driven a short distance to a street in the town.

'I'll pick you up in the morning, ladies,' the driver said, indicating a house. 'At a quarter to eight.'

As the car drove away, Victoria and Mattie stumbled their way up the path to knock on the door. It took several minutes for it to be opened. The woman standing there was small and thin, dressed in nightclothes and with her hair twisted into curling rags.

'You're late,' she snapped. 'I expected you hours ago. Follow me.'

She led them through a small hallway to the staircase. Upstairs, she showed them into a small room, crowded with two single beds, a washstand, a single wardrobe and narrow chest of drawers.

'Privy's out the back door and down the garden. And don't make a noise if you go in the night. I'm a light sleeper. Breakfast's at seven. Goodnight.'

She left the room, shutting the door behind her.

The two girls glanced at each other in the dim light from the one bare bulb hanging in the centre of the room. Victoria looked around her. 'Well, we won't be doing any cat-swinging in here.'

Mattie stifled her giggles. She was almost hysterical with tiredness and disappointment. Used to cramped and uncomfortable conditions though she was, even she had expected something better than this.

They found their way back down the stairs and stumbled down the garden path, clinging to each other in the darkness. Neither of them knew whether to laugh or to cry. Back in their room, they moved around the limited space, skirting round each other to have a quick wash, undress and fall onto one of the beds.

'Ugh! It's as hard as iron and it creaks every time I move,' Victoria groaned.

'Mmm . . .' Despite the discomfort, Mattie was already half asleep.

Forty-Five

'I'll take you and introduce you to your new colleagues,' Tim greeted them the next morning. 'I trust you will all get along.' He smiled impishly, his spectacles rising up his nose, as he led them to their places of work. 'You, Mattie, will be working in Hut Six, whilst you, Victoria, will be in the Army and Air Force Enigma Reporting Section where the translating and analysis of the messages is done. Have you any other languages other than German?'

'Only French.'

'No Italian?'

Victoria shook her head.

'Not to worry. In my humble opinion, German is more important. And, by the way, I must impress upon you both that you must not try to enter any other room or hut, nor can you talk to each other about your work. Silly, isn't it, when we're all engaged on the same goal, but there you are. Those are the rules and they must be obeyed. I should also warn you that you'll be working a pattern of eight-hour shifts throughout twenty-four hours.' They'd walked a short distance from the house when Tim said, 'Now, here you are, Victoria. This is where you'll be for the time being, but possibly only for a couple of months or so. The small hut at the side of Hut Six is being rebuilt and made bigger. It will be known as Hut Three and will work very closely with decryption operations in Hut Six.'

Tim handed Victoria into the care of a young woman who ushered her inside and closed the door.

They walked a little further and then Tim opened the door of a hut that led into a long passage with three rooms on either side. At the end of the corridor there were two larger rooms. Tim described what each room was for.

'The hut comprises four main sections really, plus smaller offices. This is the Registration Room where the messages are initially sorted and logged. Then we have the Intercept Control Room. The people in here talk directly to the intercept stations giving guidance on what they should be looking out for, particularly making sure that they are listening to the German network that is coming through the clearest to them. Different parts of the country can obviously link into different networks better than others. And then guidance is given on the type of message which would be best to break. Ah, and now we have the Machine Room. As a mathematician, Mattie, this is where you'll be working. But the other room' – he waved his hand vaguely – 'is the Decoding Room. That's where the messages are passed to once a key has been broken. They use Typex machines, which are set up to work in a similar way to Enigma, to type out the decoded messages onto strips of paper – still in German – that are then sent for translation.' He smiled at Mattie. 'That's where your friend will come in.'

Mattie glanced around the hut at the rather wobbly trestle tables and chairs. Despite the lights burning overhead, the room seemed gloomy, possibly because of the heavy blackout curtains hanging on either side of the windows, ready to be drawn at nightfall. Several people were already hard at work, their shoulders hunched, their heads bent. No one even looked up, so intent was their concentration.

'And now, just look what we have here.' Tim gestured proudly towards a machine sitting on one of the tables.

'Oh,' she said. 'It does look like a typewriter but with an extra keyboard that lights up.'

Tim laughed wryly. 'I wish it stopped at that, but it has a plugboard at the front and rotors at the rear. This machine can have one hundred and fifty-nine million million million settings. And they change the settings at midnight every day.'

Mattie gaped at him. 'And we're supposed to break it each day? It's impossible.'

Tim tapped the side of his nose. 'That's what the Germans believe and we want them to go on believing that. So, now you see the reason for such tight security.'

'You mean it has been broken?'

Tim's eyes gleamed. 'Oh yes. The story goes that three brilliant Polish mathematicians got some information from the French about Enigma and managed to construct a replica machine. How, goodness only knows. However, they have shared their knowledge with us and even given us a replica machine. You will learn more as you go along, but there are some brilliantly clever people working here who have devised all sorts of what we call "cribs". Now, let me introduce you to the woman who will act as your mentor until you find your feet.' He led her to one of the tables. 'This is Pips.'

The woman was slim with dark hair and sparkling eyes. Mattie judged she must be somewhere in her mid-forties, but her vivacity was that of someone much younger.

'I'll leave you to it, then,' Tim said and ambled away.

'Come and sit at the next table to me,' Pips said as they shook hands. 'Now, I expect you've already signed the relevant documents about secrecy?'

Mattie nodded.

'We are allowed to talk to each other about our work within this hut, but outside' – Pips shook her head – 'it's a no-no.'

'Not to anyone? Not even to people working in the other buildings?'

'Only perhaps Hut Three, because we pass our messages directly to them for translation, but absolutely no one else. It's all very hush-hush.' Pips laughed. 'That's the new phrase that means Top Secret. Now, I won't ask you any personal questions, but I'd just like to know what your forte is. Do you know why you've been sent here?'

Mattie gave a small smile and blushed a little. 'I've just completed a maths degree at – um – Oxford.'

'And have you had your results yet?'

Mattie shook her head. 'I only took the last exam on Tuesday.'

'My word, they must be keen to have you here. I'm guessing that someone somewhere in the know is expecting you to do very well. Hence your recruitment. Now, I'm not going to tell you much about myself except to say that I'm here because I play chess well and can do crosswords in record time. Sorry, if that sounds boastful – I don't mean it to be – but it's the reason I'm here.'

'Not at all,' Mattie murmured. She was about to tell Pips about Victoria and her brilliance with languages, but then decided against it. Luckily, for Mattie, keeping secrets was second nature.

She sat beside Pips trying to absorb what she was being told.

'We use cribs.'

'Yes, Tim mentioned them, but he didn't say what they were.'

'After a while, especially if you can glean that you're getting messages from the same operator, you'll find that they'll have a certain way of sending messages. All of them start off with their call sign, then the time followed by the number of letters in the message and whether it is being sent in different parts. Long messages will be split up.' Mattie nodded. So far so good – she could understand this bit.

'Then there will be two sets of three letters,' Pips went on. 'The first set tells you the type of traffic and the second is for the encoding and decoding of the message.'

Now it was getting complicated.

'Another way to find cribs is that often a particular operator will begin all his messages in the same way. Maybe with "*Heil* Hitler" or some such phrase. And there are other messages – like weather reports, for instance – where you can get repetitive language which is a huge help. And the way they sign off is well worth studying.' Pips smiled. 'You may also find that an operator will incorporate his girlfriend's name in some way. There are all sorts of little things to watch out for. Now, I'll give you this and you can be having a look at it. It'll take you a while to understand exactly what we have to do, so don't worry.'

At first it just seemed a jumble, a sheet with columns of five letters that meant absolutely nothing. She felt as if she were back in the classroom with Mr Musgrave explaining the rudiments of algebra to her. Soon, however, her natural instinct to rise to a challenge reasserted itself and under the guidance of her newfound colleague she began to make sense – little by little – of what needed to be done.

By the time the two girls left their respective huts late in the afternoon and walked the mile to their billet, Victoria said, 'I don't think I'll ever see properly again. The work's intense, isn't it?' She paused and then asked, 'Do you speak German, then?'

Mattie shook her head. 'Not really. I know enough to recognize the language, but I couldn't translate anything properly.'

'So why have you been recruited?'

Mattie pretended to be prim and proper. 'I'm not

sure I'm supposed to tell you. For all I know, you could be a German spy.'

'Indeed, I could,' Victoria murmured. 'All I've been told is that Hut Six does the deciphering, decoding or whatever the term is.'

'Yes, it seems like it. I'm a mathematician.' It sounded good to her own ears, but Mattie wondered if she was really entitled to call herself that yet. She still hadn't actually got her results. But, she argued, the powers that be, whoever they were, must have confidence in her or she wouldn't be here.

'Everyone works very hard here, all hunched over their desks,' Victoria said. 'I'm sure I'll have curvature of the spine before we're done. Still, it could be worse. It's our billet I'm more bothered about. I know we won't be spending much time there, but it's not terribly comfortable, is it? Sharing a tiny room that's hardly bigger than a wardrobe and having to go down to the end of the garden to the lavatory, even in the middle of the night. And the food is atrocious. I know there's a war on – like we're always being told – but there are limits.'

'The food's good in the canteen at work, though, isn't it? I tried it at dinner time. And it's open round the clock as we're all on shift work.'

'That's another thing. Can you imagine what that woman's going to be like when we start coming in at all hours of the day and night? She was bad enough when we first arrived. It wasn't exactly a warm welcome, was it?'

Mattie sighed. 'I expect she's glad of the money the Government must be paying her.'

'Well, whatever she's getting they – and we – are being short-changed. I'm going to see if I can find us something better, Mouse.'

Mattie smiled weakly, thinking of the cramped conditions of her childhood. But she said nothing.

They got ready for bed in the tiny room.

'I'll never sleep,' Victoria grumbled. 'This mattress is all lumpy.'

Mattie lay back. At least, she thought, with wry humour, they were not having to share the actual bed like she'd had to with her sister.

Despite Victoria's gloomy prediction, both girls fell asleep almost at once.

Three days later, Victoria announced to Mattie that she had found them a more comfortable billet. 'It's a bit further away – about two miles – but I've commandeered two bicycles for us. It's in a nice house on the outskirts of Bletchley village owned by a retired doctor and his wife.'

'Are we allowed to move?' Mattie asked worriedly.

'If we're not, I'm off – Official Secrets Act or not.' Then she grinned. 'Don't look so worried, Mouse. I've cleared it with the woman in charge here. I told her that neither of us would be able to do our work properly if we had to stay there much longer. She soon agreed we could find something else. Now, you'll love Mr and Mrs Coupland. They're a dear old couple. Well, not that old actually. He's recently retired, but Mrs Coupland is still quite sprightly and insists she'll look after us. They'd still like us to share a room as they like to keep one spare for their grown-up daughter to visit, but compared to the one we've got now, the bedroom is huge. We can join them in the sitting room whenever we want and we can have use of the kitchen too. They're a delightful couple and so anxious to "do their bit". She said if we just keep our room clean and tidy, that will be fine. She has a local lady from the village who goes in twice a week to clean the rest of the house.'

Just as Victoria had said, the couple – Mr and Mrs Coupland – were charming, making both girls feel welcome and like members of the family from the outset.

'Oh,' Mattie gasped as Mrs Coupland showed them upstairs and into the bedroom they would share. 'How lovely.'

The room was light and airy, with two comfortable-looking single beds covered in candlewick counterpanes. Chintz curtains fluttered at the window and a square of carpet made the room, though large, nevertheless cosy and welcoming. Blackout curtains also hung at the sides of the windows, to be drawn when they needed the light turned on.

'This is wonderful, Mrs Coupland,' Mattie said. 'I hope we won't be too much trouble coming in and out at different times of the day – and sometimes the night.'

'No, no, my dears. We quite understand that you're at Bletchley Park and have to work at different times.' Her eyes twinkled. 'And more than that, we know not to ask, but both my hubby and I want to help. We've always been used to him being on duty through the night sometimes, so it won't worry us. Just so long as we know you're both safe.'

'We tend to be on the same shift,' Victoria said, 'so we'll probably be coming and going together, which will make it a bit better.' She glanced approvingly around the room. 'We'll be fine here.'

'You can move in whenever you like,' Mrs Coupland said.

'This afternoon, if that's all right,' Victoria said promptly and Mattie hid her smile. Just like her new friend, she couldn't wait to move into this lovely room, even though the confines of their current accommodation hadn't bothered her as much as they had Victoria. But this room, to Mattie, was the height of luxury.

Forty-Six

'Mouse? There's a game of rounders being organized after work tonight. You interested?'

Mattie's eyes widened and she giggled. 'Me? Play sport? I'm useless, Vicky.'

'I'm sure you're not as bad as you think. Besides, it'll do you good after being hunched over a desk all day and going cross-eyed over hundreds of messages. Oh, do give it a try, there's a dear.'

'You'll have to explain the rules.'

'It's easy,' Victoria said airily.

'It might be for you,' Mattie muttered.

After they'd changed into something more suitable for playing games, Victoria and Mattie walked out onto the stretch of grass that had been earmarked for such games. Victoria explained the rules.

'The main thing to remember is that when you've hit the ball you drop the bat and run. Run like the wind, because you only score a rounder when you get right round the pitch. Just getting to one or two of the bases doesn't count. Today is just a practice to pick a team. One of the girls from one of the other huts – don't ask me which one because we're not supposed to know – is organizing a match for tomorrow, so I'm picking an opposing team. We need nine players to make it a decent match.'

A group of about ten girls were waiting. Once Victoria had instructed them how to set out a pitch, the practice began. Several of the girls had played at school and understood exactly what they had to do. They divided into two teams of six.

'Mouse, you go on the batting team. I want to see how you can play.'

Nervously, Mattie picked up the wooden bat and stood where Victoria told her to.

'Right, I'll bowl. Just give it a whack, Mouse. I'll send you a gentle one.'

Victoria threw the ball towards her and Mattie swung the bat wildly – and missed completely.

'Try again,' Victoria said, as the catcher standing behind Mattie picked up the ball and threw it back to her.

But again, Mattie couldn't hit it. On the fourth attempt, the bat clipped the ball, but sent it only a short distance.

'Try the fielding side,' one of the other girls suggested. 'You might be better at catching.'

'Doubt it,' Mattie muttered, dropping the bat and taking up a position outside the pitch.

The third time she dropped the ball, Mattie herself spread her hands and, before anyone else could say it, said, 'Look, I told you I was hopeless at anything remotely sporty.'

Victoria, standing with her hands on her hips, laughed. 'You weren't kidding, were you? I thought you were just being modest.'

'No, I wasn't.'

'Never mind, Mouse. You're good at sums and that's what really counts in this place.'

They smiled at each other.

'Couldn't she be an umpire?'

Mattie shook her head. 'I don't know the rules well enough. I tell you what, though. Tomorrow, when you play this match, I'll stand on the sidelines and cheer you on.'

'You could always bring us slices of orange out at half-time.'

'Well, I would, if I knew where to get some oranges from.'

Now everyone laughed and the practice carried on in good humour amongst them all.

Sport became one of the favourite pastimes amongst everyone at Bletchley. The men formed cricket teams in much the same way that the women had rounders matches, and a few of the men went on long cross-country runs. Victoria even joined in those sometimes; she was a keen participant in anything 'sporty', as Mattie called it. But Mattie was quite content to watch from the sidelines.

Through the days that followed after they had settled into their new billet, the work in Hut 6 – and so consequently where Victoria worked too – increased at an alarming rate.

'You know why this is happening, don't you?' Pips said in a quiet voice to Mattie.

The younger girl shook her head.

'The enemy has swept through Holland and

Belgium and now they're in France, pushing the French and British forces further and further back towards the coast. They're sending more and more messages every day and we're in danger of being overwhelmed.'

'Then we'll just have to work longer hours, won't we?' Mattie said and her words brought a smile to Pips's face.

'That's the spirit. We might have to work all night sometimes, so just warn those nice people you're living with now not to worry if you don't come home at all.' She looked archly at Mattie. 'I wouldn't like them to get the wrong idea.'

Mattie laughed. 'Neither would I. They're so good to us.'

'Like being at home, is it?'

Mattie's smile faded. 'Better, if I'm honest,' she said briefly and turned away before she would be tempted to say too much or be asked questions she'd rather not answer. But Pips's glance followed her thoughtfully. It seemed Mattie had secrets of her own to keep.

'I'm just too tired to cycle home,' Mattie said one night. 'I'm going to lie down here with my head on my coat and snatch a couple of hours.'

'I might join you,' Pips laughed, 'but I just want to carry on for a while. I think I might have got something here . . .'

Mattie knew that feeling so well, somehow instinctively knowing that at any moment she would get the breakthrough she was looking for.

She lay down on the hard floor and was instantly asleep. Pips glanced down at her fondly and fetched her own coat to lay over the girl. Then she carried on through the dark hours puzzling over a heap of messages.

When Mattie woke up and blearily rubbed her eyes, she could hear the excited chatter around her. There was even clapping and cheering. Pips was standing over her with a cup of coffee.

'We've had a bit of luck. One of our chaps had the bright idea that overtired enemy operators might make mistakes. Well, they have – several times – and we're back into the Red.'

Red was the colour that Hut 6 had given to the Enigma key used by the German air force, but they'd stopped being able to break this in the early spring. They had, however, been able to break what they called the Yellow code – the system used by the Germans when they had invaded Denmark and Norway. It had been much easier to break than the Red and had given them a lot of information on German plans. But now, it seemed, they had got the Red back too.

Mattie reached up to take the cup and drank gratefully. 'That's marvellous. Then I'd better sluice my face and get back to work.'

'Only for a few hours. The boss came in and saw you on the floor. He says I've to send you home tonight for a good night's rest. And I'll make sure Victoria goes with you. She must be working just as hard as we are.'

'I'm sure she is.' Mattie pulled herself up. 'But in the meantime, show me what's been happening – this is so exciting.'

'Do you lot in that hut ever stop working?' Victoria said as they cycled home later that night. 'You've done forty-eight hours on the trot and we're on our knees with all the stuff you're sending to us. What's going on, Mouse?'

Mattie was thoughtful for a moment. Just how much could she tell Victoria without breaking the Official Secrets Act she had signed?

'Come on, Mouse. It's only you and me and we're working on the same messages as you because you send them to us,' she added reasonably.

'The Germans are sending out over a thousand Enigma messages a day, so there's a lot of work. You probably know as much as I do.' She grinned. 'More, actually, because you're translating them. I can only understand bits of them, enough to know that they're in proper German, but I did hear a whisper that our forces are trapped against the coast near a place called Dunkirk. It seems' – she paused again and took a deep breath – 'that an armada of little ships is being assembled in Sheerness, I think it is, to go across the channel to rescue our lads on the beaches there.'

'Because of the number of soldiers to be brought back, you mean?'

'That and also because larger warships can't get close to the beaches. The smaller boats will ferry them off the beaches and take them out to sea to the bigger ones.'

'What a brilliant idea. How many do they think they'll get back?'

'They're hoping to get about forty-five thousand men back. British and other Allied troops.'

'That sounds a lot. Let's hope they manage it.'

Although Dunkirk was a defeat for the Allies, the rescue mission – Operation Dynamo – was a huge success when over 330,000 troops were rescued and brought back to the South Coast of England. But now there were new terrors. With the fall of France, Britain stood alone and it was down to Churchill's stirring speeches to rally the country.

'. . . the Battle of France is over,' he warned, 'I expect that the Battle of Britain is about to begin.'

'You know he really makes you believe we can still win,' Victoria said as they sat by the lake, which lay a short distance from the front of the house. They often came here on fine days to take a brief respite from work. 'All that stuff about fighting on the beaches. I really believe the British would do it if push came to shove.'

'I'm sure of it,' Mattie said. 'If all those soldiers rescued from Dunkirk are anything like my brother, Joe, then they'll not take that lying down. They'll be wanting to get their feet back on French soil as quickly as possible.'

'Your brother? You've got a brother? And he's in the army?'

Mattie nodded. She wasn't ready to share all her secrets with Victoria or anyone else for that matter.

She wondered if she ever would be. But she didn't mind her new friend knowing about Joe. She was proud of Joe.

'We've got leave coming up next week,' Victoria said as they cycled back to their billet later. They didn't often get the chance to go home together just now; they finished at different times, mostly because of Mattie, who had to stay until she'd finished the particular message she was working on.

Mattie yawned. 'And all I'll want to do is sleep.'

'Are you serious? I was hoping you'd come up to London with me for the weekend. You can stay at the flat I share with a friend.'

Mattie was thoughtful for a moment. The only time she'd been to London was for her interview at the Foreign Office. She'd really like to see more of the city, even if it was under wartime conditions.

'Will she mind?'

'Not at all. She's already written and said that if I ever want to bring a friend it'd be fine.'

'Does she know where we work?'

'I'm not sure. We never speak of it, but she works at the Foreign Office.'

Mattie grinned. 'Like we all do.'

Victoria laughed. 'Quite, but she really does. She's a typist.' She paused and then added, 'So, will you come?'

Mattie nodded. 'I'd love to. How long do we get?'

'Four days.'

'How generous – seeing as we've been working non-stop for three weeks and through the night sometimes.'

'We're probably very lucky to get that long, seeing as how important the work is.'

'I know.' Mattie sighed. 'It's just that it's so tiring. The concentration required is something else. But I expect it's just the same for you. You have to be every bit as accurate with your translating, I'm sure.'

'So,' Victoria said, 'we'll catch the train up to the city on Thursday night after work and be back here on Monday evening.'

'That sounds lovely.'

'Constance, this is Mattie. I call her Mouse, but no one else is allowed to.'

Constance laughed. 'Oh, just like you don't really like being called "Vicky"?'

Victoria pulled a face. 'Unfortunately, Mouse does call me that. I suppose it's only fair.'

Mattie and Constance shook hands. 'I'm delighted to meet you. I have a letter for you, Mattie. It arrived at the office this morning, so they gave it to me to pass on to you. Come into the kitchen and I'll make us some coffee. It's not real coffee, I'm afraid, but it's not too bad.'

Mattie stood still for a moment. She rarely received letters and was suddenly afraid that this could be bad news. She followed her hostess slowly and when Constance handed her the envelope, she stared down at it.

'Open it, then, Mouse,' Victoria urged. 'I can see you're worried.'

Mattie tore it open and then, as she began to read, she smiled. 'It's from my brother, Joe . . .' As she read on, her smile broadened. 'You're not going to believe this. He's on leave. Here in London – right now – and wonders if we can meet.'

'Oh, now isn't that lucky? Does he say where?'

'No. He's given me a telephone number of the hotel he's staying in and asks me to ring him if I can.'

'No time like the present. Go and try him now,' Constance suggested. 'He might be in as it's getting late. The telephone is in the hall.'

'Yes, I noticed it when we arrived.'

'Do use it whenever you want.'

'You're very kind, Constance.'

When Mattie had left the kitchen, Constance leaned towards Victoria. 'She seems very nice.'

'Oh she is. She's lovely. A bit shy, but she's extremely clever. I can't tell you any more than that.'

'Do you work together?'

Victoria shook her head and pressed her lips together as if to stop herself saying any more. Constance laughed. 'It's all right. I quite understand.'

'We arrived at you-know-where at the same time and we're billeted together. She's rubbish at sports, but she comes and supports any games we organize.' There was a pause before Victoria asked, 'How's everyone at the office? How's Charlie?'

A pink tinge suffused Constance's cheek. 'He's fine.'

'Oho, do I detect a blossoming romance? Do tell.'

'We're going out together. It's not encouraged at work, but because we work in totally different offices, I think everyone's turning a blind eye.'

'And because Daddy is Sir Michael. Does he know?'

'Oh yes. Charlie comes to the house occasionally. Mother and Father both like him.'

Victoria was quiet for a moment, wondering just what it would be like to be able to take a friend home – especially a young man – and have them made welcome.

At that moment, Mattie came back into the room.

'I'm to meet him at the Lyons Corner House in the Strand tomorrow afternoon. I've no idea where that is, but I told him I thought you would. He said to bring both of you, if you'd like to come, and he'll treat us all to afternoon tea.'

'That's very kind, but I'll be at work and then I'm meeting Charlie,' Constance said.

Mattie turned to Victoria. 'You'll come, won't you, Vicky? I'd like you to meet Joe.'

Victoria grinned. 'And you might get completely lost in London if I don't. Yes, I'd love to.'

Forty-Seven

The following day Victoria took Mattie on a tour of some of the sights of London. When it got to mid-afternoon, they made their way to the Strand where Joe had said he would meet them. The restaurant was, as the name suggested, set on the very corner of the street. Mattie, eager to see Joe, led the way inside with Victoria following. Suddenly she stopped and let out a little gasp. Victoria bumped into her.

'What's the matter?'

Mattie didn't answer but suddenly rushed ahead, weaving her way between the tables, completely ignoring the hovering waitress.

'*Dan!* Oh Dan . . .'

Victoria, following more slowly, watched as Mattie flung her arms around a tall, good-looking young soldier with brown wavy hair and dark brown eyes. Beside them another young man, dressed in the same uniform, stood grinning. He turned and his gaze met Victoria's. As she looked at him, she felt a fluttering in her stomach and her palms felt clammy. She stopped, feeling as if she couldn't go any further, but he came towards her, holding out his hand.

'You must be Mattie's friend. Victoria, isn't it?'

'Um – yes – that's right.' Suddenly, she was tongue-tied. She couldn't take her eyes off him.

He chuckled, a low, infectious sound. 'I'm Joe. Mattie's brother. And that's Dan, a lad from our street back home. They've known each other since they were nippers.'

Victoria cleared her throat and found her voice. 'They – they seem pleased to see each other.'

Again the low chuckle. 'You'd never have thought it years ago. Dan used to tease her summat rotten. She gave him a bloody nose once. Here, come and sit down. They'll finish their hugging in a minute.'

She sat down next to him, but turned her head, drinking in the sight of him. He was tall and broad shouldered with fair curly hair, cut to regulation army shortness. His face was even featured – handsome, Victoria thought – with a mouth that broke into easy, friendly smiles and blue eyes that twinkled merriment. He spoke with the same accent as Mattie. She and Victoria hadn't shared many secrets about their backgrounds, but Victoria knew her family lived in Sheffield. She found their accent rather attractive; a distinct change from the plummy, affected voices she was used to. Mattie and Dan sat down opposite them and Mattie introduced Victoria to him. He nodded to her in a friendly manner, but his gaze soon went back to Mattie, who was staring at him in just the same way. Her face was pink and her eyes sparkling.

'Oh it is so good to see you both.'

'We've been stationed together since coming back

from Dunkirk, though Joe is a long way ahead of me in rank. I have to salute him and call him "sir" around camp.'

'Well, I'm a regular and I've been in the army a lot longer than you.'

'You were both at Dunkirk?' Mattie asked, fear in her voice.

The two men glanced at each other as if they now shared their own secrets. 'Yes, but here we are like two bad pennies.'

Now, it was the two girls who exchanged a look; they knew all about Dunkirk – probably more than the two young soldiers, who'd actually been there. But they couldn't say a word.

It was a merry afternoon; the food was good and the restaurant spoilt the two young couples with extra treats and free refills of coffee or tea.

'Anything for our brave army lads,' the Nippy serving them said, bringing more cakes.

'We have to leave at five tomorrow afternoon,' Joe said, 'but are you two free earlier in the day?'

'Of course,' both Mattie and Victoria chorused and then, glancing at each other, laughed.

As the meal was coming to an end, Mattie asked, a little hesitantly, Victoria thought, 'Have you been home, Joe?'

'No, but Dan has. He keeps me posted. You tell her, Dan.'

'Are you sure?'

Joe nodded.

'What is it?' Mattie asked, sharply. 'Is Mum all right?'

Dan put his arm around her shoulders and she leaned into him. 'Your mum's fine,' he said, 'I promise, but, Mattie love, your dad's gone.'

Mattie gasped and her eyes widened.

'Maybe I should go,' Victoria said softly to Joe.

'No, no, please stay. You're her friend. I'm sure she doesn't have secrets from you.'

If only you knew, Victoria thought wryly, but she said nothing.

'What do you mean "gone"?'

'He's disappeared and Lewis along with him.'

'Oh, is that all? I thought for a moment—'

'Sorry. I'm not telling it very well.'

'The law was after them both,' Joe said. 'So they took off.'

'How's Mum coping?'

The two young men exchanged a glance again. 'A helluva lot better without them, if I'm honest, Mattie love,' Joe said.

'Your Nancy's stepped up to the plate,' Dan put in. 'She's working in a factory so she's still at home at the moment, though I understand she'd like to join the ATS. But now there's only the two of them – her and your mum – they're fine.'

'So, Toby's still in the countryside, is he? Still in Derbyshire?'

Joe nodded. 'He's on a farm somewhere. Sounds like he's loving it. Mum gets a letter from him every week.'

Mattie relaxed. She'd been gone from home so long that she couldn't imagine the chubby little boy now being eleven years old and living on a farm.

'It's good for him,' Dan said gently. 'Fresh air and good food.'

Mattie nodded. 'Mum must miss him though.' She paused and then added tentatively, 'How is she – *really*?'

Victoria couldn't fail to notice the accent on the last word. There was more behind that question than met the eye, she thought.

'She's fine. Honestly.' Dan's grin broadened. 'My mum keeps her that busy with the WVS that she hasn't time for – well – anything else.'

'I'll go home and see her as soon as I can,' Joe promised. 'Now the coast's clear.'

Just what does Joe mean by that? Victoria wondered. As the two young soldiers walked the girls back to the flat, Victoria was thinking, *So, Mattie has secrets about her family life just like I have. No wonder we get on so well – because neither of us are asking probing questions.*

The four of them met again the following morning and spent the whole day together until it was time for the young men to board the train back to camp.

As they stood on the platform a little apart from each other, Mattie and Dan together, and Victoria and Joe, Joe asked her softly, 'Will you write to me, Victoria?'

'Of course – if you'd like me to.'

'I would. Here, I've written my address on this piece of paper. It's likely to change now and again as we get posted to different places, but I'll let you know when we move. And do I write to you at the Foreign Office, like I do Mattie?'

'Yes, that's right.'

'You must both have very important jobs,' he murmured, 'but I'm guessing you're not allowed to talk about them.'

Victoria pretended to pull a face. 'It's all rather boring stuff actually. Just a lot of filing and so on, but we're told it's all very useful.'

Joe sighed. 'A bit like us really. We don't know where we're going to be sent next. It might be to North Africa. Certainly, it won't be back to France for a while. Though personally, I can't wait to take back what we lost.'

'Poor France. Fancy having a war fought in your homeland for the second time in only twenty years or so.'

'Yes, it does seem very unfair, doesn't it? Anyway,' he grinned, 'we'll do our best to keep the enemy from getting here and, one day, we'll get their country back for the French. Now, sorry, there's the whistle. I'll have to go.'

Suddenly, he grasped her shoulders and pulled her towards him, kissing her gently on the mouth. 'Take care of yourself, Victoria. I'll see you again soon.'

And then he was gone, striding towards the train, his kitbag slung over his shoulder whilst Victoria stood with her fingers trembling against her lips, staring after him.

As they walked home back to the flat, where Constance had promised to cook them an evening meal after they had said goodbye to the two young men, Mattie linked her arm through Victoria's. 'I saw Joe kissing you.'

'I know. It was a – surprise. Do – do you mind?'

'Heaven's no!' she chuckled. 'Dan kissed me as well. And *that* was certainly a surprise.'

'Was it? You seemed very – um – well – friendly from the start. I mean, you rushed to him first, even before your brother.'

Mattie stared at her. 'Oh crumbs, I did, didn't I?' She giggled. 'It was just such a surprise to see him, that's all.'

Victoria laughed. 'And if you believe that, you'll believe anything.'

Mattie shrugged. She hadn't got used to the idea herself yet, that perhaps she was fonder of Dan than she'd realized. And then she remembered how she'd felt when Dan had insisted to the Musgraves that he and she were nothing more than friends. Maybe, she admitted to herself, deep down I've always wanted it to be more.

'It was nice for you to hear news from home.' Victoria's voice, interrupting Mattie's thoughts, sounded wistful. 'To know that your mother and sister are all right. And your little brother too. Toby, is it?'

Mattie nodded and ran her tongue round her lips. 'Yes, I was glad to hear she's – um – better.'

There was something in her hesitation over the final word that stopped Victoria pressing her further. With the bits she had gleaned from the conversation over dinner, Mattie's family life sounded difficult, to say the least. It was obvious Mattie was not yet ready to confide in her new friend – if she ever would be. And Victoria could hardly condemn her for that. She wasn't being exactly open about her own background. But they were both so used to keeping secrets now – they weren't even supposed to talk about their work to each other, never mind anyone else – that being reticent about their earlier lives didn't cast a blight on their blossoming friendship. Without even discussing it, they had both decided to accept each other at face value from the time they had met on the station platform. Whatever had gone before, didn't affect their lives now.

'I'll be pleased to get back to the flat,' Victoria said. 'My feet are killing me. We must have walked miles today.'

'But I've enjoyed it, haven't you?'

'Oh yes,' Victoria murmured, and thought back to the moment earlier in the day when they had gone to the park – her park – only a stone's throw from where she lived. She'd been a bit nervous that she might see someone who knew her especially when, by pure chance, they sat down on the same park bench where she had sat so many times with Naomi and occasionally with Rose too. Even once with her mother. That all seemed such a long time ago now. She'd glanced across towards the other bench, where the man had always sat. But today, as she had expected, it was empty. She wondered what had happened to him. The picture she'd drawn went everywhere with her, encased between two sheets of tissue paper and protected by a cardboard folder.

She'd taken it to Miss Taylor's and even to Switzerland and Germany. It was with her still at Bletchley Park, stowed safely at the bottom of a drawer in their billet. Why she carried it with her, she could not have explained to anyone. She just knew it was something she had to do.

Forty-Eight

The following morning, over a leisurely breakfast, Constance asked, 'Is there anything else you want to do – either of you – whilst you're in London?'

'Not me,' Mattie said. 'It's the first time I've ever been here and although it's been wonderful, I don't think my feet will take any more sightseeing.'

Victoria chewed her bottom lip and then sighed. 'I suppose I ought to see my mother, though I doubt she'll be in.'

The other two girls exchanged a glance, then Constance said tentatively, 'What about Miss Gilbert?'

'That would be more difficult. She doesn't live in London and we must go back tomorrow. I should have written to her. She might have come up.'

'You must do it next time you get leave. Please feel free to come here any time you want to – both of you. Though be prepared, the boys won't always be able to make it and certainly not both at the same time. This has been a very lucky coincidence.'

Victoria turned to Mattie and gave a weak smile. 'Naomi Gilbert was my governess until I went to boarding school at the age of eleven. We were very close and she used to visit me at school three times every term.'

'And you spent part of the summer holidays with her, didn't you?' Constance murmured. That had been common knowledge at school. She didn't think she was saying anything that Victoria would mind.

Victoria nodded. 'We still exchange letters regularly and I saw her at the end of March just before we – um – went away.'

Mattie sighed heavily. 'Maybe next time we get a decent leave, I ought to go home.'

'Am I allowed to ask where that is, Mattie?' Constance asked, but then added, swiftly, 'Don't say if you'd rather not.'

'Sheffield.' But now Mattie said no more.

That afternoon, Victoria went to her home in Kensington, but she didn't invite Mattie to go with her. She knew the girl would not be offended. Mattie herself had been very guarded, not saying much about her own family; she would not think it strange that Victoria too was reluctant to discuss her background.

Mrs Beddows and Rose welcomed her quite literally with open arms.

'Is my mother in?'

'No. Nor will she be,' Mrs Beddows said. 'She's out to lunch and then has a committee meeting of some sort. Goodness knows what, but there's committees for this, that and the other springing up every day.'

'And your mother seems to be joining most of them,' Rose said wryly. 'Mind you,' she added with a saucy smile, 'don't tell her I said so, but it's less work for us if she's out all the time.'

'Are you getting on all right, Miss Victoria?' the cook asked. 'Still working at the Foreign Office, are you?'

Victoria nodded.

''Spect it's very busy now with all this lot going on.'

'Yes, it is, and thank you for your letters – both of you. It's so nice to get them.'

'Well, things aren't so bad for us, really. Apart from the rationing and the blackout, that is.'

'We haven't had any of the bombing they keep warning us about.'

Victoria said nothing. She was only too aware of the huge fear now that Hitler planned to invade Britain in September – only a few short months away. It was very likely that she would be one of the first to know about it, and yet she'd be unable to warn any of the people she cared about. Sometimes, such secrets were very difficult to keep.

'Have you seen Miss Gilbert recently?' Mrs Beddows asked.

Victoria shook her head. 'No, but next time I get a few days off I will try to go and see her.'

'It'd be nice to get out into the countryside. I bet you get sick of travelling about the city with all this going on.'

Victoria bit her lip; more deceit. How she wished she could tell these two women, who had cared for her for so many years, that in actual fact she was living in the countryside, as safe as anywhere and certainly safer than living in London just now. But she knew she couldn't.

*

Churchill had been right; Hitler turned his full attention on his plans to invade Britain.

'I was talking to one of the guys,' Victoria told Mattie as they carried their coffee down to sit beside the lake during the week after they'd returned to Bletchley. It was their favourite spot. They could talk without being overheard, except by the geese or the frogs. 'And before you say anything, no, we weren't talking about our work. He thinks that Hitler wants command of the skies before he tries landing here. The newspapers have said as much. In fact, they believe he's given Goering and his Luftwaffe that very task.'

'They'll have a job on their hands with our RAF lads,' Mattie said confidently.

Victoria sighed. 'It's going to be tough though.'

By the middle of July, the German air force was attacking ships in the English Channel, luring the defending British fighters over the water, perhaps hoping that if an aircraft was shot down over the sea, it would be a pilot lost as well as an aircraft.

'Goering's not getting it all his own way,' Mattie said. 'It says in today's paper that they lost thirty-seven of their aircraft yesterday.'

'What about our losses?'

Mattie shrugged. 'They didn't say.'

'Protecting the British people, I expect, from an unpalatable truth.'

Through the following weeks, the battle for supremacy of the skies raged over the South of England. Occasionally, the dogfights drifted north and the occupants of Bletchley could see them in the distance.

Shading their eyes, the two girls watched. 'I hope they don't get up as far as here,' Mattie murmured worriedly. 'If they report back that they've seen this place—'

'I think they're a little too busy to be taking reconnaissance photographs, Mouse. Besides, as long as there aren't too many of us outside, they'll only think it's an estate – which, actually, I suppose it used to be.'

'But what about all the huts? Won't they think that's odd?'

Now Victoria laughed. 'From the air, Mouse, it'll probably look like a pig farm. By the way, we'll soon be moving into that new hut right next to yours,' Victoria told Mattie as they parted to return to work. 'It's to be called Hut Three.'

Mattie giggled. 'I know, and have you seen the chute they've rigged up for us to pass deciphered messages between the two huts?'

'No. Do tell.'

'Pips showed me. When the messages have been decoded, we put them on a tray attached to a piece of string and push it through the chute with a broom handle. Then you have to pull it the rest of the way with the string.'

'You are joking, Mouse, aren't you?'

Mattie shook her head. 'No, I'm deadly serious. But it works, Vicky. It'll save running round from our hut in all weathers. And besides, we're not allowed to go into each other's huts. You know that.'

'Well, well.' Victoria shook her head. 'Whatever next?'

*

'A whole week off next week!' Victoria said towards the end of August as they took an hour's break for a walk to the lake. 'Can you believe it?'

'Actually, I'm very surprised with all that's going on. The battle for the skies doesn't seem to be over yet.'

'Perhaps it had something to do with you passing out at work the other day. You are looking very peaky, Mouse. Mrs Coupland is very concerned about you. She asked me if you'd let her husband take a look at you.'

Mattie smiled. 'They're so sweet – the pair of them. My fainting fit was probably my own fault. I was so busy that I hadn't eaten properly – or taken any breaks – for a straight eight hours. It was stupid and I won't do it again. I got a right ear-bashing from Pips and the boss.'

'Ah, so that's why the head of your hut sought me out and suggested we both take a little time off. He must have swung it with my boss. Mind you, we are both on call to come back immediately if there's a flap on. So, what are we going to do? Oh sorry – I shouldn't presume. Maybe you have your own plans.'

Mattie wrinkled her forehead. 'Not really, though I suppose,' she sighed, 'I should go home and see my mother. I had a letter from Joe last week. He's going to be there this weekend, so—'

'Oh Mattie, may I come with you?' Victoria's eyes were sparkling. The very fact that she used Mattie's proper name instead of the nickname spoke volumes.

Mattie regarded her steadily. 'Victoria Hamilton, are you falling for my brother?'

412

Victoria's cheeks turned pink. 'Well – um – he's very nice. I'd – um – just like to see him again. That's all.'

'Let's sit down, Victoria.' Mattie too used her full name. 'We must have a serious talk.'

They sat down on the grass near the lake, facing each other.

'You don't approve?' Victoria said.

'It's not that at all, it's just—' She sighed heavily. 'Let me explain. I've never said much about my family – my background – because I am ashamed of it. We come from one of the poorer parts of Sheffield. Oh, there's nothing shameful about *that*,' she said swiftly, anxious not to insult the wonderful people of her home city. 'Most of the people there are honest as the day is long, hardworking and with hearts of pure gold. They're the best neighbours anyone could have.' She paused as she thought about Dan's mother, Bella Spencer. 'But some of them – and my dad is one of them – live just outside the law. They shoplift. They steal anything they can get their hands on. I don't think my father has ever done an honest day's work in the whole of his life. And, sadly, my younger brother, Lewis, has followed in his footsteps. You heard Joe say that they'd both disappeared? Now, I'm guessing that the law was about to catch up with them so they've done a runner. So, do you really want to get mixed up with that kind of family?'

'Mattie, you can't help your relatives. It's not your fault any more than it's mine that my mother is a cold-hearted bitch, who once told me quite bluntly that she'd never wanted me.' She gasped and her hand fluttered to her mouth as if to stop more words escaping from it. Her eyes widened as she stared in disbelief at Mattie, not for what her friend had confided, but for what she herself had said. She'd let slip the secret she'd guarded all her life. And to think that even though they were now being *trained* in keeping secrets, she had blurted it out.

Mattie took her hand. 'You're right. But I thought you ought to know, though I would ask you to keep this to yourself, as, in turn, I will never breathe a word about what you've just said. Joe's a good sort – the very best. I wanted you to be aware that he's not your – class, that's all.'

Calming a little, Victoria said, 'Mattie, haven't you noticed? There are no class distinctions here at B. P. None. The professors, the heads of departments, all the really clever people treat everyone as their equals. They don't act superior in any way. Not ever. We're just all working together in a common cause. Even the little messenger girl that runs eagerly from hut to hut all day long – they all treat her the same as they treat everyone else. Maybe – when all this is over – the war will have wiped away a few class barriers.'

Mattie smiled, a little sadly. 'But enough to allow you to become involved with the likes of my brother?'

Now Victoria smiled too. 'I very much hope so. My only worry is that Joe might not want to be with someone like me. It works both ways you know.'

'If it's any consolation, he seems smitten. He never fails to ask about you in his letters even though I know he's writing to you as well.'

Victoria gasped and her cheeks turned a deeper shade of pink. 'Really?'

'Yes, really, but now,' Mattie said firmly, getting up, 'we should go back. There's work to be done.'

'Isn't there always?' Victoria laughed, but she took Mattie's proffered hand and hauled herself up.

Forty-Nine

They travelled north on the Saturday, the last day of August.

'Where are we going to stay?' Victoria asked. 'I don't want to impose upon anyone.'

Mattie smiled at Victoria's discretion. 'I'm not sure what the position will be at home, but Dan's mother, who lives in the same street, would be seriously offended if I stayed anywhere else than with them. And I think the same would go for any friend of mine.' Mattie knew that if she took Victoria to the Musgraves, who would undoubtedly make them both welcome, it would be seen as a slight to the Spencer family. When Victoria still looked a little uncomfortable at arriving at a stranger's home without invitation or warning, Mattie added, 'You'll like Aunty Bella. She's what folk call a "rough diamond", though the accommodation on offer is likely to be similar to our first billet.'

Mattie wanted to giggle at the mortified expression on Victoria's face. 'Oh Mattie, I didn't know. I'm so sorry.'

'Don't be,' Mattie said. 'You were right to move us when there was something else much better on offer. I love it at the Couplands'.'

Victoria smiled weakly. Inside she was quivering. Just what was she letting herself in for? Perhaps she'd been a bit hasty in inviting herself along with Mattie, but she so wanted to see Joe again.

They walked from the station, each carrying a suitcase. As they turned a corner, Mattie said quietly, 'This is my street.'

They both stared down its length. It looked hardly changed from when Mattie had last seen it, though perhaps a little shabbier. But there was a war on, she reminded herself. The menfolk, who would normally spruce up their houses, were either away in the forces or involved in exhausting factory work, and even a lot of the women would have taken on some kind of war work, leaving them less time for their normal domestic chores. The front steps, she noticed, were not quite as gleamingly white-stoned as usual.

'We'll call and see Aunty Bella first. She'll tell me how things are at home.' She nodded. 'I live further down the street.' She pulled a wry expression. 'I've not actually lived there for years, but you know what I mean.'

Victoria nodded, still feeling apprehensive about meeting Mattie's family and neighbours, though she reminded herself that the lady she was about to meet was Dan's mother, and she'd liked Dan.

They went down the passageway between two houses. 'We call this the ginnel,' Mattie told her. Then she opened the wooden gate that was more like an outside door into a small backyard. A woman was pegging washing onto a line strung across the yard. She glanced up at the sound of the gate opening. For a moment, she stared at them both and then dropped the wet garment she was holding back into the washing basket on the ground and rushed towards them, her arms spread wide.

'Mattie! Oh Mattie, love.' The woman enveloped Mattie in a bear hug whilst Victoria looked on in astonishment. She had never seen anything quite like it. The unrestrained warmth from a woman who was not even Mattie's mother brought a lump to Victoria's throat. Her own mother had never hugged her – not once. And though Naomi had, it had always been done with decorum. This welcome was unrestrained joy.

Mattie was laughing and disentangling herself. She turned. 'Aunty Bella, this is my friend, Victoria.'

Bella reached out towards her and for one moment Victoria thought she too was going to be clutched to the woman's ample bosom, but instead Bella merely grasped both her hands. 'You're very welcome, love. Come in, come in. You must be gagging for a cuppa. Then we'll go down and see ya mum, Mattie, love. Things are so much better since—' She paused and glanced at Mattie, a question in her eyes.

Mattie nodded. 'Yes, I do know about Dad and Lewis leaving. Joe told me.'

'He's here this weekend. Is that why you've come?' Bella led the way inside and gestured that they should both sit down at the table.

'Partly, but once I'd heard Dad was no longer here, I planned to come and see Mum anyway. So, how is she – really?'

'Much better.' She glanced at Victoria. Understanding the meaning behind the look, Mattie said, 'It's all right. You can speak freely in front of Victoria. I don't mind her knowing.'

'Good friends, are you?'

Mattie nodded and said simply, 'The best.'

Victoria smiled her agreement.

'Then you're very welcome here, love. Mattie's like one of our family. And talking of family, did you know our Jane's in the ATS, same as your Nancy?'

'No, I didn't know that. In fact, I didn't know that Nancy had actually gone. I knew she wanted to—' She hesitated, not wanting to distress Bella. 'So, you're on your own too. Well, I mean, you've got Mr Spencer, but . . .'

Bella laughed raucously. 'I don't see much of him either. He works long hours now he's back at the steel works doing war work. But me and your mum help each other along.'

'Aunty Bella, you always have. I don't know what we'd have done without you.'

Bella flapped her away in embarrassment, but Mattie could tell she was touched. 'So,' she said again, coming back to her question. 'How is Mum?'

'Not drinking at all, Mattie. It's for Toby, she says. Vowed she wouldn't touch another drop until he comes home and she said it was easier to give up altogether than to ration herself.'

Mattie nodded. 'I've heard that said before.' She paused and then added hesitantly, 'Is she managing all right for money?'

'Fine. I give her what Joe still sends to me each week and now you – and Nancy too – are both sending a little bit an' all, well, she's doing very nicely. Me an' her spend a lot of time together. The WVS keeps us both out of mischief.'

'And Dad and Lewis?' Mattie asked quietly.

Bella shrugged. 'Best day's work they ever did, running off.'

'Was the law after them?'

Bella hesitated for a moment, with a swift glance at Victoria, obviously wondering if it was really all right to be quite so open in front of her. 'No one knows, but we all think that was probably the reason.'

There was silence between them before Bella said, 'Now, what's this about you and Dan?'

Mattie's eyes widened. 'What – what d'you mean?'

'Well, is there owt going on?'

'We're writing to each other. We're just friends, that's all.'

'You sure? 'Cos I reckon it's a bit more on Dan's side. Now, I don't want either of you getting hurt, 'cos, though he's me son, I love you like a daughter an all.' She turned towards Victoria. 'D'you know owt, love?'

Victoria smiled. 'I couldn't possibly say, Mrs Spencer.' But when she gave a broad wink, they all collapsed in laughter.

'Hello, Mum,' Mattie said, as she opened the back door and stepped inside. She was on her own this time as Victoria had insisted that she should see her mother alone at first. 'I'll follow you down in about an hour,' she'd promised.

Elsie's eyes widened and filled with tears. 'Oh Mattie!'

Then they were hugging each other as if they would never let each other go again. They sat and talked and talked until Victoria knocked on the back door and more introductions were made.

Victoria glanced around the room. 'Is Joe here?'

Mattie chuckled. 'That's the only reason she's come, Mum. To see our Joe.'

Elsie's eyes widened. 'You know him?'

Carefully, Victoria said, 'I met him in London with Mattie.' Although Mattie already knew, Victoria decided to be honest with Elsie. 'We've been writing to one another.'

Elsie smiled. 'That's nice. I write once a week to him; I'm sure our soldiers are always glad of letters. Do you write to him too, Mattie? I know you write to Dan because Bella told me.'

Mattie laughed and caught Victoria's glance. 'No keeping secrets from these two, eh, Vicky?'

Victoria saw the irony in Mattie's words. Of course there were lots of secrets they must keep from their families; even from Joe and Dan.

'Joe should be back any time,' Elsie said. 'He's gone into town to do some shopping for me, bless him. He stocks up my pantry every time he comes home. And Nancy does the same whenever she's back.'

'How is she? Is she liking life in the ATS?'

'Oh I think so. She talks about nothing else. She's learnt how to strip a lorry engine down. Who'd have thought it?'

'And Toby? How is he?'

For a moment, Elsie's face fell. 'He's fine. Very happy in Derbyshire. Bella and I are going to see him in September, if we can, though we don't want to unsettle him. I know we haven't had any bombing, but he's better off in the country. He's staying on a farm and is being very well fed. A lot better than I could manage, so I want him to stay there for all sorts of reasons.' There was a brief silence before Elsie said, after a swift glance at Victoria, 'You know about your dad and Lewis, don't you?'

Mattie nodded. 'Yes. Joe told me when we met in London.'

'I'll always love Lewis – he's my son – but I have to say, I don't like what he's become.'

Tellingly, Mattie noticed that her mother made no reference to still loving her husband.

The back door rattled and Joe staggered in under the weight of four shopping bags. Mattie jumped up and hurried to help him.

'Don't reckon you'll starve for a couple of weeks now, Mum. Hello, Mattie. I didn't know you were coming.' Then he stopped in surprise. 'Oh, hello, Victoria.'

The two gazed at each other, an action that was not lost on either Mattie or Elsie.

'I'll put all this away for you, Mum,' Mattie said, 'while you make Joe a cuppa. He looks as if he could do with one.'

'I'll make one for us all and there are some scones in the bread bin, Mattie. Bring them out and we'll have those too. By the way, how long can you stay?'

'We've both got a week off, Mum. Bella's offered for Victoria to stay with them and I thought I could stay with you, if that's all right?'

'How lovely.' Elsie beamed happily.

'I've got to go back tomorrow evening,' Joe said. There was no hiding the disappointment in his voice. 'But we'll make the most of the time we've got. I'll take you both to the pictures tonight.'

'Oh, you two go,' Mattie said airily. 'I'll stay and talk to Mum. We've got a lot of catching up to do.'

Again there was a glance between Joe and Victoria, both with a delighted beam on their faces.

Fifty

Mattie was sound asleep by the time Joe crept into the bedroom they'd shared since childhood, though now there were only the two of them, one on either side of the tatty curtain. The following morning, they both woke early and lay talking in whispers.

'Joe, I haven't told anyone else. I – I feel a bit shy about it, but I got my first at Oxford.'

'That's wonderful, Mattie. I knew you would. Have you not even told Mum?'

'Not yet, but I will before I leave.'

'You must let the Musgraves and Miss Parsons know too. And, of course, the Spencers. They were all very good to you.' Joe was silent for a moment before adding, 'There's something I haven't told Mum but I don't think I will. I made some enquiries about Dad and Lewis. They were caught dealing on the black market.' He sighed. 'They're both in gaol for a stretch.'

'Best place for 'em, Joe. I hope they throw away the key.'

'You don't mean that, Mattie.'

'I most certainly do. Look how much better Mum is without either of them around. If Dad came back, you can bet your bottom dollar she'd slip back into her old ways, despite her promise. Just let's hope he stays away even when he does get out.'

'I wouldn't bank on it. He might have nowhere else to go. And Lewis might be in the same position.' He paused a moment and then added, 'D'you think I should tell her?'

'No, let's keep it to ourselves for now. It would upset her to know about Lewis.'

'But it's a bit deceitful, isn't it?'

Mattie didn't answer. Her life now was full of necessary deceit.

After a pause, Joe said, 'So what d'you want to do today?'

'I think you two lovebirds should spend it together without me playing gooseberry.'

'I do like her, Mattie, but I'm not sure her family will think I'm good enough for her.'

Mattie gave a very unladylike snort of laughter. 'Don't you worry about that. One thing this war is doing, it's a great leveller of the class system. And besides, I have the feeling that Victoria will do exactly what she wants to do, never mind what anyone else says. Women are now being treated with a great deal more respect.' She thought about Bletchley Park, where the women were treated equally alongside the men, respected for their individual talents and the valuable work they were doing. She hoped it was now the same in the factories where women were helping to build Spitfires and tanks.

'Oh well, I'm afraid the end of the war is a long way off. We'll just enjoy the present. And now, I'm going to get up and go and find her.'

After Joe and Victoria had set out for a day in the city, Elsie and Mattie concentrated on household chores until Bella arrived mid-morning to share elevenses.

'D'you know, I quite like this chicory coffee now,' Elsie said, pouring the dark liquid into three mugs.

'Tha can get used to owt in time, love,' Bella laughed. 'Though I don't reckon I'll ever come to terms with Spam.'

As they sat down together, Bella asked, 'Now, what is it you're doing, Mattie?'

Fortunately, Mattie and Victoria had agreed the same story to be told to anyone at home – both in Sheffield and London – who asked.

'We're both working for the Foreign Office in London.' Craftily, they'd agreed on the word 'for' instead of 'at'. 'Victoria started there as a typist and I got a job as a filing clerk. That's how we met.'

'Couldn't you get something better than that, with all your qualifications?' Elsie said.

'It's a start,' Mattie laughed. 'You have to start at the bottom and prove yourself. Besides, it's the war. You have to go where you're sent.'

'Really? Can't you choose what you want to do?'

Mattie shook her head, still confident that they were accepting her cover story.

After Joe had left, Victoria seemed a little lost. The two girls went shopping in the city, visited museums and parks, but everywhere only seemed to accentuate how much Victoria was missing him already. On the

Wednesday, she said, 'Mouse, would you be offended if I went back to London?'

'Of course not. Do you want me to come too?'

Victoria shook her head. 'I don't mind either way. What do you want to do?'

'If you don't mind, I'll stay with Mum the rest of the week. It's so long since I saw her and goodness knows when we might get a decent leave again. We've been very lucky to get this one.'

'You could always faint again,' Victoria chuckled, then she added, 'but I will go back, if you don't mind. I've really enjoyed meeting your mum and Dan's family, but I want to try to see Miss Gilbert if I can before we have to go back and I *suppose* I ought to see my mother. So I'll see you back at B. P. on Sunday evening.'

Mattie nodded. 'Have a good time.'

'I'll try.'

On the Friday evening, Mattie told her mother and Bella that she was returning to London on the Saturday.

'I want to be ready for work on Monday,' she explained, 'and the trains from here are very iffy and usually packed with troops moving all over the place, though goodness knows where they're going to and from. And it could be much worse on a Sunday.' She didn't tell them that her ultimate destination was Bletchley and that, in these uncertain times, it might be so much easier to get there from London. She knew she could stay at Constance's flat any time.

The three of them talked late into the night, until

Bella said just after midnight, 'I really must go home. My Rod'll wonder what's happened to me.' She hugged Mattie hard. 'You take care of yourself, lass, and mind you write to us.'

The train was crowded, as Mattie had anticipated, though the soldiers travelling with her politely made sure she had a seat. Arriving in the capital, she went at once to Constance's apartment, where, to her surprise, she found that Victoria was already there. 'I came back yesterday from seeing Miss Gilbert – or Naomi, as she now insists I call her, even though I find it difficult – with the intention of visiting my mother, which I did this afternoon. My welcome, if you can call it that, was decidedly frosty, so after I'd had a chat with the cook and the maid, I came back here. But why have you come today? I thought we were meeting back at work tomorrow?'

'I just had a feeling that the train services – especially from Sheffield – might be very dodgy on a Sunday.'

'Constance has been telling me that the RAF have been heavily engaged in air battles over the South Coast.'

'Really?' Mattie said, keeping her face straight. Both the Bletchley Park girls were fully aware of this already, but it didn't do to tell anyone else, not even Constance, who still worked at the Foreign Office.

'I'll start dinner, shall I?' Constance said. 'Unless you want to eat out, of course?'

'No,' both girls chorused and Mattie said shyly, 'You're such a good cook, it's as good as going to a restaurant.'

'And a lot cheaper,' Victoria teased.

'Flattery will get you everywhere,' Constance laughed.

A little before five o'clock, when Constance was clattering pots and pans in the kitchen, Mattie said, 'What's that awful noise?'

'Oh my God! It's the siren.' Victoria said. 'That's an air raid warning. Connie—' She ran into the kitchen. 'Leave everything. We must get to the nearest shelter. Where is it?'

'I haven't the faintest idea,' Constance said calmly. 'But I don't think they'll come here.'

At that moment there was a huge crash not far away and the windows rattled ominously.

'Oh, perhaps you're right. Come on, let's get a few things together and go and find out where it is.'

'What sort of things?'

'Something to eat and drink. I'll see to that. You and Mattie get some blankets off the beds.'

'Blankets? Why do we need them?'

Constance shrugged. 'We could be there half the night. And wherever the shelter is, it might get awfully cold in the middle of the night. It is September now, you know.'

'Right. Mouse!' Victoria shouted. 'Come and help me.'

Ten minutes later, they were locking the door to the apartment and joining the rest of the residents trooping down the stairs.

'Mr Henderson—' Constance hailed an elderly gentleman struggling to descend. 'Here, let me carry your bag.'

'Oh thank you, mate.'

'Are you going to the shelter?'

'Yes. Orders is orders,' he laughed wheezily.

'Then we'll follow you. We've no idea where it is.'

He continued to cling to the rail and walk slowly down the stairs.

'Come on, you lot, let's get down,' came an impatient voice from behind them.

'You're holding the job up.'

At that moment another crash sounded, a lot closer this time, and the people behind them surged forward. Constance only just managed to catch hold of Mr Henderson's arm before he fell.

'Look what you're doing,' Constance shouted angrily.

'Then get a move on. If you can't go any faster, move to the side and let us past.'

Victoria and Mattie moved to walk down behind the old man and Constance, whilst others behind surged past them, clattering down the stairs and into the street. After what seemed an age, although it was only a few minutes, the four of them reached the foot of the stairs.

'Now,' Constance asked, as they emerged into the street, 'which way?'

'To the left. It's at the end of the next street. You girls go on ahead.'

'Absolutely not,' Victoria said firmly. 'We're sticking together.' She took hold of the old man's other arm. 'Take it easy. There's no rush.'

As if to contradict her there was another crump

of a bomb falling, but a little further away this time. Victoria didn't even flinch.

'They're going for the docks,' the old man muttered. 'They'll take a pounding.'

They walked along together, matching their pace to the old man's.

'Here we are,' he said at last.

'Why, it's the tube station,' Constance said in surprise.

'Aye, safest place there is around here,' the old man said.

They settled down together and spent the remainder of the night making sure Mr Henderson was as comfortable as it was possible to make him, and looking after each other. There was not much sleep to be had; the ground was cold and hard and frightened children cried incessantly. They emerged in the morning to see little damage in their local area, but the news from the dock area was heartbreaking.

'We'd better make our way back to you-know-where as soon as we can,' Victoria said grimly to Mattie. 'We've work to do.'

Back at the apartment, they ate breakfast, packed their suitcases swiftly and hugged Constance.

'No idea when we'll be able to see you again, but we'll write to you in the normal way.'

'What do I tell the boys if they turn up here?'

'I think they've both guessed that we're doing some sort of work that we can't talk about,' Mattie said. 'They're always being told "Be like Dad, keep Mum" – Dan told me in his last letter – so I think they know not to ask awkward questions.'

'Not like your mum and Aunty Bella, Mouse,' Victoria chuckled and, turning to Constance, she explained, 'They asked us outright what we were doing.'

Constance's eyes widened. 'Whatever did you say?'

'The story we'd agreed; that I'm a typist at the Foreign Office and Mattie is a filing clerk there and that's how we'd met.'

'And do they think we live here – all of us together?'

'Actually, they didn't ask that, did they?'

'I just wondered if they'd questioned why you didn't give them a proper address rather than using the Foreign Office for your mail.'

Mattie laughed. 'I don't suppose it occurred to them to ask. Now, come on Vicky, we ought to get going. The trains might not be running normally and also, it's Sunday.'

As Mattie had predicted, their journey took longer than usual.

'We're having to check all the lines for damage,' an official told them at Euston, 'before we let any of the trains go, but you should make it back to Bletchley by tonight.'

'Oh thanks for nothing,' Victoria muttered, but not loud enough for the harassed man to hear. He was hardly responsible for Hitler's bombing raid. But he was right about one thing: they did make it back to Bletchley station just as the daylight began to fade. As they walked towards their billet, Victoria stopped and lifted her head towards the sky.

'Listen,' she said.

Mattie stopped walking. The evening was still and calm. 'I can't hear anything.'

'Exactly. Isn't it wonderful?'

'Oh come on, I'm exhausted. I can't wait to climb into Mrs Coupland's lovely feather bed.'

Fifty-One

Letters from Joe now came more frequently to Victoria than to his sister, but she generously shared his news with Mattie, even though she didn't actually let her read the letters. Mattie understood perfectly; she was now receiving letters from Dan that she wouldn't show to anyone else, not even her dearest friend, for that was how she regarded Victoria now.

Cocooned in their own little world, news of what was happening in other parts of the country was haphazard, usually gleaned from Dr Coupland's newspapers – often days later – when they had time and energy to read them. It wasn't until anxious letters from both Joe and Dan began to arrive that Mattie and Victoria understood just what was happening.

'Of course, we should have been the first to know with all the messages we read,' Victoria said.

'In a way, yes, you're right, but my German's not good enough to understand them fully. Besides,' Mattie grinned, 'even once a message is decoded, we can't sit there reading it. It has to be on its way.'

'It's the same for us, and of course the messages

434

are dispersed amongst us so we don't get a full picture.'

'Joe says that London is being bombed night after night. They even hit Buckingham Palace. He wants to know if we're all right.' Victoria met Mattie's gaze and her voice trembled. 'He – he thinks we're both still in London.'

'I know. So does Dan, but we can't tell them anything, Vicky. We mustn't even hint that we're – elsewhere.'

'Can't we? Not even just to say that we're not in the city?'

'No, not even that,' Mattie said firmly. 'We could be imprisoned if we say anything – or even shot.'

'Oh, I don't think . . .'

'You're not paid to *think*, Vicky. Just to translate, as I am to decode.'

'But we've got to say *something*, Mouse, else they'll go up to London to see for themselves. We can't have that.'

Mattie chewed her lip. 'Tell you what, let's just say that when we're at home – which they'll take to mean Constance's apartment – we go to the underground station near there. And that's not lying, because that's what we do when we *are* there.' She hesitated for a moment, her mind working quickly. 'And that, of course, the Foreign Office, which is where they both think we actually work, has very good arrangements for shelters.' She giggled. 'We're not saying we use them.'

'Do they?'

'What?'

435

'Have good shelters?'

'I haven't the faintest idea, but they must have, surely.'

'I don't like not being truthful with the boys. They're worried about us and that's – rather nice.' There was a wistful tone in Victoria's voice; being worried over wasn't something she was used to.

'We can't tell them *anything* approaching the truth, Vicky. Thousands of lives depend on our secrecy.'

Victoria sighed. 'I know. You're right, and we'll do what you say and try to make them accept that we keep ourselves safe.'

'If the enemy ever got wind of this place,' Mattie said, 'and bombed it, it would be catastrophic. Not only for the loss of life here, but for all those service men and women out there we'd no longer be helping. The war could go on a lot longer because of it.'

'You really think that the work we're doing is helping to shorten the war?'

'I'm sure of it.'

The two girls gazed at each other solemnly, both understanding that a little deceit to the boys was an insignificant price to pay.

'And I'll tell you something else,' Mattie said, 'even when it's all over, we won't be able to talk about it to anyone for years, probably never.'

'I know,' Victoria whispered.

In the autumn of 1940, Hut 6 had a miraculous breakthrough; they broke the Enigma code – which they called the Brown Enigma – used by the Luftwaffe to guide their bombers to their targets. Around midday each day, the targets were named and

Bletchley were able to forewarn the RAF. Not only could warnings be given to the towns and cities, but the pilots knew where to intercept the incoming enemy aircraft.

'You know they warn other places that aren't actually targets too, don't you?' Mattie told Victoria. 'Just so that the enemy won't guess we've broken their code.'

'It must be saving a lot of lives,' Victoria murmured, proud to think that she was playing such an important role in the war. 'They'll be able to sound an air-raid warning and get folk down into the air-raid shelters in time.'

'And factory production – it'll be saving a lot of factories from getting destroyed,' Mattie added, 'because not so many bombers are getting through.'

But there were days when the girls and their colleagues were downcast by failure.

'We haven't managed to decode Brown Enigma for the last four days now,' Mattie moaned in the middle of November as they got ready for bed. She was almost in tears. '*Four days* when the bombers got through and we could do nothing to help stop them.'

'I know,' Victoria said huskily, feeling her friend's pain just as acutely. 'And one of their targets was Coventry. They destroyed the cathedral there. It's on the front page of Mr Coupland's paper. Did you see it?'

Mattie nodded, her voice shaking as she whispered, 'And we couldn't do a thing about it. We couldn't warn them.'

'Get into bed, Mouse. I'll fetch you some hot milk. Mrs C won't mind.'

Victoria sat on the edge of Mattie's bed whilst they both drank hot milk.

'Have you heard,' Victoria whispered, 'about this new machine that your boss and some of the other mathematicians and scientists have designed? They think it's going to revolutionize the speed at which codes can be cracked.'

Mattie shook her head.

'It's supposed to be able to do the work of ten Enigma machines at once. They'll be building several of them and recruiting Wrens to operate them.'

'Oh now I understand what they've had us doing. We've had to find a crib and then create what Pips calls a menu that gets taken somewhere else. I had no idea where, though. I bet it's to that new machine.'

'Now, lie down and I'll tuck you in. You'll see, you'll be back into the Brown code tomorrow.'

Victoria was right and by the time she and Mattie reported for duty the following day, the Brown code had been broken again.

Early in December, both Mattie and Victoria were on duty when a message was passed through from Pips in Hut 6 to Hut 3. She bit her lip as she sent the tray on its way and glanced at Mattie, who was engrossed in the message she was working on. Pips made a sudden decision. She left the Machine Room and knocked on the office door of the head of Hut 6. As she entered, she was met by a fug of tobacco smoke. The boss always seemed to have a pipe in his mouth. It was almost as famous as Churchill's cigar.

'Hello, Pips. What can I do for you? Problems?'

'Yes.'

'Sit down and tell me what's worrying you.'

'I've just deciphered a message and sent it through for translation. Now, my German isn't as good as that of the girls in Hut Three, but I did pick up a smattering in the last war. I *think* the bombers could be on their way to the North tonight . . .' She ran her tongue around her lips. 'Most probably Sheffield.'

He met her gaze. 'Warnings will be sent in the usual way to several cities as a cover, Pips.'

She nodded. 'I know, but Sheffield is where Mattie's family lives.'

'Well, I'm sorry. You can't tell her.'

'I know, but I'm worried that her friend, Victoria in Hut Three, might get the message to translate and . . .'

'Ah, I see.' He rose from his chair. 'I'll have a word with my counterpart. You go back to your work and not a word to anyone.'

'No,' Pips whispered.

Moments later, the two heads of Huts 6 and 3 were deep in discussion.

'Wait here. I'll just see if I can find out where that particular message has gone.' He returned a few minutes later and pulled a face. 'I'm sorry, but it seems that Victoria is translating it as we speak.'

'Then you must have a word with her. On no account must she tell Mattie. It's not that I don't trust either of them. I do – implicitly – but the temptation to try to let her family know might be too strong for Mattie.'

The head of Hut 6 returned to his own office whilst the head of Hut 3 now had the unenviable job of speaking to Victoria. When he knew she had had time to deal with the message properly, he sent for her.

'Sit down, Victoria. I understand you have just translated a message that indicated that Nazi bombers might be heading to northern towns and cities tonight. Quite possibly one of them being Sheffield.'

'Yes, I have, and it's been passed on in the usual way.'

'Good.' He paused, fiddling with a pen on his desk. He cleared his throat. 'Victoria, I understand that you have a close friend working in Hut Six, and that you actually share a billet together.'

'Yes, I do.'

He cleared his throat again. 'You do understand, don't you, that you must say nothing – nothing at all – about that message? No doubt you both know that you should not discuss any work that passes through your hands with anyone other than those in your own hut.' Before she could speak, he rushed on, 'Oh I know there must be the temptation sometimes because you are, in actual fact, dealing with the same work – the same messages – but . . .'

Victoria remained silent, just staring at him, keeping her face expressionless.

'In this case, it is vital, Victoria, that you don't say a word to her. If Mattie felt compelled to try to warn her own family—'

He didn't need to say any more. Victoria understood. Not one word must ever escape from Station X that they had the slightest inkling of where the enemy bombers might strike.

'Northern towns and cities – several of them – will be warned in the usual way in good time to let the local population seek shelter.'

Victoria nodded. She understood only too well. She could not say a word to Mattie – not now or ever.

As she left the office and went back to her desk she realized that some secrets were a lot more painful to have to keep than others.

A few days later, Mattie received news from Joe:

Sheffield's been badly bombed on two nights. Mum's safe and so are Mr and Mrs Spencer. Both Dan and me have got compassionate leave, so we're going up there to make sure they're all right. Evidently no bombs fell on their street so they were very lucky . . .

'Do you want to go home?' Victoria asked worriedly, feeling sick that she was betraying her dearest friend. 'I'm sure the boss would let you.'

'No. Joe says they're unharmed. That's all that matters. He does say that when they come back, he and Dan are going to try to squeeze in a night in London. He wonders if we can meet them.'

'Oh dear. He still thinks that's where we are, doesn't he? All this secrecy is getting to be a bit of a pain,' Victoria said crossly, her pangs of guilt sharper than ever.

'But it's so necessary, Vicky. We must stick to the rules.'

'I know,' Victoria murmured, wondering if Mattie would be so understanding if she knew the whole truth. Aloud she said, 'We can only ask.'

Fifty-Two

'Amazingly, my boss has said "yes",' Mattie told Victoria. 'What about yours?'

'He's agreed too, but we can only have one full day away.' Victoria rather suspected that the two heads had consulted each other and – both knowing the full story – had agreed to an exceptional leave in the circumstances. But Mattie must still be kept in ignorance. 'When did Joe say they'd be in London?'

'Arriving Tuesday, and they've got to leave very early on Thursday from King's Cross to get back to camp.'

'Good,' Victoria smiled, 'that'll fit nicely, we can go up on Tuesday evening and then we can catch the milk train to get back here in time to report for duty on the Thursday morning. We don't want to run into them or have them find out that we're even leaving London.'

The 'boys', as they now referred to Joe and Dan, were already at Constance's flat when they arrived.

'Quick,' Constance hissed, when she heard Victoria's key in the door and came running. 'Hide your suitcases in the hall cupboard. Don't let them see them or they might start asking questions.'

There was a bit of scuffling and giggling in the

hallway, but then the three of them went into the kitchen, smiling innocently.

After all the initial hugs and kisses and exchange of greetings, Mattie said, 'So how are things at home?'

'Fine,' Joe said. 'They're all OK. The Musgraves are safe too. I checked. Our street wasn't hit at all, though a house in the next street took a direct hit and demolished the shelter they'd built in the back-yard. Three people were killed.'

Mattie gasped and her eyes widened. 'Anyone we know?'

Joe shook his head, whilst Victoria shuddered inwardly and was thankful it had not been Mattie's family or friends involved. The city had received the usual warning, but of course the valiant RAF couldn't stop all the bombers getting through.

'They went for the residential areas on the first night and then, three nights later, came back and targeted the industrial area,' Dan said. 'A lot of folks reckon that they made a mistake the first night and hit the wrong area, so they returned to do the job properly,' Dan said.

Joe shook his head as if he didn't agree. 'I'm not so sure. I reckon they meant it. They mean to demor-alize the population as well as hit industries.'

'You're probably right. We just ought to be grateful that none of our family and friends were hurt. At least, I hope they weren't. I must write to Mr and Mrs Musgrave. They'll know about all the teachers who were so good to me.'

Mentally, Victoria crossed her fingers but said nothing.

'Now I have a surprise for you,' Constance said. 'I'm taking you all to the Four Hundred nightclub tomorrow night. They have live music and you can dance all night if you want to.'

'But it's a members-only club, isn't it?'

Constance winked at Victoria. 'It is, but Daddy's a member and he's got tickets for all of us. Charlie's coming too.'

The boys slept on the floor of the lounge and the following morning they all decided to have a lazy day if they were to be up until the early hours. Charlie arrived in the early evening and fitted in very well with the young men in uniform. They both knew he too worked at the Foreign Office and recognized that even though he wasn't in uniform, he was still engaged in valuable war work.

He kissed both Mattie and Victoria on the cheek. 'You both all right? Everything going well?'

'We're fine, thanks.' Mattie laughed. 'Anyone would think you hadn't seen us for ages instead of only this morning.'

Charlie gaped at her for a moment and then a flush crept slowly up his face. 'Well – we – erm – don't get much time for chit-chat at work, do we? I – um – hardly ever bump into you.'

'That's very true.' She turned and introduced him to Joe and Dan. The awkward moment was smoothed over and it was a merry party of six that made their way to the club. The band played tirelessly and it seemed that everyone there was intent on enjoying themselves. They all danced until their feet ached.

'Just so long as Hitler doesn't decide to spoil things,' Joe said.

'I don't think they'll come tonight,' Charlie said. 'It's foggy. We do love foggy nights in London.'

They had a wonderful evening, laughing, drinking and dancing. Constance and Charlie were expert dancers, but Mattie, Joe and Dan had never had lessons. Mattie and Dan shuffled around the floor, giggling and holding each other tightly. As for Victoria, with a practised partner she could probably have outshone anyone else on the floor, but she didn't care. She was in Joe's arms and that was where she wanted to be. They danced close to each other, and she tactfully followed his lead even though the steps were none that any dancing teacher would have recognized.

'D'you realize it's three o'clock in the morning,' Dan said. 'We'll have to go back to the flat and pick up our kit bags and head for King's Cross. We daren't miss the early train, else we'll be on a charge. And that wouldn't look good for Joe.'

Victoria and Mattie glanced at each other. They were catching the early morning milk train to Bletchley. Things were working out very nicely. They could wave the boys off and pretend they were going to bed, when in fact they too would be packing their suitcases and heading to a different railway station.

'Right. We'll get a cab,' Charlie said. 'Leave it to me.'

Only moments later, the six of them were piling into the vehicle and heading back to the flat.

'A quick cup of coffee for you two boys,' Constance said pointedly, 'and then it's off to bed for the rest of us.' She winked at Victoria and Mattie. They already knew that, occasionally, Charlie stayed the night, but that Constance's parents would not approve.

Another secret that must be kept.

'Well, I think we got away with that,' Victoria said, as the two young soldiers left the flat.

'I'm so sorry,' Charlie was contrite. 'I almost let the cat out of the bag. I thought they would know.'

'Charlie,' Victoria said, pretending severity, 'you should know that no one must know where we really are. All anyone has been told is that we're working for the Foreign Office, which they naturally think is in London. And we don't disabuse them.'

'I know,' he said with a hangdog expression.

Victoria laughed and patted his cheek. 'No harm done. Now, we must love you and leave you both.'

Perhaps Victoria would not have been so calm if she had heard the conversation between Dan and Joe as they waited on the draughty platform for their train.

'Charlie seems a nice bloke,' Dan began.

'He does, but did you think there was something odd about the way he greeted Victoria and Mattie?'

Dan wrinkled his forehead. 'Not really. Should I?'

'Well, they're all supposed to be working at the same place and yet it felt like he hadn't seen them for a while.'

'I expect it's quite a big building. Maybe they work in different offices and don't meet up with each other very often. He said as much. I mean, we know a lot of chaps at camp, but you can go days without seeing someone.'

'Yeah, I expect you're right, but—' Joe hesitated.

'But what?' Dan prompted.

'I just get the feeling that they're not actually living and working in London at all. Have you never thought it odd that we write to them care of the Foreign Office and not to a home address?'

'No, to be honest, I haven't.' Dan paused and then asked, 'So where do you think they are?'

'I don't know. But they're both very clever girls. I reckon they'd be wasted as a typist and a filing clerk, don't you?'

'Oh Lord, you don't think they've got involved in – in special duties? You know, like becoming agents or spies or something?'

'I very much hope not,' Joe said soberly. 'But there's not much we can do about it if they have.'

'They always seem to be there when we let them know we've got leave. Surely, if they were away somewhere, they wouldn't be able to do that, would they?'

'Probably not.'

'We could always go up to London next time we get some leave without telling them in advance,' Dan suggested. 'And surprise them.'

'It might be us who get the surprise.'

The girls got back to Bletchley just in time to go on the nine o'clock shift, desperately hoping that no one would notice the effects of not having been to bed at all the previous night.

'It was worth it, though,' Mattie giggled as they cycled home at the end of the day, wobbling with tiredness. 'Just to see Joe and Dan.'

Victoria sighed blissfully. 'Yes, it was. But goodness knows when we'll have the chance of another decent leave that will coincide with them.'

'We can always write to them more often than we do now.'

'I know, but it isn't the same, is it?'

'No,' Mattie said with a sigh. 'It isn't, but we've plenty to do to keep ourselves busy.'

'Haven't we just?' Victoria said wryly.

In the early months of 1941, Victoria was a little restless.

'All sorts of clubs and societies have been organized, Mouse. What do you fancy doing?'

'Oh I'm not much of a one for joining anything.'

'Then it's high time you were. Come on, let's do something. I promise I won't try to drag you to anything sporty.'

Mattie grinned. 'It wouldn't be any use if you did.'

'Mind you, I'm hoping the lake will freeze over. One of the girls in my hut said they went skating on it last winter. That'd be fun.'

Mattie pulled a face. 'I don't think I'd like that. I'd fall over and break my arm or something daft and then where would I be?'

Victoria wrinkled her forehead, thinking. 'What do you think of Scottish Country Dancing then? Some of the girls say the fellers wear kilts. That must be a sight to behold.'

Mattie pulled a face. 'I've got two left feet, Vicky. It's the same as sports. It must be something to do with co-ordination. I'd be useless. I've never had dancing lessons. When we went to that night club in London, Dan and me just shuffled round the floor.'

'Well, it didn't matter there, did it? The floor was so crowded.' Victoria chuckled. 'It's just an excuse to get close to your feller, isn't it?' She wrinkled her brow as her thoughts returned to what she could persuade Mattie to join. 'There are various musical groups, choirs and such. Can you sing?'

'I don't know. I've never really tried.'

'There's a drama group. Fancy acting?'

Mattie shook her head. 'Heavens, no!'

'We'd better not try the fencing group. I don't want you let loose with an épée and killing a valuable member of Station X. I know, what about bridge or chess?'

'I wouldn't mind either of those. Perhaps chess. Pips goes to that. Tell you what, why don't you go to your sporty clubs and I'll go to chess.'

'Yes, all right, that's what we'll do, but this evening we'll go to the cinema, if you're up for it.'

'That'd be lovely. Which one?'

'The Palace in Fenny Stratford. It's only about half an hour on our bikes.'

Mattie grinned. 'Just so long as it's not raining.'

As they cycled side by side along the country lanes, they chatted together, safe in the knowledge that they could not be overheard. It was even more secure out here in the open than whispering in their bedroom at the Couplands' home.

'Have you seen the bevy of Wrens that have arrived, Mouse? What are they doing here?'

'Disappearing into one of the huts from which, I might add, there are some very peculiar noises.'

'Ah, that'll be that new bombe machine that's been developed. They say it's called that because it ticks. I don't know if that's true or not. Are we allowed to have a look?'

Mattie snorted with laughter. 'Don't be daft, Vicky. We're not allowed to know anything that goes on in any of the other huts. You and I break the rules a bit by talking about what we do. All I know is that the work must be pretty intense. Those poor girls stagger out after a shift looking exhausted.'

'There's one thing, though,' Victoria laughed. 'A lot of them have got a lovely billet.'

'Have they? Where?'

'Woburn Abbey.'

Fifty-Three

The cold weather eased and the nights grew lighter. It was good to see the bright colours of the spring flowers blooming in the villagers' gardens and the trees beginning their annual growth as the girls travelled to and from work each day.

'Have you heard?' Victoria said as they cycled home on a warm spring night early in May.

'Shouldn't think so,' Mattie chuckled. 'We're not allowed to hear much.'

'Well, there's a whisper going around that our navy has had a couple of pieces of good luck recently, though to be fair it was believed to be following the advice of one our chaps here,' Victoria added loyally. 'A German weather ship was captured near Iceland and they retrieved some paperwork on Enigma settings and then a couple of days later, one of our warships captured a U-boat and guess what?'

'I can't. Go on.'

'They actually got an Enigma machine and cipher books. It's going to make a huge difference to the naval team here.'

'Oh my. That's fantastic.'

*

The London Blitz had continued relentlessly since the previous September, but one weekend early in May was later said to be the worst raid of all. Ironically, it was to be the last of the nightly bombardments, though, of course, spasmodic attacks on the capital went on. A couple of days later Mattie was waiting outside Hut 3 for Victoria to join her for their usual morning coffee break. Her face was solemn.

'Let's get our coffee and go down to the lake. I've got something to tell you. And I don't want to be overheard.'

Victoria's mouth was dry and her heart began to beat faster. Was it news about Joe?

'Pips had some bad news and she's had to go to London. Her husband and her stepdaughter were killed in the bombing at the weekend.'

Victoria gaped at her. 'Oh how dreadful. Poor Pips. I haven't met her yet, but I've seen her coming and going from your hut.'

'We still work together. She's been very good to me. I shall miss her.'

'She'll come back, won't she?'

'Knowing her, I think so. She's the sort of person who would deal with that sort of personal tragedy by burying herself in work.'

They were both silent for a moment, wondering how Pips would cope with such a devastating loss.

'I hope Constance is all right. Should we get in touch with her?' Mattie said quietly.

'To be honest, I think they'd let us know from the Foreign Office.'

'What about' – Mattie was hesitant now – 'your mother?'

'Mrs Beddows and Rose have my address.'

'But what if . . .' Mattie's voice faded away.

'A bomb dropped on the house and they were all killed?'

'Well, yes.'

'I think I'd hear somehow,' Victoria said casually, but she did not enlighten Mattie any further.

At the end of the month, there was a buzz of excitement through the park that not even the strictest rules could stop.

'You know our naval section have been tracking the *Bismarck* after she sank our ship, *The Hood*, don't you?' Mattie whispered to Victoria in their bedroom after they'd put their lights out. The name of Germany's biggest and most feared battleship was known to everyone.

'Yes, go on.'

'Well, they told the admiralty that she'd been damaged and was heading to France, presumably for repair.'

'Did they decrypt a message to that effect?'

'Not exactly, but it was something to do with where the messages were coming from that made them think that, but the admiralty were sceptical. Anyway, we had a bit of luck in our hut today. One of our girls was dealing with a message on the Red—'

'That's the Luftwaffe Enigma, isn't it?'

'Yes.'

'Go on.'

'She spotted the word Brest.'

'The French port?'

'Exactly. What had happened was that a Luftwaffe officer was enquiring if his son was all right because he was on the *Bismarck*. And the reply was,' Mattie's tone was triumphant, 'that the ship was on its way to Brest.'

Victoria sat up and stared through the darkness towards Mattie's bed. 'Never.'

'True. I promise. So, of course, it was all hell let loose then to get that snippet of news sent through. Proof that she was indeed heading towards a French port.'

Victoria lay down slowly. 'So, if our navy finds it and sinks it, that German officer will have been instrumental in – well – causing it. And what if his son is drowned?'

There was silence between them until Mattie said quietly, 'It's war, Vicky. Just think of all those poor men we lost when it sank our ships.'

'I know you're right, of course, but just sometimes it's very difficult to be exultant at the loss of life, even if they are our enemy.'

There was no reply from the other bed and Victoria knew that Mattie had fallen asleep. But she lay awake for quite some time remembering – in the secret of the night – the handsome Kurt. Though she hardly ever thought about him now, Victoria couldn't help thinking back fondly to the time when she'd thought she was in love with Kurt. She knew better now; her love for Joe was very different. Even so, she didn't wish Kurt – or his fellow countrymen – any harm.

This war could be beastly at times.

To everyone's amazement, at the end of June, Hitler broke his pact with Russia and invaded the country.

'What is he thinking of?' Victoria said, stabbing at Mr Coupland's newspaper. 'He's mad.'

'Well, we all know that,' Mattie said calmly. 'But just think, he's turned his attention away from us.'

'Possibly, but to take on the might of that country . . .'

'All the better for us,' Mattie said reasonably.

Victoria laughed. 'You sound like the wolf in Little Red Riding Hood.'

'Let's just hope the Russian *bear* can defeat him. Save us the job, won't it? Meanwhile, we'd better get going. We're both on the night shift . . .'

Whilst perhaps the pressure eased a little on the civilian population, the occupants of Bletchley Park were as busy as ever. By October, Hitler had neared the gates of Moscow but a greater shock was to come. In early December, Japan attacked Pearl Harbor, bringing America into the war.

'I expect we'll get a few Yanks here eventually. We're all on the same side now.'

Mattie giggled. 'I think we always were. America has helped us an awful lot with supplies, you know.'

'Well, yes, there is that.' Victoria sighed. 'I just wish we could get to see the boys more often.'

'They don't seem to be able to get leave so much now, do they?'

'Not long enough for us to meet up, anyway. Maybe they'll manage something near Christmas. Anyway, come on, Mouse. We'd better go.'

None of them had managed any leave before Christmas, but early in January, Joe got in touch with Dan to say, 'I've got two days' leave coming up. Can you wangle some at the same time?'

They were now at different camps, but still managed to communicate now and again by telephone although it wasn't easy and sometimes needed the telling of little white lies.

'I'll do my best. If you don't hear any more from me, I'll meet you at King's Cross a week on Wednesday. I'll get the earliest train.'

'Are we telling the girls?'

At the other end of the crackly wire, Dan chuckled. 'Absolutely not. We'll book in at that B and B we always go to and turn up at the flat in the evening.'

When Constance opened the door to them a week later, her eyes widened and her lips parted in a startled gasp. 'What are you two doing here?'

'We've come to see our girls. Are they home yet?'

'Er – no.' She hesitated, clearly flustered. Then, with a sigh, she said, 'You'd better come in. Would you like a drink? I've got a very nice bottle of single malt.'

'Oo, that sounds great.'

The two soldiers made themselves comfortable on Constance's sofa. 'So, how's things? Are you all well?'

'Yes, thanks.'

'When will they be home?'

'Erm . . .' Constance fidgeted. She kept sitting down and then jumping up with the excuse of fetching them some nibbles.

'Constance – what's going on? You're like a cat on hot bricks.'

'Um – they're not here,' she blurted out at last. 'You really should let them know when you're coming to London.'

'Spur of the moment decision,' Dan said smoothly. 'We didn't know if we could both get leave at the same time.'

The excuse sounded plausible to Constance, who was wracking her brains to think of an equally logical reason for their absence.

'They're on holiday. They've – um – gone away for a couple of days.'

'Constance,' Joe said quietly, 'you're the world's most awful liar. I don't believe you. Now, where are they?'

'They're in the country.' This at least was true, but still the boys didn't believe her.

'Where?'

Constance looked away from Joe's steely gaze and shrugged. 'I really couldn't say.'

The two boys glanced at each other.

'I think,' Dan said slowly, 'that we seem to be putting you in a very awkward position. Look, perhaps you can answer just one or two simple questions because this is worrying us both.'

Constance said nothing, neither agreeing nor disagreeing. She just looked at them with anxious eyes.

'First of all, have they gone abroad?'

458

Constance shook her head.

'Are they likely to?' Joe asked.

Again, she shook her head.

'So, they're in this country, but not in London?'

'I can't answer that,' Constance said huskily. 'We all work for the Foreign Office – you know that – and we've all had to sign the Official Secrets Act.'

'Just one more question,' Joe said. 'And then we're taking you out to dinner and we won't ask you anything else. Scout's honour. Are they safe?'

Now Constance was able to say, 'Yes, I promise you that. As safe as anyone in this country at the present time.'

Joe sighed. 'Well, that's all we want to know really.'

'So, all letters come to the Foreign Office, do they, and then get sent on to them?'

'You said you wouldn't ask anything else,' Constance said.

'Ah, trouble is,' Joe said with a grin, 'we were never in the Scouts.'

The conversation ended on a laugh.

But as they waited on the platform for their respective trains the following evening, Joe said, 'I've been thinking.'

'Hey, steady on.'

Joe punched Dan's shoulder lightly.

'What about?'

'All this cloak-and-dagger stuff.' Joe glanced around them, just to make sure no one could overhear their conversation. 'Something happened at camp last week that made me wonder.'

'Go on.'

'We have this corporal who's a regular. He was injured at Dunkirk but not severely enough to be invalided out of the army. He's recovered now and is back with the rest of us, but he told me the powers that be don't think he could ever fight abroad again.'

Dan shrugged. 'Fair enough. So, he'll be given duties here, then. Drill instructor or something, won't he?'

'Have you ever heard of the Y Stations?'

'No.'

'They're listening stations dotted around this country to pick up enemy signals.'

'Wouldn't he need to know Morse code for that?'

'Ah, but that's not what he's going to do. Evidently, these signals are copied out very carefully and then sent by despatch rider to be decoded at a top-secret location somewhere down south. And that's what he's going to be doing. Every day he'll be taking these messages to – well – wherever. He wouldn't tell me exactly where it was. I tried pulling rank on him, but even that didn't work.'

Through the fading light, Dan stared at him. 'Ah, I see what you're getting at. At least, I think I do. You think that Mattie and Victoria, because of their cleverness – and let's face it, they beat us into a cocked hat when it comes to brains – could be working at this hush-hush place?'

'I do. I think they are – as they're telling us – working *for* the Foreign Office, but not actually *at* it.'

Dan was thoughtful for a few moments. At last, he said slowly, 'That would make sense. If they're

460

outside London but not too far away, they'd be able to get back there fairly easily. And when we've told them in advance that we're going down, they must have been able to wangle leave and be there to meet us. The crafty little monkeys.'

'But you can see why, can't you? If they've had to sign the Official Secrets Act, they can't say a word. Not now and possibly not for years to come. Signing that, you know, is very serious.'

'Is it?'

'Very. Breaking it can carry a prison sentence.'

'Then,' Dan said seriously, 'we'll just have to trust them, won't we?'

'Yes. And not ask any more awkward questions.'

Fifty-Four

It was a shock to everyone when Singapore fell to the Japanese in February 1942. Back in London on leave overnight, Victoria and Mattie discussed it with Constance. This time, the two boys could not get leave.

'I've been wondering about Celia,' Victoria said as they sat down together to eat the meal that Constance had prepared.

Constance glanced at Mattie. 'I don't suppose you know who she is, do you?'

Mattie shook her head.

'Oh sorry, Mouse. There was a girl at our school called Celia whose parents were out in Singapore. After we left school, we, that's Connie, Charlotte and I, went to finishing school in Switzerland and Celia went to the Slade art school. What she did after that, I don't know.' She turned to Constance. 'I haven't kept in touch with her, have you?'

'No, but I could perhaps find out about her. Her father was someone important out there, wasn't he?'

'All I can remember was that he worked for the British Government.'

'It should be fairly easy for me to make enquiries at work, then. I'll do that.'

'Let me know – if you can. I hope she's all right.'

Word came through from Constance a few weeks later that Celia's family had left Singapore just before the Japanese had entered the country and Victoria breathed a sigh of relief. Now, of course, the section dealing with Japanese intercepts at Bletchley was in full flow, but Mattie and Victoria were not actively involved.

'Let's take our coffee down by the lake,' Mattie suggested one warm afternoon in June.

'Yes, let's. It's lovely and sunny.' Victoria sighed. 'Squashed into those little huts, you almost forget what it's like to be outside. It'll be nice to get a bit of fresh air.'

Mattie chuckled. 'It is a bit of a squeeze at times, isn't it? But everyone's very friendly.'

'You have to be. It'd be unbearable if there was tension in the air.'

Mattie glanced around her as they sat down on the grass before saying in a low voice, 'Did you hear about those two girls from my hut who had a row in the canteen over some chap?'

'No. Do tell.'

'I don't know if I should.'

'It sounds as if plenty of folks have heard it already. Go on.'

'Evidently some chap from one of the other huts – I don't know which one – has been flirting with both of them and they were vying with each other as to which one he had confided the most to about his work. They were saying things that neither of them should have said to anyone – let alone in loud voices in the middle of the canteen.'

'Jealousy, was it?'

Mattie nodded and bit her lip. 'They were hauled up and dismissed at once. Sent packing in disgrace.'

'No!' Victoria paused and then asked, 'What about the chap?'

'I don't know.'

'He should have known better.'

'Perhaps he thought it didn't matter – just talking to others here. We've all signed the Act, I know, and we know not to discuss anything outside the gates, but in here – well, I expect he thought it was safe.'

'Mm, but we're not really supposed to talk to folk from the other huts, now are we? We were told that at the off,' Victoria said. 'I mean, I think we're all right. You and me. We're working on the same messages, aren't we? And besides, we trust each other.'

Mattie smiled. 'Yes, we do.'

Victoria lay back on the grass and closed her eyes. 'Oh, this is the life. At least, these stolen moments are. I could easily go to sleep.'

'Please don't, Vicky, else we'll be in trouble too.'

'Just five more minutes, then we'll go back in.'

They were silent for a few moments, both soaking up the sun.

'What do you want to do after all this is over?' Mattie said, her voice sounding drowsy.

'For a job, you mean?'

'Mm.'

'Haven't really thought about it.' Victoria was

silent for a moment before saying softly, 'There is one thing I'd like to do, but it's nothing to do with finding a job or a career.'

The silence lengthened before Mattie prompted gently, 'Go on.'

Reluctant to share the secret – even with Mattie – that she'd held for so long, Victoria said slowly, 'I'd like to find out about my father.'

'Your – your father?'

'I know nothing about him. He's just a name on my birth certificate and I hadn't even seen that until I had to get a copy of it before coming here. All I've ever been told is that he was killed at Passchendaele before I was born. I'd just like to find out more about him. Where and when exactly he died and if there's a grave I can visit.'

Mattie sat up suddenly and, leaning on one elbow said, 'I know someone who might be able to help you.'

Victoria opened her eyes, shading them against the sun with her hand. 'You do?'

'Pips – in my hut – she was out there, at the Front, as a nurse in the last war.'

'The one who lost her husband in the Blitz in London?' Now Victoria sat up and stared at her friend. 'Was she at Passchendaele?'

'I'm not sure, but I know she was near Ypres for a lot of the time.'

'That's near Passchendaele. The battle was actually the third battle of Ypres, but always known as Passchendaele.'

'Was it? I didn't do much in the way of history.'

'We didn't at school but I've read a lot about it. Mainly because of my father, I suppose.'

Hesitantly, Mattie asked, 'Hasn't your mother told you about him?'

'She won't have his name mentioned.'

'Too painful, I suppose,' Mattie murmured. 'What about his parents?'

Victoria shrugged. 'No idea. I don't know anything about any of my grandparents. What about you?'

'I – um – know my mother's parents are both dead. Joe found out.' Mattie paused for a moment, remembering the time Joe had confided in her about his search for their maternal grandparents. 'You mustn't tell Mum, Mattie,' he'd made her promise. 'As for the other side . . .' Mattie's voice tightened. 'I'd rather not know, to be honest.'

Victoria stared at her but asked no more questions. If Mattie wanted her to know any more, she would tell her in her own good time. Victoria was not one to pry. She had plenty of mystery in her own life, but now, she didn't mind sharing this particular secret with her friend.

'Come on,' she said, getting up. 'We'd better go back. I don't want to get dismissed.'

'Me neither. I love it here.'

For a moment, Victoria was thoughtful. 'D'you know, Mouse,' she said slowly, surprised by what she was saying, 'despite the cold in winter, the draughty huts, the cramped working conditions, the night shifts and even that first awful billet, yes, I love it too.'

They smiled at each other, knowing that it was

their friendship that was the best thing of all about their life at Station X.

'Pips, this is my friend, Victoria. I don't know if you've actually met her properly before, but would you mind if she asked you some questions?'

The two girls had waylaid Pips as they all left for their billets at the end of a long day.

For a moment, Pips looked startled. 'Well, it rather depends . . .'

'Oh, not about work,' Mattie said hurriedly. 'It's – it's more personal. Some advice, really.'

Pips's expression relaxed. 'Of course not. I have seen you in the canteen and around the park, Victoria, but no, strangely, we haven't spoken before.' She chuckled. 'Even though we've been here over two years. All this secrecy doesn't help one form friendships, does it? We're all too scared of saying something we shouldn't. Anyway, how can I help?'

'Mattie says you were near Ypres during the last war.'

'I was, yes. I was with an independent flying ambulance corps and we moved about quite a bit, but we always seemed to end up back near Ypres.'

'Were you there the whole time?'

'Almost. I was injured in early November 1917' – Pips smiled wryly – 'disobeying orders.'

'You!' Mattie gasped.

'Yes, me.' Pips chuckled. 'I was quite a rebel in those days. Still am, if I'm pushed.'

'I can't believe it. You're always reminding us about the need for secrecy here and obeying the rules.'

'It was different then. We were saving lives physically. Here, it's our keeping quiet that will save lives.'

'May I ask you what you did? When you were injured, I mean.'

Pips's eyes twinkled. 'I went into no man's land to rescue a reconnaissance pilot from his crashed aircraft. Getting back to our trenches I was shot in the leg.'

'Were you sent home because of that?'

'Only to recover from my injury. Infection was rife out there and it was the best action, though' – she pulled a face – 'I wasn't happy. I went back as soon as I could, but that particular battle was over by then. Anyway, what was it you wanted to ask me, Victoria?'

Victoria took a deep breath. 'I know very little about my father – my mother won't discuss him or his family. All I know is that his name was Richard Hamilton and that he was killed at Passchendaele. I just wondered if there's any way of finding out if he has a grave and where it is.'

'You'd like to visit it once all this nonsense is over?' Pips asked gently.

Victoria nodded.

'Would the War Office help, d'you think?' Mattie asked.

Pips laughed. 'I think they're a little preoccupied at the moment. I suggest your first step would be to write to the Imperial War Graves Commission. Their head office is in Maidenhead, but be prepared for it to be some time before you get an answer.' For a moment she was thoughtful. 'It wouldn't be any good at the moment, but after the war, I could write to a member of my extended family who stayed in Belgium after the last lot. William. He married a Belgian nurse and he lives not far from Ypres. He tends all the local cemeteries from the Great War – for both sides – so he's been allowed to stay. I'm sure he'd be happy to do some research locally for you.' She lowered her voice. 'Mattie, do you remember someone bringing a strange telegram that no one could understand into our hut a few weeks ago?'

Mattie nodded. 'But you knew what it was about, didn't you?'

Pips nodded. 'It was from William. His nephew is a Spitfire pilot and he was shot down in Belgium. He managed to get to his uncle's farm near Ypres and William sent the telegram hoping it would eventually reach me because I would understand it.'

'I do remember that,' Mattie smiled. 'We were all so pleased. A bit of good news, for a change.'

'So, at the moment, I know William is all right and, after the war, I'd be happy to get in touch with him for you, Victoria.'

'Thank you, Pips,' Victoria murmured. 'I'll just have to wait a little longer, I suppose.'

As Pips moved away, Victoria whispered, 'She's nice, isn't she?'

'Lovely,' Mattie agreed. 'She's been very kind and helpful to me. I wouldn't have had a clue what was going on when I first arrived, if it hadn't been for her.'

'Well, thank you for introducing me to her. Now, come along, Mouse, we'd better get home. No doubt Mrs Coupland will have a lovely meal waiting for us as she always does.'

Fifty-Five

The routine of the next few months was interrupted now and again by something out of the ordinary happening; sometimes good, sometimes bad. But in November there was really something to celebrate.

'Did you know?' Victoria whispered to Mattie one night as they readied for bed.

Mattie yawned. She'd had a long and hectic day and couldn't wait to snuggle down beneath the covers in the warm feather bed. 'I probably don't until you tell me.'

'They've started calling the information we produce "Ultra intelligence".'

'Well, of course it is. No one else does what we do, now do they?'

'And there's something else. There's been a lot of extra traffic because of what's going on in North Africa—'

'Don't I know it,' Mattie said wryly.

'So, they're planning to build a proper brick block for our hut and yours to move into. We certainly need more space. I don't know about you, but we're so crowded now, we're nearly sitting on one another's knees.'

'*Lebensraum*,' Mattie murmured sleepily, as she

pulled the covers up to her chin. 'More living space.'

Victoria stiffened and stared down at her friend. Her mind flew back to her time in Germany when she had heard the expression so often; Hitler's demand for more *lebensraum* for his people.

'Yes,' she said softly, 'that was what started this whole sorry mess.'

But Mattie was already asleep.

They were both on a run of night shifts and when they reported for duty the following day, a ripple of excitement and jubilation was spreading through the whole of Bletchley Park.

'I don't expect you've heard yet,' Pips said, when she met them just outside the huts as they were arriving and she was leaving. 'Rommel has been routed near El Alamein. He's on the run. Monty' – this was everyone's affectionate name for General Montgomery – 'has taken thousands of prisoners and destroyed about three hundred enemy tanks.'

'That is good news,' Victoria said. 'They'll be ringing the church bells next.'

'Oh I think they very well might,' Pips said seriously. 'This is the first real victory we've had.'

Pips had been right; on Sunday 15 November church bells throughout the land rang for the first time since the threat of invasion in 1940. There was even a peal from the devastated Coventry Cathedral where, miraculously, the spire and bell tower still stood.

As New Year came, there was a greater feeling of

optimism. As the Prime Minister had said in a speech at the Mansion House shortly after Montgomery's victory, 'Now this is not the end. It is not even the beginning of the end. But it is, perhaps, the end of the beginning.'

'We're moving, did you know?'

'Shh.' Mattie glanced nervously round the canteen at Victoria's words.

'I don't think it's a secret,' Victoria said. 'No one's going to fail to notice us moving all our stuff into the new buildings.'

Mattie placed her plate on the table, sat down and picked up her knife and fork. 'So, are we all going? Both huts?'

'Oh yes. We work so closely together, it would be silly not to. The laugh is, though, we're still going to be called Hut Three and Hut Six.'

'Sensible, I suppose. That's what we're known by.'

The move into Block D took place in February.

'Well, at least we don't have to transfer messages with a broom handle anymore,' Mattie joked. 'Now we've got a proper conveyor belt system.'

Victoria laughed. 'We have, and it'll be kept extremely busy. I think it will hardly ever stop.'

In May 1943, an RAF raid gave cause for further satisfaction, though the success of this dangerous and daring mission by a special squadron was tempered by sadness as several aircraft and their crews were lost. The target was the industrial region of the Ruhr to attack the dams there. With the invention by Barnes

Wallis of a bouncing bomb, which skipped over the surface of water like a child playing 'ducks and drakes', two of the dams – the Möhne and the Eder – were breached, causing catastrophic flooding and destroying power stations. The Sorpe Dam too was badly damaged.

And so it continued, the hard work punctuated by success and failure, not only within the walls of Bletchley Park but in the wider theatre of war too. Towards the end of the year there was a definite feeling of anticipation, of excitement. Joe wrote to both Mattie and Victoria: *Dan and I have wangled some leave for the beginning of December. Can you both get time off too?*

At once the girls requested leave and, to their astonishment, were granted it.

'Oh I can't wait to see them both,' Mattie said as they travelled to London. 'It seems ages since we saw them.'

'It *is* ages since we saw them, Mouse. Letters are all right, aren't they, but they're not the same.'

'I feel sorry for all the wives and sweethearts whose chaps are abroad in North Africa or somewhere. At least ours have still been here.'

'Mm, just waiting for their moment to get back into Europe.'

'Yes,' Mattie said in a small voice. 'I do realize that.'

They had a wonderful two full days together and Constance and Charlie joined them each evening. On the last night, when they were all sitting in Constance's apartment, Joe said solemnly, 'We haven't been told anything officially yet, but we all get the feeling that the top brass is planning something big for next year. Now, we know none of you can tell us anything – even if you do know something – but we want you to know that we're ready for it.'

'In fact,' Dan said with a lopsided grin, 'We can't wait for something to happen. We feel as if we've been kicking our heels for four years.'

'Actually,' Joe added, 'we're very surprised we haven't been posted abroad.'

'Well, you've been training new recruits for most of the time since Dunkirk, haven't you, Joe?' Dan said. 'But I'm surprised I haven't been sent overseas.'

Joe shrugged. 'It must have taken a time to build up all our supplies again; weaponry and so on. We lost almost everything at Dunkirk. And they've got to keep some of us here as home defence.'

'True, but I reckon when the time comes for us to get back into Europe, we'll both be going.'

The girls glanced at each other and Charlie looked a little rueful, though he said nothing. He'd learnt over the years of war to keep quiet. He'd always been allowed to say that he worked for the Foreign Office, if he'd been pressed for an answer as to why he wasn't in uniform, but even that hadn't sufficed on occasions and he'd often been subjected to verbal abuse and ridicule.

'So, what we're saying,' Dan said, 'is that we might not see much of you next year.'

'But you'll keep writing to us, won't you, wherever we are?'

'Of course,' Victoria and Mattie chorused.

There was a steady build-up of work at Bletchley Park throughout the early months of the year and, as spring turned into summer, the number of messages increased and security tightened even more. Leave became even harder to obtain. Now, there was another equally important task. Everyone who was concerned with the actual decoding and translation of messages was aware of a subterfuge by the Allies. They wanted the German command to think that an invasion of Europe – which was taken for granted by both sides as something that would happen sooner or later – would take place across the narrowest part of the Channel near Calais. In fact, the landings were planned for Normandy, but it was paramount that the enemy were persuaded to move a great part of their defensive troops and weaponry away from there.

Elaborate deceptions were put in place and Station X was tasked with watching out for clues in the messages that these had been discovered and, more importantly, believed. They also confused the enemy even further by pretending that landings might take place through Norway. This evidently found credence with Hitler because he sent one of his fighting divisions to Scandinavia only weeks before D-Day happened. The workload, and the anxiety to keep up the accuracy of decoding and translating, increased. Mattie, Victoria and their colleagues often worked around the clock, staggering off duty to sleep for a few hours only to return to their desks as soon as possible.

Dr and Mrs Coupland were acutely aware of the toll on the girls' general health and made every effort to look after them. Mrs Coupland gave them good, healthy meals as much as the rationing would allow and Dr Coupland insisted on a giving them a check-up now and again to make sure there were no serious health issues arising.

'I am permitted to,' he twinkled at them. 'I'm still registered as a locum.'

'I think we're both just so tired,' Victoria told him in the privacy of his consulting room.

'Get out into the sunshine as much as possible,' he advised. 'The cycle rides do help you to get fresh air each day but get outside whenever you can, especially while the weather's good.'

And so it was that Victoria and Mattie were sitting by the side of the lake at lunchtime one day early in June, when suddenly the sky was filled with RAF aircraft flying south, so many that for a while the sun was blotted out.

'You know where they're going, Mouse, don't you?' Victoria said quietly.

Solemnly, Mattie nodded. 'Yes, I think I do. This is it. This is D-Day.'

'And now, we're going to be busier than ever.'

'But there's something else,' Mattie whispered. 'Joe and Dan will be going.'

Fifty-Six

During the months after the Normandy landings, as they became known, correspondence from the British soldiers – now back on French soil as they had promised – was spasmodic. Weeks passed without a word from them and then a bundle of letters written perhaps over several weeks would arrive at once. The girls wrote regularly, but had no way of knowing if their letters reached Joe and Dan.

'It's nice to get them,' Victoria said, as six of Joe's letters arrived at once. 'Even belatedly, but he doesn't say he's got anything from us.'

'Neither does Dan,' Mattie said with a sigh, 'but they'll know we're writing.'

By the end of August, the Allies were in Paris, the swastika had been torn down from the Eiffel Tower and the Tricolour flew again. The Americans swept through Orléans, Chartres and Dreux to meet up with the British approaching Rouen, whilst the Germans retreated across the Seine. The battles continued and the push to reach Germany itself progressed steadily, despite a few setbacks.

Christmas 1944 came and went and the girls stayed at Bletchley. It passed almost unnoticed – everyone was so busy – but the canteen served Christmas dinners and there were dances and various social activities organized. Victoria and Mattie didn't feel like attending many; Joe and Dan weren't there.

'It's all right for the girls who have a romance going on right here – and there are several that I know about,' Victoria said, 'but I just wouldn't feel comfortable about dancing with other men. My heart belongs to Joe and I'd feel so guilty.'

Mattie smiled. 'At least we had a nice bundle of letters arrive just in time for Christmas.'

'Yes, that was lovely.'

But as January 1945 passed into February and winter gradually turned into spring, the girls received no more letters from either Joe or Dan.

'You'd think we'd hear from one of them, wouldn't you?' Victoria said, beginning to get a little anxious.

'There'll be a whole bunch of them stacking up somewhere,' Mattie sighed. 'But the worst of it is we don't know exactly where either of them are. Just "somewhere in France".'

'We'll just have to bury ourselves in our work and try not to think about it too much.'

'Easier said than done,' Mattie murmured and then added, more strongly, 'Still, we're lucky we've got plenty to keep us busy. Try not to worry, Vicky. I'm sure they're all right. "No news is good news" and all that.'

Mattie flung open the door of the room that was still called Hut 3 and stepped inside and shouted, 'Vicky – Vicky!'

At once, the head of the department appeared from

his office. 'You can't come in here. You should know that.'

'I've got to see Vicky. It's – it's important.'

'Nothing's more important than security—'

'Yes, it is. My brother's been posted missing in France and he's Vicky's boyfriend.'

There was a flash of sympathy in the man's tone but he was still obliged to say stiffly, 'I'm sorry to hear that, but you know the rules and they have to be obeyed.'

Mattie pulled in a deep breath, trying to calm her wildly beating heart. 'Then would you please tell Victoria to come out here?'

'I'll see what I can do. But first, you have to step outside – and stay there. Do I have your word?'

'This is ridiculous,' Mattie stormed. 'Anyone would think we didn't deal with the very same messages. And now, we're even in the same building.' She sighed. 'Oh all right, but please—'

'How did you learn the news?' the man asked sharply, still unwilling to accede to her request without first obtaining further information.

'My mother got a telegram and she wrote to me care of the Foreign Office. It's been forwarded on in the usual way.'

The man's expression relaxed and he nodded approval. 'I'm sorry we can't allow you to telephone from here. There's a telephone box in the village, I believe.'

'It's all right. They have a telephone at our billet. Mr Coupland used to be the local doctor. That would be all right, wouldn't it?'

'Of course. Though you must be careful not to indicate to your mother exactly where you are.' As Mattie nodded, he added, 'I'm sorry to have to say this in these circumstances, but you do understand, don't you?'

'Of course.' Mattie was calming down a little herself now.

'I'll find Victoria for you.'

A few moments later, Victoria came hurrying out. 'What is it? The boss looked awfully serious. He's given me an hour off.'

'Let's go and sit by the lake.' Mattie linked her arm with Victoria's.

'Oh Mouse, what's wrong? You've been crying. Oh no!' She stopped walking suddenly and pulled Mattie round to face her. 'It's Joe, isn't it? Tell me quickly.'

'He's been posted missing,' Mattie's voice was flat. 'Mum wrote to tell me, but, of course, her letter's taken a while to get here.'

'When?'

'About two weeks ago now, I think. That's all I know.'

'So – he's missing, not – not killed?'

Mattie nodded, unable to speak now for the huge lump in her throat. Her lovely brother Joe, who had always looked after the family, was missing in action. She knew it wasn't the worst possible news, but it was bad enough. And they didn't even know where he was or where it had happened. Maybe they'd never know what had become of him. He'd be another casualty of war; just a name on a memorial somewhere with no grave for them to visit.

The two girls sat down on the grass, not even

caring to check if it was damp or not, with their arms around each other.

'Oh Mattie, whatever are we going to do? I can't bear it.'

'Dearest Vicky, we have to. We have to be strong for each other and we have to do what Pips did when she had the awful news about her husband. We have to carry on with our work here.'

'Don't you want to apply for compassionate leave to go home and see your mother?'

'I could, I suppose, but I don't see the point. What can I do if I go home? Aunty Bella will look after Mum. I know that without even having to ask her. And the Spencers will be as cut up as we are. They were very fond of Joe.'

'Don't talk in the past tense, Mattie, please. Not yet. Not till – till we know for sure.'

'You're right. There's still hope.'

Victoria was staring out across the lake into the far distance, seeing not the view before her but Joe's smiling, handsome face. 'He's the only man I've ever really cared about,' she murmured.

'Really?' Mattie said shakily, trying to laugh through her tears. 'I've always imagined you must have had them queuing up at the door. Didn't you – what is it they call it – have a Season? Didn't you "come out"? You must have had dozens of eligible bachelors dancing attendance on you.'

Victoria smiled shakily. 'I managed to sidestep all of them very neatly.'

'Was that a new dance? The sidestep?' Mattie tried to make a joke, but it fell flat.

'Not one of them was as handsome or as lovely as your Joe.' She was silent for a long time before saying, almost in a whisper, 'There was someone once. I met him whilst I was at finishing school on a skiing holiday.'

For a moment, Mattie was struck by the chasm between their lifestyles before they had come to Bletchley Park. It was surprising that they had become such good friends and a miracle that Victoria had fallen in love with her brother. Seeing her stricken face at hearing the news, Mattie could be in no doubt now about her friend's feelings for Joe.

Haltingly, Victoria told Mattie a little about her short-lived romance with the handsome German and how it had come to an abrupt end.

'If you'd seen the things we saw that night – the one they now call Kristallnacht – you'd understand why the rumours about what's happening to the Jews in Europe has never surprised me. We have to win this war no matter what – what it costs.' Her voice broke on the last few words and she buried her head against Mattie's shoulder, allowing the tears to fall. Mattie held her close and stroked her head.

The silence lengthened between them, each feeling bereft. At last, Victoria sat up and dried her eyes.

'What about Dan? You haven't heard from him recently either, have you? His mother would let you know if – if . . .'

Mattie nodded, 'Yes, she would. And now,' she added briskly, 'we've had our hour. We'd better go in. Chin up. At least we've still got hope. Poor Pips hadn't and just look how she's coped.'

As they got to their feet, Victoria said, 'Please don't tell anyone what I told you about Kurt, will you?' She gave a wobbly smile. 'I wouldn't want anyone to think I was spying for the enemy.'

'Of course I won't. It'll be our secret.'

'Another one,' Victoria sighed. 'So many secrets.'

'Well, this is the place for them,' Mattie said, forcing herself to smile too.

They both returned to their respective rooms and carried on bravely with their work. The days were interminably long, but they were both glad of the intensity of the tasks that kept their minds busy. Only at night did the anxiety and misery threaten to overwhelm them, when they lay in their twin beds, sometimes talking, sometimes quiet and lost in their own thoughts until blissful sleep claimed them at last.

They'd decided that they ought to tell the Couplands. Such news, sadly, was all too common and was not classed as 'a Bletchley secret'.

'Oh my dears, how dreadful for you,' Mrs Coupland said, clasping her hands in front of her. 'We understand just how you feel. Our daughter's husband was posted missing for over a week at the time of El Alamein until he was located in hospital. He recovered and went back to the front line. As far as we know, he's still safe, but that week was torture. You poor things. If there's anything we can do, you must tell us.'

'Is it ever going to ease up a bit?' Victoria grumbled as they cycled home after a long shift. 'Two girls have gone off sick today because of the pressure of translating everything you're sending through. I don't know how you're deciphering everything so quickly.'

'Don't tell anyone,' Mattie began.

'As if I would, Mouse.'

'Because they'll be under such stress now, the Germans are making mistakes in their encoding. They never used to – at least not like they are doing now. I suppose they're panicking and that makes them careless. We were always able to find a few cribs, but now they're making it easy-peasy.'

By the time April arrived, there was a definite optimism in the air, but there was still no further news of Joe.

'What about Dan?' Victoria asked Mattie. 'You've still not heard from him, have you?'

'His mother's written to say that as far as they know he's all right, but they've not had any letters from him recently either.'

'So we've just got to carry on. Surely, it can't last much longer.'

Mattie shrugged. 'Who knows, when you've got a madman in charge. Any sensible commander would see that his cause is hopeless now and he'd surrender to save a lot more lives being lost.'

'Hitler won't give in until the Allies are knocking on the door of his bunker.'

The war went on until May. There were successes and failures on both sides; sometimes the Germans had a victory, sometimes the Allies, but overall it was the latter who made steady progress.

And then, early in May, as they cycled home after a night shift, Victoria said, 'So, it looks like it's all over, then. Could you understand the message from Admiral Dönitz that came through early this morning before it was passed through to us?'

'We understood enough of it. Pips told us all what it said. It didn't need decoding, only translating by you lot.'

'Unconditional surrender,' Victoria murmured. 'To be honest, I didn't think it could go on much longer after Hitler committed suicide last week.'

'And we can't tell anyone else outside our own huts.'

'No, we've got to leave that to the BBC. And, no doubt, the Prime Minister will make a broadcast.'

'Of course, it's not quite all over. There's still fighting going on in the East,' Mattie reminded her.

'But they won't want us here any longer, will they? There's not going to be much for us to do now, is there?'

'They still need the Japanese section at full strength. And I think they want us to stay on for a few more weeks too. Months, maybe.'

'What do you think you'll do long term?'

Mattie wrinkled her forehead. 'I don't know. Probably train to be a teacher.'

'But you'll marry Dan?'

Mattie giggled. 'He hasn't asked me yet.'

'He will,' Victoria said confidently.

'So what are *you* going to do?'

'I'm praying I'm going to be able to marry your

brother, Mouse. I've made up my mind to believe he's still alive. And, yes, he has asked me.'

Mattie gasped. 'When did that happen, then?'

'The last time we were together. Do you realize it's almost eighteen months since we last saw them? I'm just hoping he hasn't changed his mind. When do you think they'll all come home?'

'I – really couldn't say,' Mattie murmured.

Victoria was talking so positively, determined to believe that somewhere, somehow, Joe was still alive, that Mattie couldn't – and wouldn't – dash her hopes. But, silently, she thought, *What if Joe doesn't come back? We've heard nothing more. We don't know if he's alive or is a prisoner – or . . .*

Worse still – and this she hadn't told Victoria – Mattie had heard a rumour that in their disorderly and hasty retreat, the Germans were no longer holding prisoners of war. They were 'disposing' of them.

Her mind shied away from her worst fears.

'Anyway,' Victoria was saying, interrupting Mattie's bleak thoughts with forced cheerfulness, 'we've got a whole week off now. Let's make the most of it.'

They packed their suitcases that evening and the following morning caught the train to London, determined to celebrate once the news they already knew had been made public.

Fifty-Seven

The streets of the capital were heaving with joyous people already celebrating and it took them some time to reach the relative peace of Constance's flat. Victoria peered out of the window. 'Just look at all these folk. Oh Mattie, do let's go out and join them.'

'What about Connie? Shouldn't we wait for her?'

'We don't know where she is. She might even be out there already and if we hang about here, we'll miss all the fun.'

They needn't have worried; the celebrations were to last through most of two days, but on this first day the rejoicing crowds would pause only to listen to the Prime Minister give his speech during the afternoon and the King, who broadcast to the nation in the evening.

'Let's go to Trafalgar Square,' Victoria suggested, leading the way. The square was packed, with people climbing lamp posts or dancing in the fountains and everywhere men and women were kissing.

'Hey, beautiful,' an American soldier appeared from nowhere, sweeping Victoria into his arms and kissing her soundly. And then he was gone as quickly as he had arrived.

Mattie laughed at her friend's consternation. 'Good

job our Joe isn't here. There'd've been a serious breakdown in the Anglo–American friendship.'

Victoria, blushing furiously, straightened her jacket and muttered. 'You wait, Mouse, it'll happen to you any minute.'

And it did. In fact, it went on happening to both of them.

'Oh, what the heck!' Victoria said at last and kissed each one in return.

'Let's go to Buckingham Palace,' Mattie shouted above the cheering and laughter.

'I doubt we'll make it through this lot, but come on. We'll give it a go.'

They pushed their way through the crowds and at last reached the Mall.

'Still a way to go,' Victoria said, but they kept going.

'Don't lose me, Vicky. I haven't a clue how to get back to Connie's.'

'Hang on to the back of my jacket.'

Steadily, they made progress until at long last they were standing in the throng in front of the gates of the palace.

'We want the King,' the crowd chanted. 'We want the King.'

And then they saw the royal family come out onto the balcony; the King, the Queen and the two princesses, Elizabeth dressed in her ATS uniform. The cheering reached a crescendo and as soon as the royal party went back inside the shouts for them began again. 'We want the King.'

There was no lessening of dancing and shouting

– or kissing. The celebrating went on all night. In the early hours, Victoria and Mattie staggered back to the apartment.

'I'm shattered,' Mattie said as they got ready for bed. 'But I wouldn't have missed it for the world.'

'If only,' Victoria said, 'the boys had been with us, it would have been perfect.'

Mattie said nothing. It was as if, in all the excitement of Victory over Europe, Victoria had closed her mind to the fact that Joe might never be coming home.

Victoria and Mattie spent the following day in the apartment, sleeping until late. Constance had left them a note: *Gone to work, but will cook you a meal tonight. C x*

Victoria yawned as they sat drinking coffee, still in their dressing gowns. 'I don't feel like doing anything today.'

'Let's not, then,' Mattie murmured. 'I'm shattered. They always say when you've been extra busy, when you do stop, the tiredness catches up with you.'

'And we've been busy for the last five years.'

'But there's one thing we ought to try and do whilst we're here.' Mattie wanted to keep her friend busy, keep her believing that Joe would indeed come home.

'What's that?' Victoria yawned again.

'Make a start on finding out what happened to your father.'

Victoria stopped mid-yawn and stared at her. 'You're willing to help me?'

'Of course. If you want me to, that is. If you don't . . .'

Victoria sat up, wide awake at once. 'Oh I do, I do, Mouse. But where shall we start?'

Touched by her eagerness, Mattie, too, shook off her lethargy. 'If you can, the best place to start is with your mother.'

Victoria pulled a face. 'I don't think she'll tell me anything. She never has. I've only broached the subject on two occasions in the whole of my life and she got very angry both times.'

'She might tell you more now you're older. She must know *something*. If you – er – push her a little.'

'Darling Mouse, you can't push my mother to do anything. Well, at least I can't.'

'Is there anyone who can?'

Victoria leaned back in her chair again with a sigh. 'Not that I know. You see, I only ever met one of her friends – the one who acted as my sponsor when I was presented at court.'

Back in the real world, the difference between them was going to be more pronounced, Mattie thought, but pushing such feelings aside she asked, 'Who was it? Can you remember?'

'Pearl somebody.' Victoria wrinkled her forehead. 'Harrington. That was it.'

'Would she know anything?'

Victoria shrugged. 'I don't know, but I very much doubt it.'

'Mother, I want you to meet my dear friend, Mattie.'

Grace's gaze swept Mattie up and down and the

young woman was acutely conscious of her drab, utilitarian two-piece costume. But she lifted her chin and smiled at the smartly dressed woman in front of her. Victoria's mother was certainly not wearing wartime fashion, and an expensive perfume wafted towards Mattie as Grace held out a languid hand.

'How do you do, Matilda.' Her lip curled. 'I presume that is your proper name? I do so despise shortened names.'

'No, Mattie is my name.'

Grace's eyebrows arched in disapproval. 'How unfortunate for you. Where are you from?'

'Sheffield.' Mattie stifled the urge to call the woman 'ma'am', even though her demeanour almost demanded it.

'Oh. The North.' She paused to emphasize her words. 'Don't tell me you're employed at the Foreign Office too.'

Before Mattie could answer, Victoria said, 'Yes, she is. Mattie is a mathematical genius.'

'Really?' Grace murmured. 'You do surprise me.' She was bored now. She couldn't possibly have any interest in this girl and the sooner she could prise her daughter away from keeping company with such a person, the better. 'Now that all this nonsense is over, Victoria, I trust you will be coming home and making an attempt to find yourself a suitable husband. Though how we're to manage it now that yet another generation of fine young men has been decimated, I cannot imagine. And you're almost twenty-seven now. I fear you may have left it far too late.'

'No need, Mother. I have already found the man I wish to marry – Mattie's brother, Joe – but—'

'Victoria!' Mattie cried out, rushing to Grace's side and grasping her arms. 'I think your mother is about to faint.'

They helped her to the sofa where she sank back against the silk cushions. Victoria rang the bell and Rose appeared.

'Smelling salts, miss,' Rose said pragmatically. 'That's what we need. I'll fetch some.'

A few minutes later, Grace was recovering.

'What caused this?' Rose whispered.

'I told her I am engaged to be married.'

Rose beamed. 'Oh, what lovely news, miss. I couldn't be happier for you.'

'It seems, though,' Victoria remarked drily, 'that my mother is anything but.'

'She'll get over it.'

'What are you two whispering about? I won't have you whispering. Rose, you may go. And don't think you can't be dismissed, because you can.'

'Suits me, ma'am, but I don't think you could find a replacement easily, not now. Not since the war. Women have done all sorts in the war and domestic service is not something they'll be wanting to go back to.'

Victoria looked askance at the maid daring to answer back. Before the war, such insolence had been impossible, but now everything was changing. Every*one* was changing. But not, she thought as she glanced down at her, her mother.

Mattie looked on in amazement. She'd never heard

anything like this in her life. At Bletchley, all classes of society had mixed easily and affably, all with a mutual goal. But now Mattie was seeing the other end of the scale to her own background. Whilst she didn't think Grace Hamilton was exactly aristocracy, she was certainly acting as if she were.

Grace, now recovered, said, 'We'll talk about this later, Victoria. Are you staying the night?'

'No, Mother. We're at the apartment I share with Constance.'

'Then you will oblige me by coming here at eleven sharp tomorrow morning – on your own – when we will discuss the matter.'

'Very well, Mother, and there is something else I shall want to talk about. I want you to tell me about my father and, this time, I will not be fobbed off.'

Grace reached for the smelling salts again.

Fifty-Eight

'Mattie – this is the wonderful Mrs Beddows and Rose, whom you've seen briefly upstairs. This is my dear friend, Mattie.'

'We're very pleased to meet you, miss,' the cook welcomed her. 'Please sit down. I'll make you both some coffee. Oh, it's good to see you, Miss Victoria. How are you?' She lowered her voice. 'Rose tells me you have some exciting news.'

Victoria chuckled. 'No keeping anything from you, is there, Mrs Beddows?' She glanced round. 'Does Mrs Jones still come in daily?'

'She left to work in munitions. I don't expect her to come back, and besides' – she pulled a face – 'madam has now found out that we can actually manage without her.'

'But will you, if mother starts entertaining again like she used to?'

Mrs Beddows laughed. 'She's never stopped, miss. She's on all sorts of committees – all to do with the war effort, I have to say – and they meet here for coffee mornings, afternoon tea and dinner parties. There's something going on two or three times a week.'

Victoria stirred her coffee thoughtfully. 'Mrs Beddows – did you ever know my father?'

For a brief moment the cook looked startled before saying, 'No, miss, I didn't. That was before my time working for your mother.'

Victoria glanced at Rose with the same question in her eyes, but the housemaid shook her head. 'And mine, miss. You was about two when I started here.' She grinned. 'I was only fourteen.'

'I'd only started the year before Rose came,' Mrs Beddows said.

'Who worked here before you? Do you know?'

'A Mrs Frost, miss. But she was quite old and ill by that time. I understand she died not long after she left here.'

'And a housemaid?'

Mrs Beddows and Rose glanced at each other. 'I don't think there was one, though I think they had a daily.'

'Do you know who that was?'

'Sorry, no, miss.'

'But there was a nanny when you were little,' Rose put in helpfully. 'Before Miss Gilbert came.'

'There was.' Mrs Beddows nodded. 'But she only came after you were born. She wouldn't have known the master either.'

'What about Mother's friends? Would any of them have known him?'

'They might,' Mrs Beddows said doubtfully. 'But I'd be very careful asking around, miss. If your mother got to know—'

'Quite,' Victoria said tartly.

*

As they walked back to the apartment, Mattie said, 'So, you don't think Miss Gilbert could know anything either?'

'Doesn't sound like it?'

'What about the headmistress of that school you went to?'

'Miss Taylor? Why would she know anything? I don't think she ever actually met my *mother*, let alone knew anything about my father.'

'I just wondered if, when you were enrolled at the school, she'd've wanted details about your background.' She giggled. 'It sounds as if it was quite a posh school. Maybe they wanted details of your breeding history.'

Victoria smiled but took Mattie's suggestion seriously. 'It's possible.'

Mattie stopped suddenly and gazed around her. 'Oh Vicky, just look at all this devastation.' Her gaze roamed over the bombed buildings. Work to clear the sites had already started, but it looked like it was going to be a never-ending task. She thought about her home city, Sheffield, and knew it had suffered a similar fate. And then there was Liverpool, Hull, Coventry and many more towns and cities that had felt the full wrath of Hitler's bombers. 'It's going to take years for this country to recover. And to think of all the folks who've been lost. It doesn't bear thinking about.'

'We'll survive. The Brits always do,' Victoria said, tucking her arm through Mattie's. As they began walking again, Victoria added, 'Tell you what, why don't we take a trip into the countryside one day this week? I wouldn't mind seeing my old school again. Would you come with me?'

'Are you sure? I wouldn't fit in in a place like that.'

'Oh Miss Taylor's not like my mother. She's a sweetie. She'll make you very welcome – especially when I tell her you've been to Oxford. She'll be most impressed. It's her ongoing ambition to get at least one girl into either Oxford or Cambridge every year.'

'Well, if you're sure . . .'

They travelled there on the Wednesday. Tucked away in the countryside the school had hardly been affected by the war. 'Although,' Miss Taylor told them as she welcomed them both into her sitting room, 'we did take in several evacuees out of a sense of "doing our bit". Now,' she smiled at them both, 'I'm not going to ask what you two did in the war. With your talents and backgrounds, I can make an educated guess.'

Victoria wondered if Miss Taylor had been asked for recommendations amongst her well-bred young ladies for 'special duties', though she would not ask.

'Whatever it was,' the headmistress went on, 'I'm delighted to see you safely through it, though you do both look rather tired. I hope you can get a well-earned rest for a while before you need to start thinking about what you're going to do in the future. And I understand,' she turned to Mattie, 'that you, my dear, got a first in mathematics at Oxford. That is a real achievement. Congratulations.'

Mattie smiled, taking to this woman at once and not at all intimidated by her. 'I had the help and support of some wonderful teachers, right from primary school. I wouldn't have got there at all if they hadn't taken me under their wing.'

Miss Taylor smiled, accepting the compliment to her fellow professionals. Mattie had never lost her accent, nor had she ever tried to. Despite her home circumstances, she was proud of being a Sheffielder and would never deny her roots.

'I hope you don't mind us coming,' Victoria began.

'I'm delighted to see you again, Victoria, and to meet you, Mattie. We're always very pleased to see "old girls".'

'May I ask you something?'

'Of course.'

'Did you know anything about my father? I just wondered, when I was accepted here, if you knew anything about my – my background.'

'Have you not asked your mother?'

'Several times – most recently this week, but every time she gets either angry or very upset. She won't tell me a thing. She wouldn't even give me my birth certificate so I obtained one, but all that told me was his name and his occupation. Richard Hamilton, officer in the British Army. It's not much to go on, is it? And the only other thing I know – which was what my mother did tell me – was that he was killed at Passchendaele but even then, I have no actual date.'

Miss Taylor wrinkled her forehead. 'The only thing I can suggest is either Somerset House or the Imperial War Graves Commission, and of the two, I think the latter is likely to be your best bet, at least to start with.'

'That's what Pips suggested,' Mattie said excitedly. 'Pips is someone I work with and she was a volunteer nurse during the first war. She served a lot near Ypres.'

'Passchendaele was actually the Third Battle of Ypres,' Miss Taylor said.

Mattie nodded and said simply, 'She was there.'

'Pips also told us,' Victoria said, 'that if we were able to find out a little more information, she has a relative who was with them as a stretcher bearer. He still lives in Belgium, very close to Ypres. She said she was sure he'd be willing to help.'

'He married a Belgian nurse and never came back to England,' Mattie added.

Miss Taylor smiled. 'You sound as if you've got several avenues to explore, but, on second thoughts, I would recommend you gather as much information about him as you can first. Is that really all you know?'

Victoria nodded.

'Then I should get his marriage certificate and his birth certificate.'

'Somerset House again, then?'

'I think so.' She paused and then added, 'On your own birth certificate, did it say "deceased" by his name?'

'No.'

'I'm not sure if it does on a child's birth certificate but I do know it often does on a marriage certificate, where it gives the names of the fathers of the bride and groom and states if they're deceased.'

Victoria stared at her. 'Do – do you mean that if I get their marriage certificate, it will give me the names of both my grandfathers?'

'It should do, yes.'

'Oh my,' Victoria breathed.

'And then you can get other certificates. You could build up quite a family tree.'

Mattie said no more in front of the headmistress, but as they walked back down the long drive and out of the school gates, she said, 'Well, after what we've been doing for the last five years, this little mystery should be a doddle to crack.'

The following day they journeyed to see Naomi, who made them both welcome. She was still teaching at a local primary school.

'I really enjoy it,' she told them. 'It gives me so much more time to myself than when I was a live-in governess, though I wouldn't have missed my time with you, Victoria, for the world.'

But when Victoria turned the conversation to her own family, Naomi shook her head. 'I'm sorry, I really don't know anything about your father, dear.'

As they returned home, Victoria said, 'Our conversation with Miss Gilbert . . .'

'She kept reminding you to call her "Naomi".'

Victoria chuckled. 'I know, but I find it difficult. Could you call your old teachers by their Christian names?'

Mattie wrinkled her forehead, thinking of the Musgraves and Miss Preston. 'No,' she said at last, 'I couldn't. Anyway, what were you going to say?'

'Our conversation with her about the evacuees reminded me of Charlotte, a girl Connie and I knew. I wonder what happened to her. I must ask Connie. She might know.'

Constance didn't know anything about Charlotte, so Victoria said, 'You know, we ought to have some sort of reunion.'

'That's a good idea. I'll see what I can do.' Constance was silent for a few moments before asking softly, 'Have you still not heard anything from either of the boys?'

Victoria and Mattie exchanged a glance and then shook their heads, both acutely aware that all their family tree searches and questions about old friends were merely a cover for the real anxiety that lay constantly at the back of both their minds.

Fifty-Nine

Victoria and Mattie returned to Bletchley at the end of the week. They were each asked by the individual heads of their huts if they would be willing to stay on for another few months. 'We don't anticipate that things will wind up here completely until next year. A lot of you are leaving, of course, but if you've nothing lined up, perhaps you'd like to stay and help.'

Both Victoria and Mattie agreed at once.

'Let's just hope the Couplands won't mind us staying.'

Mr and Mrs Coupland were delighted. 'It's like having our daughter back home.' Mrs Coupland beamed. 'And you're no trouble at all.' So Victoria and Mattie decided to stay at Bletchley for as long as they were needed.

'There's just one thing,' Victoria said to her superior at Bletchley. 'I'm trying to find out what happened to my father . . .'

'Oh dear. Was he a casualty?'

'So I understand, but not in this war. In the last lot.' She went on to explain.

'Right,' he said, when she had finished. 'Now the pressure's off a bit here, I'll do my best to help. You follow the routes you have mentioned. I'll make one or two enquiries on your behalf.' He tapped the side of his nose and she knew not to ask questions.

Victoria had already sent for three certificates and when they arrived, forwarded by Constance, her hands were shaking as she opened the long envelope in the privacy of their bedroom at their billet.

'A marriage certificate and a birth certificate, but no death certificate.'

'There's a note,' Mattie said, picking up a piece of paper that had fluttered to the floor when Victoria pulled the papers out of the envelope. Victoria unfolded the note first. It was handwritten by the official who had obviously carried out the work on her behalf.

'He says he's enclosing the documents I requested, but was unable to locate a death certificate. He suggests I try the Imperial War Graves Commission too.'

'Let's look at what he has sent.' Mattie was as excited as Victoria. 'Wait a minute,' she added, jumping up, 'I'll find a sheet of paper and we can start a family tree.'

Moments later, she was sitting down again, a pad on her knee and her pencil poised. 'Right, go on.'

Victoria pulled in a deep breath 'I'm almost afraid to look.'

'Start with the marriage certificate. I think it's common sense to work backwards.'

'Right. Here goes.' She unfolded the first sheet and read out the details to Mattie, who scribbled quickly.

'It gives their names. Richard Hamilton, bachelor, and Grace Overton, spinster.'

'And their ages?'

'Richard was twenty-five and Grace was nineteen.'

'Date of marriage?'

'The twenty-sixth of January, 1917.'

'That's before Passchendaele started,' Mattie murmured. 'Perhaps he was home on leave.' Then briskly, she said, 'Right, next question. Where were they married? It's usually near the bride's home. That might give you a clue where she came from, if she won't even tell you that.'

'St Mary's Church, Whitechapel.'

'Ah,' Mattie said, scribbling furiously. 'Over in London. What else does it say?'

'Richard's profession was a major in the British Army. Blimey, a major! She hasn't got a profession. It's been left blank. That figures,' Victoria muttered. 'She's obviously been a lady of leisure all her life.'

'Anything about their fathers?'

For a moment, Victoria was silent. Then slowly she lifted her head and met Mattie's gaze. 'His father is Montague Hamilton, KBE.'

'My goodness. A knight of the realm.' Mattie grinned. 'I knew you were posh.' Excitedly, she added, 'We can look him up in the library.'

'Burke's.'

They giggled together, the excitement of their findings making them giddy.

'Now, be sensible, Victoria,' Mattie said, trying to restore their concentration. 'What about your mother's father?'

Victoria turned back to the paper in her hand. 'Charles Overton, deceased.'

'Oh that's a shame.'

'At the time of their marriage,' Victoria went on, 'Richard was living at Haversham Manor. Presumably that was his family's home – but I've no idea where that is.'

'I think it's a village somewhere in Kent, but we'll look it up. What's your mother's address?'

'It's given as being in the same place.'

'So why did they get married in Whitechapel and not where they both lived?'

'That's a mystery that needs cracking. Mother knows, but—'

'She won't tell you. So,' Mattie went on, 'what are their fathers' occupations?'

'Hers doesn't give one, because he was "deceased", I suppose, but Sir Montague's is given as "land-owner".'

'Oh my, I bet he's got a country estate.'

They both looked up at the same moment and spoke together. 'We'll go there.'

'Do you think we should?' Victoria added, suddenly a little doubtful. 'I don't want to upset anyone. I mean, if my father did die in the last war – even if either or both of his parents are still alive – it would stir up unhappy memories.'

'Dearest Vicky, I don't think unhappy memories need stirring up. I'm guessing they will have thought about him every day of their lives and will do so until the day they die. That's if they *are* still alive now.'

'I expect you're right.' Victoria still hesitated. 'Let's leave it until next time we get some leave. I'd like to hear from the War Graves Commission first. I'll write to them.'

Mattie sighed. 'Perhaps you're right. We ought to have a bit more information before we go blundering in.' Mattie eyed her friend and then whispered softly, 'I expect you're a bit nervous, too, aren't you? I know I would be. Years ago, Joe found out that our grandparents – my mother's parents, that is – had died. I had such mixed feelings. I was sad because I'd never get to meet them and yet I just know that I'd've been very nervous about turning up on their doorstep. They might very well have sent me off with a flea in my ear. I gather there'd been a huge family fallout when my mum married my dad. Why on earth she did, God only knows. I certainly can't blame them for disapproving of him.' She eyed Victoria. 'But our Joe is a very different kettle of fish. He's nothing like our dad.'

Victoria smiled. 'I'll take my chances.' Then her face clouded. 'I just wish we knew for certain, Mattie, what has happened to him. One way or – or the other. I mean "posted missing" tells you nothing really, does it? You'd think we'd've heard a bit more from someone by now, wouldn't you?'

'It might take a while yet. And for Dan too. It must be pretty chaotic out there, Vicky. We'll just have to be patient.'

'Yes,' Victoria said softly. 'You're right there.'

'Now,' Mattie said firmly, 'in the meantime, we'll keep ourselves busy with this little puzzle. Let's have a look at your father's birth certificate. That'll tell us even more.'

'Born at Haversham Manor, on the nineteenth of April, 1892. We know about his father and it says here that his mother was Francesca, formerly Hodges. His father's occupation again is given as landowner.'

'Then,' Mattie said firmly, 'we definitely need to go there.'

Bletchley Park seemed little changed, except that there was less urgency to their work now and fewer people about. The block where they worked was just the same but, it seemed, there were changes to come.

'I'll be leaving at the end of August,' Pips told Mattie. 'I think there'll be one or two family weddings coming up now it's all over.'

'How lovely.'

'Has your friend done any more about trying to find out what happened to her father?'

Mattie explained what action they'd already taken. 'There were some intriguing facts on the certificates she got and we intend to follow them up once she's heard from the War Graves Commission.'

'It might be a while before she does hear from them. Sadly, they must be very busy just now.' She paused and then added, 'Have you heard from your brother and your young man?'

Mattie shook her head. 'No, we've had no more news about Joe after he was posted missing and I haven't heard from Dan either for months.'

'Stay hopeful. All sorts of strange things can happen in wartime.'

Pips turned away before Mattie could say anything.

In truth, the younger girl did not know what to say. She was acutely aware that Pips had not been able to have any hope.

'Have you heard from the War Graves Commission yet?' Mattie asked as they cycled home one evening during the following week.

'No, but I was going to tell you when we got home. Did I mention that the head of my hut promised he'd try to help?'

'No, you didn't.'

'To be honest, I thought he was just being kind, but it seems he really meant it. He asked me into his office today and told me that he'd made several enquiries on my behalf and there is no record of a Major Richard Hamilton being killed at Passchendaele. There is a reference to a Richard Hamilton on the Menin Gate, he said, but he doesn't think that was him. There was no age given, but he was a private and on my birth certificate it definitely said he was an officer in the British Army.'

'And a major when he got married.'

'Precisely.'

'But he did say' – Victoria ran her tongue around her lips – 'that he'd found out that a Major Richard Hamilton was invalided out of the army in October 1917 after being wounded at Passchendaele.' They both stopped cycling and Mattie stared at her.

'Invalided out? So – he didn't die out there, then?'

'Not if that's him – no. Though he could, of course, have died a little later of his injuries.'

'But then his death would have been recorded here surely? In England.'

'You'd think so, wouldn't you?'

'Do you think,' Mattie whispered, 'that he didn't die? That – that he could still be alive?'

'He could. He'd only be about fifty-three now, wouldn't he?'

'So . . .' Mattie was almost more excited than Victoria. 'We've got two days off together next week. Let's go to Haversham Manor. We should be able to get there by train.'

'Do – do you think we should go? I mean, he must know about me surely. If he'd wanted to find me, he'd have come looking for me, wouldn't he?'

'I don't know,' Mattie said truthfully. 'There's a real mystery behind all this. Why would your mother say he was dead, if he wasn't? Why won't she tell you anything about him or his family? She didn't even tell you about her own family, did she? Why was it all such a big secret? Maybe she didn't even tell him or his family about your birth. I could have understood it if we'd found out you were illegitimate, but you're not.'

'Unless, of course, I'm not Richard Hamilton's daughter,' Victoria said quietly, 'and I'm someone else's. She might very well have wanted to keep that quiet. And perhaps, when he got back, he didn't want anything to do with either of us when he realized I couldn't possibly be his child. I mean, if he came home in October, it's a bit tight for a full-term pregnancy by my birthday in June, isn't it?'

Mattie smiled wryly. 'Well, we're used to solving mysteries and cracking secrets, aren't we?'

'We are indeed. But is this one we really want to solve?'

'Only you can decide that, Vicky.'

Victoria was undecided over the next few days, but as their leave approached, she finally said, 'All right, we'll go, but I think we should brace ourselves for a disappointment. It might be very awkward, or even downright nasty.'

'I can cope if you can, and I'll always be there for you, Vicky. You're not on your own anymore.'

Victoria, warmed by her friend's words, said, 'Right, we'll go.'

Sixty

They paused at the gates leading into a long driveway. In the distance, they could see a mansion.

'Reminds you of Bletchley a bit, doesn't it?'

'Or your school. All these big places seem to have long driveways.' Mattie glanced around her. 'There's even a lake. And just look at those smooth lawns.' As they neared the house, they could see a profusion of pink roses on either side of the path leading up to the steps to a terrace in front of the house.

'Don't they smell wonderful?' Mattie said, breathing in the perfumed air.

'Mm.' Victoria murmured absently. Mattie knew she was feeling nervous.

'Don't worry. What have you got to lose?'

'Nothing, I suppose. I just . . .' She sighed heavily. 'I suppose I'm apprehensive; first, of how they're going to treat us and second, of what I might find out. I mean, the whole situation seems very odd, to say the least.'

Mattie laughed wryly. 'Well, I doubt very much you'll find that your father is a tea leaf.'

'Oh Mouse. You can't help who your relatives are even if there's a thief amongst them.'

'Exactly!' Mattie retorted and Victoria had the grace to look sheepish.

They climbed up two sets of steps to the front door and stood a moment. 'Go on then, ring the bell.'

Victoria pulled on the old-fashioned bell-pull and they waited what seemed an age until the heavy oak door opened slowly.

A tall, straight-backed man, probably in his sixties, dressed in a morning suit with a crisp white shirt and black tie looked down on them.

'Good morning,' he began but then, as his gaze came to Victoria, he jumped physically and his mouth opened on a silent 'oh'.

'Good morning,' Mattie said politely. 'We're sorry to bother you, but could you tell us if anyone called "Hamilton" still lives here?'

The man was still gazing, transfixed, at Victoria, who, under his stare, began to blush. At last he found his voice. 'Won't you please come in?' His voice was unexpectedly shaky, as if he had had a huge shock. 'I think the master would like to see you.'

They stepped inside the large oak-panelled hall with heavy, ornate furniture and gazed around them.

'If you wouldn't mind waiting just a moment.'

'Isn't he courteous?' Mattie whispered. 'One of the "old school". I shouldn't think there're many of them left now.'

Victoria didn't answer. She was looking round the hall and the grand staircase sweeping up to a gallery landing, the walls lined with paintings, presumably of family ancestors.

Suddenly, she stiffened and gave a tiny gasp as her

gaze fastened on a particular portrait hanging at the top of the staircase. 'Oh Mouse,' she breathed, 'just look.'

Mattie looked up at the full-length portrait of a young woman dressed in a pale blue 1920s-style dress. Short, curly blonde hair framed a sweet face. A soft smile curved her lips and her mischievous eyes stared straight at them.

'It's you,' Mattie breathed.

'Well, not quite. She's older in that portrait than I am now.'

'That's true. So, who . . . ?'

At that moment, the butler returned and with a little bow bade them follow him to the morning room. He ushered them into a sunny room. A man and a woman were sitting side by side on a sofa. The man was distinguished-looking, in his mid-seventies, Mattie reckoned. He had silver hair brushed smoothly back. But it was the woman at his side to whom Mattie's gaze went. There was no doubt that it was the woman in the portrait on the stairs, though now she too had silvery hair and a few wrinkles lined her face, but none were so deep as to alter her appearance from her young self. She was clinging to the man's hand with both of hers.

'Oh Monty,' both Victoria and Mattie heard her breathe. 'It's her. It has to be.'

Slowly, they both rose and moved towards the two young women standing, still a little uncertainly, just inside the doorway. Their eyes were fixed on Victoria.

'You,' the man began, his voice unsteady, 'must be Victoria.'

Victoria met his gaze, trying to read in its depths what he was feeling. 'Yes, I am,' she whispered.

With a little cry, which startled both girls, the woman released her hold on her husband and stretched out her hands towards Victoria. 'Oh my dear, dear girl. How we have longed for this day – for this moment.' She grasped both of Victoria's hands as if she would never again let them go.

At her side, the man turned to the butler, who was still hovering. 'Benson,' he said, his voice still shaky, 'would you please ask Major Richard to join us in the morning room?' As the butler gave his customary bow and began to turn away, the man added, 'And I think you'd better give him a little word of warning.'

'Come and sit down.' Then, as if she had suddenly become aware of Mattie and remembering her impeccable manners, the woman included them both. 'You, too, my dear.' But it was to Victoria that her attention returned at once. Still clasping her hands, she led her to the sofa, leaving Mattie to find her own seat.

The man – whom Mattie now took to be Sir Montague – smiled at her and ushered her towards a chair. 'Are you a friend of Victoria's?'

'Yes, I'm Mattie Price. We work together. That's how we met.'

'And where might that be?'

Mattie smiled at him, but said nothing.

He stared at her for a moment and then nodded slowly, seeming to understand that he should ask no more.

There was a sound at the door and everyone's eyes turned to see a tall man, in his early fifties, standing there. He was clean shaven with a strong jawline and dark eyes. His dark hair was greying a little at the temples and he was leaning, quite heavily, on a walking stick. His gaze at once found Victoria, and Mattie turned to see her friend rising slowly to her feet. Her eyes were wide and her lips were parted in shock. 'It's you,' she stuttered. 'The man in the park.'

Richard was moving across the room. And now, too, Victoria was moving towards him, watched by the other three.

Standing close to him, looking up at him, she asked simply, 'Are you really my father?'

Richard smiled down at her. In his eyes was a light that had been missing for many years. 'Can there be any question when you look there' – he nodded at the woman still sitting on the sofa – 'at your paternal grandmother? If there had ever been any doubt – and there wasn't – we have the proof before our eyes right now.'

'I have so many questions, but perhaps . . .'

'I will answer anything you ask,' he said softly. His voice was deep and rich and there was no denying the sincerity in his tone as he added, 'And with complete honesty.'

'I should go,' Mattie murmured, getting up. 'This will all be very private, I'm sure.'

'No, please don't go.' Victoria turned to her father. 'Mattie is my dearest friend. Nothing will ever go beyond these four walls that we don't want to. I can promise you that. And besides,' she glanced at Mattie with a tremulous smile, 'one day soon, I hope, she will be my sister-in-law, though' – her eyes clouded with sadness – 'at the moment, we can't be sure of anything.' Victoria pressed her lips together. She couldn't bring herself to say any more at the moment.

'It sounds as if we have a lot to talk about.' Richard said. 'Sit down, Mattie. Please. You are more than welcome to stay.'

Mattie sat down again a little nervously. Perhaps these grand people would not be so welcoming when they knew more about her family.

For the next two hours they talked and talked. First, sitting beside her grandmother, Francesca, and holding her hand, Victoria told them about her life until this moment. Of her mother's coldness and disinterest, how Grace had actually told her she'd never wanted her, how the servants and her governess had been the only ones to show affection to her. How she had felt some compulsion to draw the man in the park and had carried his likeness with her always. How she still had it safely hidden in the bottom of her suitcase even until this very day. The poignancy of her lonely, isolated life made her grandmother wipe tears from her eyes.

And then slowly, haltingly at first, Richard began to tell his side of the story. 'What is the saying? "Marry in haste and repent at leisure"? I'm afraid that's what we did. I was wounded in late 1916 and brought back to England. I was hospitalized in London, where your mother was a nurse.'

'A nurse!' The exclamation burst from Victoria's lips before she could stop it. 'Good heavens!'

Richard smiled thinly. 'She was a very good one. And very caring.'

Victoria stared at him. Could they really be talking about the same woman? Then she pulled her mind back to what he was saying.

'It was what you would call a whirlwind romance and we were married before I was sent back to France. I wanted to know that she would have some security if anything happened to me. She would have my pension and the allowance that I get from the family's estate.' He glanced across at his parents. 'Mother and Father didn't exactly try to stop us getting married, but they did advise caution. We hadn't had time to get to know one another, they said. Wartime circumstances are not the best of times to fall in love.' He paused a moment, realizing that perhaps his daughter might be following a similar path. But for the moment, he went on with his own story. 'I'm afraid . . .' He was tactful enough to emphasize his next words. 'In *our* case, they were right. Of course, I didn't know at the time, but when I returned to the front at the end of September, just in time for the last few weeks of Passchendaele, Grace was pregnant.' He paused, remembering a bleak time. 'I was wounded again the very first time I went back on the front line – more severely that time, in my leg, and by now I was also suffering from shell shock. I was invalided out of the army altogether.

'When eventually I came out of hospital, Grace wanted no more to do with me.' He glanced apologetically at Victoria. 'She was angry – incandescent with rage, I think the phrase is – that she was pregnant. And despite having been a nurse, she was not prepared to be tied to an invalid husband for the rest of her life. At that time it was not clear whether shell-shock victims would make any kind of decent recovery.' He glanced with affection at his parents. 'But with Mother's and Father's love and care I eventually got well again, although it did take a few years.'

'He was too ill at that time to stand up to her,' Sir Montague put in. 'He'd done enough fighting. We installed her in our London house—'

'That's *your* house?' Victoria said.

Sir Montague nodded. 'And we've paid her a generous allowance all these years. We always hoped, you see, that one day she would let us see you. Every year, on your birthday, we sent presents and begged her to allow us to visit you.'

Victoria turned pale. 'I – I never got anything from you.'

'What about Christmas? We sent gifts then too.'

Victoria shook her head. 'I didn't even know you existed. Any of you. As I got older, I asked her to tell me about my father, but she wouldn't say a word.' Now she looked at her father. 'Why didn't you divorce her?'

There was a silence between the other three until her grandmother said gently, 'Times are changing now, my dear, and we must try to alter our ways and perhaps even some of our deepest-held beliefs, but until now, divorce has been something that has never been contemplated in our family.'

Mattie said nothing. It wasn't her place, but it was

the same in her world, though for very different reasons. Her family could never afford to pay for a divorce, though she would dearly like to see her mother free of the man she'd married. It seems mistakes could be made in all classes of society. Even the wealthy were not immune from making hasty and disastrous decisions. She looked across at Richard Hamilton. He was the epitome of an officer and a gentleman, but his face was lined with the years of disappointment and the separation from his daughter had obviously never been what he'd wanted for a moment. He was speaking again and his words almost broke Mattie's heart, so what they must be doing to Victoria, she daren't think.

'When we married, I truly believed your mother loved me as much as I loved her. I don't know what changed her. Whether it was my injuries and illness she couldn't cope with or what, I don't know.'

'But you said she was a nurse. Surely . . . ?'

Richard shrugged. 'You'd have thought so, wouldn't you? But I found out later that she was a volunteer nurse – just for the duration of the war. She wasn't fully qualified in the normal way.'

'Ah, not dedicated, then?' Victoria said.

Richard shook his head. 'I wondered for a time if she'd met someone else, but it seemed that wasn't the case. She just wanted to lead her own life without the encumbrance of a husband and family.'

'Do you think she was what we'd call a "gold digger"?' Victoria said candidly. 'She saw an easy life of luxury as your wife.'

'I wouldn't like to say that—'

'But it's probably true, because, believe me, that's the life she has lived and still does.' She frowned. 'But what I still don't understand is why she wouldn't let you see me. Even, since she obviously had no affection for me, why she didn't let you take me.' She glanced around. 'Or am I being presumptuous that you would have wanted me?'

All three chorused at once. 'Of *course* we wanted you.'

Gently, Lady Hamilton said, 'My dear, perhaps it is difficult for you both to understand.' In her kindly way, she included Mattie. 'Life in our—' she hesitated to use the word uppermost in her mind – class – instead, she added, 'world has its own strict social rules. I believe that your mother desired a certain way of life and in marrying Richard she thought she'd found it. What she didn't bargain for was being married to an invalid.'

'Or,' Victoria whispered, 'getting pregnant.'

With this, none of them could argue, for it was obvious to them all that the last thing Grace had wanted was to be saddled with a child.

'But, in a strange way,' Lady Hamilton went on, 'you became her meal ticket. She decided that she would be a war widow, an object of sympathy. A divorcee would have been barred from so many of the social circles to which she craved admittance. And once she'd created this story, she could hardly let us see you, could she? The pretence had to be upheld.'

'But couldn't you have demanded access to me? You could have stopped her allowance.'

'We did threaten that once,' Sir Montague joined in. 'But she said she'd not only create a huge scandal with a messy divorce, but also take you right away so that we'd never even know where you were. At least, this way, Richard could see you from time to time whilst you were growing up, even if he daren't make himself known to you. We knew you were being cared for and educated well.' He glanced at her and his voice broke a little as he added, 'At least we *thought* you were being properly cared for. It must have been a cold and lonely existence for you, my dear. I am so very sorry.'

Victoria shrugged. 'I didn't know any different at the time. Besides, children in our class' – Victoria had no compunction in using the word – 'often don't see much of their parents. They're brought up in the nursery or the schoolroom and then sent to boarding school. I was never short of material possessions and my governess was an absolute darling. I still see her as often as I can.' She paused and then added, 'But I don't understand why I was never allowed friends of my own age at home.'

'No doubt she was afraid that her secret would be discovered. Children are notoriously inquisitive. She didn't want awkward questions being asked. Hence, she wouldn't tell you anything about your father. She couldn't.'

Victoria nodded slowly, understanding everything now. She was silent for a moment. Then she glanced around at her newfound relatives. 'So,' she said slowly, 'you have paid for my education, my trips abroad – everything. And I suspect the allowance I've been receiving since I was twenty-one also comes from you.'

Richard nodded. 'And don't even think of trying to refuse it, because I won't let you. I have been unable to be close to you for years. The only times I could even see you was on a Friday in the park. I used to go up to London every week just on the off chance of seeing you. So, please allow me a morsel of pride that at least I am helping you.'

Victoria smiled wryly. 'Mother has already said it will stop if I dare to marry Joe.'

Richard shook his head. 'She can't stop it. When you reached twenty-one, the allowance was set up in your name to be paid into a bank account in your name only. She can't interfere with that. Whatever you do, my dear, your allowance will continue. I promise you that.'

'What if you don't approve of Joe?' Mattie dared to ask.

They all glanced at her almost as if they had forgotten she was there. 'If they truly love each other, I don't mind who he is or what his background is,' Richard said. 'All I would ask is that they're very sure before they marry that it's what they both want. Where is he, by the way? I can't wait to meet him.'

Victoria and Mattie exchanged a glance before Victoria whispered hoarsely, 'We don't really know. Neither of us have heard from him for quite a long time. The last we heard, he'd been posted as "missing".'

Sixty-One

Lady Francesca Hamilton organized an early dinner so that the two girls could eat before they left to return to Bletchley.

'Tell us a little about yourself, Mattie, though we're not prying, I promise you,' Richard asked as they sat down around the large table in the dining room.

'I'm a very proud Sheffielder,' she said, with a grin. 'Most of us are honest and hardworking. A few are not and sadly, my father is one of them. To put it bluntly, he's never done an honest day's work in his life.'

For the next half an hour, Mattie told them about the hardships of her early life, now letting out secrets that even Victoria didn't know, and ending, 'If it hadn't been for the kindness of a neighbour and of my teachers, I would probably still be there.'

'Mattie got a first in mathematics at Oxford,' Victoria said, as proudly as if the success had been her own.

'My dear girl, that is some achievement for anyone,' Sir Montague began, 'let alone—' He stopped suddenly and then added, 'I'm sorry, that was tactless of me.' But Mattie only grinned.

'Don't apologize. I've tried to keep my background secret for so long – even from Victoria.'

The two girls exchanged a glance across the table.

'As I have mine,' Victoria said softly. 'But now we can share them all.'

'So many secrets,' Mattie murmured, but only she and her friend understood that there were many more secrets that neither of them would probably ever be able to share with anyone else, not even their nearest and dearest. Though they both had the distinct feeling that the others around the table guessed that what they had been doing through the war – and were still involved in to a certain extent – could not be discussed. This was confirmed for Victoria's father and grandparents when Sir Montague offered to have the chauffeur drive them home only to be told politely, but firmly, by his granddaughter, 'Just to the railway station, please.'

Sitting together on the train, Victoria leaned her head back against the seat. 'What a day! Who'd have thought, when we set out this morning, that by evening I'd have found myself a whole family.'

Mattie chuckled, delighted for her friend. 'And best of all, they seem willing – eager almost – to meet Joe. That's good of them, you know, especially after what I told them.'

'It's better that they know the truth now than think we've kept anything from them.' Victoria touched Mattie's hand. 'Thank you for being so open and honest with them. It can't have been easy for you.'

Mattie laughed wryly. 'It wasn't, especially after having kept it all so secret for years. I just hope Joe won't be angry with me.'

'He won't be. Joe is just as honest as you are. He

wouldn't want to start with deceit and lies. I can't wait for him to meet them now. If only,' she added wistfully, 'we knew if he's still alive.'

'Vicky,' Mattie was again standing outside the room where Hut 3 was now, still not daring to go in, but she'd knocked on the door and asked the girl who'd answered it to summon Victoria.

Victoria felt her heart lurch as she saw Mattie's solemn face. 'What is it? What's happened?'

'To be honest, I don't know, but I've had a telegram from Aunty Bella. It just says "Come home at once stop urgent stop Bella".'

'Then you'd better go. Will your boss give you leave?'

'I think so. I haven't asked him yet, but he's pretty good usually. And now things aren't quite so hectic . . . I'll – I'll explain as much as I can.'

'Just do what you need to, Mouse. Show him the telegram and tell him about – about Joe. How we've still heard nothing. That should be enough, surely.'

The two girls gazed at each other, fear in their eyes.

'What – what if it is about Joe?'

'Let me know at once, won't you?'

''Course.'

Within an hour, Mattie had cycled to their billet, packed a bag and was standing on the station platform waiting for the next train to take her north.

She ran most of the way from the station to their street, pausing only to catch her breath before she plunged down it to Bella's house near the top of the road.

She burst in through the back gate and rapped on the door. 'Aunty Bella—' she began as the door rattled and began to open, but when she saw who was standing there, she threw herself into his arms.

'Oh Dan. *Dan!* You're back. You're safe. Oh thank God.' She pulled back and then kissed him firmly on the mouth. His arms were tightly around her.

'Darling Mattie,' he said at last, pulling back a little. Then she caught his expression. Although he was obviously pleased to see her, she could see that there was something still troubling him.

'What is it? Isn't this – you being here – why Aunty Bella sent me a telegram?'

'No, she sent me one an' all. We only docked last night and I got it when I came ashore. I managed to get compassionate leave.'

'Then – then – Oh no! Is it Joe?'

Swiftly, Dan shook his head. 'No, I'd no idea until Mum just told me that he'd been posted missing. I'm so sorry, Mattie. After D-Day we got sent to different areas and communication between the ordinary soldiers was difficult. I did try to find out where Joe was but I haven't heard anything for months.' He smiled wryly. 'And we were a bit busy.'

'I can understand,' Mattie whispered.

'The reason my mum sent a telegram to you,' Dan went on, 'is because there's trouble down at your house. Your dad's back.'

The three of them went down the street. Rod had offered to go too, but Bella said, 'You keep out of it for now, love.' Despite the anxiety in her face she'd smiled. 'We'll send for reinforcements if we need 'em.'

As they walked, Bella explained. 'He came back three days ago and I left it for a bit. You never know, he might have changed . . .'

'Fat chance,' Dan muttered and, silently, Mattie had to agree with him.

'But he's worse than ever and your mum's slipping back into her old ways because of it. He's nasty to her. I reckon he's been hitting her, though she won't admit it. But she's back on the bottle, Mattie, even after her promise. But, to be honest, for once I can't blame her.'

'What about Toby? Is he home yet?'

'I think that's another reason your mum's been upskittled. He doesn't want to come back. He's got settled on that farm in Derbyshire and loves the life. Don't forget, Mattie, he's sixteen now and he will have changed a lot. He's grown up from being a little boy into a young man. You can't blame him for not wanting to come back here, but your mum was counting on him coming home.'

'What about Nancy?'

'Nowt's been said about her, really. I wouldn't be surprised if she didn't stay in the forces. She's taken to that life, an' all. An' I don't expect you'll come back here, will you?'

Mattie glanced swiftly at Dan. He was frowning as he marched down the street. For the moment his whole focus was on the trouble in Mattie's home and sorting it out. He, too, wished Joe was back home. *But is that ever going to happen?* he wondered. In the meantime – until they knew for certain – he'd have to stand in for his best friend.

They let themselves in by the back door to be met by a wall of shouting and saw Sid standing in the middle of the kitchen waving his arms and shaking his fist.

'I can see you've got out of line while I've been away. I'll put a stop to all this gallivanting with 'er from top o' t'street.'

Bella, unafraid, waded in. 'Oh aye, an' who's "'er from top o' t'street", when she's at home. Cat's mother?'

Sid turned and his lip curled. 'And you can hop it. I don't want you in my house again.' Then he spotted Mattie. 'Well, well, well, look what the cat's dragged in. Her High an' Mightiness. And what have you been doing through the war? I see you're not in uniform.'

Mattie moved into the room. 'Something a damned sight more useful than I bet you've been doing. Where've you been, Dad? Gaol?'

Sid clenched his fist and began to raise his arm but Dan stepped forward. 'I wouldn't, if I were you, Mr Price.'

'An' who do you think you are, coming interfering with a man in his own house?' Sid blustered, but he let his arm drop.

Mattie turned to her mother, cowering in her chair by the range. She noticed at once the purple bruise on the left-hand side of Elsie's face. Her mother's eyes were glazed, just like they used to be, and her hands were shaking.

'Oh Mum,' she whispered. Then she whipped round to face her father again, anger emboldening her.

'Get out! Get out of this house and stay out. We don't want you back.'

'Oh aye, and who's going to make me, eh?'

'Joe will, when he gets back. So you'd best go now, because when he gets home—'

'He's not coming home,' Sid interrupted with a malicious smile.

Mattie stopped and stared at him. 'What d'you mean? Of course he's coming back.'

Slowly, Sid shook his head. 'He's never coming back. Haven't you been told? He was shot after being taken prisoner.' His lip curled. 'T'Germans didn't keep many prisoners after D-Day. They were too busy trying to save their own skins. Anyone they caught was taken into t'woods and shot.'

Elsie gave an anguished howl like a wounded animal and beat her chest with her fists.

'Are you sure it's true?' Dan said later. After Sid's startling announcement, there had been little more they could do. They had managed to calm Elsie. Though she was still weeping copiously, they were silent tears of hopelessness now. They sat with her until Sid had gone out to the pub.

'He'll come back in a worse state than ever and knock you about some more,' Bella had said worriedly. 'Come home with us. You can stay with us as long as you want.'

But Elsie had been adamant. 'No, I'll stay here.

I don't really care what he does to me. If my boy's gone, I don't want to live anymore anyway.'

'Oh Mum, please don't talk like that,' Mattie said. Her heart was breaking too, but she had to be strong for her mother.

And there was still Victoria she would have to break the awful news to. However was she going to do that? Whilst they'd had no definite news, there'd always been hope, but now . . .

Back in their own home, Dan repeated his question and added, 'How's he got to know anyway, before your mum's heard officially?'

'I should have asked him. I wasn't thinking straight.' Mattie could say no more, because it was information she'd learnt at Bletchley Park. She knew that what her father had said – about no prisoners being kept alive by the enemy after D-Day – was thought to be true.

There was silence in the Spencer kitchen except for the sound of Bella clattering pots and pans as she prepared a meal that it was unlikely anyone would feel like eating.

'I'll have to tell Vicky,' Mattie whispered.

'Would it be better to wait until you get back? Telling someone something like that over the telephone is awful. Besides, I would wait a day or so to see if your mother gets an official letter.'

'I'm due to go back tomorrow. I can't take any more time off.'

'So am I,' Dan said.

Overhearing this, Bella said, 'Then we must try to persuade your mum to come here. Once he knows you've both gone, he'll be up to his tricks again.'

'It's good of you, Aunty Bella, but that won't solve the problem long term, will it? Toby's not coming home and goodness knows when Nancy will be back and what she's going to do in the future. If only Joe—' Mattie stopped, choking on the words.

'I still wonder how your dad knew,' Dan said, pondering, 'when your mum obviously didn't.'

Mattie wiped away the tears that had filled her eyes and took a deep breath. She must be strong. 'Perhaps there was a letter and he found it and opened it. I should've asked him, but I was so shocked.'

Dan frowned. 'He would have told her, wouldn't he? He would have flung it at her in some sort of perverse triumph. Joe was her golden boy. Your dad would have been gloating.'

Mattie sighed deeply. 'Now that I could believe. He was always jealous of Joe and Joe was the one who stood up to him.'

'You didn't do so badly tonight, love.' Dan put his arm around her shoulders and hugged him to her. 'Now, let's get to bed. We ought to try to get some sleep.'

Mattie went into Jane's room. Lying in the narrow bed, she buried her face in the pillow trying to muffle the sobs she could no longer hold back. The bedroom door opened and she felt someone sit on the edge of the bed. Then Bella's comforting arms were around her and she was sitting up and weeping against the older woman's shoulder.

'There, there, love. Let it all out.' She sat there,

rocking Mattie, until the exhausted girl fell asleep. Bella laid her down gently and tucked the covers around her tenderly.

'Poor lass,' she murmured. 'No one should have to put up with what you've had to in your young life. But my Dan will be good to you, I promise you that.'

With a heavy sigh, Bella crept out of the bedroom, closing the door softly behind her.

Sixty-Two

The following morning, Mattie sluiced her face at the washstand in the bedroom, dressed and packed her suitcase. Brushing her hair, she scarcely recognized the pale face staring back at her.

The other three were waiting for her. 'I'll walk you to the station,' Dan said, 'but you must try to eat some breakfast first.'

Mattie shook her head. 'I couldn't. Really, I couldn't.'

'Don't worry, love. I've packed you some Spam sandwiches. Maybe you'll feel like eating a bit on the train.'

Mattie smiled weakly.

'Now, off you go, the pair of you. And don't worry about your mum. Me an' Rod will keep an eye on her. If he does owt else to her, it's the police I'll be fetching next time and I'll tell him as much.'

'I ought to go down and see her again before I go.'

'I don't think she'll be up yet. It's early. She – doesn't get up very early of a morning now.'

Mattie stared at Bella for a moment before nodding. She understood only too well what Bella was implying. Elsie would be sleeping off the effects of the bottle, and with the news she'd received last night, was there any wonder?

The fresh morning air revived her. She linked her arm through Dan's as they walked to the station.

'I've got to go back tonight, Mattie, but before I go, Mum and me are going to try to get your mum to come and sleep at ours. She didn't ought to stay down there on her own with him.'

'I don't think you'll manage it, but it's good of you both to try.'

They reached the station and found their way to the correct platform. Gently, Dan took her shoulders. 'We're family now – well, almost. When I get demobbed, we'll talk about getting married.'

'You – you haven't actually asked me yet, Dan.'

'Haven't I?' He sounded genuinely surprised. Then suddenly he grasped her hand and dropped to one knee. 'Darling Mattie, will you marry me?'

Suddenly, there was the sound of clapping and cheering around them as others, waiting for the train, saw the soldier proposing to his girl.

'Say "yes", lass,' a woman shouted. 'Don't let a handsome young soldier like him get away. Mind you, if I was thirty years younger . . .'

Laughter rippled along the platform as Mattie, blushing furiously, pulled him up. 'Of course I will, you daft 'aporth. What a time and a place to pick!'

'No time like the present.' His face sobered. 'P'raps it wasn't the best place, but, like the old girl said, I don't want *you* to get away.' He kissed her hard and then helped her into a carriage where willing soldiers' hands pulled her aboard.

'We'll look after her, mate,' one soldier called out and Dan hollered back, 'That's what I'm afraid of.'

There were loud guffaws and much waving as the train moved off.

'Sit here, duck,' the soldier who'd shouted to Dan gave her his seat. Mattie smiled her thanks and sat down. The soldiers laughed and joked all the way and always included her. Mattie was grateful. Her tears weren't far away. She was experiencing a tumult of emotions; happiness at Dan's proposal – that went without saying – and worry over her mother. But overriding all that was her heart-wrenching distress over her brother. Just how was she ever to tell Vicky that now there was no hope that Joe was coming back?

She'd decided to go to London first, to Constance's flat. She needed to talk to her before she faced Victoria. She didn't have to be back at Bletchley until the following morning and she could catch the early morning milk train and be there in time. Besides, she rather felt her superiors would be understanding in the circumstances, especially now the pressure was somewhat less.

Her feet dragged with weariness and sorrow as she walked the final few steps from the tube station. She rang the bell and leaned against the door jamb until she heard footsteps on the other side and the door opened and a beaming Vicky stood there.

Tears sprang to Mattie's eyes. 'Oh Vicky – you're here,' she said unnecessarily.

Vicky was taking her arm and pulling her into the flat. 'Indeed I am. And look who else is here . . .'

'Vicky – I need to talk to you. There's something I have to . . .'

Mattie stepped into the sitting room. A tall, handsome young soldier came towards her, his arms outstretched.

Mattie felt the blood drain from her face. She felt dizzy and sick and her knees gave way beneath her. Everything went black.

She came to on the sofa with three pairs of anxious eyes peering down at her as she whispered, 'Joe, oh Joe. I thought you were dead.'

'No, here I am, large as life and twice as ugly. It took a long time to get back. I sent word, but it obviously hasn't got through.'

'It's not that. I've just been home. Dad was there. He – he's been knocking Mum about . . .'

Joe's face darkened. 'Has he now? Then I'll have to go up home and sort him out once and for all.'

'Joe – they think you're dead. He told us you'd been shot after being captured.'

'Ah. Yes, that.'

'Joe?'

'I was captured alongside several others. They took us deep into a wood and machine-gunned the lot of us. It was a miracle that I was only caught in the leg. I fell down and several others fell on top of me. I lay there for ages, terrified that they would make sure we were all dead, but they didn't. They drove away and all was quiet. There were only two of us out of about thirty who survived. The other lad had been hit in the arm and my injury wasn't so bad that I couldn't walk. Luckily, we were still in France and we managed to get to a farm. The farmer was friendly, overjoyed because the Allies were coming. He hid us in his hay loft and his daughter dressed our wounds every day and brought us food. We stayed there quite a long time until the farmer told us that the Germans were finally gone and that the British had arrived. Eventually, we found our way back to our rearguard lines, but our unit had moved on by then and so, although we were taken care of, they didn't really seem to worry too much about getting us home.' He grinned. 'Mind you, to be fair, they did have rather a lot on their minds and neither of us were fit to fight anymore. Everything was really coming to an end then but things were in turmoil. I got back to the coast eventually. I sent messages – I promise you I did – but it was absolute chaos. And then, it was all over, but still I couldn't seem to get passage back home. I'm so sorry you've all been so worried.'

'You're here now, but we must send word to Mum. She's in bits, Joe, saying she doesn't care what happens to her now you're not coming back.'

'Let's go to the nearest post office and send a telegram,' Victoria said. 'Come on, Joe. We can't let your poor mother go on grieving like that.'

'Send it to Aunty Bella, Joe,' Mattie said. 'Dad might get it and – not tell her.'

Victoria's eyes rounded. 'Would he really do that?'

'Oh yes,' Joe said grimly. 'If you're sure you're all right, Mattie, we'll go now.'

'I'll look after her,' Constance assured them. 'You just go.'

At the post office, it was Joe who sent the telegram to Mrs Bella Spencer:

TELL MUM I'M ALIVE AND WELL STOP TELL
DAD I'M COMING FOR HIM STOP JOE

'That's quite an expensive telegram,' the girl behind the counter warned him but Joe only grinned.

'I don't mind what it costs. I'm back from the dead.'

'I ought to be going with you, Joe,' Mattie said worriedly later that evening as they were finishing the meal that Constance had prepared. 'But I daren't just go AWOL.'

'I don't want you to,' Joe said. 'Constance, that was the best meal I've had since the last time I was here. I don't know how you do it on the rationing.'

'Thank you, kind sir,' Constance said, smiling.

'How about I go with you, Joe?' Victoria said. 'I've been granted three days' leave.'

'I'm not sure I want you seeing what's going to go on,' Joe said.

'Darling Joe, we're going to be married, aren't we? And despite what people often say, you *do* marry your partner's family. Unless, of course, you've changed your mind.'

'Never,' Joe said. He clasped her hand tightly as they sat together on the sofa. 'But I'm not sure your family are going to be very happy about me.'

Over the last hour or so, Victoria had told Joe and Constance all that had happened when she and Mattie had visited Haversham Manor.

'They know all about the Price family,' she said now.

'They do? You – you told them?'

'No, Mattie did.'

She saw Joe glance at Mattie as she began to apologize, 'Joe—'

Swiftly, Victoria interrupted her, saying, 'And before you tell her off, I'm glad she did. We're not going to start our married life with secrets and deceit.'

Deliberately, she did not meet Mattie's gaze; there would always be secrets they could not share with Joe and Dan.

'What – what did they say?' Joe asked hesitantly.

'All my father said was that as long as we loved each other and that we were sure, then he'd give us his blessing. He's really looking forward to meeting you.'

'And your mother?'

Victoria shrugged. She said nothing, but her meaning was clear.

Joe pulled in a deep breath. 'All right, then. If you're sure, I would be glad to have you with me. I just hope you're prepared for what might happen. It won't be pretty.'

Victoria hugged his arm to her side. 'We'll face it together.'

Joe and Victoria travelled north as Mattie returned to Bletchley. They went first to see Bella, who hugged Victoria like an old friend, but it was the sight of Joe that brought tears to her eyes. 'Eeh, lad, you had us worried. Am I glad to see you. Now, sit down, the pair of you. Yer dinner's all ready. I'm sorry Dan had to go back before you got here, but he daren't be late reporting back.'

'This is so kind of you, Mrs Spencer,' Victoria began, but Bella waved aside her thanks.

'It's nowt, love, not for family. And you're almost one of the family now, aren't you?' She glanced archly at them. 'Or at least you soon will be. And please call me Aunty Bella or even Bella, I don't mind which, but I can't be doing with all this "Mrs" stuff.' She laughed. 'I keep looking round thinking me mother-in-law's come back to haunt me. Not that I'd mind,' Bella chattered on. 'She was a dear old soul. We always got along well. Now, eat up,' she said as she placed plates of food in front of them. 'Then we'll go down and beard the lion in his den.'

An hour later Joe, Victoria and Bella walked down the road and into the Price household. Sid was sitting at the table calmly reading a newspaper whilst Elsie cowered in her chair, a fresh bruise on her face.

Victoria crossed the room, pulled a stool close to Elsie and sat down, taking hold of her hand. Bella moved to sit in the battered armchair opposite. Together the three women watched whatever was going to happen.

Sid looked up at Joe with a sneer on his face. 'Oh, it's you. I hoped you were dead.' Then he nodded towards Victoria. 'This your fancy piece, is it? Where d'you find her? On a street corner?'

Joe lunged towards him, grasped his shirt neck

and hauled him to his feet. But all Sid said was, 'I'd mind what you're doin', if I was you. I've got back-up now.'

Joe frowned but it was Elsie's quavering voice that said, 'Lewis is back. He arrived late last night. He's upstairs.'

'Is he now? Thought you'd both come back and carry on your nefarious activities here, did you? Well, you can think again.'

'Oh can I, indeed? And who's going to stop me, eh? Who's house is this? It's not *hers*. It's my name on the rent book.'

'Aye, but who pays it, eh? You tell me that.' Joe released his grip, pushed Sid away from him and took two strides towards the door that led to the stairs. 'Lewis,' he bellowed. 'Get down here.'

A few moments later heavy footsteps sounded on the stairs and Lewis appeared, his eyes still heavy with sleep, but they opened wider when he saw his brother. Then he grinned. 'Ey up, mate. Good to see you.'

Joe was staring at his brother, taking in his appearance. It seemed as if Lewis had grown taller; he had certainly broadened out. His hair was cut short and he was clean-shaven. He was wearing khaki trousers with his braces hanging down either side, a sleeveless vest and heavy boots.

Joe pointed at the trousers and boots. 'They're army issue. Where did you get them?'

'I was given 'em when I joined up two years ago.'

'You? Joined up?'

'Aye, I did, but I didn't want any of you to know

I'd got meself into a bit of bother and it was either enlisting or going to prison again, and I fancied taking me chances with Hitler's bullets rather than being beaten up in gaol. Once was quite enough.'

Joe's lip curled. 'Well, that's where you'll end up if you take up with him again.' He nodded towards their father.

Lewis glanced at Sid too and his grin widened. 'Ah, but you see, brother dear, I have no intention of going back to me old life.'

'Wha . . . ?' Sid began.

'Sorry, Dad, but I've learnt me lesson. I like the army life, it's a good one, if you play it straight, and I mean to. I've signed on as a regular.'

But Sid wasn't done yet. 'They'll not keep you when they find out about your past. You've done one stretch in gaol that I know about.'

'That's where you're wrong. They know it all, but you see, I got a medal for bravery on D-Day and now I'm going to be a drill instructor. Oh, I'm staying in t'army, Dad, and there's nowt that you can do about it. I've got me life sorted out and it's staying that way.' He moved further into the room. 'And now I'll say "hello" to Mum. I didn't see her last night.'

As he moved to stand before her, they all watched his expression darken when he saw the bruises on Elsie's face and noticed her still clutching the bottle like a drowning woman. His fists clenched at his sides as slowly he turned to look at his father.

'You did this?'

Sid shrugged as he sat down again at the table.

'She's been getting out of hand while I've been away.'

Now it was Lewis who crossed the room and grabbed his father's shirt, just as Joe had done. He hauled him to his feet. 'You an' me are going outside and I'm going to give you the pasting of your life. By the time I've finished with you, you'll be sorry you ever came back.'

'Ey, lad. You and me are pals, aren't we?' Sid was whining now. 'I taught you all I know. We could make a killing round here now on the black market. I've got contacts . . .'

'Not anymore, Dad.' Lewis paused and then, pulling him even closer, his spittle rained on Sid's face as he said, 'D'you know summat, it makes me sick to me stomach to call you that name. I swear I'll never call you "Dad" again. You've never been a proper father to any of us. Now, outside, you piece of—'

'Hang on a minute, Lewis.' Now it was Joe who put a restraining hand on Lewis's arm. 'Don't wreck your chances of a good life, mate. Let's just get rid of him.'

'Eh?' Lewis's eyes widened. 'My God! You don't mean—'

Joe laughed aloud. 'Lor', no. He's not worth either of us dangling at the end of a rope for. No, we'll get the police here. I'm sure they'd be very interested in all the stuff that's stashed in various corners of this house, starting with under the beds, to say nothing of the wash house.'

'You wouldn't . . .' Sid began to bluster. 'You wouldn't grass on your own father.'

'Like Lewis said, you've been no sort of a father to any of us,' Joe said grimly. 'And, yes, we would and we will, unless you get your stuff together right now and disappear. And this time, make sure it's for good because next time, I won't hold Lewis back. In fact, I'll join him.'

Sixty-Three

Sid gathered a few belongings together and was gone within an hour. Where to, no one knew or cared.

'Now, Mum,' Lewis said gently, squatting down in front of her. Victoria was still sitting beside Elsie, holding her hand. 'I've got a full week's leave and I want to see you back on track before I have to report back.'

For the first time since Sid had arrived home, Elsie smiled. She held out a half-empty bottle and said, 'Pour this down the sink, will you? I won't be needing it anymore.'

'You sure? You could wean yourself off it gradually. If you go cold turkey—'

But Elsie shook her head and glanced at Bella. 'Thanks to Bella, I've been off it for a long time. It's – it's only when he comes back that I fall again. It shouldn't be too bad for me this time and it's better to stop it altogether. I've done it before.'

'She has,' Bella agreed. 'It was tough, but she did it, Lewis, and she can do it again. I'll make sure of that. We'll get back to doing our WVS work. They still need us, Elsie love.'

'But when I go, you'll be on your own, won't you? I'm still afraid he'll come back once he knows both

Joe and me have gone. When is Toby coming home?
I'm surprised he's not here already.'

Tears filled Elsie's eyes but bravely she said, 'He's
not coming back. He wants to stay in Derbyshire
and work on the farm.'

Lewis was silent for a moment before saying softly,
'Can't blame him, I suppose. It'd be a good life for
him. Perhaps you could move out there, Mum, to be
near him. We could mebbe find you a little cottage
to rent.'

But Elsie shook her head. 'No, I'm a city girl. The
open countryside frightens me a bit, to be honest.
And besides, Nancy will be coming home. I had a
letter from her last week. When she gets demobbed
she's coming back here and taking up her old job at
Coles. She's decided not to stay in the ATS after all.'

'And you're all right with that, are you, Mum?'

'Oh yes. Nancy's altered, Lewis. She helps around
the house a lot more now and we get on very well
together. And she'll contribute to the expenses. She's
said so.'

Lewis didn't look convinced, but when he glanced
up at his brother, Joe nodded. 'Mum's right. She's
not the selfish cow she used to be. Sorry, Vicky.' He
added swiftly, but Victoria only smiled.

'And now,' Lewis said, standing up, 'if that's
everything settled, I want you to introduce me to this
lovely lady, Joe, who, I gather, is your girlfriend.'

'Fiancée, actually.'

Victoria stood up and went to Joe's side. He put
his arm about her. 'This is my reprobate brother,
who, I am delighted to hear, has changed his ways.'

He held out his free hand to Lewis and the two brothers shook hands. 'I couldn't be more chuffed, Lewis.'

Back in London, Joe had to leave the following morning but not before Constance had said, 'I'm trying to organize a reunion for the four of us girls who were at finishing school together, but, of course, I now want to include Mattie, Dan and you. And my Charlie, of course. Do you think you and Dan can sort out some dates when you could get here?'

'That sounds wonderful, Constance. I'll let you know. Perhaps we could do it at the same time that Vicky wants to take me to visit her family. I'm a bit worried about that, but Mattie's told me they're lovely people.'

'They are by all accounts. And besides, I think Vicky will go her own way in life and she wants to marry you. I doubt anyone could stop her.'

But even after Constance's words of encouragement, Joe felt very apprehensive the day that Victoria took him to Haversham Manor.

'Do relax, darling,' Victoria tried to reassure him. 'I'm sure they don't bite.'

The visit was, in fact, a huge success; Richard Hamilton and Joe had plenty to talk about and the older man was interested in Joe's plans to stay in the army for the foreseeable future.

As they all sat on the terrace at the rear of the house after luncheon, Sir Montague said, 'Now, we have a suggestion for you two young people, but no one is going to be offended if it's not what you want. We – that's the three of us – would like to have your wedding here at the Manor and we just wondered if you'd like to have a double celebration with Mattie and Dan. We've plenty of rooms to accommodate some of your guests – like your family, Joe – and there's a very nice hotel for others to stay at if there are too many for us to have here.'

Victoria and Joe glanced at each other.

'Don't say anything now,' Sir Montague said hastily. 'Talk about it. See what you and the others think and let us know.'

'That's more than generous of you, Grandfather,' Victoria said. 'We'll certainly think seriously about it and we'll ask Mattie what she thinks too.'

As they journeyed back to London, Joe said, 'I can't believe they've made such an offer. They can't dislike me, can they?'

'Darling, they love you already. Grannie told me just before we left. They couldn't be happier with my choice. And my father whispered to me that he can see how much we love each other. He's happy for us too.'

'So, how do we tell Mattie and Dan?'

'Ah, now I think you'd better leave that to me, there's a dear. I don't want you wading in with your size tens. I know just how to handle Mouse.'

The party the following Saturday evening went off with a swing. Georgina arrived on her own.

'No boyfriend, Lady G?' Constance said.

'I've been far too busy running the farm to feed

the nation to be thinking about such things.' But there was a twinkle in her eye as she said it and Constance had the distinct feeling that there was someone in the background, but that perhaps the friendship was too early for the young man in question to be thrust into meeting a bevy of Georgina's friends.

Georgina was delighted to meet Mattie, Joe and Dan.

'Good Lord,' Joe said, shaking her hand. 'I've never met a real "lady" before. Am I supposed to bow?'

'Don't you dare,' Georgina laughed and they fell into an easy conversation.

'Celia's not here,' Victoria said, looking around.

'No, she's abroad, but she sent her love and promises we'll all meet up the next time she's back in England.'

'And what about Charlotte?' Victoria asked.

'She's supposed to be coming. Ah, there's the doorbell. That might be her.'

They heard muffled voices in the small hallway and then, a few moments later, Constance returned with Charlotte close behind her. But behind her came a very tall, broad-shouldered fair-haired man in the immaculate uniform of the American Army.

'Ladies and Gentlemen,' Constance said, smiling broadly, 'may I introduce Mr and Mrs Greyson Miller.'

There was a brief silence and then squeals of delight from Georgina and Victoria, who both rushed to hug Charlotte.

Later, as the guests mingled freely, Charlotte

explained to her friends how she'd met Grey, as she called him. 'He was stationed near where I was working with the Jewish refugee children. That's how we met. The Americans were – are – enormously generous and often came to help out at the centre we ran. Isn't he a dish?'

'He most certainly is. So, will you be going to live in America?'

'I expect so,' Charlotte said dreamily, her gaze still on her handsome husband. 'But I don't care where we live as long as we're together.'

There was lively chatter until well into the early hours and several toasts to each happy couple. At last, Constance closed the door on the last guests, leaving only herself, Victoria and Mattie to stagger to their beds.

'Just one more toast before you go to bed, girls. Charge your glasses.'

They stood in a small circle. 'Wha's the toast, then?' Mattie said, slightly slurring her words.

'To friends,' Constance said. 'Old and new.'

The other two echoed her words and took a sip out of their glasses.

'And now,' Constance said, setting down her glass, 'I bags the bathroom first.'

Left alone, Victoria and Mattie regarded each other solemnly. 'There's just one more toast for us, isn't there, Mouse?'

'I know,' Mattie whispered and raised her glass. 'To Bletchley Park and all its secrets.'